LINDSAY McKENNA

brings you the story you've been waiting for—
the intense, emotional romance between
two of MORGAN'S MERCENARIES' most
beloved characters: rugged, mysterious
Major Mike Houston and vulnerable,
beautiful Dr. Ann Parsons.

* * *

**"I need you," Mike rasped, placing his
hand against her cheek and guiding her
face upward.**

In one heated moment out of time, all Ann
had longed for was finally happening. It was
all so crazy. So mixed-up. Yet as she lifted her
chin and felt his strong mouth settle upon her
lips, nothing had ever felt so right. So pure.
So devastatingly beautiful. His strong arms
moved around her back and she felt him
pull her against him.

There was no mistake about his gesture; it was
clearly that of a man claiming his woman....

* * *

"Lindsay McKenna continues to leave her
distinctive mark on the romance genre with...
timeless tales about the healing powers of love."
—*Affaire de Coeur*

MORGAN'S MERCENARIES

LINDSAY McKENNA

HEART OF THE JAGUAR

Silhouette Books

Published by Silhouette Books

America's Publisher of Contemporary Romance

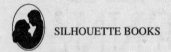

SILHOUETTE BOOKS

MORGAN'S MERCENARIES:
HEART OF THE JAGUAR

Copyright © 1999 by Eileen Nauman

ISBN 0-373-48371-6

All rights reserved. Except for use in any review, the reproduction or utilization of this work in whole or in part in any form by any electronic, mechanical or other means, now known or hereafter invented, including xerography, photocopying and recording, or in any information storage or retrieval system, is forbidden without the written permission of the editorial office, Silhouette Books, 300 East 42nd Street, New York, NY 10017 U.S.A.

All characters in this book have no existence outside the imagination of the author and have no relation whatsoever to anyone bearing the same name or names. They are not even distantly inspired by any individual known or unknown to the author, and all incidents are pure invention.

This edition published by arrangement with Harlequin Books S.A.

® and TM are trademarks of Harlequin Books S.A., used under license. Trademarks indicated with ® are registered in the United States Patent and Trademark Office, the Canadian Trade Marks Office and in other countries.

Printed in U.S.A.

To all my wonderful readers
who have been with me over the years.
You *are* the greatest!

Prologue

"**O**h, hell...I'm dying...."

The thought slammed through Captain Mike Houston's spinning mind and then, in disgust, he uttered the desperate words out loud. Sliding his long, muddied fingers along his camouflaged right thigh, he looked down to see bright red blood spurting like a pulsing fountain. A bullet had ricocheted off a tree and nicked his femoral artery, and he was bleeding like a butchered hog. Instinctively, because he was trained as a paramedic, he put direct pressure on the wound with his dirty hand.

Lying in the midst of the Peruvian jungle, Mike knew there wouldn't be any rescue coming. No, the helicopter he'd been in had been shot down by Eduardo Escovar's drug cartel mercenaries, who were intent on hunting him down and murdering him. As far as Mike knew, he was the only survivor of the flaming wreckage. The redness and blisters on his forearms, the tightness of his face, told him he hadn't gotten away without being burned. Gasping, he threw back his head. Sweat trailed down the sides of his hardened face as he began to feel each single beat of his heart in his heaving chest.

Though he'd leaped from the falling bird before it hit the triple canopy of trees, Mike knew his Peruvian army team hadn't survived the attack. The helicopter had been hit by a rocket at five hundred feet and had slowly turned over on its side like a wounded, shrieking eagle, twisting around and around until it hit the thick jungle cover.

In the distance, he could hear flames from the downed aircraft still snapping and popping. He heard the excited voices of Escovar's men as they searched through the jungle, hunting for any survivors. It was only a matter of time now, actually. A pained, one-cornered smile twisted Mike's mouth. Helluva place to pack it all in: in his mother's homeland. She was Quechua Indian and had been concerned when he was assigned by the U.S. Army to teach Peruvian soldiers how to begin ridding their land of the cocaine lords. She'd wept in his arms, pleading with him not to go down there, that he'd die.

Well, it looked like she was right. Mike scowled. At twenty-six years old, he didn't want to die. Hell, he'd barely lived yet. He'd only been an Army Special Forces officer since he graduated from college at age twenty-two. He had his whole career—his whole life—ahead of him. But as he lay in the shallow depression, the surrounding green, leafy jungle effectively hiding him, the soft, spongy ground beneath him damp with rotting vegetation, he began to feel light-headed. That was the first sign of shock, he noted coldly. *Pretty soon I'm going to dump, my blood pressure will drop through the floor and I'll lose consciousness and die.* It would be like going to sleep.

Still, he'd been in so many close calls over the years as he'd directed Peruvian army teams against the continuing battle with drug lords in the highlands of this jungle country that he believed he might have a chance. He had luck—his mother's Indian luck. She prayed for him constantly. It made a difference.

He could feel his heart thudding hard in his chest. And, he became aware of the pulse of blood through his body. The sticky red substance had completely soaked the material around his thigh. He tried to put more pressure on the wound. No, he thought gravely, this time there would be no help, no helicopter coming, no relief to make up the difference. He knew that the copilot had gotten off a mayday message shortly after they were hit because he'd heard him scream out their location as the out-of-control helicopter plunged toward earth. But who knew if anyone had picked up the transmission? There was little chance of a rescue being organized.

The heavy jungle growth felt comforting to him. In his green-and-tan camouflage uniform, he was well hidden. With a mirthless smile, Mike lay on his left side, placing his arm beneath his head like a pillow while his right hand closed more firmly over his hard, massive thigh. It was only a matter of time. Escovar's men were local villagers. They knew how to hunt and track. They'd eventually pick up his trail. He hadn't been able to hide his tracks this time. Usually, he was just as good as they were in hiding his whereabouts, but not on this misty, cool morning. Blinking through the sweat dripping off his bunched brow, Houston looked up through the wide, wet leaves.

Humidity lay like a blanket above the canopy. On most days, sunlight never reached the jungle floor. His eyes blurred briefly and everything went hazy. The beat of his heart became pronounced. As he lost more blood, his heart pumped harder, trying to make do with less. It was a losing battle. His mind was shorting out, too. He wondered if he'd bleed to death before the cocaine soldiers found him. He hoped so, because what they'd do to him wouldn't be pretty. He laughed to himself. The Geneva Convention didn't mean a damn thing down here. Its declaration of the rights of prisoners was a piece of paper in some far-off land. Here, the law of the jungle prevailed. Any prisoner taken could expect horrendous, painful torture until death released him from the agony. To torment one's enemy wasn't just permitted, it was a right.

Pain throbbed up and down his leg. He had to try and get his web belt around his thigh and make a tourniquet. Mike laughed at himself once again. Why the hell was he trying to save his own miserable life? So Escovar's men could finish him off, an inch at a time? He kept his hand gripped on his thigh. *No belt. Screw it. I'll die instead.* He shut his eyes, the black, spiky lashes resting against his ashen, glistening features. Ordinarily, he looked like a Peruvian Indian, his skin not copper colored, but a dark, dusky hue that hinted at the *norteamericano* blood interfaced with Indian.

He spoke Spanish and the Quechua language as easily as he did English, thanks to his mother's influence.

"Never forget your upbringing, Michael!" she would remonstrate, shaking that small, brown finger in his face. "Your father might think you're all *norteamericano,* but you are not! Your heart belongs to my people. Your spirit belongs to the Jaguar Clan in the jungles of Peru. Never forget that."

Mike chuckled softly, his face pressing into the scratchy leaves and branches where he lay. He was weakening further. In spite of the humid hell that surrounded him, he felt cold, and he was dying of thirst. Oh, for a drink of water right now! Somewhere in his hazy mind, he knew he was going to go through every classic symptom of shock as the blood leaked out of his body. For a moment, he felt lighter, the heaviness of his body, the belts of ammunition he wore criss-crossed around his chest no longer pulling him downward. Despite his tightly shut eyes, he saw the dull, whitish yellow glow of clouds that always embraced the jungle. The light always reminded him of his mother's belief that the clouds were actually the veil between the worlds. On this side was the "real world," she'd told him, when he was a child on her knee, listening as she spun story after story of her Indian heritage. But the other side...ahh...that was the world of the shamans and the Jaguar Clan. It was a world full of magic, danger, mystery and terror. Only trained medicine people could go between the worlds and come back alive from the experience. Anyone else foolish enough to try it would die.

I'm dying now. I'm going between the worlds. Part of him, the *norteamericano* side, laughed derisively at the thought. But his mother's Indian blood, that part of him connected deeply with Mother Earth, believed it. Until now, Mike hadn't really thought much about his mother's belief system. In these moments before his death, her words were more important to him than he'd ever realized.

Mike heard the shout of a soldier no more than a hundred feet away from where he lay. He knew he'd done a bad job of hiding himself beneath the damp, rotting leaves and branches that filled the shallow depression he'd dug, but his leg wound had taken most of his attention. Now consciousness was draining from him. His fingers began to slip away from his wound and he felt the pulse of warm blood spreading across them. He didn't have the strength to hold pressure over the bullet hole in his thigh any longer.

He was breathing shallowly now. His heartbeat was growing weaker. He was dumping. His blood pressure would plummet any second now, and he'd die. Opening his eyes, he saw nothing but that humid, moist veil to another world. Funny, he couldn't see anything else anymore. He supposed that was part of dying. Blinking away the sweat running into his eyes, he realized he no longer felt its sting. Yes, he was definitely going through the dying process. He began to lose his fear of being discovered. Absorbed by the white-and-gold light that now surrounded him, he realized the cold that had been flowing up his legs and into the center of his body had stopped. He blinked again.

A voice inside his head told him to look down at his arm, which was flung out before him. He shifted his gaze slightly across the surface of the ground, thinking he would only be able to see the white light. But he could make out his darkly haired arm, the camouflage material torn away, leaving the lower part exposed.

His vision was changing. As if he were looking at his arm through a microscope, Mike saw each black hair and his darkly tanned flesh beneath. His focus moved to his large-knuckled, heavily scarred hand. Suddenly, he felt something shift within him.

The feeling wasn't that noticeable, just a vague sense of readjustment. Mike wasn't sure what caused it, but there was a rumbling feeling in his chest, like a heavy truck grinding up a steep hill in low gear.

Sounds blurred around him. The drip, drip, drip of water falling from the leaves was amplified, while the shouts of the soldiers dissolved. Mike felt oddly uncomfortable, but his pain was nearly gone. Even the throbbing sensation in his leg had disappeared.

Puzzled, Houston blinked and continued to stare dazedly at his outstretched arm. The sight of it was his last hold on reality, he figured. Pretty soon, his vision would dim and he'd be gone—forever, this time. He felt lighter and lighter, all the noises and the pain slowly dissolving. He felt as if he were whirling and the sensation made him dizzy as it became more and more profound. His gaze clung to his dirty, bloodied arm, as if he were trying to absorb one last reminder of his physical body before he died. A part of him didn't want to die. It was his Indian spirit fighting, he guessed.

All of Mike's focus was drawn to the dark hairs that carpeted his forearm. Suddenly some of the hair began to turn a deep gold color. The black hairs remaining took on the shape of black crescent moons all over his now golden-haired arm. What the hell was going down? He didn't have the strength to utter the question. His mind spun. He couldn't think straight any longer. He watched, mesmerized, as his forearm continued to change. Gasping he saw his long, callused fingers transformed into claws. He was no longer staring at his hand, but the huge paw of a big cat! What was happening? Was he hallucinating? That was it. He was hallucinating just as he was dying.

A new strength began to flow up his right arm, a startlingly powerful, pulsing sensation of life triumphing unexpectedly over death. Groaning, Mike rolled onto his back. He closed his eyes, unable to comprehend this strange new feeling. As the warmth and power tunneled up his right arm and flowed into his thickly corded neck and head, he felt changes. Unusual changes. He felt his teeth elongate in his mouth. Strangely, miraculously, he began to regain his senses.

His left arm began to feel like his right one. Then his torso felt like it was shifting—expanding here, narrowing there. The warmth flowed down into his legs and he felt them change shape, too. He was dying, that was all. Dying. But if this was death, why was his heart beating so powerfully in his chest? He opened his mouth and took in a deep, ragged breath. Air flowed into his lungs, life-giving and galvanizing. *What's going on?* His mind wasn't working right. His senses were suddenly, inexplicably acute. Even more so, his sense of smell was heightened. He could scent the soldiers and detect the direction they were coming from. Even better, he could hear them as he'd never heard them before.

Mike rolled onto his stomach. He shouldn't have been able to due to his wound, but he did. The jungle had taken on different colors to him—not the shades he was used to seeing. Soft light surrounded every leaf, branch and tree. Everything was connected by that river of slowly moving light.

The first soldier was nearly upon him. Mike crouched and waited. Anger tunneled through him as he saw the man lift his rifle and quicken his pace toward where he lay hiding. The soldier was dressed in camouflage fatigues and heavily armed, his black eyes narrowed with a sort of savage pleasure. There was no denying his murderous intent, and Mike sensed this intruder into his domain had tortured many victims and enjoyed their pain, their screams. Blinking, Mike saw a dark gray color around the man. It wasn't at all like the clear, unbeguiling light he saw around the plants and trees. No, this man's light was murky. *Evil.*

Instinctively, Mike crouched, every fiber of his being set to defend himself. He didn't know where the strength came from, but he felt his hind legs tense, lower slightly, and then he lunged out of his hiding place, his body a projectile, his claws aimed at the man's exposed neck.

The soldier shrieked and tried to halt. Too late! Everything went black in front of Mike. As he slashed savagely at the soldier's neck, he heard the man's scream die in his throat. Within seconds, three more soldiers arrived. Though Mike did not see them, he heard their choking cries and screams of surprise, felt the powerful, flowing movement of his well-muscled, sleek body. The only thing he knew was that his life was at stake and he had to kill them before they killed him.

Once the killing was over, he felt blackness rimming his vision, the gold-and-white light rapidly beginning to fade. With a groan that seemed more like a low growl to his ears, he felt himself running, or more appropriately, loping. He could feel the slap of leaves against his body, but he couldn't see anything! His energy began to seep away. Strength left his legs, flowing up through his torso. He felt the damp earth beneath his hands and he suddenly collapsed onto it with a groan. The light was gone; the darkness rapidly moved toward him. He was dead. He was sure of it as he lay there on the jungle floor, covered in the humid mist that divided this world and the next.

Houston regained consciousness slowly. Prying his heavy lids open languidly, he stared upward. He lay on his back, hidden by the thick, luxuriant growth around him. Yes, he could see the dark silhouettes of the trees outlined in the mist. But something was different. What? His mind was groggy and he was having trouble remembering much of anything. Above the dense, humid white clouds above the canopy, the sun had shifted. It was almost dusk, he realized.

Little by little, strength flowed back to him. He groaned and rolled slowly onto his left side. Recalling his deadly wound, he propped himself up against a tree and groggily looked down at his right thigh. Blood was everywhere across his lower body. Yet where was the wound? Weakly lifting his hand, his fingers trembling badly, he tried to find the rip in the material where the bullet had entered. There was none. Frowning, he tried to think. It was impossible.

Was he dead and just didn't know it? Looking up, he realized he felt different, but very much alive. He dug his fingers into the damp, rotting leaves to assure himself of the reality of his surroundings. As he continued to stare down at the place where his wound should have been, he realized something else had changed. The entire front of his uniform was splattered with blood. He hadn't been wounded in the chest. What would cause blood to cover the front of shirt? Moving his hand slowly up his wrinkled, muddy uniform, Houston realized the blood had dried, stiffening the fabric. The metallic odor clung nauseatingly to his flaring nostrils.

How did he get covered with so much blood? It couldn't be his own. His mind railed at the illogic of it all. Lifting his head, Mike slowly tried to absorb everything around him. Yes, he was still in a jungle. The same one he'd crash-landed into, as far as he could tell. Monkeys screamed in the distance, their howling somehow comforting him. A few colorful parrots flew above him looking for a night perch before dusk ended in darkness.

As his gaze dropped from the jungle around him to his left arm, hanging at his side, he felt a jolt. There were gold hairs on his arm. Gold and black. He frowned, thinking he was seeing things. Using what little strength he had left, he lifted his arm and stared at it. What the hell? His vision blurred and then cleared once again. There, on his forearm near his wrist, was an irregular patch of gold hair with two black crescent-moon shapes. This couldn't be real, he reasoned. As he moved his fingers across the patch of hair, his heart thudded hard, once, in his chest. It was fur. Soft, short, thick fur, surrounded by his own hair. But as he explored it, it disappeared beneath his fingertips.

Overwhelmed, Houston leaned his head back against the tree and drew several deep breaths of air into his lungs. His senses were no longer as acute, but he heard voices not too far from where he lay. Escovar's men? Snapping his eyes open, Mike waited. For some reason, he didn't feel danger. That was silly, too. Just moments ago, several of Escovar's men were going to kill him. Confused, Mike narrowed his eyes and gazed toward the sound.

An aged white man, barefoot and wearing dark blue pants, with a jaguar skin draped over his shoulders, appeared out of the jungle in front of him. Houston raised his eyes to the gray-haired man's bearded face and met his crinkled gray eyes. The old man nodded in greeting and exposed strong white teeth in a welcoming smile. The man's two cohorts came toward Mike, an African man and a young Indian girl with willow green eyes.

"I was told you were out here," the old man said, leaning heavily against a staff that had brightly colored macaw feathers attached to its top. He touched the claw necklace around his neck and chuckled. "I see your guardian has left you your life, hombre. We will take you back to the village. You will be safe with us. Come...."

Chapter 1

"Mike? Mike, it's time to get up!"

Groaning, Houston turned on his side, jamming his face into the feather pillow. Damn, he thought groggily, he'd had that nightmare again. A flashback really, the same one he'd had a hundred times before...

"Mike?"

"Uh, yeah...I'm awake...." he muttered.

Where was he? Rolling over, he forced his eyes open. The plain timbers of the Santa Fe architecture of the room met his eyes, reminding him he was no longer in the jungle. The sounds were different here. He heard the crow of a nearby rooster and the soft snort of some horses in a corral. As he blinked the sleep out of his eyes, he heard the lowing of cattle, too. Oh yeah, he remembered suddenly. He was staying at the Donovan Ranch near Sedona, Arizona. Helluva long way from his normal digs.

He shoved himself upright in the old brass bed, the covers falling away to expose his naked chest and upper body. When he got the chance, he never slept with clothes on—even pajamas—preferring nakedness instead. All too often in his work he had to sleep in his fatigues, ready to leap up and start moving at a moment's notice. In fact, sleeping in a bed was a luxury for him.

Savagely rubbing his face to wake up, Mike felt the stiff prickle of beard beneath his fingers. He'd had that post-traumatic-stress-disorder dream again, reminding him of who he really was, of what made him different from other men, other human beings. Scowling, he shook his head and sent the fragments of memory back into the depths of that cauldron, his subconscious. *More like Pandora's box with an ugly twist,* he thought with a sleepy grin.

What time is it? he wondered, shoving his feet from beneath the covers and placing them on the cool cedar floor. The clock on his bed stand said 0800.

Dr. Ann Parsons had called him from the next room, he realized belatedly. The alarm clock must have gone off and he hadn't heard it. *Damn.* He'd promised Morgan Trayhern that he'd meet him at 0800 to get the details of his next mission. Grunting, Mike launched himself out of bed and stretched. He liked the feeling of each group of muscles in his body bunching, stretching and relaxing. Arcing his arms over his head, he closed his eyes and appreciated his physical strength. It was one helluva body, one that had more scars on it, had taken more blows and survived more than most.

Exhaling loudly, he ran his fingers through his military short, dark hair and headed to the bathroom that adjoined his room. As he padded across the pale gold floor, he remembered his nightmare. A smile cut across his thinned lips as he opened the door to the shower and turned it on. Nine years had passed since that incident in the jungle, and at thirty-five years of age, he still dreamed about that miraculous, life-changing event.

As he stepped into the pummeling stream of hot water for his morning shower—another luxury—the steam roiled in clouds around him reminding him of the endless twisting clouds that haunted the jungles of South America. He grabbed the soap and began to briskly wash himself. There was nothing like a hot shower to get the blood flowing and wake him up. For the first hour of the morning Houston was a bear of sorts, until he was fully awake and had poured a cup of good, black espresso down his gullet. Then and only then was he human and not growling or snarling at everyone. Mike had a reputation of being a grizzly in the morning.

Soaping his left arm, he blinked away the water running in rivulets across his face. Grinning, he studied the burn scars on his darkly haired arm, reminding him of his escape from the flaming copter that had been shot down. Various white scars from shrapnel that had exploded from the craft after it had crashed were also visible reminders of that day he'd faced death and won.

But he no longer saw a tuft of gold fur with black crescents across it. Scrubbing his arm, Mike turned his face into the stream of hot water. That old shaman from the village, Grandfather Adaire, had informed him that Mike's guardian had guided him to rescue Mike and care for him. It took nearly a week of rest in that remote jungle village known as the Village of the Clouds before Houston had been in any shape to decide whether he wanted to live or not.

Mike recalled how his men at the military barracks just outside of Lima called him *El Jaguar,* or the jaguar god—the man who had returned from the dead. Jaguars were believed to be the only animal able to do that, according to legends about them that abounded throughout South America. Everyone had thought Mike died with the other men of his squad in that crash. But he hadn't. And he never told anyone of his strange adventure through life, death and life again. They'd have called him loco—crazy. No one would ever know the truth of what had really happened out there.

Only that old shaman, his white hair sticking out around his head like a hen's nest, seemed to know exactly what had happened. Mike had been too weak to question him. Inca, the young Indian girl from Brazil with the willow green eyes and long black hair, had fed him nourishing soup, kept him warm and tended him hourly in a hut near the shaman's dwelling in the village. For that entire week, Inca had cared for him like he was a newborn baby. She was only eighteen years old, an orphan who had been adopted by Adaire and his wife, Alaria. Every time Adaire dropped by to see how well Mike was recovering, the old shaman would laugh the laugh of a man who knew an inside joke. Only Mike didn't know the joke and the shaman didn't seem particularly desirous of letting him in on it.

After washing his hair, Mike quickly rinsed, shut off the shower and climbed out. Rubbing himself briskly with a thick, white, terry-cloth towel, he reveled in the sensations it created across his goose-bump-covered flesh. Funny, but since that incident nine years earlier, he'd become far more aware of his body than ever before. He had walked away from his experience in the jungle with a sense of pleasure about his tall, strong physical form that he'd not had previous to his brush with death. Sometimes he felt like a great, giant cat stretching. And if he ran, he could feel the joy of blood pumping through him, the incredible power in his muscles. It was a euphoric sensation, one that he'd come to enjoy.

Hurrying through the rest of his morning duties, Mike quickly dressed in his camouflage fatigues, put his spotless, shining boots on and placed his beret in the left epaulet of his blouse. Taking one more look in the steamy mirror, he saw staring back at him a man who looked like one tough hombre, in his opinion. His blue eyes were large, though more often they were narrowed, focusing on something that would catch his wary attention. Tiny white scars stood out against his recently shaved jaw. The many lines at the corners of his eyes and the slash brackets on either side of his pursed mouth shouted of his military hardness. He was a major in Special Forces and damn proud of it. He'd survived thirteen long years in the Peruvian jungle, where life was often snuffed out in a heartbeat by vengeful drug lords.

Glancing at the watch on his hairy wrist, he realized he'd better get a move on. He'd just hurry out to the kitchen, grab his very necessary cup of espresso and gulp it down before meeting Morgan. And he was anxious to get to that meeting for another reason beside the fact that he was late. Though Mike had enjoyed the peace and quiet of this ranch, he had discovered other, greater benefits to staying there—such as spending time with the good doctor. Dr. Ann Parsons had been assigned to tend to Morgan and his wife's recovery, while Mike had been assigned to keep guard. And he certainly hadn't minded working with the pretty M.D.

Even better than seeing his boss today, Mike decided as he opened the door to his bedroom, he'd get to sit and look at Ann once more. Smiling to himself, he realized he was looking forward to that pleasure most of all. Even though she also worked for

Morgan at Perseus, a high-level, supersecret government entity, he wouldn't see her after today. Houston wanted to take every opportunity to absorb her beauty before they parted ways. Sighing as he walked down the gleaming hallway, he knew he could easily fall in love with Ann. If he allowed himself to. The price that they'd pay, however, would be too high. Besides, his keen interest in her was only one-sided. Yes, they'd shared a number of heated, promising kisses over the last two months, but she wasn't really interested in him as much as he wished she were. Ann was afraid of commitment, Mike realized. Why, he didn't know.

The memory of her sweet, soft mouth beneath his made him go hot with yearning all over again. Ann enjoyed their stolen moments together, there was no doubt. So why did she keep pushing him away? He'd seen the desire in her thoughtful blue-gray eyes after one of their torrid, hungry kisses. Had felt her tremble deliciously in his arms. The hunger in her eyes went all the way through him. So what had stopped her every damn time? Mike was confused. He'd tried to get Ann to open up, to talk about it, but she wouldn't. It was like hitting a damn brick wall. But he didn't press Ann any longer. Because although this was the first time in a long time he found himself wanting a woman, being with Ann wasn't a game with him, either. Mike didn't see her as a one-night stand or someone to amuse himself with while he was here in Arizona. He, too, was wary of having a relationship and he knew he couldn't have things both ways. But what really did he want with her?

The realistic side of him told him that even though he could fall hopelessly in love with her if he threw caution to the wind, their relationship could go nowhere anyway. Not with his jaded past. Not with his dangerous present and future. His heart ached. He reluctantly admitted that he'd felt a lot of things for Ann over the past two months and there wasn't a damn thing he could do about it. Maybe, Houston ruminated sadly, it was just as well she kept her distance from him—for whatever secret reasons she held. Anyone he had ever loved had died. It was that heartbreakingly simple. A fact. And he had no desire to see Ann die. *Hell...*

More than anything, Mike respected Ann. She had started out as an Air Force flight surgeon and her training also included work as a psychiatrist. Now a medical doctor for Perseus, she was very good at what she did. Her work with Morgan had often placed her in danger; she was frequently assigned to fly in and pick up wounded mercenaries when they got into more trouble than they'd bargained for. Mike decided that maybe Ann had made a pact with herself a long time ago not to get involved with military types. Oh, he didn't blame her there. Hell, a military man could be alive one moment, dead the next. And where did that leave the woman who loved him? Alone, without the man she'd hoped to have around for a long, long time. Her lover gone—forever.

Too bad. She's a looker. Tall, leggy, self-confident, she had a gutsiness he admired. There was nothing about the thirty-two-year-old doctor that didn't appeal to him. Pity she didn't see him in the same light. Maybe her womanly instincts warned her how different he really was. Maybe she was picking up on his secret life and it was scaring her away from him....

Mike turned the corner and headed to the kitchen. Hell, any woman who took one look at his hard-bitten, scarred countenance and heard of his fearsome reputation would run the other way. He was one mean son of a bitch and he had his actions in Peru to prove it.

Down there they called him the jaguar god because he seemed to have nine lives like the most powerful hunter in the South American jungle—the dreaded, mystical jaguar. The drug lords feared Mike and they damn well should. Those bastards had destroyed his mother's helpless people, and as long as Houston could take a breath into his body, his whole life would be geared to eradicating them from Peru.

Maybe that's why no women wanted to become involved in a long-term relationship with him. They wouldn't be the focus of his life or his attentions. Houston couldn't blame them. Still, he'd miss Ann Parsons like hell. Her soft, exploratory kisses, the hunger she sparked in him would be no more. It was a damn shame. For she was a woman who could not only turn his head, but even make him consider devoting a little time to her instead of the one-man war he waged continuously against the cocaine lords....

When Houston reached the kitchen, he heard voices. Groaning inwardly, he realized it was Ann's honeyed, cultured tone and

Morgan Trayhern's deep, probing voice. Mike was so late the meeting was already underway. As he headed for the espresso machine, he heard them in the living room talking animatedly, like the good friends they were. Ann had worked for Morgan almost from the time he'd created Perseus many years ago. It was then he saw the note beside the tiled sink, next to the espresso machine "In case you oversleep," it said in Ann's "doctor scrawl." No one could read her writing but him, and he'd teased her about it mercilessly during the eight weeks they had been at the Donovan Ranch baby-sitting Morgan and his wife.

Mike hurriedly snapped on the machine. Ann had ground the coffee, put it in the small basket and filled the steel container with fresh water that would soon be boiling, ready to percolate his desperately needed espresso. A mirthless, one-cornered smile cut into the hard planes of Mike's face. Though Ann didn't like him to the degree he fancied her, she had a good heart. She'd even taken pity on the likes of him.

Houston poked his head around the entrance to the living room of the cabin he was staying in on the ranch. They'd agreed to meet at his cabin and he saw Morgan, dressed in a pair of jeans and a red plaid, flannel shirt, sitting at the end of a leather couch, near the open fireplace. Ann stood in front of the blazing flames, which brought out the red and gold highlights in her shoulder-length sable hair. She was rubbing her long, thin surgeon's hands together vigorously, warming herself.

Mike was chilly, too, but it was wintertime in Arizona, so what did he expect? When Ann lifted her chin and her blue-gray eyes met his, he grinned a little sheepishly.

"Morning," he rumbled.

"Is it? You haven't had your coffee yet, Major Houston, so I know better than to engage you in polite social conversation."

His boyish grin broadened in embarrassment. He saw Morgan frown and look first at Ann and then at him.

Houston nodded. "Yeah, you're right, Doc. I'm just an old snarly jaguar before I get my espresso. I'll be in shortly. A good fairy all but made my java for me and it'll be ready pronto." He winked at her. "I owe you, Ann...."

"Take your time, Mike," Morgan murmured with a forgiving

look. He lifted a heavy white mug from the coffee table and took a sip. "Today we're not in a hurry."

Mike saw Ann's eyes sparkle mischievously even though her face had a deadpan expression. As he stepped back into the kitchen, he remembered the blush that had spread across her long, sloping cheekbones when he'd winked at her. She always reacted to his playful charm with some discomfort. He wondered why and lamented once more that Ann had never opened up to him about her past or why she couldn't fully embrace him now. Her kisses said one thing, the fear he saw in her eyes quite another.

Damn, but the woman was pretty. Did she realize she held his heart in her hands? Did she want today to be goodbye? He'd dreamed torrid dreams of loving her completely. The closest they had come to that was the day they had shared a picnic down at the creek. He'd accurately read her desire that time, and when he'd kissed her, she'd asked him to touch her intimately, to explore her with his hands.

In the molten heat of the moment, as he'd stretched out on the blanket beside her, she'd frozen. Mike had sat up, for he had no desire to push himself on her. She had apologized and quickly pulled her blouse back over her shoulders, before getting up and hurrying away. Her face had been flushed and he could tell she was embarrassed by her behavior.

It was so frustrating! Everything about their relationship was on again, off again. She wanted him. She was afraid of him. Or maybe she was afraid of herself? Mike pondered that angle as he waited for his espresso to brew.

Ann was a type A personality who didn't know how to rest or relax. She had to be doing something every single minute of her day. In his book, people like that were running away from something. So what was Ann running from? Sighing audibly, Mike scowled. If only she'd lower those walls she held around herself and talk to him. If only...

The aromatic odor of the espresso drifted toward him as he stood expectantly over the machine. Ann had often made a wry face at his need to drink only black, thick espresso, but hell, in South America it was the drink of choice, besides maté, Argentina's national drink. He'd been raised on espresso since he was a small kid, following his mother into the kitchen as she made her own cup each morning.

Picking up the note with his scarred fingers, he shook his head. He couldn't figure Ann out. Most of the time around the ranch she pointedly ignored him. His job was to run patrols and keep Morgan and Laura safe from possible drug-cartel attacks while they holed up and tried to heal from the kidnapping ordeal that had torn their lives apart, quite literally, at the seams. Ann had come because she was a qualified psychiatrist and Laura's state had been rocky and unstable at first.

Mike ran his fingers across the ink on the note. Since she'd been staying at the hideaway cabin on Oak Creek with her husband, Laura spent an hour in therapy every day with Dr. Parsons, and Mike wasn't surprised that Ann had helped Laura Trayhern tremendously. God knew, he wanted to feel the effects of Ann's undivided attention on him. Grinning darkly, he told himself that he'd change, too, if given the chance to be the center of *her* focus. But thus far, Ann evaded him whenever possible. So why did she obviously enjoy his kisses so much when he eased her into his arms? He could feel all her walls melt away as they kissed.

Was Ann prejudiced against his skin color—the fact that he wasn't a pure white, Anglo male with all the trimmings? Perhaps she couldn't bring herself to admit it to herself, much less him. Questions, so many damn, unanswered questions. And today was the last day he'd ever see Ann. His heart squeezed with pain. With need.

As he poured the espresso into a small, delicate white cup with his large hands, he sighed in frustration, mentally preparing himself to shift gears and talk business with Morgan Trayhern. At least Ann would be in the same room with him and he'd get one last moment with her. He felt like a man being sent to the gallows and having his last wish fulfilled, but hell, there was no love life for him where he was heading. None at all. The only thing waiting for him was a bullet or a machete with his name on it. No, Peru was his hell. Whatever small piece of heaven he'd been afforded had died years earlier, and Houston knew that with his karmic track record—the many men he'd killed over the years—heaven wasn't about to grant him a second chance at anything. With a careless grin, he shrugged his shoulders as if throwing off the grief and chains of the past, and headed toward the living room.

Chapter 2

Mike sauntered into the living room after taking his first, rejuvenating sip of the dark, fragrant liquid. He chose a leather wing chair opposite Morgan, in front of a coffee table littered with magazines. Ann was holding her own cup of coffee between her hands, standing with her back to the snapping, roaring fire. She refused to look him in the eye, some of the flush still lingering on her cheeks.

"I overslept," Mike growled in Morgan's direction, studying his boss's somber features. The man who had hired him was internationally famous. Morgan headed up Perseus, a high-tech mercenary operation consisting of men and women, mostly from the military, who were hired to perform dangerous missions around the world. Though Perseus was privately owned by Morgan, there wasn't a government in the democratic world that didn't hire his renown services. Like Morgan, whose honesty and strong military background kept this clandestine ship of state running smoothly, his people were the best at what they did. Most people, when they heard the word *mercenary,* thought of a turncoat bastard who had no allegiance except to the bottom line: money. Not so at Perseus. Trayhern's reputation for integrity was well known by almost every government in the world. He and his team were revered for coming to the aid of those who were in trouble and, for whatever reason, were without their country's legal or political protection.

Because Trayhern had been wronged by his own country, had been labeled a traitor and been in hiding for nearly half his life before his name was cleared with the help of his wife, he knew the disastrous results of not being able to reach out to some powerful entity for help.

As Mike leaned back and relished each sip of his espresso, he noticed once again the white scar that ran from Morgan's left temple all the way down his recently shaved cheek to his jaw, a mute testimony of his surviving on a hill in the closing days of the Vietnam War. There, he'd been a captain in the Marine Corps, and responsible for a company of men that had been wiped out and overrun by the enemy. Only he and one other man had survived. And then his troubles had really begun. Now that he was nearing fifty, Morgan's black hair was peppered at the temples with silver though his square face was still hard, shouting of the rigid discipline of his military background. Because he was a hero in Houston's eyes, Mike had agreed to act as Morgan and Laura's bodyguard during this rather bland two-month stay in rural Arizona.

"You ready to talk?" Morgan asked him with a slight grin. "Ann's been warning me about you being snarly without your espresso."

"Yeah," Mike rumbled, "she might as well have set up an IV and poured it directly into my veins this morning. Sorry I overslept." He glanced at Ann, who refused to meet his gaze. Mike was too much of a gentleman to say *why* he'd lost so much sleep last night. The reason was that he'd cornered Ann and asked her why she was evading him. It had turned into a frustrating, angry confrontation and he'd ended up silencing her with a kiss—a kiss that had nearly been both their undoing. Ann had almost lost control of herself. He had felt her unraveling in his arms. And that's when she'd pushed him away. It had been a miserable night for them, he acknowledged. She'd cried and he'd held her. Yet as he rocked her in his arms, she'd still refused to give in to him and

talk about why she kept him at arm's length. One thing he knew
for sure, she didn't trust him. That hurt Mike deeply and his heart
ached with sadness.

Cocking his head in Ann's direction, he saw a slight, strained
smile cross her full lips as she lifted the cup and took a sip of her
coffee. Her eyes were still puffy looking this morning. He wondered if she'd cried more after tearing out of his embrace and
fleeing to her room last night.

Morgan nodded. "It was a good day to sleep in." He picked
up a file and handed it across the pine coffee table to Mike.
"Here's your pay and a little extra bonus for taking this mission
on. I know you didn't have to."

As the manila file slid into his fingers, Mike placed his cup on
the table. Opening the folder, he saw a check for thirty thousand
dollars, plus papers detailing all his duties over the last two
months.

His brows raised. "This is a little much, boss."

Morgan grinned and crossed his legs. "I know soldiers like you
don't enjoy baby-sitting jobs like this one. But you knew the drug
lords involved, and you knew their habits and techniques. I know
you'd rather be down in the Peruvian jungles chasing them than
sitting up here for two months playing watchdog." He motioned
with his finger toward the check Houston was holding. "I'm grateful you took the mission, pabulum or not, Mike. That's our way
of thanking you."

Houston had heard several times from Ann how generous Trayhern was with his employees, as well as the charities they supported. Now Mike was getting a firsthand taste of it. "Hell," he
muttered, "this is almost a year's army pay for me."

Chuckling, Morgan nodded. "It probably is. There's a first-class
airline ticket there also, reserved under your assumed identity of
Peter Quinn. You've got a flight out of Phoenix at 1500 hours
today aboard Veracruz Airlines. They make a fueling stop in Mexico City and then you fly directly into Lima."

The man was excessively generous, Mike decided as he found
the airline ticket. He frowned as he saw another check beneath the
ticket. Setting the folder down in his lap, he muttered, "What's
this?" His eyes widened considerably. It was a check for a hun-

dred thousand dollars, made out to the Sisters of Guadalupe Clinic in Lima, Peru.

"Laura was telling me how, in your spare time, you work with two old French nuns down in the barrio, the poor section of Lima, using your paramedic skills alongside the nuns' homeopathic treatments. She said you'd established the medical clinic eight years ago to help Indian children who couldn't afford medical help." He waved his hand toward the check Mike was holding. "That's a donation to your clinic, Houston. Laura hinted that the clinic was usually running on hope and faith, and that you could use a lot more supplies." His eyes grew thoughtful. "Maybe this will keep the wolf...or jaguar...from your clinic's door for a while."

Mike swallowed hard, his Adam's apple bobbing as he held the check. The paper felt as if it were burning his fingers. "This..."

"Speechless for once?" Ann teased with a soft laugh.

Mike twisted his head to look up at her. That unreadable doctor's facade generally in place on her oval face was gone. He waited for such moments because her openness gave her unusual features a warm attractiveness. Her nose was long and thin and had obviously been broken at one time because there was a slight bump on it. She was narrow all over—narrow oval face, narrow hands and skinny but shapely legs. Her eyes were one of her finest features: large, intelligent and widely set. Her mouth, which was now curved gently, hinted powerfully to him of her soft, vulnerable side. Mike hungrily absorbed her countenance, and he managed a slight grin. Ann was trying desperately to be civil to him.

He saw the darkness in her eyes and could feel her fear. Was she as sad over their parting as he was? His heart said yes. Although his intuition didn't make sense at all to him, now was not the place or time to pursue it. He was sure Morgan didn't know about Ann's on-and-off relationship with him over the past two months, and he'd keep it that way—for her sake.

"Yeah, you're right—I usually have a comeback for almost everything, don't I?"

Ann nodded. "Without fail, Major Houston. One of your most reliable traits."

"I'll take that as praise, not an insult, Dr. Parsons." A little of her old, teasing self was resurfacing, and Mike was glad. The last

thing he wanted was to make Ann feel bad, and he sure as he
had managed to do that last night. Before he left, he knew he'c
have to draw her aside, privately, and apologize. He didn't wan
their friendship to end on a bitter note. Ann deserved better thar
that and so did he.

She shrugged her shoulders delicately. "Take it any way yo
want, Major. I'm always open to options."

How he wished she really were! Laughing deeply, Mike re
turned his attention to Morgan. "This is unexpected."

The warmth in Morgan's eyes belied the expressionless masl
he usually wore over his features. "Needed, according to Laura,'
he said. "I like to help out the less fortunate. God knows, I wa
one for long enough, Mike." He scowled at the memory of th
atrocities he'd suffered.

Mike stared at the check. "Thank you. You have no idea hov
much this is going to help. I was trying to figure out a way t
keep the clinic open. I'm afraid our little charity isn't seen as ver
worthy by the rich and powerful in Lima. The children are dark
skinned Indians, not poor little Anglos in need. Believe me—" hi
voice shook with sudden emotion "—this is going to help mor
than you'll ever know." Mike vaguely recalled talking to Laur
about his clinic once, a fleeting conversation he'd completely for
gotten about. The woman didn't forget anything! And she was jus
as generous and giving as her very wealthy husband.

"We're glad to do what we can, Mike. From now on, you
clinic is on *our* donation list. The sum might go up or down
little, but at least you'll know that every January, you'll be re
ceiving enough money, I hope, to keep those doors open to th
Indian children and their families." Leaning forward, Morgan tool
a second manila file from the coffee table and handed it to Ann
"Here are your marching orders, Ann. You were asking me where
I was sending you next. Well, take a look. I think you'll b
pleased."

Ann smiled warmly at Morgan as she took the file. "Thanks.
love new missions."

Mike saw how comfortable Ann and Morgan were with on
another and realized they almost had an older brother–younge
sister relationship. It was obvious Ann loved Morgan and re

pected him. Hell, who wouldn't? Still, Mike felt a twinge of longing because he wished Ann would bestow such a warm, trusting
look in his direction. But he knew that would never happen after
today, and he found himself lamenting that fact far more sharply
than he should. Such was the effect the good doctor had on him,
although she pretended to be oblivious of the way he mooned over
her like a jaguar did over a lost mate. Mike suspected Ann really
missed nothing. She was a trained therapist. She was taught to
observe nuances of body language, tone of voice and subtle expressions. No, she knew he was powerfully drawn to her, but she
wasn't interested, that was all. And although that left him confused
and frustrated, he realized it was for the best. He wasn't exactly
the kind of man who could give her what she needed, in light of
his own past.

Sighing, Mike leaned back in the chair, stealing a moment to
watch Ann unobtrusively. He rarely got such a chance, and since
they were parting today and he'd never see her again, he wanted
to take this opportunity to absorb her into his heart one last time.
In some ways, he was like a greedy thief, and he felt a little guilty
about it.

Ann chuckled as she placed the coffee cup on the dark wood
mantel above the fireplace. "I hope it's a warm place, Morgan!
I'm freezing here." She opened the file in her hands. "Hawaii or
Australia would sure be nice," she hinted with a smile.

"Oh," Morgan murmured, "you're going someplace warm, all
right, but neither of those countries."

Ann picked up the airline ticket and opened it.

Mike saw her broad brow wrinkle instantly. And then she
snapped an unsettled look in *his* direction. He almost asked why,
but then she pursed her lips and began sifting through the rest of
the papers, reading intently.

"Morgan," she protested in a strangled tone, "what's going on
here? This isn't an assignment for another mission." Ann stared
accusingly at Houston again. "These are orders to go down to *his*
clinic in Lima and help him out for six weeks."

"Yes," Morgan murmured, sipping his coffee contentedly, "it
is."

Stunned, Houston looked at Ann's upset features and then at

Morgan. "What?" He couldn't have been hearing right. His hear
pounded briefly in his chest as he sat up at full attention. Ann wa
coming to Lima with him? The news staggered him. Elated him
Worried him. He saw the undiluted fear in Ann's eyes as neve
before. His hands wrapped around the arms of the chair. What wa
going on here?

Waving her thin hand across the file, Ann sputtered, "Morgan
this isn't a mission assignment. This—this is—charity work!"

"It's a mission," Morgan soothed. "A very important one
Laura and I think you're the perfect person to help Mike get thi
little clinic up and running." He smiled slightly, satisfied with hi
plans. "As a matter of fact—" he glanced down at the gold Role>
watch on his wrist "—there's a load of medical supplies bein;
trucked from Mesa, Arizona, over to Sky Harbor International Air
port in Phoenix right now. Ann, you will be responsible for ove
fifty thousand dollars' worth of medical supplies once you tw
land in Lima. And then I expect you, with your usual precisio
and organizational skills, to take the six weeks and get Mike'
clinic up to full speed like it should be."

Gasping, Ann shut the folder with finality. Her eyes flashed
"You *planned* this, Major Houston."

Mike's mouth dropped open and he quickly snapped it shut
"Now, just a minute, Ann," he muttered as he unwound from th
chair and stood up, "I didn't know anything about this." And h
hadn't. But he felt her anger directly. Those gray-blue eyes of her
turned icy cold when she was upset. Disliking the fact that he wa
being accused of something he was innocent of, he looked at Mor
gan. "Tell her, will you?"

"Mike knew nothing about this, Ann. It was actually Laura'
idea. We spent several evenings planning it out, making the nec
essary phone calls and getting everything lined up."

Glaring at Houston, Ann closed her fingers tightly over th
folder. "Morgan, one thing I learned about this Peruvian cowbo
in the last two months I've spent here is that he's a master o
manipulation."

"Oww, that hurts," Mike protested. Not that it wasn't true
"Sure, I rob Peter to pay Paul, so to speak, in order to get th
money I need to finance our military efforts down in Peru, but—"

"You've got a mind like a steel trap," Ann accused in a low voice. "You probably purposely dropped the information about your clinic to Laura because you know she has such a soft heart for people who are in trouble or need help."

Anger stirred in Houston. One thing he didn't like was being wrongly accused. He saw the desperation in Ann's eyes and heard the raw pain in her voice. He was receiving so many confused emotional signals from her that he didn't have time to sort them all out. Keeping his voice soothing, he rasped, "Look, Ann, I had *no idea* when Laura buttonholed me about a month ago, and nosed around about what I did down in Lima, that she'd take the information and do something like this with it."

"Ann, calm down," Morgan said in his deep voice. "This isn't a prison sentence."

"Really?" Ann glared steadily in Houston's direction.

"Really," Morgan repeated. He sat up and placed his cup on the coffee table in front of him. "Why be so upset? It's spring in Peru. It's warm. It's a beautiful country and Lima is one of the most sophisticated and affluent cities in South America. I've arranged everything for you. There'll be a van waiting at the Lima airport. The medical supplies will be loaded into it and Mike can drive you to the clinic. There's another car there waiting for you. It was bought earlier and registered in the clinic's name, since the clinic's got a nonprofit status. You can use it to drive back and forth to the nice apartment we've rented for you." He smiled at her. "For once you aren't going to be flying around in a helicopter with a flak jacket and helmet on, wondering if you're landing in a hot fire zone. This is a pretty safe assignment. Quiet. Probably pretty boring, but I'm sure it will be immensely satisfying to you emotionally. It isn't that you don't like children. I know different."

Houston prowled restlessly around the perimeter of the living room. He watched Ann give him livid, stabbing looks of raw accusation every now and again, despite the fact that Morgan had an incredibly soothing effect on her—any woman, in fact. Mike wished he had the skill, but didn't. "Look," he protested in frustration, "if Ann doesn't want to go, there's nothing I can do about that. But maybe I can take the edge off things a little bit for her." He leaned down and picked up the thirty-thousand-dollar check.

"Here, put this with the rest, since you're going to have to put up with me six weeks longer than you thought." He handed Ann the donation and the personal check Morgan had written out to him. He could see the fear deep in her eyes. Anger warred with sadness and heartbreak within him. Trying his best to gather his strewn emotions, he rasped, "You want to run a clinic, it takes money. So here it is. And if you're pissed off and distrusting of me and my intentions, well, that's okay. I know the truth—I had nothing to do with this assignment of yours. I won't be around the clinic that much to be a pain in the ass to you, anyway. Fair enough?" He put both checks in her hands. Her gaze wavered as she met his hard, angry eyes.

Houston turned, shook Morgan's hand, thanked him and left. He needed to get out of the house and calm down. As he went out the front door, the coolness of the Arizona morning hit him. Throwing back his shoulders, he descended the wooden steps quickly and headed toward the corral. *Damn! Everything's screwed up. Everything!* As he took long, steady strides, Mike rubbed his aching chest.

But although this wasn't how he'd planned things to go with Ann, a tiny part of him was euphoric that she would be coming to Lima with him. He would have more time with her, even if the opportunities to see her would be severely limited down there. As he halted at the corral, where twenty Arabians were feeding, he placed his elbows on the uppermost rung of the pipe fence. The metal felt cooling to him, to his smarting anger and frustration.

Closing his eyes, Houston tried to wrestle with all his emotions. Ann thought he'd set this whole thing up. It was obvious she hadn't believed Morgan when he'd explained that Mike had nothing to do with it. Her anger was real. And so was that terror banked in her eyes. Closing his fists, Mike took a deep, unsettled breath of air into his chest. No matter how hard he tried, he couldn't erase the sweet power of Ann's mouth upon his, her incredible, hungry response to him. But although her mouth, her body signaled one thing, her mind held sway over her actions. What a helluva fix he was in now! More than anything, Mike wanted to somehow convince Ann that he was innocent of dragging her on this assignment. Judging from her anger, she probably wasn't going to give him an opening very soon to explain. Maybe, on the flight down to Lima, she'd cool off and he could reason with her. He hoped so. Or maybe Morgan could soothe her because Mike certainly couldn't!

"Morgan, I don't want to go down there," Ann declared.

He shrugged and sipped his coffee. "Calm down, Ann. This is an excellent assignment." He smiled up at her drawn features. She looked cornered but Morgan didn't really want to let her out of this one. Worried that Escovar, one of the most powerful of all the drug dealers in South America, was going to go after Mike Houston in earnest once Mike was back in Peru, Morgan wanted a backup. He didn't want to tell Houston of his concerns for his life, but if Mike got into trouble, Morgan wanted someone with the best medical skills on the planet nearby. And even though Ann was only in her early thirties, she was a top professional in the field.

Ann didn't know why he was sending her to Peru to be near Houston. Morgan didn't want to put that kind of pressure on her. Besides, from everything he and his wife could see, there was a mutual attraction between the by-the-book doctor and the hot-headed, passionate major whose Indian blood kept him running headlong into dangerous scrapes with Escovar. Yes, Ann's cool, calm and collected personality would be a good match for Houston, whose zealous attempts to destroy every drug dealer he could find in Peru could be his undoing.

Morgan admired Houston tremendously, and he'd just gotten information from the highest government sources that Escovar had recently renewed his efforts to take revenge on Houston. In fact, Escovar had just doubled the price on his head. Morgan had no doubt Mike had his own network of spies to warn him of Escovar's movements, but Morgan wanted a safety net for him. And Ann, who was all science and facts, was a good chess piece to put into play down there. She could keep tabs on the footloose major and save his neck, if necessary. No, it was best that Ann go there thinking she would be slaving away in a small clinic. Morgan didn't want her flying in those drug-raid copters and getting shot at. He knew that Houston's network of helicopters could ensure that he was within an hour's ride of Lima should anything terrible happen to him. And Ann would be there waiting, ready with her surgical skills to save his sorry life.

Smiling to himself, Morgan sipped more of his coffee. There was no one better than Houston to go up against Eduardo Escovar. But Morgan wanted insurance for him of a different sort. He felt intuitively that Houston liked Ann—a whole lot. And maybe, just maybe, the hotshot jungle fighter would ease off on the throttles just a little bit, take a few less risks if he knew he had someone to return to in Lima after one of his bloody raids deep in the mountains. *Maybe...* Morgan admitted his plan was risky in itself. It was obvious Ann thought Houston had maneuvered things to get her on this assignment. And in Houston, she had more than met her match. Chuckling to himself, Morgan marveled over the attraction he saw between the cool, level-headed scientist and the passionate jaguar god of Peru. It was the molten steel being thrust into a bucket of icy water. What a combination! Morgan knew the sparks would fly. Secretly, his money was on Houston to endure her scalpel-like reactions and slowly but surely wear her down. Beneath Ann's genius mind, beneath that cold, scientific rationale that fed her intellect, was a hot-blooded woman who was afraid to step out of her ivory tower and experience being wild and free in a man's arms. And these weren't just any man's arms Morgan was pushing her toward.... He was betting that Houston could handle her. Time would tell, though.

"The flight to Peru will be a good shakedown cruise for both of you," he told Ann in his rumbling voice. "A nice chance to talk over how you want to run the clinic for Houston."

Ann glared at Morgan. "I'm not happy about this assignment. At all."

He lifted his hand. "Just be patient," he urged gently. "Mike isn't the monster you make him out to be. He's all-heart if you give him a chance."

That was exactly what Ann was afraid of—Mike Houston's passionate, wild heart. He frightened her. More so than any other man. And in less than three hours, she'd be forced to sit beside him on that airplane. How was she going to deal with her fearful emotions?

* * *

Ann tried to contain her feelings as she sat in the first-class section of the Veracruz flight. Mike Houston, dressed in a pair of dark brown slacks, a short-sleeved, white silk shirt and camel hair sport coat, sat across the aisle. She studied his rugged profile. It reminded her of the harsh granite of the Andes beneath them. They'd been in the air for hours since picking up fuel in Mexico City for the long flight to Lima.

Her conscience prickled. She knew she was being grumpy about this assignment and she didn't like herself for it. Generally, she was unflappable in every situation. Nothing ever caused her to swerve from her focus on saving lives, not even bullets flying around her. This man, this army major, had really unsettled her in ways she'd never thought possible. How could she be so drawn to Mike? *How?* It scared her to even think of him in that way. Ann thought herself incapable of ever falling in love again since— She slammed the lid shut on her memories before she felt the pain of them. Somehow being around Mike made her feel vulnerable once more. He was mysterious; there was something about him she couldn't put her finger on and it bothered her immensely. He was unlike any man she'd ever met—or had been attracted to. Her gut told her that dealing with him would be like handling nitroglycerine—one false move and the attraction between them would explode into something more.

She was a coward, she admitted to herself. A certifiable coward. Mike had been honest and aboveboard in his genuine interest in her. He hadn't manipulated her in this regard. After all, she'd enjoyed his kisses, his incredibly tender explorations, as much as he obviously had. There was no fault in this, really. She was an adult. She had willingly kissed him and wanted his continued caresses. Even now, she felt her lower body tighten with such need of him that she wanted to cry. The past was too strong for her to overcome, though. If she knew Mike for a longer time, those walls might dissolve. And that's what Ann was really afraid of. Six weeks in Lima with him around on a daily basis would surely unlatch a door in her heart that she'd thought would remain closed forever.

Anxiety raced through Ann. She felt bad and wanted to apologize to Mike for accusing him, though she wasn't so sure he was completely innocent of getting her assigned to Lima. She watched out of the corner of her eye as he sipped some amber-colored whiskey. He'd barely spoken a word to her for hours now and he only communicated when she asked him a question. He was still angry with her, despite the fact that he seemed to have cooled down considerably after his outburst in front of Morgan. He'd even apologized to her later as they were packing to leave the ranch. She'd stiffly accepted his apology, but she'd seen the sadness in his eyes, and had fought the tears in her own.

Ann didn't want to hurt Mike, but she knew she had. She could barely stand herself as a result. He was a man of incredible courage, an officer and a gentleman. The kind of man she could fall in love with, if she allowed herself. That's why going to a foreign country and being under Houston's protection was unnerving. She would *have* to rely on him because she was unfamiliar with Peruvian culture. Her rational mind didn't like being out of control like that. Ann had always relied upon herself, all her life. If she got into a scrape, she managed to get herself out—alone, without help.

Yes, she'd dreamed of Mike, of their kisses, of being with him completely. Her emotions unraveled when she was around him, and she felt needy, hungry in a way that she'd never felt before. The thought of six more weeks in his powerful and persuasive presence scared her more than bullets or bombs exploding around her.

Manipulation was something Ann despised. It brought out every conceivable dark emotion within her. But then, she'd been manipulated once, by a master similar to Houston, so why shouldn't she be wary of him? She'd fallen for an Air Force pilot after the one love of her life had died in a plane crash. Robert Crane had said every word, given her every look and done everything she'd ever dreamed that a man might do for the woman he was falling in love with—and she'd fallen hopelessly for him. Now she knew that what she felt for Robert had not grown out of love, but out of the grief and loss of her one true love. At the time, Ann hadn't realized that, of course.

The realization came soon after Crane had lured her into bed.

Once he'd "caught" her, he'd up and left. When Ann confronted him about it a week later, he'd laughed at her and told her the awful truth: he was a hunter, she was the hunted. His quarry. She'd been prey to be taken, used and then thrown away. The humiliation and shame of that disastrous time in her life had branded her forever. Never did Ann want to be manipulated like that again. Yet somehow Houston had gotten beneath her considerable armor. It must be his South American blood, his passion for life, that had breathed hot, molten desire into her heart. Daily, she fought her feelings for him. Daily, she tried to shrug off his heated looks, his gentle teasing, and yes, those wonderful kisses that opened her up inside and made her bare her vulnerability.

Ann closed her eyes and sighed raggedly. What was Houston's real intent? At thirty-two years old, she wasn't stupid or naive. She'd seen the looks he'd given her. She wasn't a young thing who didn't recognize in his dark blue, assessing eyes the smoldering hunger of a man who wanted a woman. He *wanted* her. She felt his longing for her, his unqualified interest. The raw, painful truth was Ann wanted Mike as much as he wanted her. And she was too much of a coward to even try to disentangle herself from the past and reach out to him. She was simply too scarred and too scared. What little emotion she had left was deeply hidden and protected within her. She just didn't have what it took to freely love Houston.

Sighing, Ann wrapped her arms across her chest, closed her eyes and tried to sleep. It was gloomy in the plane now, the lights very low. Most of the people around them in the first-class cabin were already asleep—except for her and Houston. Part of her just couldn't believe that he hadn't dropped several hints to Laura about his struggling clinic to get Ann down here in Lima with him. She knew enough about his dangerous job as an army liaison between the U.S. and Peruvian military resources to realize he had learned how to be very adroit in touchy political situations. She knew Houston had hobnobbed with the rich and powerful at fashionable dinners and society events in Lima. He was a smooth talker. Too smooth, she decided with a frown. Like Robert Crane, a little voice warned her stridently.

As an adviser and the commanding officer representing the U.S.

Army, Houston had to have a lot of skills in place. He had to have the ability to employ U.S. policy and get it to jibe with Peru's political philosophy at the same time. While working out in the field, which was obviously what he loved the most, he coordinated well-planned attacks against the cocaine lords in the jungle highlands. After a successful battle or raid, he'd work his way through the chain of command all the way up to the president of Peru, letting the government know what went down and how many millions of dollars of cocaine wouldn't flow north as a result. Houston handled a big budget and was responsible for keeping ten helicopters flying around the clock, chopping away at the cocaine warlords' domain.

Exhaling forcefully, Ann wondered why a man with such skills would have to manipulate her into coming down to his clinic. The thought made her open her eyes and sit up. She moved across the aisle to the empty seat next to him. Houston lifted his massive head, his dark blue gaze settling warily on hers.

"I just want to know one thing," Ann whispered fiercely. "Why the hell didn't you ask me, face-to-face, for my help? If you wanted me to come down here and help out, why didn't you come to me instead of pulling strings with Laura and Morgan to maneuver me into this corner?"

She saw the hand lying on the armrest slowly flex. She studied the many scars across it and knew every one was a story in itself. The scars were like mini badges of courage in her mind. Then she saw a flinty, cold look come in to his eyes. She felt iciness around him, aimed directly at her.

"Don't you think," Houston growled, leaning forward and nailing her with a glare, "that I would have if I thought you might do it? Sure, the thought crossed my mind, but that was *after* I'd told Laura a little about the clinic."

Ann gripped the seat, her fingers digging into the fabric. "You're saying you're innocent?" She tried to contain the hysteria she was feeling. Mike was so close, so very, very male, and her heart cried out for him, for his embrace. She hated herself for attacking him. He looked completely stunned by the force of her verbal assault. Once again she was hurting him. But she had to protect herself from Mike somehow, keep him from melting her down, little by little. Especially now that they would be working together at the clinic. He'd broken her resistance at the ranch. He would do so again down there, and Ann felt trapped and desperate. She just couldn't give in to her heart. If she did... No, it was too scary to even contemplate.

"For once," Houston rasped, "I am innocent." Reeling from her unexpected attack, he felt his anger explode. "Don't you think I know you don't trust me? You've made that pretty damn obvious, Ann." He set his empty glass down on the table in front of him and leaned slowly toward her, his eyes becoming slits. "Have you ever asked yourself why in the hell I would want to drag someone unwilling down to Lima and spend six weeks with her? That's kinda like throwing two male jaguars into the same pen. You sure as hell know they're territorial—that a male jaguar won't put up with another being in his territory. And they're sure as hell gonna fight each other to the death because each one can't stand the fact that the other is invading his turf."

He exhaled and growled, "One thing I'm not, Ann, is a victim. If you think for one second that I'm looking forward to your sulking, pouting demeanor while I'm working with those two little nuns, whom I love like grandmothers, you're very mistaken. As far as I'm concerned, you can get off this plane at the airport, execute an aboutface and climb right back on for a return flight to the States."

Stung, Ann glared at him, her heart beating hard in her breast. She saw the raw hurt in Mike's eyes, heard it in the rasp of his voice. Oh, why was she doing this? It was as if all the desperation she felt was being fueled by her underlying fear and turning her into this woman she'd never met before. Helpless to stop her response to him, she whispered harshly, "You're very good at twisting words, Major. But then, that's your job, isn't it? Get the dishonest politicians to play ball with you, fund you and your men, your activities. Cross lines in the sand and get both bullies to play the same game together?"

His lips curled away from his teeth. "Dammit, Ann, you're stepping way out of line now. I don't mind if you attack me personally or question my ethics, which you seem to think are very badly flawed, but when you go after my men, who put their lives on the line every day, that's where I draw *my* line in the sand.'' His gaze drilled into her shadowed, frightened eyes. ''Those men have wives and kids and extended families, yet they get paid a pittance to leap out of those choppers and face well-armed cocaine soldiers in the highlands. It's not fair and it's not right. But I'll be damned if some Harvard-graduate medical doctor is going to look down at them. My men are some of the bravest soldiers in the world. Their families are in jeopardy because of what they do, so they're risking more than their lives, they're risking the lives of their loved ones, too.''

Gasping, Ann straightened. The air was tense and she felt his low growl move through her like a tremor from an earthquake. His demeanor had changed to one of controlled violence—aimed at her. She saw the spark in his eyes, like the gleam of a predator stalking her. Fumbling internally, Ann knew she had started this attack. She deserved his reaction. The wounded and vulnerable part of her would rather deal with a man's anger than a man's love. And right now, her heart was hurting so much in her breast she wanted to cry out, throw her arms around Mike and just hold him as she knew he would hold her. If only she wasn't so frightened. Smoothing her gray, light wool slacks against her thighs, she took several breaths before speaking. The danger emanating from Houston shook her. He'd pulled out all his guns, probably hoping she'd back down.

''Okay,'' she whispered, holding his glare, ''I'll apologize for the remarks I just made about your men. They grew out of my anger. I own it and I'll admit it.''

Houston slowly straightened, his gaze never leaving hers. ''You still think I engineered this whole thing to get you down to Lima, don't you?'' He'd give anything to make her realize he was innocent of this. But the look in her eyes told him differently.

''There's no question in my mind about that,'' Ann growled back.

''For what possible purpose?'' he asked, his voice cracking.

Surprised, Ann placed her hands on her knees. ''Why, the obvious one, Major.''

''What? That I like you? That I admire your brains, your gutsiness? I made no bones about that when we worked together up north.'' He'd have said more, but people were looking in their direction. Even now he would protect Ann from prying eyes and ears.

''And I'm sure those aren't the only things about me you admired,'' Ann sputtered, feeling heat move up her neck and into her face. She felt uneasy talking about the attraction between them, but dammit, there was no denying it! Oh, she was blushing! Of all the times to blush!

Houston forced himself to lean back in his seat, a mirthless smile slashing across the hard planes of his face. The pain and raw need he felt for her were mixed with anger and frustration. He'd never expected Ann to assault him like this. ''And here I thought you were without imagination, Ann. I was wrong, I guess, wasn't I?''

The innuendo struck her full force. Ann saw and felt his derisive laughter as he tilted his head back and allowed the low, growling sound to escape from his throat. She had that coming and she knew it.

''You know what, Doctor?''

She met his ruthless gaze. ''What?''

''I have a really tough time thinking you're not a machine. I've seen a lot of medicos in my lifetime, but none of them came across as icy and brittle as you. I heard Morgan say you were one of the best. Well, you're going to have to prove that to me. I won't allow you to step a foot in that clinic with your kind of by-the-book bedside manner. I've seen it for eight weeks now, and I'm certainly not going to subject two nuns who work tirelessly for the poor to your iceberg tactics. As a matter of fact, I don't think you've allowed yourself to be human for a helluva long time. You're happy in your little ivory tower. That's fine. Down there at the clinic, we're all touchers and huggers, and you'll probably misread that, too. Some of the children coming in are orphans off the street, abandoned because their parents were unable to feed one more mouth. Those kids get a lot of hugs, embraces and love showered on them by the three of us.''

With a shake of his head, Houston rasped, ''And if Miss Anglo with her highfalutin Harvard medical degree thinks she's stepping into our humble abode like the proverbial Ice Queen to order us poor half-breeds and stupid Indians around like we're brainless, she has another think coming. No, I don't want you down in Lima with me, if the truth be known, Ann. Not like this. I'm used to working with people who have heart, who have a passion for living life and who aren't afraid to show their vulnerability. Do me a favor? When you get off this flight, stay at the airport. I'll make sure you get the very next flight back to the States.''

Chapter 3

By the time their jet touched down at Lima's International airport, it was 0600. Pink touched the rim of the horizon, and ordinarily, Mike would have enjoyed the spectacle of color set against the darkness of the Andes mountains, where Lima sat loftily overlooking the Pacific Ocean. Disgruntled, unable to sleep and generally grouchy because of his head-on clash with Ann, he strode off the plane. His heart ached with grief over the loss of the trust he'd forged with her on the ranch. How could he have fallen so helplessly and hopelessly in need of her in two short months? Maybe he was more lonely that he realized. But it was more than loneliness, he realized. He knew now that he wasn't the kind of man who could go through life without a good woman at his side. The tragedy and loss he had endured in his past had told him he had no right to ever try and reach out and love again. Mike never expected to find love again—nor did he want to. He'd always thought of himself as a doomed man. Because of his dangerous life-style, he'd always known it was just a matter of time until his body became meat for buzzards. And then Ann Parsons had walked into his life and he'd begun to dream once more of happiness. What a fool he was.

The dark smudges under Ann's glorious eyes told him she didn't feel much better than he did. Dammit, he wanted to apologize for some of the things he'd said to her in anger earlier. Somehow, she got to him, and he lost his normal ability to hold on to his temper. *Great. Just great.* More than anything, Mike didn't want to leave her with hurtful feelings between them. Ann deserved better than that. He owed it to her to make amends and try to heal the bad blood between them.

Slowing his gait, he waited for her to catch up. One nice thing about first class was that they were off the plane first. He slung the black canvas knapsack he always carried with him over his left shoulder. As Ann approached, he saw that her dark hair was in mild disarray, and he had the maddening urge to reach over and comb his fingers through the thick, gleaming strands, which shimmered with highlights of gold and red. *Better not,* he warned himself. *She'll take my hand off at the elbow.* And then he grinned carelessly. He knew it would be worth it, because she'd once allowed him the privilege of sliding his fingers through her silky hair in one of their stolen moments—in the heat of a hungry, searching kiss.

Once Ann was beside him, he continued toward the terminal. Even at this time of morning, Lima airport was busy. Mike wasn't surprised. Peru's capital was a twenty-four-hours-a-day city. It was cosmopolitan, upscale and surging ahead because of the influence of Japanese investors and the huge population of Japanese people who had left their island home to settle here. They brought money into the economy, and over the years Lima had become the third largest enclave of Japanese in the world. Only Sao Paulo, Brazil, had a larger population outside Japan.

As he stepped into the terminal, he saw a huge crowd of people waiting for folks to disembark from their flight. Too bad he didn't have a special somebody waiting for him. Someone like Ann. Hell, he had too much of the romantic left in him. Or maybe being with a woman he was so drawn to had stirred up that vat of loneliness he'd stuffed deep down inside of him. No, the army was his only wife, and this was one time he was regretting that dictate. Well, it didn't matter anyway, because Ann didn't want him. And if she hadn't before, she sure as hell didn't now after his stupid, stupid remarks to her in the heat of their argument on board the aircraft.

At customs Mike dropped easily into Spanish, Lima's main language. Japanese was a close second and one that he'd mastered with a lot of difficulty over the years because of his position with the Peruvian government. He remained on guard, always looking around. Now that he was back on Peruvian soil, he had to be alert or he could be killed. The young lady behind the desk, obviously Castilian Spanish with her golden skin, thin proud features, black eyes and shining black hair, smiled at him. Mike felt a little better just seeing a pleasant expression on someone's face for a change.

At the check-in desk, he launched into conversation with the ticketing agent about a van that was due to bring the medical supplies, to be carried in on the next flight. In the meantime, he saw Ann halt a few feet away and observe the busy, crowded terminal. She didn't look like a doctor in that moment. No, just a very thin, tired woman. His conscience ate at him big-time. Thanking the agent, Mike turned and sauntered over to where she stood just outside of the streams of people coming and going in the terminal.

"I've never been to Lima," Ann confessed without looking up at him. "This airport reminds me of the Chicago terminal—huge, bustling and busy twenty-four hours a day. I just never imagined it." Mike's presence, especially in the fog of her exhaustion, was overwhelming to her. Ann felt herself seesawing between going with him to the clinic and remaining at the terminal to catch the next flight back to the States. She saw the anguish in his dark eyes, the fatigue clearly marked on his own hard features, and felt a wonderful blanket of protection and care settle around her. She knew that feeling came from being with him. She tried to tell herself that his care didn't mean anything. However, she was too tired to fight the truth of what she felt emanating from him. And she knew the rawness she felt in her chest was her own longing for him.

She'd had a long time on their flight to feel her way through her jangled feelings, her confusion, her fear and her needs. Although she lay in her chair, her eyes closed, Ann hadn't slept because she'd been too upset. How had she come to feel so much for Mike while at the ranch? *How?* No matter what she did, the answer didn't seem forthcoming. Ann had sworn never to fall for a man again...not with her bad track record. How had Mike eased himself into her life? Was it that boyish smile he flashed at her in unexpected moments, always catching her off guard? Was it his obvious passion for living life fully and for the moment? That dancing glint in his eyes that broadcast such warmth and tenderness toward her every time he looked at her? His hot, searching kisses? The way he touched her, fanning coals of passion into wildly flaring flames? It was more than sexual, Ann admitted darkly. She *liked* Mike. His integrity. His continued efforts to help the poor and defend them. She approved of his morals and values. There was nothing, really, *not* to like about Mike Houston, she sourly admitted. Absolutely nothing. Except for the mystery she felt around him—that mystical quality she couldn't pinpoint with her razor-honed intellect. Not all the academic degrees in the world could outfit her to deal with someone like Houston.

"Maybe," Mike growled, despite his attempt to take the sting out of his tone, "if you give Peru half a chance, she'll seduce you like she did me when I came here more than a decade ago." He heaved an inner sigh of relief. At least Ann was talking civilly to him once again. But then, she hadn't slept, either, so he knew she was probably feeling more like a walking zombie right now and the blame game was low on her list of priorities.

Pointing toward where they had to walk to get to the baggage claim area, he added, "They call Lima the Jewel of the Pacific. The city sits up on the slopes of the lower Andes and looks out over the dark blue Pacific Ocean. The first time I came here, I didn't know what to expect. My mother had told me many, many stories of Lima, and how beautiful it was—the apartments that had flower boxes on their balconies and the trees that made the city look more like a park than a maze of steel-and-glass sentinels. She loved this city." Mike risked a glance down at Ann. Even though she was a good five feet nine inches tall, she was still short in comparison to him.

She refused to look up at him. The way her full lips were pursed told him that he'd hurt her earlier with his nasty, spiteful comments. Ruthlessly, Houston absorbed her aristocratic profile. She had high cheekbones, like his Indian ancestors did. With another sigh, he dropped his gaze to her pursed lips once more. *To hell with it.* Somehow, he had to change things so that they parted on good terms at least. He took a deep breath, reached out and gripped her arm gently, forcing her to look at him.

"Listen," he muttered darkly as her expression changed to one of shock as he touched her, "I'm sorry for what I said to you on the plane. It wasn't right and—"

A cry for help halfway down the terminal ripped through the early morning air. People began to slow down or hurry a little faster.

Scowling, Mike dropped his hand from Ann's arm, instantly alert. "Now what?" he growled.

Ann looked in direction of the sound. She could hear a woman sobbing and screaming for help. She saw Mike Houston peering above the heads of the crowd. "You're taller than I am," she exclaimed. "What do you see? What's going on?"

Grimacing, he glanced down at her. "Someone's in trouble. Medical trouble. Come on...." He took off in long, loping strides.

"Mike! Wait!" Ann hurried to catch up. He was a tall, broad-shouldered man and he cut a swathe through the crowds in the airport terminal. She wasn't so lucky and was stopped repeatedly. As she hurried along in his wake, she found herself admiring the way he ran, with a boneless, swift grace that reminded her of a large cat. Perhaps a cougar loping along silently, yet with remarkable power. Other people seemed to sense it, too, for Houston was never elbowed, stopped, nor did he have to change direction. No, the masses parted for him like the Red Sea had for Moses. Ann realized she was witnessing that impenetrable mystery about him in action now. No wonder they called him the jaguar god.

Mike's eyes widened as he made his way through the large circle of people that had formed. In the middle was a woman crying hysterically. A young woman, very pretty, well-heeled and dressed in a purple business suit. He knew her well. It was Elena Valdez, wife of Antonio Valdez, one of the most prominent and powerful businessmen in Lima. What the hell was happening?

"Step aside," Mike growled, opening a path to where Elena stood sobbing, her fists against her mouth. She was from one of the old aristocratic families of Peru, of pure Castilian blood. Normally aloof and serene, her mascaraed eyes were running dark streaks like war paint down her cheeks, her red lips contorted as she stared down at the floor. Mike followed her wild, shocked gaze.

"Antonio!" he rasped. Houston suddenly spun on his heel and roared at the crowd, "Give us room!"

Miraculously, everyone took a number of steps back widening the circle. There on the floor, ashen and unmoving, was Antonio Valdez. The thousand-dollar, dark blue pinstripe suit he wore went with the short, sleek black hair combed back on his narrow skull. His red silk tie looked garish next to his pasty flesh as Mike sank to his knees.

"Antonio—Tony!" He gripped the businessman's shoulder. The man did not respond. Sensing Ann's presence, Mike snapped his head up as he placed two fingers against the man's neck.

"Cardiac arrest," he stated shortly. "No pulse..." He leaned down, his ear close to the man's nose. "No breath." He jabbed at his backpack, which he'd dropped nearby. "There's a bag-valve mask in there. Get it. An OPA, too." He ripped at the man's tie, the silk of his shirt giving way under the power of Mike's efforts. Then he tipped the man's head back to create an airway. He heard Elena sobbing wildly.

"Oh, Mike! Mike! Antonio was just walking with me. Everything was fine. Fine! And suddenly...suddenly he grew very pale and groaned. He collapsed, *mi amigo*. Oh, Mike! Help him! Help him!"

Jerking the tie from Tony's neck, Houston shot a glance at Ann, who was on her knees, digging furiously in his backpack. All the tiredness, the cloudy look in her eyes, had dissolved. When she looked up, protective green latex gloves in hand, he reached out and took them. With expert swiftness, he donned them. "Get the goggles, too. If he vomits, I don't want it in our eyes."

"Right!" Ann handed him a pair of plastic goggles. Her hands trembled slightly as she placed the white OPA, a plastic device known as an oropharyngeal airway, into the patient's mouth. This device would keep his tongue from falling back and blocking his breathing passage once they started pumping air into his lungs.

Ann grabbed the bag-valve mask and moved once more to the man's head. She knelt and settled the translucent, soft plastic mask over his face. The mask was attached to the blue, oval-shaped rubber bag that would start pumping air into him.

Mike watched her get into position. She leaned over the man, ready.

"Have you got paramedics posted here at the terminal?" she demanded, squeezing the appliance.

"Hell, no." Mike looked up and barked at a younger man dressed in business clothes. "You! Get to a white phone! Call security for help. Tell them we've got a cardiac case in terminal three. Tell them to call an ambulance, pronto!"

"Sí, sí!" the man shouted, and he turned and worked his way through the crowd.

"Okay, let's get on it," Ann whispered.

Mike appreciated her cool efficiency as he knelt on the other side of Antonio and placed his hands just below the man's sternum. He laid his large palm flat against his chest, then nodded in her direction. "Give 'em air. Two breaths."

"I know CPR."

He heard the warning clip of her voice. Scowling, he concentrated on his part of the two-person procedure. After two breaths, he leaned over Tony and delivered a powerful downward push over the sternum. The heart lay under that long, flat bone that held the rib cage together.

In moments, they were working like a well-oiled team. Houston forgot the pandemonium around them, forgot Elena's sobbing. He counted to himself, his mouth thinned, his nostrils flaring.

Two minutes into the process, he rasped, "Stop CPR." Anxiously, he placed his fingers against Antonio's neck.

"No pulse." He leaned down, praying for the man to at least be breathing. "No breath."

"Do you know him?"

Houston gave a jerky nod as he repositioned his hands. "Yes. Start CPR."

Ann squeezed the bag-valve mask, delivering a long, slow dose of oxygen into the man's chest cavity. She saw the patient's wife kneel down at his feet, sobbing and praying. She was so young and pretty—she couldn't be more than in her late twenties.

"How old is he?"

"Forty-five."

"Perfect age for a CA."

"Yeah, isn't it, though?" Mike continued to push down on the man's chest again and again. He kept looking at Tony's color. "Damn, this isn't working."

"How long before an ambulance arrives with a defibrillator machine?"

"Too long," he muttered. "Too damn long. Stop CPR. We're going to do something different."

Ann watched as Houston jerked the shirt completely away from the man's chest. She saw him ball up his fist. She knew what he was going to do. In the absence of a defibrillator, which with an electrical shock could jolt the heart into starting again, a medic could strike the sternum with a fist. Sometimes, though rarely, the hard, shocking blow would get the heart restarted. It was risky. She noted the strain on Mike's face, the glistening sweat on his wrinkled brow. His eyes had turned a dark, stormy blue, and she knew all his focus was on his abilities as a paramedic, despite the many other emotions he had to be feeling.

"Is he a friend of yours?" she asked, holding the man's head steady as Mike prepared to strike his chest.

"Yes. A damn good friend. God, I hope this works," he said.

Mike measured where his fist would strike the man's sternum. He gripped Tony's shoulder to hold him in place. Raising his arm, he smashed his fist downward in a hard arc. Flesh met flesh. He heard his friend's sternum crack loudly beneath his assault.

"Come on! Come on!" Houston snarled as he gripped the man's lifeless shoulders and shook him hard. "Damn you, Tony!" he breathed into the man's graying face, "don't you *dare* die on me!" He put his fingers against his neck.

"Nothing," he growled.

"Do it again," Ann ordered in a hushed tone. She saw the fear in Houston's eyes.

"He's dumping on us...."

"I don't care. It's all we got! Hit him again!"

For a split second, Ann met his distraught eyes. And then he balled his fist again. Once the sternum was broken there was a danger that any further strikes to jolt the heart could create lacerations in the liver and possibly the heart itself, from fragments of bone that had been broken by the first blow. Antonio could bleed to death as a result.

"You mean son of a bitch," Houston growled at Tony as he raised his fist. "You live! You hear me?" Then he brought his fist down just as hard as the first time.

The man's whole body jarred and jerked beneath the second blow. Ann held the man's head and neck in alignment and continued to pump oxygen into him. She watched as Mike leaned over to check for pulse and breathing. Whether it was because she was already numb with tiredness and drained emotionally, she didn't know, but for a split second as he leaned down, snarling in Spanish at his friend, she thought she was seeing things.

Houston's growling voice wasn't human any longer. It sounded to her like a huge jungle cat. It shocked her, the primal, sound reverberating through every pore in her body as he leaned over and shook Antonio. She sensed an energy in the air, pummeling her repeatedly like wildly racing ocean waves. She realized it was emanating from Houston as he leaned over Antonio, almost willing him to breathe again.

"You're not dying on me," he rasped, striking him even harder than before, in the center of the chest. "Live! Live, you hear me?"

Ann blinked belatedly. As Houston struck the man a third time, she knew she was seeing things. His head disappeared, and in its place she saw the golden face of a jaguar or leopard, black crescent spots against gold fur. She was hallucinating! Shaking her head, she closed her eyes and opened them again. Mike was leaning over his friend, his fingers pressed insistently against his neck. My God, what was happening? What was she seeing? For the first time, Ann clearly realized that she was on a mission with an incredibly attractive man whose power was beyond her own rational mind.

"Tony!" he pleaded hoarsely. "Don't die on me! Don't!"

Houston's plea shook her. Gone was the hard soldier's mask. She trembled at the raw emotion of his voice. Tears stung her eyes. What a horrible thing to come home to—seeing a good friend go into cardiac arrest and then watching him die. Ann was ready to tell Mike that it was too late. Only seven percent of people suffering from a heart attack ever revived with the help of CPR.

Again she gazed up through her veil of tears. She no longer heard the onlookers or felt them closing in on them, inch by inch. She watched as Houston hunkered over the older man, gripping him by the shoulders and giving him a good, hard shake. Yet again Houston struck him in the chest.

"Mike—" she begged.

"Wait! A pulse! I've got a pulse!" He gave a cry of triumph and watched intensely as the man's face began to lose some of its grayness. "Bag 'em hard," he snapped. "Pump all the oxygen you can into him." He grinned tightly and put a coat beneath the man's legs to elevate them slightly. Leaning over him again, he called, "Tony? Tony, you hear me? Open those ugly eyes of yours and look up at me. It's Mike. Mike Houston. Come on, buddy, you can do it. Open your eyes!" And he shook him again, all the time keeping a firm grip on his friend's arms.

Houston watched the dark lashes tremble against the man's pasty features. "That's it, open your eyes. I'm here. You're gonna be okay. Come on, come on back. You're too mean to die yet...." Then he grinned as Tony opened his dark brown eyes and stared groggily up at him.

Almost immediately, the patient started gagging. Ann removed the bag valve mask from his face, took out the breathing appliance and threw it aside. She quickly replaced the mask, holding it there until she and Mike were both sure he was getting enough oxygen and was breathing well on his own.

Houston heard Elena cry out her husband's name as she bent over him.

"Calm down, Elena," he coaxed, reaching across and soothingly moving his hand against her thin shoulder as she gripped her husband's hand. "He's okay...." Mike wasn't sure how okay Antonio really was. He knew the man had suffered a massive heart attack. How bad, they'd only know after a series of tests at the hospital.

Risking a look up at Ann, who was still kneeling at Tony's

head, delivering the life-giving oxygen, he saw tears sparkling in her eyes. They caught him completely off guard. Returning his attention to his friend, he reached down, got his stethoscope from the bag and listened intently to his heart. It was a good, strong beat. Then Mike took his blood pressure.

"Eighty over sixty," he announced with satisfaction.

"It could be better," Ann said.

Grimly, Mike deflated the blood pressure cuff. "Give him five minutes. He's not dumping on us. Color's flooding his face. His capillary refill is better," he murmured as he pinched the index fingernail of Tony's right hand. Normally, the capillary refill took two seconds or less to flow back into the pinched area. It was a good indicator that the heart was pumping strongly and normally, supplying the life-giving substance to even the farthest extremities of the body.

"Three seconds?" Ann asked.

Houston nodded. He waited to recheck the blood pressure, but five minutes seemed to take forever. Glancing at his watch, he wished the second hand would move faster.

Elena was speaking in hushed tones to her husband. When Tony tried to reach up and touch his wife's wet, pale face, Mike grinned. "You're gonna be fine, Tony. But right now, keep your hands off Elena, you hear me? Just lie there and let your strength come back." He glanced at Ann. "Stop bagging him."

She nodded and watched as he took another blood pressure reading. Houston's expression was intense and hard now. She was seeing his professional side as a paramedic once more. He was very good at what he did. He had an incredible confidence that radiated from him like the sun sending energy earthward. She watched as his thinned lips relaxed. A cocky, one-cornered smile tugged at his mouth as he removed the stethoscope from his ears and settled it around his thick, well-muscled neck. When he looked in her direction, she felt incredible tenderness coming from him. It wasn't for her, but she basked in that invisible glow just the same. In that moment, he looked like a little boy, his blue eyes sparkling with unabashed joy.

"One-ten over eighty. He's stabilizing. He's through the worst of it."

"Yes," Ann quavered, giving him a trembling smile of triumph. "He's going to live...."

Houston stood with Ann at his side as the ambulance paramedics took Antonio Valdez away on a gurney. Most of the crowd had disappeared now that the life-and-death drama was over. Without thinking, Mike put his hand on her shoulder. "Hell of a welcome to Lima."

Ann felt the warm strength of his hand. She recognized his gesture for what it was. People in the medical field had to be devoid of emotion, keep ahead of the curve in any emergency, think rationally and stay calm when everything around them was shaking apart. She lifted her chin and met Mike's blue gaze, absorbing his touch, the energy that seemed to tingle from his hand into her shoulder. It made her feel safe and cared for. His touch felt like life itself throbbing through her. It wasn't the first time she had felt this unusual sensation. Now it was far more palpable and comforting. A soft smile flitted across her face. "Yes, it was...but you were good. Very good. You knew what to do." Her heart expanded wildly. How could she stand the thought of not being near Mike? Suddenly, Ann realized how much her life had changed since he had walked into it.

Digesting the feelings that overrode her normal fears, she understood for the first time how much Houston had become a part of her, and vice versa, it seemed. They had been a good team. They'd worked as one. Perhaps it was due to sleep deprivation, but there in the Lima terminal Ann listened to her heart more closely than she had in a long time.

Houston absorbed that hesitant, fleeting smile Ann gave him. How beautiful she was, even though her hair was in mild disarray and her white blouse rumpled from the long flight. "So were you. We're a good team, you and I." And then he grinned. "Even if we do fight like dogs and cats." He didn't want to remove his hand, but he knew it was best. Allowing it to fall back to his side, Mike thought he saw a fleeting darkness in Ann's wide, intelligent eyes. Unable to interpret what it meant, he cocked his head. "Let me at least buy you a good cup of espresso before I leave for the clinic. It's the least I can do to thank you for helping save Tony's life. I owe you one...."

Ann frowned. "I'll take the offer, but what makes you think you're leaving this terminal without me?" For better or worse, she had made a decision to stay—because of her feelings toward Mike. She was scared to death, but she had to take the risk. Her mind screamed at her that she was a fool, but her heart was expanding with such joy over her decision that she felt breathless. Inwardly, she knew she was making the right choice, regardless of her dark, haunting past.

Scowling, Houston halted abruptly and turned to face her. There was surprise written on his features. "You made it very clear you didn't want to be down here with me," he began slowly, his voice low with raw feeling. Tony almost dying had left Mike more vulnerable than usual. He was afraid to believe what he'd just heard. His heart pounded briefly to underscore his need for Ann. His fear. Mike searched her calm features. Her eyes shone with hope. The fear was still there, but it had lessened. What was going on? Stunned by her words, he rasped, "Or was I hearing wrong?"

"You didn't hear wrong, Mike. I changed my mind, that's all. You got a problem with that?" Ann held his flaring look of surprise. She felt an avalanche of that powerful energy deluge her momentarily. She remembered how, when she was bagging Antonio, she'd seen the awe in people's faces as Mike worked over the man. All eyes had been riveted on him as he struggled to save his friend's life.

There was no question in her mind why Houston was not only a leader, but one that few people, including herself, could resist. Even if it was dangerous to her wounded heart. She was too afraid, still, to admit for sure why she agreed to stay on. Only time would tell, and another six weeks would hopefully yield the answer she was searching for.

Her mouth twisted wryly. "This is probably the sorriest decision I'll ever make, Houston, but I'm sticking it out down here for six weeks. With or without you. I honor Morgan's commitments. I go where he sends me." She saw hope burning fiercely in Mike's eyes, and more...much more....

Mike just stared at her for a moment. Here was the confident, gutsy woman he knew lived inside her, but who he'd rarely seen. The question *why are you staying?* was almost torn from him, but he forced the words back down. Whether Ann knew it or not, he had a powerful, ongoing connection with her. He sensed a lot more about her than she realized. He knew she was scared, but he also sensed her feelings for him—feelings that had existed all along but that she'd refused to share with him. Now, for whatever reason, she was doing that. Euphoria robbed Mike momentarily of words. Was it possible that she was going to allow their relationship to grow? The thought was heady. Wild. Full of promise. At the same time, he felt full of fear for an uncertain future. Those he cared for died. She would die, too. No, he had to keep his distance. He had to protect her from himself at all costs. His whole life was committed to killing Eduardo Escovar. Mike was in a death spiral dance with the drug lord and he had no room for a woman in his life. Especially a woman like Ann Parsons. Another part of him, one that surprised the hell out of him, reveled in her decision to remain with him in Peru, regardless.

Ann watched a slow grin crawl across his face. Houston had such a strong, chiseled mouth. A beautiful mouth, she admitted. One that she wanted to feel against her lips again and again. For whatever reason, she felt bolder than she had in a long time. Maybe seeing Antonio almost die had ripped away something inside her, made her realize life was precious and should be lived in the moment, not hidden in some dark closet of fear.... Chagrined, Ann cut off the thoughts and feelings that seem to grow like grass whenever she was around the charismatic army officer.

"Well," she challenged, her voice husky, "are you going to stand there gawking or are you going to buy me that espresso you promised?"

Snapping into action, Houston slid his hand around her upper arm and guided her forward. "No, ma'am, I'll buy you that well-deserved cup of espresso." He felt edgy with fear. He was raw with wanting. Wanting her. Breath-stealing elation raced through him as Ann strode at his side. This time she didn't seem to mind his hand on her arm. Indeed, it was as if she liked it there. But Houston didn't fool himself. They'd just been through a very intense life-and-death situation. He found it normal that medicos automatically drew close to one another for emotional support after a crisis was over. It was only human, he warned himself. Still, his fingers tingled wildly as he felt the slip and slide of Ann's light wool blazer against the white silk of her blouse, the firmness of her flesh beneath it. He reveled in the pleasurable sensation, feeling once again like a greedy beggar taking whatever crumbs she'd unknowingly thrown out to him.

Had Antonio's heart attack triggered her own need to live life more fully? To possibly reach out to him? Grinning recklessly, laughter rumbling up from his chest, he said, "This has been one wild ride so far, Dr. Parsons, and the day is young yet...."

She raised one brow and glanced up at him as they walked. "I give you that," she replied, her pulse speeding up. The undisguised happiness in Mike's eyes affected her, left her aching to kiss him, to feel his hands slide around her torso as he pulled her uncompromisingly against his body. She longed to experience his sweet assault upon her senses once again, and it almost overwhelmed her.

When Mike glanced down at her, he realized in that split second that Ann had dropped her guard, because she was grinning, too. There was bright color in her cheeks, and she looked damn beautiful when she blushed. Instantly, she turned away to avoid his eyes. But not even that could mar Houston's happiness at her decision to stay in Peru.

To hell with it. Mike threw all caution aside. "Come here...." he murmured huskily as he drew Ann out of the traffic of the busy terminal. Backing her against the wall, he leaned close to her. In her eyes he read the need she felt for him, and registered in every fiber of his being. The connection between them was as palpable as the feel of his fingers as he grazed the slope of her flushed cheek.

"I need you," he rasped, placing his hand against her cheek and guiding her face upward. The driving need to kiss her and the need he saw in her eyes made him let down his own guard for this one, exquisite moment. He saw her eyes widen momentarily, heard her breath hitch. He sensed her emotional response, and it felt damn good washing through him. Smiling tenderly down at her as he lightly brushed her parting lips with his, he saw the fear in her eyes dissolve. Yes, she wanted this as much as he did.

For one heated moment out of time, all the terminal sounds, the people's voices, faded from Ann's awareness. All she'd longed for moments ago was happening. Somehow, Mike had known she needed him. It was all so crazy. So mixed up. Yet as she lifted her chin and felt his strong mouth settle upon her lips, nothing had ever felt so right. So pure. So devastatingly beautiful. His strong arm moved around her back and she felt him pull her against him. There was no mistaking his gesture; it was clearly that of a man claiming his woman.

Her lashes swept downward and the ache inside her intensified as his mouth skimmed hers. How good he tasted! She inhaled his very male scent into her quivering nostrils, slid her hands upward against his barrel chest, her fingers digging convulsively against the fabric of his shirt, marveling in the strength of his muscles tightening beneath her exploration. His mouth slid surely against her lips, rocking them open even farther, his tongue thrusting boldly into her mouth. She gave a moan of sweet surrender as she lost herself in the fiery, hungry mating. All that existed in that moment was Mike, his maleness, his tender domination of her as a woman yielding to him in almost every way possible. Oh, how stupid she had been not to give herself to him sooner!

His mouth moved possessively and she responded just as hungrily and boldly to his dizzying assault. With him, she felt a primal wildness she'd never felt with any man. He brought out her earthiness, her need to be her untamed, untrammeled self. His hand slid behind her head, holding her, trapping her so he could taste her even more deeply. The sweet hotness and longing built between her thighs as she felt him grind his hips demandingly against hers. There was no mistaking his need of her. Ann felt urgency and frustration. Her fingers opened and closed spasmodically against his thickly corded neck. She couldn't get enough of him and drowned in the splendor of his tender assault upon her.

Ann wanted the hot, branding kiss, the sweet, unspoken promise between them to last forever. As Houston began to ease his mouth from hers, she cried out internally, not wanting to cease contact with him in any way. Yet she knew they must. She was sure they were making a spectacle of themselves in the corridor. People were staring at them but for once, Ann didn't care. Mike had somehow dissolved all her fears, her need to be proper and prudish out in public. He tore away her doctor's facade and stripped her naked, revealing her hot, womanly core of primitive needs and desires. As she looked dazedly up into his narrowed, gleaming eyes, she had never felt so protected or desired.

His face was alive with feelings—for her. Ann saw it in his burning look, his mouth only inches from her own as he stood over her, his arm continuing to press her tightly against him. She tasted him on her lips. She felt the masculine hardness of him against her abdomen and her own heated response to his hunger. Never had Ann felt more alive than now. Never. Her breath was shallow and gasping. She tried to speak.

"No..." Houston rasped thickly, "don't think for once, Ann. Just feel. Feel!" he ordered, and captured her glistening lips one more time.

Sinking against him, her knees like jelly due to his renewed assault on her senses, Ann felt the world skid to a dizzying halt. Only Mike and she existed. She no longer cared what anyone thought as she held him tightly against her, her breasts hard against his chest. Their hearts were pounding; she could feel his as if it were inside her. The sensation was shockingly beautiful and one she'd never experienced before. The sandpaper quality of his beard against her cheek, his hot, moist breath, the taste and power of him as he grazed her lips repeatedly, almost teasingly, left her aching painfully. She wanted to feel him inside her, filling her, taking her, making her his in every conceivable way. Whatever fear had held her was gone now, and in its place, a fierce desire for Mike welled up, surging through her like a tidal wave.

Gradually, ever so gradually, Houston forced himself to ease back from Ann's lips. Lips made of the wild honey he'd found only in the jungles of Peru. Honey that was so sweet it made him dissolve beneath her searching, innocent mouth. There was no question he needed her. None. And as he opened his eyes and stared down into her dazed blue-gray ones, he knew she needed him, too. She was trembling with need of him. But so was he. He regretted kissing her here in the terminal. Anywhere else would

have been better than here. The painful knot in his lower body
attested to the poor choice of location. He wanted to love her
thoroughly, to indelibly print his essence within her. Wanted so
badly to claim her and make her his woman it was nearly his
undoing. The fierceness of his desire for Ann was far more than
just sexual, because he was in touch with every subtle essence
within her—from her emotions to her spirit. Ann didn't know that
but he knew she could feel his bond with her as much as he did.
That much was clear in the awe he saw reflected in her eyes, the
questions about what she was feeling.

"Shh," he whispered, grazing his thumb across her wet lips.
"just feel, Ann. Just feel.... It's real...all of this is real, I promise
you. You aren't imagining anything." He closed his eyes and
rested his brow against hers, letting himself sink back into that
invisible connection that he'd allowed to fully form between them.
Once Ann could talk to him about her feelings and openly confide
in him, he vowed to tell her all that had happened to him in the
jungle. Another part of him told him he was crazy for allowing
her to get close to him. Did he want to put her in that kind of
danger? How could he? But Ann would have to know the truth
very soon. She had to make her own decision about whether he
was worth desiring or not.

Easing away, Houston cupped her shoulders and gently moved
her away from him. Ann's face was flushed, her eyes soft and
filled with desire—for him. Never had he felt stronger...or more
protective. His mouth curved ruefully.

"Would you like to go freshen up in the ladies' room?"

Swaying uncertainly in his embrace, Ann nodded. Looking
around, she felt embarrassment flooding her. Many people had
stopped to watch them. "Oh dear...yes, yes I would...."

Mike nodded and placed his arm around her. "Don't worry,
folks around here understand lovers. They aren't staring at us because we kissed, you know. Down here, everyone loves lovers."
He guided Ann toward the women's rest room up ahead.

Grateful for his humor, his protective demeanor against the
many prying eyes, Ann tried to contain her escaping feelings. She
pushed strands of hair away from her face and forced herself to
breathe more evenly. *Lovers.* The word flowed through her. Yes,

he wanted to be Mike's lover. Every cell in her body was aching
'ith need of him, more than ever now. Just being close to him
/as feeding that brightly burning fire that had roared to life in her
uring his searching, hungry kisses.

Reaching the ladies' room, Ann forced herself to walk into it.
he felt drunk. Drunk with pleasure and desire. Somehow, she had
) pull herself back together again. At the washbasin, she sloshed
old water repeatedly into her face until she felt some semblance
f order returning to her. She spent a great deal more time in there
an was necessary; it took a good ten minutes to gather herself.
lotting her face, she quickly ran a brush through her mussed hair
nd put lipstick back on her soft, well-kissed mouth.

All of her carefully orchestrated life had just exploded. Com-
letely. Ann was no longer thinking with her head, only her heart.
he switch was shocking to her. All her life, she'd allowed her
ead to rule her, not her emotions. In Mike's presence, all she
'anted to do was feel—and then feel some more. What was going
) happen? Could she control herself where he was concerned?
he felt like a teenager with her hormones running away from her,
ke she had no control over anything. All she had to do was think
f Mike, allow his hard features to gel before her, and she grew
ot and shaky all over again. Ann thought it was because she'd
enied her real feelings for him throughout the last two months.
his time his kiss had ripped the lid off Pandora's box.

Groaning, she took a deep breath, talked sternly to herself and
:ft the rest room. She found Houston standing across the corridor,
is back to the wall, his arms crossed over his chest. How calm
nd centered he seemed! Ann stood there for a moment, envying
is obvious control. He looked fine. He looked like nothing had
appened. But it had. Something life-shattering had occurred
/ithin her when he'd held her minutes ago. Something so pro-
ound, so deep had occurred that Ann needed time to try and
nderstand what had taken place.

As if sensing she was there, he turned his gaze to her. In that
istant, her heart responded violently, and again that sense of
varmth and protection he gave her overwhelmed her. Suddenly
izzy, Ann leaned against the wall, unsure of what was happening.
nstantly, she saw Mike straighten and walk directly to her.

Before he could say anything, she held out her hand. "I'm okay I really am."

He smiled a little and placed his hand on her left arm, just in case. "You look beautiful," he whispered huskily. And she did Her lips were soft from his kisses, her eyes velvet with desire. The flush across her cheeks was still there, and as he drew her back into the traffic, he thought she looked like a teenage girl who had just experienced her very first kiss from the boy she had a crush on.

Ann leaned against him as he placed his arm around her shoulders and led her along. Grateful for his understanding, she managed to murmur, "I've *never* felt like this, Mike. *Ever.*"

Chuckling indulgently, he pressed a kiss to her hair. "I told you Peru would cast her spell on you. Down here, magic happens all the time."

"Magic? Humph. More like a sledgehammer to my head, if you ask me." Ann heard him laugh deeply over her remark. She felt his steadying care and she acquiesced to his superior strength.

"Well," he drawled, giving her a teasing look, "maybe our kiss had a little something to do with that?"

Refusing to be baited, Ann tried to give him a dour look. "You don't have to look like a satisfied cat about it, Houston."

Preening a little, Mike broadened his grin into one of boyish delight. "That kiss has been a long time in coming. And there' no way I'm apologizing for it. Ah, here we are." He halted. "This is just what you need—espresso to settle your nerves."

Ann laughed a little as they stood in front of the restaurant "Oh, sure, coffee to soothe my jangled nerves. Right." They stood looking at the small café with its red-and-green-striped awning.

"I always stop here, at Federico's Place, to get my espresso when I'm coming in off a long flight." Mike gestured to the brass and-glass doors. "Come on. He's got the best espresso in Lima. swear it."

Once they were seated at a small round table covered in expensive white linen and decorated with colorful flowers in a cut-glass vase, Ann smiled gratefully at the waiter. When he delivered their coffee a moment later, she cautiously sipped the tiny, fragile cup of espresso, and studied the man before her. Mike Houston was simply too large for the white wrought-iron chair, the table or even this small café. But it was there that he frequented because the owner, Federico, had recognized him instantly. There had been a lot of backslapping, smiles and greetings. And it seemed the two young waiters knew him, too. She was beginning to wonder who Houston didn't know, but then, he'd been down here more than ten years, and in his line of business, it was good to know a lot of people.

"Well?" Mike demanded. "What do you think?" He'd already drunk half of his espresso, while Ann had only hesitantly tasted hers. He supposed she was like that with everything in her life: cautious and slow. Why? She had that shadowed look back in her eyes as she lifted the English china cup to her lips and looked at him over the rim.

"It's sweet...and tastes surprisingly mild." Ann set the cup down. "I thought it would taste bitter because it's so concentrated."

Chuckling, Mike finished off his first cup. A second magically showed up seconds later, Federico himself brought it over with a flourish. Mike nodded and thanked the restaurant owner. "What you poor folks up in *Norteamérica* get for coffee beans, is a sin," he said to Ann with a laugh. "*Sudamericanos* aren't stupid." He raised the cup in toast to her. "We keep the *best* beans down here, and that's what you're drinking—Andean coffee raised on slopes so high that the condors fly over them daily. Coffee growing in some of the finest, richest lava soil in the world. It *has* to taste good."

Ann couldn't help but smile. "You are so passionate about everything. I've never met anyone like you before." It was Mike's passion that was somehow encouraging her to tap into her own desires on such a primal, wonderful level of herself as a woman.

His reckless grin broadened. "My mother often told me when I was a young kid growing up that if I didn't *love* whatever I was doing, I'd eventually curl up and die. She told me to do things that made my heart sing, that made my heart soar like the condors that hang above the Andes." He sobered a little and sighed. "She was a woman of immense intelligence, I realized as I got old enough and experienced enough to really understand what she was telling me.''

''To live life with passion,'' Ann murmured. ''That's not one I've heard of late.''

''So,'' Mike said, ''do you live your life with passion? Do you love what you do as a medical doctor?''

''I like what I do. It feels good to be able to stop a person's pain, to stop death from cheating a life...but passion? I don't know about that.'' She frowned and picked up her cup once again. ''I certainly don't live with the gusto you do.''

''A little while ago,'' Mike murmured in a low intimate tone, as he turned the tiny cup around and around between his massive, scarred hands, ''I saw a different Ann Parsons out there. Not the one I knew for eight weeks in Arizona. This woman, the one I kissed today, was—different. Provocative...passionate...committed...''

''Translated, that means what?''

''Just that I felt a much different woman,'' Mike said in a whisper, so that no one could eavesdrop.

Avoiding his heated look, Ann tinkered nervously with the cup in her hands. ''Mike...give me time. I—I'm just not prepared to say much right now.''

Holding up his palm in a gesture of peace, he added huskily, ''You're a woman of immense feelings. I understand. You're like a deep, deep well of water. Not many are privy to the real feelings you hide so well.''

Ann couldn't deny any of it. Stealing a glance at him, she whispered, ''I don't know what happened to me today, Mike. Maybe something changed in me when I saw Antonio almost die. I usually protect myself from personal feelings in these situations....'' Her words trailed away as she became pensive. Mike deserved her honesty here. Setting the cup down, she forced herself to add, ''I guess your passion for living life with emotion has rubbed off onto me a lot more than I realized. Watching your friend almost die probably shook that loose in me. It was time, I guess....''

Mike nodded, feeling the gravity of her statement. She was being honest on a level he'd never experienced with her before— due to that magical connection forged between them earlier, in that beautiful moment when he'd kissed her. He decided to return some of her honesty. "When I was trying to save Tony, I was afraid," he admitted. "I was afraid he was dead. I wanted him to live so damn bad I could taste it. I could feel myself willing my heartbeat, my energy or whatever it was, into his body. And when I looked up at you in that moment, I felt hope. It spurred me on." With a shrug, he added a little shamefacedly, "I can't tell you what went on between us in that split second, I only know that something did. And somehow, it gave me hope when I didn't really have any left."

"All that in one look," Ann murmured as she sipped the espresso. "I'm amazed, frankly." Still, she felt good at Mike's sincere praise, at the admiration in his eyes. She liked the feeling.

"You have a very healing effect on people, whether you know it or not," Houston said sincerely.

"Something else happened back there, Mike," Ann began hesitantly. "I think what I saw may have been a result of sleep deprivation." She saw him frown. With a wave of her thin hand, she said, "Not that it was bad. It was just...shocking."

"What happened?"

"Promise you won't tell me I had a brief, acute psychotic episode?"

"No problem. You're sane and well grounded." Interested in hearing her experience, Houston asked, "This happened while we were bagging Tony?"

"Yes. At one point," Ann continued, setting the espresso aside and folding her hands on the table, "something changed. You got far more intense than before. You'd hit him twice in the chest and he hadn't started breathing again. I know you were desperate. You wanted your friend to live. That was normal behavior, but..." She folded her hands "...then something happened, and I can't explain it or even begin to get a handle on it."

"What?" Mike's scowl deepened. He saw a flush stain Ann's cheeks. "Something that upset you?"

"It didn't upset me exactly, Mike. I just felt these incredible waves of energy striking me, like waves from the ocean, only...they were coming from you. I actually felt buffeted by them as you leaned over Tony, working so intently with him, willing

him to live. And then, the silliest thing of all, I saw this shadow
or something.... It descended over you. Well, part of you. And it
was only for a split second. I'm sure it was a sleep-deprivation
hallucination...."

"*What* did you see?" he demanded darkly.

Taking a deep breath, Ann dived into her experience. "I saw
this dark shadow appear above your head. It just seemed to form
out of nowhere. I'm not sure anyone else saw it." Moistening her
lips and avoiding his sharp, glittering gaze, she added, "I saw it
come over you like a transparency of some sort, fitting over your
head and shoulders." Embarrassed, she gave an awkward laugh,
and said, "For a moment, it looked like a jaguar or leopard over
your head. I no longer saw your face, your profile. Instead I saw
this huge cat's head and massive shoulders. Well," Ann murmured
wryly, risking a look up at him, "I'm sure by now you think I
experienced a psychotic episode."

Mike shrugged. "Down here," he muttered uncomfortably, "I
carry a name."

"Excuse me?"

His brows knitted and he stared down at his espresso cup. "I
have a nickname...." He heaved a sigh. Lifting his head, he met
her frank blue-gray gaze. "I'm sure you'll hear it sooner rather
than later, so I might as well tell you myself. I'm called the jaguar
god. It's a reputation I've garnered over the years. The cocaine
lords started calling me that a long time ago. The name stuck."
He grimaced.

"It's not a bad name," Ann murmured. "Why are you so uncomfortable with it?"

Mike sat up and flexed his shoulders. "Someday, Ann, I'll tell
you more about it. More than likely my friends at the clinic will
fill your ears about me, about the legend surrounding me, until
you're sick and tired of hearing that name."

Ann frowned. "You mean there's more to this? I wasn't seeing
things?"

Mike rose and pulled some sols from his pocket. "You're a
trained therapist. You know how sleep deprivation and emotional
stress can make you hallucinate during intense moments of crisis,"

he said, deciding that the truth would have to wait. He couldn't risk her rejection of him. Not after that nourishing kiss. "Come on, that van should be ready by now and those medical supplies loaded in it."

Chapter 4

Despite her extreme fatigue, Ann was wide awake as Mike drove the heavily loaded van from the airport to one of the poorest sections of Lima. She tried to minimize in her mind the power and influence of his hot, melting caresses, but it was impossible. It was almost as if her lips were still tingling from his branding, unexpected kiss. She tried concentrating on the road ahead of them, noticing that Mike avoided most of the major freeways and took smaller streets. He probably knew this city like the back of his hand. Even more, Ann was aware of his heightened state of alertness. He was behaving like a soldier out in the bush rather than a man driving in the relative safety of a city. It didn't make sense and she wondered what dangers lay ahead of them.

One thing for sure, Mike was right about Lima. The city was set like a crown jewel on verdant green slopes and surrounded by the raw beauty of the Andes, which towered like a backdrop in the distance. The day was sunny, the sky a soft blue, and Ann found herself enjoying her first views of the city.

"Lima reminds me of Buenos Aires," she said to Mike, as he turned down a dirt road that led into a poor section, what he called a barrio.

Nodding, Mike divided his attention between driving and watching for enemies. He was on his own turf now, and the drug lords had hundreds of spies throughout the city looking for him, trying to pin him down so that a hit squad could corner and murder him.

"Lima and Buenos Aires are a lot alike," he said, distracted. "Plenty of trees, bushes and flowers all over the place."

"Nothing like New York City?"

He grinned tightly. "That place..."

"For once we agree on something," she teased. Moments later, the scenery changed as they crept down the dirt road, which was rutted with deep furrows where tires had chewed into the soil. The winter rains had left the area in a quagmire as usual, and the city certainly wasn't going to waste money on asphalt paving in a barrio. Houston's gaze was restless, his awareness acute. His eyes were scanning their surroundings like radar. Ann felt uncomfortable. Or more to the point, endangered. By what? Whom?

When Mike saw her brows dip, he tried to lighten the feeling of tension in the truck. "Hang around and you might decide I'm not the bad hombre you think I am." He winked at her and delivered a boyish smile in her direction to ease the concern he saw in her eyes. "I've got six weeks to change your mind." He scowled inwardly. What was he saying? He was loco, he decided. There was no way to have a relationship with Ann. Though he'd always known that, the truth of it hit home as he drove through the city. He couldn't place her in that kind of danger. He simply couldn't. The price was too high for her—and for himself.

Ann slanted a lingering glance in his direction. Houston had taken off his sport coat and rolled up the sleeves of the white cotton shirt he wore revealing his strong, massive forearms which were covered with dark hair. The window was open, allowing the spring air to circulate in the van, mixed with the scents of fires and food cooking in pots in the nearby village. "Where are we now?" she asked, sitting up and rearranging the seat belt across her shoulder.

"This is the barrio our clinic serves," Houston said with a scowl. "My home away from home."

"Where do you live the rest of the time?"

"Anywhere in Peru where I can find the drug lords first before they find me and my men,'' he answered grimly. ''Usually I stay at the BOQ—barracks officers' quarters—up near the capital when I come in off a mission.'' He took a beeper from his belt and looked at it. ''Matter of fact, they know I'm here. I've already got five phone calls to make as soon as we get this stuff to the clinic.'' He snapped the beeper back onto his belt.

Ann shook her head as she surveyed the neighborhood. Most of the ramshackle houses were little more than corrugated tin held up with bits of wood, with cardboard as siding. Huge families crowded the doorways as Ann and Mike slowly drove by. ''No one should live in these conditions,'' she murmured. ''The city at least ought to put sanitary sewage systems into a place like this. So many children will die of infections from drinking water from open cesspools.''

''You've got the general idea.''

She heard the tightness in Houston's voice and studied the hard set of his mouth. As they drove deeper into the barrio, living conditions deteriorated accordingly. People were thin and hungry looking, their dark brown faces pinched. They were wrapped in rags and threadbare clothing to try and keep warm. As Mike drove, more and more people greeted him, calling out and lifting their hands in welcome. He called back, often by name, and waved in return.

''It seems like everyone here knows you.''

''Just about.''

''Because of the clinic?''

''Yeah, mostly. Sister Dominique goes around once a week and makes house calls. She carries her homeopathic kit from house to house, family to family, doing what she can.'' He shook his head. ''Oftentimes it's not enough.''

''Hopeless?''

''No,'' Mike said, making a slow turn to the left, down another very narrow street lined with cardboard shacks and crowded with people. ''Never hopeless.'' He grinned suddenly. ''I hold out hope for the hopeless, Ann, or I wouldn't be down here doing this stuff. No, the clinic makes a difference.''

Ann admired his commitment to improving the sad conditions. ''Can't governmental agencies help you?''

"They won't," he said, gesturing toward a redbrick church ahead, its gleaming white spire thrusting above the mire of human habitations. "Peruvians in Lima don't view Indians as human. We're animals to them. Big, dumb brutes to be used as pack animals, is all."

Frowning, Ann said, "You said you were Yaqui?"

"My mother's part Yaqui, from Central America, and part Quechua Indian. She was born in Peru, but her family moved north to Mexico when she was six years old."

"How did your mother meet your father?"

"When you get me good and drunk sometime, I'll tell you," Mike told her with a grin.

He braked the van and turned at the redbrick church, which was surrounded by a white picket fence. Despite the mud, filth and poverty of the neighborhood, the Catholic church was spotlessly clean, with no trash littering the well-kept green lawn. The church stood out like a sore thumb in the dirty barrio, but Ann supposed it was a symbol of hope. A beacon of sorts. When he drove the van to the rear of the church, she saw a one-story brick addition to the building.

"That's the clinic," Mike told her proudly, slowing down. Putting the van into Reverse, he backed up to the open gate of the picket fence. "Sisters Dominique and Gabriella live here. They're the ones who are in the trenches every day, keeping the clinic doors open for the people."

Ann saw at least fifteen mothers with children standing patiently in line outside the doors. Her heart broke as she noticed their lined, worried faces. Some carried babies in thin blankets, pressed tightly to them; others had crying children who clung to their colorful skirts. They were all Indians, Ann observed.

Houston turned off the van and set the brake. He glanced over at Ann. The devastation in her exhausted eyes spoke eloquently of how deeply moved she was by the horrible conditions the Indians lived in. She was easily touched, he was discovering, and it said something about her he'd already known intuitively. Still, he wondered how she would fit in with the nuns here, and he worried that the cool demeanor Ann had displayed toward him when they'd worked together on the ranch might put the nuns off. "The two little old nuns are French. They're from Marseilles, and they're saints, as far as I'm concerned. They've been ministering to the poor since they came here in their twenties. They're in their seventies now and should've retired a long time ago, but they're like horses in a harness—it's all they know and they have hearts as big as Lima. They speak French and Spanish and some English.''

He wrapped his hands around the steering wheel and gave Ann a measuring look. ''I know how you reacted to me off and on for eight weeks up in Arizona. They don't need a *norteamericana* coming in here and telling them what to do. They're homeopaths, not medical doctors. If you don't know anything about homeopathy, try to suspend your disbelief about it, watch them work and watch what happens to the patients they serve before you make any judgment about it, okay?''

Ann met and held his searching gaze. Because she'd kept him at a distance until now, he probably thought she would carry on that way here. ''You're remembering my attitude toward you in Arizona and predicting that I'll treat everyone at this clinic the same way?''

Mike castigated himself. ''There are times when I wish I had more diplomacy, but lack of sleep is making me a little more blunt than usual.'' He opened his hands over the wheel in a helpless gesture. ''I owe you an apology.''

Ann accepted his apology—the second one to come from him since they'd traded parries on the plane. ''Look,'' she said, sighing wearily, ''I understand your being wary. I know I haven't been easy to get along with. But let's just forget our personal feelings about one another, shall we? I have a commitment to honor in Morgan's name for the next six weeks. In a clinic situation or a hospital environment, I'm not the ice queen you think I am. So don't be concerned that I'll ride roughshod over two old nuns. I've got better things to do with my time than pick at them or complain about what type of medicine they practice. No, I don't know a lot about homeopathy. But it obviously works or they wouldn't have been using it here for fifty years, would they?'' But despite her assurances to Mike, Ann knew she would have to make an effort to suspend some of her rational approaches and training. Her medical background was different from a homeopathic practitioner's. This was another situation in which she would have to yield her scientific bent to a more mysterious, even mystical kind of medicine. If she was going to survive these six weeks, she understood that she had to adjust to Mike's world, and that included the nuns' medical procedures.

Mike saw Ann struggling to not be hurt by his request. That said a lot about her. She was confident and didn't let her ego get in the way of better judgment. "I didn't mean to accuse you of being close-minded. It's just that I know a lot of conventional medicine types in the medical field who look down their nose at homeopathy. Hell, the clinic was so poor financially that we couldn't afford to buy the prescription drugs we needed, so homeopathic meds took up the slack instead."

"I'll stand back and let them run the show," Ann promised. "I'm here to assist. All right?"

Satisfied, Mike nodded. "I just don't want any misunderstandings, Ann. God knows, I'm going to be busier than a one-armed paper hanger this next week. I don't have time to come down here and put out brushfires between you and my grannies, that's all." And then he smiled and held her warming gaze. "Otherwise, I think they'll fall in love with you."

She smiled tiredly in return. "Thank you for your brutal honesty, Major. I generally don't cause 'brushfires.' I'm in the habit of putting them out."

"Touché," he murmured with a sour smile. "Okay, let's go inside...."

"Mon petit chou!"

Mike halted just inside the door. Sister Gabby, who was holding her stethoscope on the chest of a baby being held by a young mother, called out in welcome. She raised her soft, frizzy white head, her brown eyes sparkling.

"Mon petit chou, you are home!" she cried. "Oh! How long it has been! We missed you!" Patting the baby with her paper-thin hand, she bustled forward putting the stethoscope around her neck. Then, she threw open her arms and hugged Mike with a fierceness that always surprised him. Sister Gabby was four feet

eleven inches tall—a dwarf in comparison to him. Yet she was strong. Very strong for her age. And she was a giant in his eyes, towering over everyone with her warm heart, her grace.

He gently embraced the nun, dropping into French. "Grandma Gabby, I have great news. Look who I brought with me. This is Dr. Ann Parsons from the States. She's a trained emergency-room physician and she's going to assist you and Granny Dominique for the next six weeks." Mike eased the nun around, praying that Ann would smile.

To his relief, as he brought the two together for introductions, Mike saw Ann's exhaustion melt away before him, leaving a warm, radiant woman whose blue-gray eyes shone with incredible happiness as she reached out and gently enclosed the old nun's hand between her own, and greeted her in flawless, beautiful French.

"Sister Gabriella, I've heard so many wonderful things about you from Major Houston, here. It's a great honor to meet you."

"Ah, call me Sister Gabby, please." The nun directed a beaming smile up at Mike, who had draped a protective arm around her thin, hunched shoulders. "This young one, the one we call 'my little cabbage,' is the true saint around here. And we are so glad to have your help, Dr. Parsons! The Lord knows that we can use a medical doctor of your experience around here, eh?"

Ann smiled pleasantly and released the nun's hand, noticing her dark blue habit which did not cover her silver hair, and the gold crucifix that lay against her thin chest. Although the nun was in her seventies, Ann saw that her aging face was strong and beautiful. And Gabby's adoring gaze never left Houston's. There was no denying the love and admiration the old nun had for the army officer.

"'*Mon petit chou*'?" Ann inquired sweetly, looking directly at Houston, who promptly avoided her inquiring gaze. "Is that the major's name?" Her smile grew as she watched Mike become highly uncomfortable. She knew it was an often-used endearment in France for someone who was precious and beloved. She just found it a little hard to picture big Mike Houston being called a "little cabbage." There was nothing little about this man.

Tittering, Sister Gabby said, "Oh, yes. You know—" she

wagged her finger up at Mike "—when this young army officer came to us a decade ago with the offer to build us a small clinic to help the poor, we knew a miracle had walked into our lives. Michael is named after the archangel, the destroyer. But he was an answer to our prayers, believe me! Do you know that he built this clinic by hand, brick by brick, over a year's time? Instead of destroying, he built."

"Granny..." Mike protested, "I really don't think Dr. Parsons wants to hear the history—"

"Sure I do," Ann answered, smiling softly as she devoted her full attention back to the tiny nun. "So, he built this clinic for you?" She was enjoying Houston's obvious embarrassment as he shifted from one foot to another, his hands behind his back. Let him squirm. It was good for his soul.

"Ah, yes! He had only the help of the poor who live around our church. Every day he would come here from his dangerous duties and roll up his sleeves—" she pinched his massive biceps with pride "—and he would lay brick! He talked the Lima government out of the old brick and he raised money for the concrete. He was a one-man army! That is when Sister Dominique and I decided to give him a nickname. Now, you know his *other* name," Gabby said in a conspiratorial tone, "but that doesn't really tell of what lies in his heart. So we decided to call him 'my little cabbage' because that's what he was to us, to our people and to the poor we serve—so very precious and beloved by all of us." She reached up, her parchment-colored hand patting Mike's barrel chest. "Beneath this shirt beats a heart of gold, Dr. Parsons. His generosity, his care of the poor is so great! But his heart is even more large and giving!"

"Granny!" Mike protested. "I really don't think we have time to talk pleasantries right now, do you? Dr. Parsons will get bored hearing about me. While I get some help unloading supplies from the van, why don't you introduce her to Sister Dominique?"

Ann chuckled to herself. She liked watching the old woman ruffle Mike's feathers, she decided, as Sister Gabby caught her hand and led her down the narrow hall to another room in the clinic.

"Ah, yes, of course, *mon petit chou.* Time is short! I know you cannot stay long. It is dangerous for you to be too long in one place, eh? Yes, come, come, Dr. Parsons...."

Ann glanced over her shoulder at Houston. He had relief written all over his features. As she proceeded down the narrow hall she saw four different examination rooms. They were pitifully equipped, she realized. The tiny nun moved quickly, switching from French to Spanish as she stuck her head in each of the rooms to tell the awaiting patients that she'd be back in just a moment.

The last room in the clinic was actually an office of sorts. It was the smallest space, and there was a badly dented metal desk in the center of it with another nun in a blue habit seated behind it. Her white hair was cut very short and her wire-rimmed glasses were perched on her very fine, thin nose as she dug through a huge, teetering pile of papers.

"I swear, Gabriella," she muttered without looking up, "we *must* get these homeopathic cases into the files! I am looking for Juan's records. I do not remember what homeopathic remedy we gave him six weeks ago! I must find it!"

"Tut, tut, Dominique," Gabby said, tapping her smartly on the shoulder. "We have a visitor, a medical doctor who is going to help us for six weeks! Dr. Ann Parsons is from the United States. Meet Sister Dominique."

"Eh?" Dominique looked up, her pinched face very wrinkled. Her gray eyes narrowed as she looked Ann up and down. Placing her hands on her hips, she said, "Well, a *real* medical doctor? How did this happen?" Then she suddenly grinned, and Ann saw that all her front upper teeth were missing.

Sister Dominique's handshake was surprisingly strong. Ann smiled. "Major Houston was partly responsible for getting me to volunteer." She released Dominique's hand. "It looks like you could use a file clerk in here?" she added, eyeing the cabinets, which were partially open with all kinds of files sticking out of them.

Sister Dominique looked sadly around at the chipped and dented office furnishings. "I need a clerk. I need five new file drawers." She waved her arms around the stuffy little room. "I need more space!"

"Now, now, Dominique," Gabby chided, waving a finger at

her, "be patient. *Mon petit chou* is home and said he's got two *new* file cabinets for us! He's getting the men to help bring them back here. Isn't that wonderful? He said a *norteamericano,* Señor Trayhern, gave a huge donation to us! Our prayers have been answered—again!" She clapped her hands delightedly.

Dourly, Sister Dominique griped, "Why does God always answer our prayers at the last minute? I swear, Gabby, we must be saying them wrong. There must be something to the process we have obviously overlooked, eh? We pray and pray and pray for *years,* and finally, just when we think the clinic will close, or we just can't go on, He decides to drop us a few crumbs to keep going. No," she muttered, scratching her silvery head, "we must be going about this wrong. Perhaps we need to get up at four a.m. to pray instead of six a.m.?"

Ann smiled gently. Sister Dominique had a vinegar personality, but the tall, lean woman's burning gray eyes sparkled with hints of wry amusement, too.

"I think that God heard you plenty, this time," Ann answered warmly. "Wait until you see what all Mike is bringing out of that van for your clinic. And that donation was for a nice sum—a hundred and thirty thousand dollars to put into the bank for equipment to help you at the clinic."

Both nuns said, "Ahh..." as they looked at each other. Gabby broke into a high-pitched cackle and moved around the desk to hug Dominique. And as they embraced, both nuns began to cry.

Ann found herself with damp eyes as the nuns sobbed on each other's shoulders, their French and Spanish strewn between their joyous bouts of weeping. Digging into her leather shoulder purse, Ann found some tissues and handed them out to each of them.

"Thank you," Gabby sniffed, blotting her eyes. "Oh, this is such a wonderful miracle!"

"*Mon petit chou* made this happen, I'll bet," Dominique told the other nun briskly. "He can squeeze blood out of a turnip, that one!"

"And how many times has he had to do it for us? For our clinic?" Gabby sighed, blowing her nose loudly.

"We must get back to our patients," Dominique reminded her starchly, throwing her tissue into a nearby garbage container. "Dr.

Parsons, why don't you come with me? You can sit and watch and listen. For the next few days, I want you to just get acquainted with what we do, with our patients. They are quite wary of Anglos, you know. Word must get out in the barrio about you. And then—'' she raised her eyebrows, which were so thin they were almost nonexistent, ''we will have a hundred people or more lined up and waiting when we open the clinic doors at seven a.m. No medical doctors ever come down here. No, you will be a curiosity. And they have heard so much about modern medicine that they will think you are heaven-sent to help them with their ills.''

''Ah,'' Gabby said with a sigh, ''they will bring their crippled, those that need surgery, thinking that she can do all those things they cannot afford.''

Dominique grunted and walked quickly around the desk, her long, thin arms flying. ''We'll deal with that when it happens, Gabby. Come, we all have much work to do!''

When he returned to the clinic later that day, Houston poked his head into the largest room, a five-bed area he added on to the original structure two years ago. He found Ann and Sister Dominique standing on either side of the bed of a little girl whose head and right eye were bandaged. The girl's mother, a Quechua Indian, held the child protectively in her arms. As he approached, Mike softened his footsteps across the spotlessly clean hardwood floor, studying Ann.

She sat on the bed, facing the little five-year-old and unwrapping the dressing. He noticed she had changed into a white jacket, her stethoscope hanging around her neck, a blood pressure cuff hanging out of her left pocket. Sister Dominique stood behind her, explaining in detail the child's condition.

The low, honeyed tone of Ann's voice drifted toward him. He halted and watched, unnoticed by all of them except Sister Dominique, who raised her head imperiously, met his gaze and gave him a tight smile of acknowledgment before brusquely returning her attention to the other women. Mike smiled to himself. Sister Dominique never missed a beat.

Curious about Ann's bedside manner, he decided not to make his presence known to her. He knew he should get going. It was dangerous to be at the clinic too long. After unloading the supplies, he'd left for a while to return phone calls and check on some of the operations he had set up, figuring he'd give Ann time to get to know the nuns and see how the clinic worked. But now that he'd returned, he knew it was foolish to stick around. Ann's and the nun's safety had to come first over the selfish yearnings of his heart to stay just a minute or two longer. And his presence at the clinic put them at risk.

But just the way Ann tenderly unwrapped the dressing and gauze from around the child's head made his skin prickle pleasantly with desire for her. He saw the gentle strength in her face, her eyes warm with compassion, her voice low and soothing. And the child seemed to react positively to her ministrations.

For the next five minutes, Houston simply absorbed Ann's presence as she went about her duties, in a manner that indicated her work came as naturally as breathing to her. The child had tripped while carrying a stick and stabbed herself in the right eye. The wound was messy but Ann, with Sister Dominique's help, washed it out and examined it closely. To Mike's relief, Ann was willing to allow Sister Dominique to dispense a homeopathic remedy, Symphytum, in order to reduce the swelling of the tissue and help the injured eyeball heal. He liked the way she worked—with swift, efficient motions—and he realized that came from a lot of field experience under extreme and dangerous conditions. A smile tugged at his mouth as he allowed his hands to drop from his hips.

Mike waited until Ann was getting up before he made his presence known. "Half of healing is the love you put into it," he murmured as he finally approached.

Ann turned in surprise. How long had Mike been in the room? "I didn't hear you come in," she said.

"I didn't want to be heard."

Sister Dominique chuckled. "He's the jaguar god, Dr. Parsons. That is the mysterious part of him and his *other* name. Anyone who lives in Peru has heard of him. He walks like the silent jaguar he is named for. His enemies know his deadly abilities. They fear him. Just as his archangel namesake did, he destroys his enemies, but he does it for the common good and protection of the people. You need not fear him, though. He is like a shadow, you know?"

She came over and patted Mike's shoulder. "He is a good shadow, not a bad one. His enemies want to see him hanged by his feet and stripped of his flesh, one inch at a time. With us—" she smiled benignly up at him "—he's a silent, watchful guardian who protects us and helps us to heal others. No, do not be upset that you did not hear him coming. You are safe with him. Always."

Mike watched Sister Dominique leave the room as the woman tucked her daughter, who was probably staying overnight for observation, into the bed. The other four beds held what looked like worse cases, mostly older men and women. He watched Ann gather up the extra bandages and place them in her pocket.

"How are you getting along?"

Ann walked up to him, her exhaustion dissolving beneath his caring gaze. "Fine." For a moment she thought she saw Houston's eyes change, but it could have just been the fatigue lapping at her that made her think there was something stirring in the depths of those dark blue eyes of his—something so warm and good that it seemed to come out and wrap around her briefly in an invisible embrace. It had to be the jet lag, she told herself, or her imagination was just overactive from being around Mike. Ever since that breathless kiss at the airport, her mind had been creating flights of fantasy.

"You're looking beat, Ann. You've got dark circles under your eyes the size of the Lima airport." Mike said wrapping his fingers under her left arm and leading her toward the door. "I've got to get to my office. How about if I drop you off at your apartment? I think you need about twenty hours of sleep and then you'll feel a hell of a lot better." And he would feel a lot better knowing she'd been safely delivered to her apartment.

Ann walked at his side down the hall. "A hell of a lot better than I look?" she baited, a sour smile edging her lips.

Houston grinned. "Now, *querida,* I would *never* say that." He shook his head. "Nope, in my own male, Neanderthal way, I'd say you can't make a looker look ugly." He'd become painfully aware of how his endearment had struck her when he saw Ann's features grow soft. The word *querida* meant "darling" in Spanish and he'd allowed it to slip out by mistake. He must be tired. Or maybe, in his heart, she was already his woman. Inwardly, Houston fought against himself. He simply could *not* see Ann in that way. He had to protect her, not leave her open to a dangerous life by his side.

Heat suffused Ann's cheeks. Self-consciously, she stuffed the stethoscope into her pocket. Anything to halt the frisson of need that burned through her as Mike's endearment touched her. The intimacy he automatically established with her was shattering. In that moment when he'd looked down at her and spoken that one word, Ann had wanted to step into his arms, drown herself in the rough splendor of his mouth and be loved senseless by him. The raw desire in Mike's eyes made her tremble inwardly. Rubbing the back of her neck, she said, "You *are* terribly old-fashioned." Did he know how *much* he affected her? Ann would just die if he did. She tried to cover her reaction by remaining busy, focusing on little details around the clinic.

"Yeah," he said with a chuckle, "I'm a throwback to the caveman type, I know. As you get used to me, I'll rub off on you and you'll see my bite's not as bad as my bark." The high flush in her cheeks, her nervous gestures told Mike how much his intimacy with her had affected her. He felt her emotional response rock through him like the powerful gust of wind that struck before a storm poured its life-giving rains upon the jungle.

"Somehow," Ann murmured, picking up her purse, which Sister Gabby had stuffed into a drawer of the old metal desk, "I doubt that. Sister Dominique was telling me earlier that there's a reward offered for your head. Never mind the rest of your body." Ann shifted uneasily and searched his suddenly hard, expressionless features as he walked easily down the hall and out the clinic doors with her. "Is that true? The nuns told me a lot of what you do down here." Worry ate at her more than she liked to admit. Mike was so passionate about living, about life. How could anyone want to snuff out this magnificent warrior's life? How? Reeling from the shock that anyone would have a price on his head, she made an effort to look at Mike in the new light. In Arizona, he had been vague about his work in Peru. Now the truth was ugly and frightening to her.

"Nuns don't lie," he said abruptly, opening the door to the

sedan for her. Houston warily looked around the church grounds. It always paid to be alert, no matter how tired he was.

Inside, Ann put on her seat belt and waited until Mike climbed in. She wanted to stop asking questions, but they just kept tumbling out of her mouth. As he drove the car slowly away from the church, she asked, "Well? Is it true? There's a huge price on your head?"

Grimly, Mike nodded. "Let's talk about more pleasant things, shall we?" He saw the shadowed look she gave him. She really *cared* about him. He could not protect himself against the waves of her roller-coaster emotions. The worry, anguish and fear she felt for him affected him powerfully. But if she knew how deeply he sensed her every emotion, she'd be mortified.

Ann rested her head against the seat. "Okay." She sighed and closed her eyes. "I need a hot bath, lots of hot water, I feel so dirty...."

It was on the tip of his tongue to tell her that no one in the barrio had ever experienced a hot bath, but he swallowed his comment. He could tell she was tired by the pastiness of her skin, and he noticed how tight and stressed she had become. "A hot bath can do wonders," he agreed.

Ann whispered, "Yes, it will, but you know what? Nothing will take away the pain of caring for that last little girl we saw at the clinic," she murmured. "It just breaks my heart. She's going to go blind, Mike, and there's nothing we can do for her—no surgery available.... I wanted to cry for her."

Mike glanced at Ann before turning his attention back to the foot traffic along the dirt road. "You might as well get used to it, *querida*," he said, the endearment rolling off his tongue once again. "You're going to see heartbreaking cases every day you step into that clinic to work. It's not a pretty sight."

Mike's endearment took the edge off the sorrow she felt for the child, and his deep voice was soothing to her tension and tiredness. But she also heard the anguish in his tone. There was no question of his commitment to the clinic, to the poor. "Those nuns think you walk on water," she said softly. "They adore you."

"Humph, if I step into water I'll sure as hell go down just as fast as the next poor bastard. My grannies are a little biased toward me, so you have to take some of what they say with a grain of salt.''

Through her barely opened eyes, Ann realized he was blushing, his cheeks a decided ruddy color. Lips parting, Ann whispered, ''Maybe I drew too quick a conclusion about you, Mike. You are a person of unnerving mystery. I have more questions than answers about you.''

He cut her a wry look. ''Now, don't go believing the nuns. Every once in a while they stretch the truth a little.''

Her lips pulled into a careless smile and she met and held his gaze. ''You mean you don't want to suffer from a good reputation?''

Chuckling, Mike flexed his fingers against the steering wheel. ''You're hearing only one side of the story.''

''I ask you and you don't answer me. So what choice do I have but to believe what others say about you?''

He winced. ''Touché.''

''So, there really is a reward for your head on a silver platter?''

He saw the genuine worry in Ann's eyes once more and he tried to minimize the danger of his situation. ''Thirty pieces of silver or something like that...'' he muttered.

''Don't get defensive, Mike. It isn't every day I hear of such a thing. You seem to blow the whole thing off. If I had a bounty on my head, I'd never come back to Peru.''

Mike glanced briefly into her drowsy eyes. ''Trust me, I'm on guard twenty-five hours a day, eight days a week. Yeah, some drug lords would love to have my head served to them on a silver platter. But that reward has been offered for seven years now and no one has collected it yet. I don't intend to give my enemies the pleasure, either. I'm going to keep hitting them, disrupting their trade and fighting to take back the Indian villages they enslave for their nefarious ends.'' His mouth reflected the grimness in his voice. ''No matter how long it takes.''

Ann felt a sweeping surge of power gather around him; it wasn't visible, but she could sense it. In some ways, the sensation reminded her of what she'd felt around Mike at the airport earlier, when he'd saved his friend's life. The pupils of his eyes dilated, making them look huge and black, with only a thin ring of blue around them. His features hardened to emphasize his words.

"I know plenty about the drug lords because Morgan's mercs have been working in the Caribbean, Brazil and Peru on assignment against them," Ann said, watching as they drove out of the barrio and onto the asphalt streets of a more upscale area. "When Morgan and three or four of his mercs were kidnapped by two drug lords down here, I found out a lot more than I ever wanted to know."

"Drug lords are the living scum on the face of Mother Earth," Mike growled. "I'll spend every breath I breathe taking those bastards down and apart. No, I'm their nightmare, believe me. That's why there's a ten-million-sol reward for my head." He saw Ann blanch as he mistakenly revealed the true price his enemies offered for his death.

She stirred and sat up, rubbing her face. Heart beating wildly in her breast, she said quietly, "That's more than thirty pieces of silver. Has anyone tried to kill you?"

Mike wished they could talk about something else, but he knew he owed her the truth—before it was too late. "Sure, many times." He frowned. "That's why you have to be careful, too, Ann. You stay alert everywhere you go. The clinic has never been a target—yet. So far, Eduardo Escovar, one of the drug lords who's after me, has respected the sacredness of church ground. But they've hit the barrio three times in the last seven years. People have been killed by the raids they've made, thinking I was in the area when I wasn't. Thank God, none of the bombs they planted around the barrio went off. The people there know about the druggies and their soldiers. They watch the clinic grounds and they protect those two sisters. I try and vary when I go to the clinic to help out. I never have the same schedule twice, to keep them from setting up an ambush for me. And the nuns are never told beforehand when I'll be coming in. I just show up unannounced."

Shivering, Ann felt suddenly cold. She shouldn't be; the late spring afternoon was warm and pleasant. Rubbing her arms, she wrestled with the harsh truth that Mike's life was on the line every day. "How can you live like this? The stress would kill me."

His mouth curved tightly. "I guess what it boils down to is that my passion to see my people free of oppression is stronger than my need to worry about my own neck.'' He tasted the fear and the care warring within her. Helpless, Mike could only try to buffer her tumultuous emotional state. Would Ann withdraw from him now? He knew the stakes were too high for her to even consider a relationship with him, and he could see in her eyes that she was realizing that truth now. It was best if she did. Maybe hard reality would make her care less for him than before. He hoped so. It was the only way he could be sure she remained safe.

''And you've evaded capture by them for seven years?''

''So far, so good.'' He turned onto a main avenue lined with trees. Traffic was heavy, but it was always that way in this section of the city, where the rich and powerful lived in tall, spacious apartment buildings. Morgan Trayhern had not been stingy in getting Ann posh quarters, that was for sure.

''And,'' Ann wondered in a low tone, ''is that because of this jaguar they talk about?'' She touched lightly on the topic because every time she mentioned it, Mike closed up and retreated from her. She admitted she was more than just a little curious about this new and surprising facet to him. According to the nuns, the man was a living legend among the Indians in Peru. They idolized him. Because he was also a part of the people due to his Indian blood, they saw him as a spokesman, leader and protector. Mike had such broad, capable-looking shoulders beneath the white cotton shirt he wore. Just how many responsibilities did he really carry? Ann was getting an inkling of his role in Peru and it filled her with a mixture of awe and terror.

She shouldn't be in awe of any man, she thought, berating herself sharply. Awe had gotten her into the worst nightmare of her life. No, no man should be put on a pedestal and worshipped. Bitterly, Ann hoped she'd learned that lesson. It was so easy to want to put Mike on just such a pedestal, though.

When Houston didn't reply to her question about the jaguar, she added, ''The sisters said that among the Indian population, people refer to you as the jaguar god.''

Shrugging, Mike muttered, ''I get called a lot of things. Believe me, you'll want to put cotton in your ears when you hear some of the not-so-nice descriptions that I'm sure you'll be privy to in the next six weeks.''

"I feel you evading me on this, Mike. Why?"

As he pulled into an underground parking facility beneath a relatively new apartment building made of steel and glass, he shot her a quizzical look and then devoted his attention to finding a parking spot. "There's a lot I need to tell you, to fill you in on," he admitted slowly. "But we're both a little beat right now and I'd like to save it for another time."

Ann nodded, though her exhaustion seemed to have melted away from her as her curiosity was aroused. "Yes...that would be fine...."

Mike pulled into a parking slot near the elevators. He frowned and shut off the car engine, all the while looking around the gloomy depths of the garage. No place was safe, as far as he was concerned. "I'm being more than a little selfish about all this," he admitted in a low tone as he held Ann's gaze. "I was glad I didn't have to leave you in Arizona. But I also knew the risks of your being here and you didn't." He shrugged as if trying to rid himself of some invisible load he carried. "It's not too late to get back on that plane, you know." He hated suggesting it, but it was the only right thing to do. Ann shouldn't stay if she was afraid of becoming too involved with him, or putting herself in danger because of him. No, she had to make an informed decision on this. Unconsciously, Mike held his breath and waited for her answer. The smart thing to do was get her on a plane going north as soon as possible. But his heart cried, "no!"

Pain ripped through Ann's chest; it was as if she were physically connected to Mike for a moment. Something was going on inside her and she didn't understand it. Briefly touching her heart region, she closed her eyes and avoided his searching gaze. Taking a deep breath, she opened them again and looked directly at him. "I think it's time for a little honesty here." She barreled on. "I'm scared, Mike. Of you. Of myself. And now this...this situation where you could get killed at any second." Swallowing hard, she felt tears burning her eyes and forced them back. "I'd be a liar to say it doesn't bother me, because it does. Horribly, if you want the truth.

But..." She gave him a helpless look and drowned in the burning blueness of his gaze.

"But?" Houston croaked, tension radiating through him as he felt and saw her wrestling with so many unspoken emotions.

"How could I have let myself feel so much?" Ann whispered brokenly. "How?"

He sat very still. Tears trickled down her face, down the taut flesh of her pale cheeks. "Maybe we cared for one another in Arizona and we were just too mule-headed to admit it to each other."

His words were spoken so softly that they felt like a whisper through the tumultuous halls of her mind. She closed her eyes, the pain nearly unbearable. Risking everything, she opened them once more. "Yes...I care for you. God knows, I tried to deny it. I tried to bury it. Dammit, Mike!" Tears splattered down her face. "Damn you...damn myself. Oh, hell, I don't know how it happened...or why...it just did."

Her cry cut through his heart. Acting on blind instinct, he leaned forward and slid his arms around her, pulling her against him. At first she tensed, but within moments, she surrendered to him, her head coming to rest against his jaw. She felt soft and good in his arms, wherever their bodies touched. Mike closed his eyes and pressed a kiss into her hair. He could smell the spicy, faint scent of the perfume she wore. It did nothing but accentuate his need for her. All of her.

"I've never seen someone fight so hard not to care for another person as you have," he whispered hoarsely. "And I know you have your reasons, *querida*." He tightened his embrace around her momentarily. Her hand moved languidly up his arm and he relished the sensation her touch caused. "I should be sorry as hell that this has happened, because my being with you puts you in danger. A danger I'm not willing to expose you to..."

Ann buried her face against his neck. "Hold me," she quavered. "Just hold me?" Right now, she felt like a frightened little girl rather than a woman. Her past haunted her. On top of that, the realization that Mike's life was in constant danger added a new pain to her awakening heart, just when she was trying to reach out and allow herself to love once again—despite her fears.

He pressed small, soft kisses to her hair, her temple and wan cheek. He tasted the saltiness of her tears, the dampness of her flesh beneath his mouth. "I should have told you earlier about the danger that surrounds me," he apologized thickly.

Ann shook her head and buried her face more deeply against him. "No..." she murmured, "how could you? I wouldn't let you. I was still running scared. I was in denial about you...about how I really felt toward you...." Unhappily, she muttered, "And I'm a therapist—I should know better."

Houston brushed several thick strands of hair from her cheek. "Welcome to the real word of people, Doc. You're really one of us, after all...."

The rumbling sound in his chest was comforting to Ann and she managed a slight laugh. "I guess you're right, Mike."

"I know I am." His hand stilled against her cheek. "Do you want me to take you to the airport? You can walk away. If you stay...I can't make any promises about us. Not ever...."

Slowly Ann eased out of his arms. She met his grave, shadowed gaze. "No...I want to stay, Mike. I want...need to explore what we have or don't have—danger or no danger."

Chapter 5

Tension thrummed through Mike as he watched Ann look around her newly rented apartment. It was posh, filled with expensive antique furniture from the Queen Anne period. He checked the dead bolt and the other lock on the door. Below, in an unmarked car, he had Pablo, one of his best soldiers, waiting and watching outside the apartment complex. Escovar's spies in the city were in the hundreds. They all knew Mike's face. They all knew what to do if they saw him: call one of the roving hit squads in Lima—whichever was closest. Then a van filled with the best mercenary soldiers the drug lords could buy would come screeching up, determined to murder Houston and anyone with him.

Rubbing his neck ruefully as Ann looked around the large apartment with obvious delight, Mike knew he had to get going. To stay longer was putting her at risk, whether she knew it or not. As she emerged from the bedroom, he met her halfway down the carpeted hall. Reaching out, he drew her into his arms. She came willingly.

"I've got to get going," he said gruffly against her thick, silky hair as she rested against him.

"You can't stay?"

He groaned. Mike understood the invitation: Ann wanted him to make love to her. But as he ran his hand across her slumped shoulders, he remembered the depth of her exhaustion. "Now, *querida,*" he teased, "if we even thought of trying to love one another, we'd fall asleep halfway through. I don't know about you, but when I take you all the way, I want to be wide awake." Why had he said that? Houston was angry with himself. He had no right to lead her on like this. But his heart was overflowing with need of her. Ordinarily, he resisted such temptations, but Ann was unraveling his emotional control in every possible way and he was helpless to stop her. Somehow, he knew he had to try.

Ann smiled softly and languished in the strength and protection of his embrace. "You're right," she murmured. "I'm so tired I can barely walk...or think."

"See?" Mike said with a slight smile as he eased her from his arms. Her eyes were dark with exhaustion, but he ached to take her even now. "Will a stolen kiss do?" His heart beat fiercely as she lifted her chin and gave him that tender smile filled with undisguised desire. His hands automatically tightened on her arms.

Wordlessly, he leaned down, swept her deeply into his embrace and took her offered lips. How soft and sweet they were! He found himself starving for her. His hands moving of their own accord, he eased them down her back as her own arms came up and encircled his neck. The soft firmness of her rounded breasts made fire burn through him. He heard her moan as he lightly caressed the curve of her breasts. Shamelessly, she pressed her hips against his.

The warning in the back of his mind took over. He had stayed alive this long because he never disregarded it. Reluctantly, he tore his mouth from hers. Fire burned in Ann's eyes as he stared hungrily down at her, cupping her shoulders to steady her, as she swayed in the aftermath of their searching kiss.

"You're one hell of a kisser," he rasped. "Take that hot bath you mentioned. Go to bed, *querida.* I'll drop by and see you sometime tomorrow." He frowned. "And keep your dead bolt on that door, do you hear? I've got a key for it and the other lock."

Vaguely, Ann heard his instructions, heard the concern in his voice. Her mouth tingled. She stared dazedly up at him and her body responded hotly to his narrowed eyes, the primal animal sense she felt emanating from him. For a moment—just a split second—she thought she saw the yellow-and-black eyes of a jaguar instead his blue ones. She had to be hallucinating again from sleep deprivation.

"Okay..." she whispered. "I'll see you soon?"

Caressing her hair, he murmured, "Count on it...."

The apartment seemed so void and lonely after Mike left. Ann dutifully slipped the dead bolt in place and locked the door. She moved to the bathroom, fatigue robbing her of all thought. Her first day in Lima had been by far the most aching, hungry and mysterious she had ever spent in her life. Mike was more of an enigma than ever. Yet she knew unequivocally that she needed him—and wanted to explore how she felt about him. Somehow, she had to put the brakes on her out-of-control feelings where he was concerned, she thought as she readied herself for bed, then climbed wearily between the sheets. As sleep claimed her completely, she had a vivid, colorful dream.

Ann found herself standing by the clearest, most inviting looking water she'd ever seen. The oval-shaped pool was a collecting spot, a depression in the soft earth of the Amazon basin. The humidity that forever blotted out the sun and made the sky look like translucent mist moved above her like a living, breathing thing. As she stood naked and barefoot beside the magical-looking pool, she watched like an awed child as that mist gently twisted, turned, took shape and then dissolved, only to writhe into another form or momentary pattern once again. The swirling humidity made the sun look more like a lightbulb hidden behind heavy fabric.

I should be cold, she thought. But she wasn't. The delicious warmth and humidity of the jungle enveloped her like an invisible blanket. It felt wonderful to be free of her bra and panties and all her clothes! Stretching her arms over her head, she laughed fully, her voice muted by the surrounding trees and lush green foliage beneath the rain forest canopy.

Returning her attention to the glistening, smooth surface of the pool, Ann swore she could feel Mother Earth breathing, in and out...in and out.... As she threaded her fingers through her loose, straight hair, Ann could feel the humidity making the strands curl slightly. What did this place remind her of?

As she gazed about the area, she saw broad-leafed plants, no more than a foot high, growing here and there. Grass did not survive beneath the triple canopy; there wasn't enough sunlight to encourage it. The banks of the pool were scattered with decomposing leaves that had fallen from above and small branches that had been knocked off the trees, perhaps by a colorful parrot or a monkey. The decay that surrounded her wasn't repugnant to her as she knelt down on her hands and knees. No, the ground was soft and yielding, almost like a resilient skin to Ann as she pressed her palms against it, testing it gently in slow, delicious exploration. The odor was sweet—surprisingly sweet and clean smelling.

The faint scent of a flower caught her flaring nostrils and she turned to find a huge silk cotton tree next to the pool, its roots large, thin flat gray wings arching out from the main trunk like flying buttresses. There were at least eight "wings" holding the massive, tall tree in place. On one of them, she noticed a clump of darker leaves and an array of bright, colorful flowers springing from it, hanging over the pool like a series of Christmas ornaments. The flowers smelled like vanilla, and she leaned back on her heels, closed her eyes and drew the fragrance deep into her body.

This place in her dream felt like a birthing chamber to Ann. Slowly opening her eyes, she absorbed that realization within her. Yes, that was it. This very special jungle in the Amazon basin was a living incubator of Mother Earth. By some grace, she'd been allowed into the birthing chamber where expressions of love became life itself. An incredible sense of awe flowed through her as she continued to slowly gaze around her perfect Eden. Ann had had no idea the jungle was this beautiful. It truly was a primal region, as it had given birth to so many beautiful plants, animals and flowers.

Leaning down, she trailed her fingers across the glasslike surface of the quiet pool. The water was invitingly warm. She watched the tiny wavelets become ripples and then disappear halfway across the pool's expanse. Laughing, Ann leaned out over the edge of the bank and looked at herself in the mirrored surface.

How young and happy she appeared! Much younger than her thirty-two years. Smiling delightedly, she admired her reflection. There were faint freckles scattered across her nose and cheeks, which she usually hid with makeup. She saw the bump on her nose—but this time, for some reason, she felt no shaft of pain when she focused on it. That was a miracle in itself, Ann decided. But then, this place she was in was truly magical.

Her gaze moved to her eyes—her best feature, she felt. They were wide and shining. She looked like a child who had just stumbled into a storybook place. Her eyes were no longer ringed or dark looking. Instead, they were sparkling with gold in their depths and shining with joy. Ann felt so happy here and wondered if it was sinful to feel this euphoric. She couldn't recall the last time she'd felt like this, if ever. Her gaze fell to her softly parted, full lips. She had a nice mouth, she decided. It was often pursed, but as a physician, she had to maintain a certain demeanor.

Something whispered to her to slip into the pool's inviting depths, where Ann could see the dark brown of decomposing organic matter scattered on the sandy bottom. A sudden urge overwhelmed her and for once she became utterly spontaneous. Easing her feet into the pool, she was surprised at how warm, how soothing it felt. The water seemed to tug gently at her feet and ankles, calling her to slip farther into its depths. Ann realized the oval shape of the pool reminded her of a woman's womb. That made her feel comfortable and she moved effortlessly into the warm, clear water.

As the liquid enveloped her, dampened her hair, she sighed softly. This wasn't just water, this was energy-ladened, living water. As her feet touched the soft, mushy bottom, she found herself standing with the water just above her breasts. Moving her arms slowly through the clear liquid, she marveled at the energy that stirred provocatively around her. The water wasn't moving, but she felt some force slowly swirling upward from her feet, ankles, knees and thighs. The sensation was lulling and she moaned softly, closed her eyes and floated, her arms and legs outstretched. It felt as if a thousand tiny hands were massaging every inch of her body, and she never wanted the sensation to cease.

As she rolled over on her back and floated, she felt the rest of her hair absorb the living, charged water. Closing her eyes, Ann heard the soft rush of air being drawn into the forested area and felt everything around her begin to slowly expand in order to take in that necessary breath of air. There was no doubt that Mother Earth had given her entrance to her own womb. Ann, a woman, was being blessed by being allowed into the center of the living planet, the womb of Mother Earth, and partaking in the creation of life.

Tears stung Ann's eyes as she realized the enormous gift she was being given. Slowly opening her eyes, she rolled over and found herself at the opposite bank. Her gaze moved to the red-and-yellow flowers that hung over the pool. They called to her. She could hear them, their tiny voices high and filled with such love. They begged her to take the spike of flowers and lace it among strands of her hair. Again spontaneity overwhelmed her, and Ann stood up and gently snapped the end of the spike. The fragrance of vanilla surrounded her as she carefully wound the orchids through her hair.

As she climbed out of the pool and looked down, she could see the red-and-yellow flowers like a brilliant, living crown of fire and sunlight surrounding her head. Even more surprising was that Ann could feel the throbbing, pulsing warmth of those flowers sending wave after wave of sensation from her head downward. Each tiny wavelet moved farther and farther through her as she stood there, appreciating the feeling within her body. As the energy reached her breasts, she felt herself respond sexually, and for a moment that caught her off guard. But as the lulling, stroking movement of the wavelets continued to undulate through her, she sank to the bank of the pool, lay down and closed her eyes.

The golden light and fire made her breasts grow firm and she felt herself suddenly wishing Mike, whom she needed so desperately, was here to touch her, to cup her breast and then place his mouth across the rigid nipple and suckle her gently, provocatively. The moment she wished for that, the energy flowed like the power of a flooding river on the rampage to the center of her body and began to throb wildly between her thighs. Caught within her wish to share this with Mike, she moaned with longing. The throbbing ache continued and she moved her hips in a rhythmic motion, wanting Mike, wanting him to hold her, move his fingers in a rocking motion and slowly open her thighs. Oh, to be touched, to be softly stroked now! The ache built and so did the fire. The energy of the flowers continued unabated, and then she felt a blossoming between her thighs, an incredible shower of golden light bursting forth, as if there was another kind of birth, another creation occurring within her.

A hot, lava-like warmth spilled through her and she sighed with pleasure, holding her arms against herself as the heat and light exploded not only upward in a dizzying spiral of pleasure, but down out of her.

The energy spiraled around her legs and plunged deep into Mother Earth. In that moment, Ann felt a part of the sky and a part of the earth as never before. She felt more alive, more connected to every living, breathing thing than she could ever recall. Slowly, ever so slowly, that sensation began to dissolve. Ann cried out in protest and sat up. No! No, she didn't want to lose this feeling! This incredible sensation of being attached to Mother Earth and feeling her breath, her heart beating and the throb of life pulsing through every cell in her body.

Somewhere in the background, she heard a doorbell ringing— once, twice, three times. Doorbells didn't belong in jungle dreams. With a groan, Ann turned over on her side, her hair swirling across her face and tickling her nose. The tickle took her out of her heated dream state. *Damn.* Forcing her eyes open, she blinked several times. Where was she? It took her a long, groggy moment to remember.

The doorbell rang again. Insistently.

"All right!" Ann grumbled as she sat up and threw off the light cover. The soft lavender curtains over the window of the pale pink bedroom kept light from flooding in, and she was grateful, because it appeared that the sun was shining brightly outside. Rubbing her face, she felt irritated. How badly she wanted to remain in that torrid, luscious dream. Even now, as she forced herself to stand up, Ann felt the last remnants of the warm pulsation between her thighs. It was a wonderful feeling, one that she hadn't experienced in a long, long time. How many years had she tried to deny her own sexual needs? To suppress her sexual appetite and tell her body no? Too many. Far too many. Until now...until Mike had crashed unexpectedly into her life.

Stumbling to the end of the bed, Ann groped for her pale tangerine silk robe. She pulled it over her knee-length, white silk nightgown.

The doorbell rang again.

"All right!" she muttered defiantly as she hurried down the carpeted hall. "Just hold your horses, dammit!"

Pushing her hair away from her face, Ann tried to reorient herself. Yes, she was in Lima, Peru, not her home in the suburbs of Washington. No, it wasn't winter outside, it was spring. She hurried through the living room toward the door. Fumbling with the locks, she managed to dislodge the dead bolt. Twisting the knob, she jerked the door open and glared out at the trespasser who had awakened her out of that very provocative dream.

"Mike!"

Houston's brows flew upward as he stood in the hall with groceries and a bouquet of flowers in hand. Ann stared drowsily at him. Her hair was in disarray, her blue eyes were clouded with sleep and her delicious mouth was parted and looking so damn kissable. Her tone, however, had little civility. She was upset, that was for sure. He gave her a faint shrug and tried a one-cornered smile of greeting to ease her irritation.

"I woke you up, didn't I?"

Ruffled, Ann blinked again. Was she dreaming? "This is a nightmare...I want to go back to bed and keep on dreaming," she muttered thickly as she turned on her heel and moved back into the living room.

Nonplussed, Mike stepped into the apartment. "Well, okay...go ahead," he murmured.

"No...I'm sorry, Mike. I'm just...not here...." Ann had to try and wake up. She felt drugged, groggy. As she stood near the beautifully carved coffee table of dark red mahogany, she rubbed her face.

Mike shifted the groceries and shut the door behind him. "It's afternoon," he told her apologetically as he moved past her toward the kitchen. "Two p.m. I thought you'd be up by now. There wasn't any food in the place, so I thought I'd bring some over so you wouldn't starve to death when you woke up.'' He'd miscalculated her need for sleep, and felt badly. Under the circumstances, he had to see Ann sooner rather than later because the longer he stayed in Lima, the greater the danger. It was only a matter of time until one of the drug lords' spies identified him.

Ann sighed loudly. "I can't wake up, Mike. Don't talk to me right now. I've got to take a hot shower. Maybe then I can shake this off—this dream, the jet lag...." She turned and disappeared down the hall toward the master bathroom.

Chuckling indulgently, Mike watched her leave. Did Ann realize just how pretty she looked? How she made that silk robe move in such a provocative, teasing way? Sighing, he shook his head and continued on to the kitchen. He wondered if Ann realized the power she had over him as a woman. Normally, she wore the facade of doctor and therapist in his presence. Even the clothes she chose were mannish looking and understated, usually dull gray or brown. Mike understood why. She was a professional and needed to appear that way at all times. But there was so much to like about her feminine side—the side she seemed so unaware of. He wanted to help her discover the hot, unbridled woman within her. How selfish he was becoming when it came to her. Not even his past, which loomed like a nightmarish warning in front of him, could stop his desire for her.

After setting the groceries on the spotless, white-tiled kitchen counter, he decided to make Ann a cup of espresso. Yes, that would wake her up, he thought, pleased with the idea. He'd surprise her with a cup. She could drink it while she prepared for her shower. That was something he'd like someone to be thoughtful enough to do for him. No one had, of course, but he wanted to do it for her. She looked so pretty and vulnerable when she was sleepy. Her "I'm in charge" look was no longer placed like a mask over her soft, flushed features.

Ann had just shed her clothes, the shower creating clouds of steam as she adjusted it to just the right temperature, when there was a circumspect knock at the antique white-and-gold bathroom door.

What now? Ann's mind just wasn't functioning. Jet lag combined with stress and staying up too long had her in an unrelenting grip. Usually she could wake up very quickly and be cheerful. Today she desperately needed a shower in order to raise herself.

The circumspect knock came again.

Jerking at the knob, Ann only belatedly realized she was naked. Quickly stepping behind the door, she glared out from behind it. Mike was smiling lamely and holding out a cup and saucer in her direction.

"Espresso. I thought you might like some before your shower. You look like you need a good jolt to wake up from all that jet lag." He offered her the cup.

Looking down at it, Ann realized there was cream in the espresso. Houston must have observed that she took cream and sugar in her coffee in Arizona.

"Is there sugar in there, too?" she croaked, to make sure.

His mouth curved. "Yeah, just the way you like it, *querida*. Here, take it." For a moment, he wondered if she would. There was such sleepiness still present in Ann's eyes as she looked up at him. He wanted to reach out, take her into his arms, lead her down the hall and love her awake. He brutally squashed the thought. *Distance*...he had to keep his distance from Ann. He couldn't keep being intimate like this woman. Calling her darling didn't help, either. Frustrated, Houston felt torn up inside.

"Come on," he urged, trying to lighten the mood. "There are no strings attached to this. I just took pity on you, that's all...."

Touched by his boyish smile, Ann reached out and took the proffered gift. "Thanks...this is going above and beyond the call of duty, Mike. I'll be out in a little while, okay?"

"Sure. No hurry." He glowed at her tender look of thanks.

Ann started to close the door.

"How do you like your eggs?"

The door halted. "What?"

"Your eggs. How do you like them?"

She scowled. "I don't eat breakfast. You know that."

His brows moved upward again. "No, I didn't know that. At the ranch, I was always done with breakfast and was just coming back after my morning tour when I'd see you in the kitchen. You always had coffee in your hands.... You don't eat breakfast?"

She heard the incredulousness note in his deep voice. "No," she answered lamely, "I don't. I...I...oh, never mind."

Mike saw Ann become flustered. He realized she was naked and hiding behind the door. Soft clouds of mist were leaking out into the hall. "No problem. I'll fix you something you'll *want* to eat. Get your shower, Ann."

She eased the door shut. The fragrance of the espresso drew her. She took a sip and groaned over the luxury of his thoughtful gift. She was being a real grouch and he was being understanding about it, taking her in his stride. The jet lag was turning her into a harpy eagle, she decided unhappily. Taking two more quick sips of the thick, sweet coffee, she smiled. This was just what she needed. How did Mike know? Her heart whispered that he cared enough to want to make her happy.

As she climbed into the welcoming stream of the shower and slid the glass door closed, Ann sighed and thrust her head beneath the water. Yes, this was perfect! How long she stood beneath that soothing, massaging spray reliving that torrid, delicious dream, Ann had no idea. She finally emerged from the eye-opening shower and toweled herself off. Then enjoyed the luxury, finishing the rest of her espresso.

Wrapping a thick yellow towel around herself, Ann padded quietly from the bathroom to her bedroom. A wonderful, spicy odor filled the air and she found herself automatically inhaling the delicious smell. Whatever Houston was fixing in the kitchen sure made her hungry!

That was odd, too, that she should feel this hungry. Like a starved wolf, in fact. Ann laughed softly at herself. Mike seemed to be giving her an appetite for a lot of things.

After pulling on a pale pink tank top, Ann chose a pair of well-worn, dark gray wool slacks. Most of the clothes she'd packed were still in her suitcases. She'd been so tired last night that she'd done little more than take a quick bath and drop, literally, into the beautifully carved mahogany, queen-size bed. She'd slept deeply. Wonderfully. The only thing missing had been Mike—being in his arms and sharing the lovemaking that had occurred in her torrid dream.

As Ann riffled through her second suitcase, she tried to find a

long-sleeved blouse to put over her tank top. She always felt less
a target if she wore big, oversize blouses to hide her body, her
breasts. Men didn't stare at her that much if she was cloaked in a
blouse and then the standard white smock she wore as an MD.

"Damn..." she muttered, and gave up. Luckily, she found her
comb and brush and went back to the bathroom. Even more luckily, she found her toothbrush and toothpaste.

When Ann had finished her toilet, she glanced up into the gold-
framed mirror. Steam still clung to the edges of it and gave her
reflection a very soft, beautiful look. Far prettier than she felt, that
was for sure. Her sable-colored hair gleamed with reddish gold
highlights even though it was still damp and hung unceremoni-
ously around her shoulders. Still, the dark frame of her hair emphasized her blue-gray eyes and the flush across her cheeks.
Touching her light dusting of freckles, Ann muttered, "Oh
well..." She refused to be embarrassed by them for once. Usually,
she wore just enough makeup to hide them from the world. Today
she didn't care. Mike had always said she probably looked beautiful au naturel. Well, today he was going to see her that way.

Her stomach growled. Rubbing the grumbling area with her
hand, she hurried down the hall toward the kitchen, where all those
wonderful smells were originating. Ann felt unparalleled joy at
seeing Mike again so soon. Maybe today they would have
time...time to explore one another at a delicious, leisurely pace.
She found herself eager just to sit and share the afternoon with
him. She'd never allowed herself such intimacy with Mike when
they were at the Donovan Ranch together. What a fool she'd been,
she realized, wanting to explore what might be.

She halted at the entrance to the sunny, pale yellow kitchen,
which contained every conceivable modern appliance. For the first
time, Ann really looked at Houston as he worked busily over the
stove. He wasn't in uniform, but casually dressed in a pair of dark
brown slacks and a cream-colored polo shirt that outlined his magnificent chest to perfection.

Ann noticed once again just now, how terribly good-looking
Mike really was. Although he was tall, he was medium boned and
not heavy. There was an incredible grace to his movements as if
he didn't have joints at all. He reminded her of a sensuous cougar

on the prowl—dangerous and mystical. At the ranch, he'd always worn pressed, starched army fatigues. She liked the way those dark brown slacks emphasized his narrow hips and showed the curve of his butt and his thick, powerful thighs. Yes, he was definitely in good physical shape, there was no doubt.

Disgruntled by her heated thoughts, Ann began to realize the depth of her need for Mike. Normally, she never looked at men in this way. Before Mike, men were to be distrusted, not appreciated as she was appreciating him right now. Hell, it had to be that dream she'd had earlier, spilling into reality, Ann decided. How she would love to feel that alive, that sensual, and have her five senses that lushly awake and receptive! Oh, what a change from how she normally allowed herself to feel! Her heart told her that Mike could make her feel that way. Eagerly, Ann looked forward to some quiet time spent with him today—and tonight. Yes, tonight...

Her gaze moved from Mike's body to his face. He wasn't handsome, at least, not in the conventional sense. But Ann found herself appreciating his square-jawed face, that nose that had been broken too many times to count, the white scars that told how much a warrior he was. Most of all, she found herself wanting to be kissed, to be seduced by this man of mystery who was cloaked in legend and myth.

His mouth was perfect, Ann decided—the most perfect part about him. His upper lip was slightly thinner than his full, flat lower lip. It was a mouth used to giving orders and having them carried out in an instant. She looked forward to those times, she hesitantly admitted, when his mouth would change from that thinned expression of hardness and military authority, and soften, one corner lifting in an amused, teasing smile.

Yes, there was much to enjoy about Mike Houston, Ann admitted. She could feel her breasts start to tingle as she studied the shape of his mouth. As her gaze moved down to absorb his strong, lean body once again, she could feel a slight throbbing ache begin between her thighs. Frustrated with herself for not being able to quench the longing, one she'd never experienced with any man in her life to date, Ann cleared her throat. Despite her head's shrill warning to not allow herself to get involved with Houston, she couldn't help admiring him.

Houston lifted his head and saw Ann leaning in the doorway, her arms wrapped defensively across her breasts, looking at him with that soft, provocative smile of hers. He was more than a little aware of the heat in her eyes—for him.

"Hey, look who just rose from the dead!" he crowed.

"Very funny, Houston." Ann grinned unwillingly as she moved to the kitchen counter.

He noticed she looked damn pretty in that sweet little pink tank top, which outlined her upper body very nicely. She had beautiful breasts. What would it be like to touch them, to feel the soft curve of them flowing into his large hands? The thought was incendiary. Torturous. Instantly, Mike shoved it away. He instinctively knew that if he complimented her on her outfit, she'd never wear it again. Ann always wore bulky clothes, clothes that hid her slender, beautiful body. It didn't make sense. Most women would kill to have a body like hers. That, or diet their life away to achieve it.

"Go sit down in the breakfast nook," he urged her. "I just made a second cup of espresso for you. You'll see it there. I'll have my welcome-to-Lima lunch ready for you in a jiffy."

Ann laughed a little. She couldn't help it. This was a side of Houston she'd never seen before. He was like an eager little boy, not the hard-bitten soldier she knew him to be. There was warmth and teasing in his deep voice, and she melted beneath that burning blue gaze that had sunlight in its depth. Even though he'd shaved this morning, the shadow of his beard gave his face a dangerous look. It made him all that much more mysterious looking—and a danger to her wildly fluctuating emotions.

"You've been so thoughtful, Mike. Thanks...." Sitting down, Ann gratefully sipped her espresso. There were two place settings laid out next to one another at the round table covered with a bright orange, red and yellow cloth. Just as she put the cup to her lips, her gaze settled on some flowers in a crystal vase next to the grocery bags still sitting on the drain board. She choked on the coffee.

As Mike brought over the skillet and put half the contents on her plate and the other half on his, Ann coughed violently. "What are those?'' she demanded in a strained voice, pointing to the flowers on the counter. Her coughing fit subsided.

''Hmm? Oh, orchids. Why?'' He grinned as he placed the empty skillet in the sink and ran water to fill it. Grabbing the vase, he triumphantly brought the flowers over and set them on the table so they could be fully appreciated.

Ann coughed again and pressed her hand to her chest. The orchids were red and yellow. They had a distinctive light vanilla fragrance that wafted toward her.

Frowning, Mike took his seat. ''You don't like orchids?''

''Well...'' Ann murmured with a shake of her head, ''this is weird. Just too synchronistic.'' Taking her gold linen napkin, she spread it across her thighs. The spicy odor of the food before her was making her salivate.

''What's weird?'' Mike lifted a forkful of the food into his mouth. He saw a very puzzled expression on Ann's face as she continued to stare at the orchids. ''Are you allergic to orchids? Is that it?''

She waved her hand nervously. ''Uh, no...no.''

Chewing his food thoughtfully, he planted both elbows on the table and tapped her plate with his fork. ''You act like you've seen a ghost or something. Come on, eat before you get any skinnier and I lose you to a stiff breeze.''

Ann fumbled around and found the fork. ''I just dreamed about these very same orchids,'' she muttered as she looked, for the first time, down at the colorful meal on her plate.

''Yeah?'' Mike smiled, suddenly feeling very pleased over that. ''A good dream, I hope?''

Ann moved the food around on her plate and refused to look at him. ''Maybe it's jet lag,'' she groused, ''or maybe it's this mystical place. Or you. I don't know....''

''You're muttering again, Doctor,'' he teased, eating voraciously. ''Come on, dig in. I'm a pretty good cook, as you well know.'' He had usually made lunch and dinner for them at the ranch in Arizona.

Ann set the fork down and reached out for the spray of orchids. The petals felt firm and waxy beneath her fingertips. They were a bright yellow, the inner lip red. Very red. The entire shape of the orchid reminded Ann of a woman with her thighs open and beckoning. Flushing heatedly over the unexpected thought, she quickly pulled her fingers from the flower and forced herself to pick up the fork again.

"Why did you bring orchids?" she demanded.

"Well, uh, just on a whim, that's all." Mike watched her scowl deepen. "You don't like flowers?"

"Yes," Ann said, "I like flowers." She forced the food into her mouth. It was surprisingly delicious. "What is this?"

"The meal?" He saw the surprise in her expression. Relieved that she'd momentarily forgotten her obvious upset over his bringing flowers, he was glad to talk about the food instead. "*Huevos rancheros,* Peruvian style." He grinned a little and pointed out the green peppers, onions and fresh tomatoes among the egg mixture. "What really makes them special is adding ginger."

"They're good," she exclaimed, suddenly famished.

He preened. "Thanks."

For whatever reason, her five senses were more fully engaged than she'd ever been aware of before. It was a wonderful discovery. Odors were sharper, more distinctive. The taste buds on her tongue delectably felt each ingredient and texture. It had to be because she was with Mike, she thought. That was the only explanation for it.

A silence fell over them. It wasn't stilted and Mike was glad of that. Every once in a while, Ann would look at those orchids with a wary, unsettled and confused look. Maybe later she'd share why. Right now, all he wanted her to do was eat.

When the main course was finished, Mike went to the counter and made them more espresso. He brought out a coffee cake smothered in chopped brazil nuts and slathered with thick, sweet caramel, and sat down once more.

"Here in Peru people serve seven courses at every meal. I took pity on you and decided eggs and dessert would be enough to introduce you to our way of living down here."

She smiled a little and took a bite of her cake, which melted in her mouth. "I'm glad someone has some mercy. That was very kind of you to do all of this, Mike. I feel so pampered." She looked up to see his blue gaze growing sad. Why? And just as quickly, that look disappeared from his countenance. "No one has ever done this for me. Espresso before a shower..." She sighed and rewarded him with a soft, warm smile of gratitude.

Houston reached over and gripped her fingers momentarily. "You deserve to be pampered. Spoiled, in fact." Something in him sensed that Ann had had a very hard life. Now was not the time to speak of that, either. Mike felt frustration curdling deep within him. Time was their enemy right now. He couldn't stay much longer. He couldn't risk Ann being killed because of him. "I'm going to do it every chance I get," he promised her huskily.

Heat swept up her cheeks and Ann laughed a little shyly. She touched her face. "I feel like a teenager, not a thirty-two-year-old woman. I keep thinking it's this place—the mystery, the magic.... Like you said earlier at the airport, the way Peru seduces its visitors...."

He nodded and released her fingers, even though he didn't want to. "There is mystery and magic here," he conceded quietly, "and Indians believe in the mysticism and spirituality of this country, too."

She sobered a little. "I feel out of place here and yet, irrationally, I feel as if I belong, too." She managed a grimace. "Bane of a psychiatrist, you know? The head and eyes see something and look for matter-of-fact explanations about life, but this heart of mine is responding to you, to this country, and it is *not* rational at all...."

He regarded her gently. "Maybe the good doctor is climbing out of her head and into her heart? Peru is about passion, emotions, and yes, the magic and mystery of life and all its incredible and sometimes unexplainable facets." He saw Ann's eyes widen beautifully. Tears glimmered in their depths momentarily and then she forced them away. "I..." He searched for words. "What you're discovering, Ann, is something so special and rare that it scares the hell out of you. The mystery of life isn't so easily explained by weighing, measuring or seeing it with your eyes. Peru is probably more mystical and spiritual than any place you've been before. Right now, you're doing some major adjusting to her...but if you surrender to her seduction, you'll find out so much more about yourself, your own heart and what really makes you pas-

sionate, what makes you want to live your life to the fullest—''
He stopped abruptly.

Touched, Ann nodded. "I'm beginning to understand a lot of
things about myself of late...."

"Yeah?" He smiled slightly. "Really?"

"Oh, yes." Ann sighed. She set her plate aside. "I was just too
scared to admit it to myself, Mike—or to you—until...well, just
lately. I guess I'm still getting used to it all. I'm glad we have the
time down here, because I need it."

Houston rankled at the word *we*. He felt as if he was on the
edge of a razor-sharp sword and no matter what he did, or how
finely he tried to walk the lines with Ann, he was going to wound
her. It was the last thing he wanted.

Hesitating, Ann whispered, "I know what I feel for you is special, Mike. I've *never* felt this way with anyone."

Hope and fear sheared violently through him. He felt the depth
of her admission all the way to his soul. "Keep your distance from
me," he muttered a little self-consciously. "I'm not worth it, Ann.
Anyone who gets near me is in danger. I don't want to put you
in that spot." Yet he admitted with anguish that he was inevitably
heading somewhere with her he'd never been before. All Houston
could do was shake his head in awe of the power of his need for
Ann. Something so deep, so healing was occurring within him that
he couldn't yet put a handle on it, give it a name or even begin
to understand the implications of falling hopelessly, helplessly for
her. He felt like a child in that moment, innocent and full of hope.
And that was the last thing he should be feeling in his circumstances.

Ann nodded and reached out and covered his hand with her
own. "Danger to my heart?" she offered softly. "I feel like a
green teenager again, dumb, inexperienced...." She laughed awkwardly. She was powerfully attracted to a man of complete mystery.

Mike sensed her discomfort. He raised her hand and kissed the
back of it, holding her uncertain gaze. "Never dumb," he told
her. "Just because we're feeling things we've never felt with another human being before doesn't make us dumb. Just..." he
smiled a little "...inexperienced. Most of the time I feel like I'm

walking on clouds, not Mother Earth, when I think of you. When I picture your face, *querida,* my heart opens up like one of those orchids and I feel this warmth wash through me like the Amazon flooding in springtime. It steals my breath and all I can do is feel. And feel some more...'' Mike reluctantly released her hand. Perhaps it was the powerful spirit of love he was feeling toward Ann. That realization scared him deeply. In light of his past, there was no way he could surrender to it—or to her.

Ann stared at the orchids for a moment and then studied him in the tender silence stretching between them. ''I'm scared, Mike, but I'm not going to run this time. I'm committed to going wherever this crazy relationship of ours is heading.'' She touched the orchid tentatively.

Sadness moved through him. Ann had more courage than he did. She truly didn't realize how dangerous caring for him could be. He hated himself in that moment—his life and his commitment to the people of Peru. The price he paid was high. Right now, he felt as if it was too high, but there was no way he could turn back, and he sure as hell wasn't going to allow Ann into his world. He had to protect her and her heart at all costs. Trying to change the subject, he said, ''It's the flowers, isn't it?''

With a slight smile, Ann whispered, ''Maybe...perhaps they are part of the magic and mystery of Peru? These orchids are special, aren't they?'' She fingered the waxy petals thoughtfully.

Sighing, Houston shrugged his broad shoulders. ''I couldn't help myself,'' he admitted. ''Well, I guess I could have. There's a story to them. Right outside the grocery store this little old Quechua Indian woman has her orchid stand. She's probably in her eighties, all bent over, shivering in the morning air. I know how hard it is to get orchids, although they grow everywhere here in Peru. This is how she makes her living, to get enough food daily. I stopped and asked her what her most expensive orchid was. She studied me and asked me who was I buying them for. I told her it was for a beautiful *norteamericana* doctor. She cackled and then reached up to the top shelf of her little stand and brought down this spray of orchids. She said that you needed this particular flower.''

Ann tilted her head, lulled by his wonderful storytelling abilities.

Mike's face was open for her to examine and she began to realize how completely vulnerable he was with her. There was no hint of the pretense she'd seen in his face during those eight weeks in Arizona. None. It was as if she was meeting the same man all over again, only he was different—and far more provocative to her as a woman. It made her feel a fierce need of him.

"She said I *needed* this orchid?" Ann asked.

Chuckling, Mike finished off his coffee cake and pushed the white saucer to one side. "Yeah, she did. Now, this old lady wasn't just some bag lady on the streets, you know. She wore a leather thong around her neck, with a tuft of black-and-gold hair hanging from it."

"What does that mean?"

"Quechua Indians have a Jaguar Clan, made up of priests and priestesses. These are people who, from childhood on, are recognized as being one with the spirit of the jaguar. They're trained by the medicine man or woman of their village to carry on the sacred and secret ceremonies associated with the jaguar. Those who pass all the tests—and most don't—get to wear jaguar fur as their badge of honor and courage. "

"But what does this all mean? And what does it have to do with these orchids?"

"Patience," he soothed. "Every story that's worth telling shouldn't be chopped up or hurried along." Mike leaned back and tipped the front legs of his chair off the tile floor. His voice was filled with satisfaction. "The jaguar is considered the most powerful of all animal spirits in South America. If a person is able to survive the physical experience of meeting a jaguar in the wild, there's an exchange that takes place between them. The jaguar trades his or her spirit with the student in training. If all goes right, their spirits are forever linked after that. The student passes the last and final test, and then he or she becomes a healer, the most powerful of all healers in South America."

"Because," Ann suggested, "the jaguar somehow bestows on them this power? Is that right?" She noticed the amusement in Mike's eyes. Ann wasn't sure whether he was spinning another tale or telling the truth. She had to admit she loved listening to his unfolding story.

He held up his hand. "There's a lot more to it than I'm telling you, but basically, the power of the jaguar's spirit can be used for ultimate good or ultimate evil. If a person manages to survive their experience with a live, wild jaguar and gets the 'trade,' then they are known as a healer. If they don't, and use it for personal power, selfishness or manipulation of others, they are known as a sorcerer.

"The old woman with the orchids was a healer from the Jaguar Clan. Such people are well known for their psychic ability. It's said that they know what we are thinking and feeling. They walk into our dreams and send us messages, good or bad, sometimes as a warning of some kind. That's the power of the jaguar. He's most powerful at night. That's his kingdom and he is the lord of the jungle when the sun goes down. He's feared by four-leggeds and two-leggeds alike. So..." Mike gave Ann a brief smile "...I think she intuited something when she gave me the orchids, because they weren't the most expensive ones she had. I knew that, and I paid her twice what they were worth because something good, something healing, had gone down between us in that exchange and healers deserve to be paid for their services."

With a shake of her head, Ann whispered, "This is so weird.... I had a dream just before you came and these orchids, the very same ones, with the same fragrance, were in it...."

"Want to tell me about it?"

Flushing furiously, Ann jerked her hand away from the orchid and muttered, "No."

Mike tried to hide his disappointment. "You'll probably get a lot of stories, legends and myths from my granny nuns while you're down here. Everything is steeped in a tale, you know—the truth, B.S. and everything in between. Discernment is the operative word here."

"Still," Ann said, relieved that Mike wasn't going to press her about her very torrid dream, "stories are connections with archetypes, truth and symbols. They shouldn't be lightly dismissed."

Mike nodded sagely and smiled a little. Ann was flushing to the roots of her hair and she wouldn't meet his eyes. She was like a little girl, extremely shy and embarrassed—totally unlike her. Hmm, that old jaguar priestess knew what she was doing, all right. He laughed delightedly to himself. It was obvious Ann was struggling to use her cold, hard, left-brain logic, but in Peru, in South America, one should leave that part of the brain at home.

No, down here the mysterious right brain was what grasped all the unexplained and inexplicable happenings every day. Ann was a psychiatrist and she was going to have a tough time dealing with that, Mike could see. She kept looking at those orchids and then retreating deep within herself. He could feel her wanting to run and hide from something. But what?

Chapter 6

Houston felt his heart squeeze in his chest as he glanced at his watch. It was well past time for him to leave. He was putting Ann in danger by staying so long. Easing the chair back down to four legs, he removed the plates from in front of them. Somberly, he held her gaze and said, "There are some things I need to tell you, Ann...before, well...so you understand why I'm not worth your time or trouble." Shrugging almost painfully, he said, "I wanted to tell you before we left Arizona, but it wasn't the right time. Then, when we got here, I wanted you to get a good night's sleep under your belt before I talked to you."

Ann saw Mike's expression suddenly become serious, the darkness in his eyes and the slashes on either side of his mouth underscoring what he was going to say. "All right," she said tentatively, "I'm listening."

"You probably thought I worked here in Lima most of the time and that I'd be over to the clinic on a pretty regular basis. Right?"

She nodded. "So...you're not going to be at the clinic that often?" Ann felt disappointment in her heart when he nodded. As she watched Mike take his seat again, folding his hands in front of him, she felt a cloak of sadness and fear blanketing her. She realized those feelings were coming from Mike. Shaken that she could sense his emotions so strongly, she found her heart thudding.

"I won't be there very often. I keep in touch with my granny nuns via one of my soldiers, mostly. The last thing I want is to have Escovar's men come crashing into the clinic, murdering everyone in cold blood because they think they're going to find me there." His mouth became a thin line. "Ann, I've got the blood of enough people I loved on my conscience already." He looked at her squarely. "I don't want any more."

She felt his pain and heard it in the rawness of his voice. He looked lost in his memories for the moment and she guessed he was reliving flashbacks of friends who had died while fighting the drug lords. "Losing your men in battle is a terrible thing," she agreed quietly. "They're our extended family. People we care about and want to keep safe even if we know it's an impossibility."

Houston looked down at his heavily scarred hands. "I lost my parents, the woman I loved and my unborn son to Eduardo Escovar."

Ann gasped and felt a ripping sensation in her heart. Houston looked at her, his eyes shadowed.

"H-how terrible...." she managed to whisper, automatically placing her hand against the column of her throat, where a lump of grief was forming for him, for his awful loss.

His mouth twisted savagely. "When it happened, I was half-crazed and in shock over it. Loco with grief, they said at the barracks. I took my best squad out with me and we hit Escovar's men hard. So hard that we stood up to our ankles in blood when it was all over. Originally, I'd wanted to land at his compound. No one had ever done that because it's so heavily fortified—part ammo dump, part heavy-duty artillery and aircraft rockets. Luckily, my sergeant talked me out of that plan, in favor of a second, less dangerous one."

Houston scraped his chair back and stood up, resting his hips against the counter and wrapping his arms against his chest, caught up in that bloody nightmare from the past. "I had intended to capture Escovar's wife and children. To hold them hostage to force him to move out of Peru once and for all. And then I was going to return them to him, unharmed.'' Grimly, Mike lowered his gaze to Ann's pale face. ''We caught the family fleeing in a car about ten miles from Escovar's fortress. Everything went wrong. Instead of capturing them alive, we saw them all killed in a terrible accident.

''The driver went around a mountain curve too fast and he rolled the car carrying Escovar's family over a five-hundred-foot drop-off. They all died instantly. There was nothing we could do to save them...and God knows, we tried.'' His mouth hardened with the memory. ''Escovar saw their deaths as me getting even with him for killing my own family. That's when he leveled the ten-million-sol reward on my head. Ever since then, we've been in this death spiral dance with one another. He wants me.'' Houston's voice lowered to a growl. ''I'm going to get him first.''

A chill worked its way up Ann's spine as she saw the harshness return to Houston's face. Helplessly she opened her hands and whispered, ''What an awful tragedy.''

''I understand from Morgan you haven't had it easy, either,'' Mike said.

Ann winced. ''He told you about my family?''

''No...he didn't. He only mentioned you'd suffered a great deal.'' Mike saw the devastation in Ann's eyes and the tears she tried to hold back. He hated hurting her like this, but they had to get their cards laid out on the table. Ann had to know the truth about him and why she could not continue to care for him. She had to know that loving him would be her death warrant.

''I was an only child, Mike. My parents lived in Washington, D.C. I was working with Perseus and Morgan for two years going on missions around the Caribbean. Ramirez, a drug lord from Colombia, infiltrated our organization and quietly targeted many of Perseus members' families, including mine.'' She saw Houston's eyes narrow. Her voice became strained as she forced the words out. ''Ramirez had hit men kill my parents in cold blood. They were absolutely innocent. The police found them in their home in Fairfax, Virginia, when a phone call was made to the precinct an hour after they were executed. I was out on a mission halfway around the world when it happened. At the same time, Morgan, his wife and son were all kidnapped. One of the other mercs broke the news to me in a phone call.''

"Damn," Mike rasped. "I'm sorry, Ann." He wanted to go over and comfort her. Simply hold her because the grief in her large blue-gray eyes tore at him.

"Some days I'm still not over it, Mike. It suddenly feels like yesterday and all the grief comes rolling back over me. And the anger..." Ann raised her head, his obvious pain for her blanketing her. "So you see, we share a common background with our families being murdered by drug lords. How long ago did you lose your family?''

"Five years," he answered flatly. "And like you, there are days when it feels like yesterday, and other times it seems like a bad dream with no pain or grief attached to it at all. Everyone told me that over time, the pain would lessen, and it has. But not the memory of what happened.''

"Morgan, Laura and their son, Jason, were kidnapped," Ann murmured. "But, as you know, with the help of the Peruvian government, you and your men, and one of our mercs, Ramirez and his gang were put out of action—permanently.''

"Yeah, I remember that. I worked with that merc, Culver Lachlan. He's up in a village in the highlands, married to that Peruvian ex-government agent, Pilar Martinez, who helped him get to Ramirez. They're friends of mine, and I keep in touch with them because Escovar is trying to regain Ramirez's old territory from the villagers in that area. He's killing people up there right now, to make 'examples' of them.''

"And it's your job to stop him.''

Houston nodded and allowed his tense arms to fall to his sides. Seeing the compassion on Ann's face made him feel raw. This time, she wasn't trying to hide anything from him, and he was glad.

"Want another cup?" he asked huskily, pointing to the espresso machine.

"No...no, thanks, Mike.''

Somehow, he felt better talking to Ann about his past. It took the edge off his rage, which was never too far beneath the surface when it came to discussing Eduardo Escovar and what he'd done to utterly destroy Mike's life.

"I have to leave soon," he said, glancing at his watch again. "I don't want to, but I have to, Ann."

Terror ate at her as she studied the expressionless mask that had descended over his features now. She was beginning to understand that Mike had been shielding a lot from her. "Are you afraid that because I'm at the clinic, Escovar might attack, since he knows I'm with Perseus?"

"I'm afraid," Mike rasped, "that if Escovar thinks there's something going on between us, he'd gladly make a raid on the clinic to kidnap you. Then he'd kill you to get even with me. Or if he found me hanging around the clinic because of you once too often, he might decide that church property wasn't sacred any longer, and might come in and kill everyone there." Frowning, Mike muttered, "I don't want to take that risk."

Coloring, Ann fumbled with the cup in front of her. "I understand."

Heaving a sigh, Mike stared down at his large, scarred hands. "There's more to tell, Ann. About a year ago, I fell in love with a *norteamericana* woman, an official at the U.S. Embassy. Her name was Tracy. I was very careful about protecting her—us— what we had developing between us. We never went out in public to eat or anything like that. We kept a very low profile. Escovar found out about it, anyway. The Peruvian government is riddled with moles and word leaked out." Mike held Ann's startled gaze. "Tracy was killed in a car bomb explosion right outside her apartment one morning when she was going to work."

"God...." Ann croaked.

"You aren't going to see much of me at all for that reason, Ann. The people I love get killed because of me. I don't want to put you, my friends or my granny nuns into that position, ever." His mouth turned into a suffering line of barely withheld emotions. "The war between Escovar and me has escalated, and anyone who is dear to me will be destroyed. It's a real black-and-white situation."

Suddenly cold, Ann got up and moved slowly around the kitchen. She felt chaos inside herself. Grief mixed with yearning.

Sadness entwined with an ache deep within her. She understood her feelings—she needed Mike and wanted to pursue their relationship. But she could love him, only to lose him. Or die herself, in the line of fire. The look on Mike's face said it all; his suffering was plainly, hauntingly visible on his craggy features. For a moment, she thought she saw moisture in his eyes, but in the next second it was gone. She was probably seeing things again.

Taking a deep breath, she whispered, "So, this is goodbye, isn't it? I won't see you while I'm working over at the clinic?"

Mike watched her halt midway from the table, her arms wrapped around herself, looking terribly abandoned—and it was his fault. Turning around, he murmured, "It has to be this way." His heart was crying out for her, but his head wished she would take the next flight out of Lima and go home to safety. He wasn't sure he could stand losing another woman he cared about to Escovar. Somehow, Mike understood that Ann was his life even though he was pushing her away. If she died... Pain gutted him just thinking about it.

Ann saw gold flecks in Houston's stormy-looking eyes. She felt awful. And angry. And sad. She didn't want Mike to walk out of her life forever, but fear kept her from saying it. That same old knot was forming in her gut, the one that always started whenever she was becoming emotionally attached to someone...especially a man. Oh, it hadn't happened often, but when it did, that fear stood inside her like the Berlin Wall, causing her to retreat.

"It's just that..." Ann hesitated, searching for the right words "...I'm in a strange country with strange customs. I thought you'd be around. Someone I could talk to if I had questions, or whatever.... Oh, hell, Mike." Ann glared at him. "You're asking a lot. A whole hell of a lot."

Nodding, he rasped, "I know I am. That's why it's up to you to decide now, rather than later. I can have one of my men take you to the airport. You can walk away."

Ann slowly stood up and moved the chair away from her. Inwardly, she roiled with anger, fear and need for him as she tried to sort out what she wanted. Pacing the kitchen slowly, her arms folded tightly against herself, she tried to quiet her mind and feel her way to the truth of the situation. He remained silent as she pondered what she wanted to do.

Then she halted a few feet in front of him. She didn't know who looked or felt grimmer at the moment. Her voice was husky with strain. "Because of my past, I shut myself off, Mike. I was pretty successful at it for a long time until you crashed into my life." She saw him smile a little—a smile edged with deep sadness. She saw hope burning in his eyes and a fierce, unspoken need for her. "I'm tired of hiding, of burying myself." She sighed. "No. I want to stay. And if possible, I want to explore what we have on your terms and conditions. I don't like the danger—" she allowed her arms to drop to her sides as she added wearily "—but I don't like the other choice, either. I want a chance to see what we have, where it will lead...don't you?"

Easing to his full height, Mike nodded. Euphoria swept through him at her words. Not only did she want to stay, but she wanted to be with him, despite the danger. He approached Ann, who stood looking like a lost, orphaned child rather than the strong woman he knew her to be. A bitter sweetness flowed through him. Aching to reach out and caress her flaming cheek, Mike lifted his hand. "What I want and what I can have are not the same thing," he rasped, looking down at her, at the turmoil in her eyes. But he knew now that she had chosen to stay, he would *need* to see her. And he would have to be more careful than he'd ever been in his life. He just *couldn't* lose her. "I'll do what I can to come to you, if safety permits."

Ann bowed her head. "This is so hard for me, Mike...because of my past..." She looked up at him, tears stinging her eyes. "You're so strong and brave compared to me. I don't know if I have the guts to go the distance. I want to, but..." She watched that very male mouth curve tenderly. When Mike smiled, Ann felt as if sunlight was blanketing her and making her feel warm and safe once more. Her head warned her that being around Houston would be her death warrant. People who loved him died. Shaken by the thought, she absorbed his healing touch.

"Listen to me," he said, cupping her shoulders and giving her a small shake. "You're one of the bravest women I've ever known. What you do at Perseus is just as dangerous as what I do out in the field. So don't cut yourself down, *querida.* You've got a heart as courageous as mine.''

Ann gave him a wry look. ''Why do I have the feeling I'm going to find that out?''

His fingers tightened on her shoulders. ''I didn't mean to lead you on, Ann...I honestly didn't. But now that you are here with me, the thought of losing you—'' He broke off, his voice quavery.

She felt his powerful emotions avalanche through her. ''I know,'' she answered helplessly.

''You know,'' Mike rasped, ''I wanted to tell you before I left tonight that I like your freckles. I've never seen them before. You must have always covered them up.''

''Oh, them...'' Ann self-consciously allowed her fingertips to brush across her cheek.

''I like them,'' he told her, his smile deepening as he caressed her thick, damp hair. ''It brings out the little girl that hides inside you. She's special, you know. Pretty spontaneous, too.''

His words brought back her dream, Ann realized, as she reveled in his undivided attention. It was as if she were standing in front of an incredibly brilliant, shining sun, rather than just an ordinary human being. But he was a flesh-and-blood man and that made her scared and lured her simultaneously.

''I'm not a spontaneous person by nature,'' she muttered defiantly. ''And you know that—freckles or no freckles.'' Although, for once, Ann found herself realizing that her decision to stay— to see Mike when and if she could—would teach her to be spontaneous. Her heart entertained a notion of what it would be like to meet Mike at that magical pool she'd dreamed about. Oh! Blushing furiously over those lascivious thoughts, Ann hoped that he wasn't able to read her mind.

''If things were different, I'd have the time to find out just what is making you blush like that,'' Houston murmured as he rested his hands languidly on his narrow hips, studying her purely feminine reaction to him. But he had to go. Time was more than up for his stay at her apartment. Brushing her cheek, he whispered, ''I don't care what you say. You look beautiful when you wear your hair down and let those freckles shine through. They're the real you, you know?''

Ann blushed like a proverbial schoolgirl, and that tipped him off. Mike wanted to ask who had made her feel so embarrassed about her natural beauty, but time wasn't going to let him do that. The sight of her set his heart pounding briefly and caused a warm feeling to flow through him. He'd never felt quite like this before. Yes, he'd loved two other women in his life, but the feelings Ann stirred in him were new. She was like a wild, watchful animal around men, he was discovering.

"I've got to go," Houston murmured huskily, allowing his hands to drop from her arms. "I'll be in touch as soon as I can. Through one of my men. He'll use the password *orchid,* to let you know he's my emissary and not one of Escovar's spies."

Ann followed him to the door of her apartment. "All right. Is...where you're going...dangerous?" She knew better than to ask, but her silly heart was in control of her at the moment.

Mike looked out the door through the peephole before unlocking the dead bolt. "Now you're going to worry about me?" he teased, trying to gently parry her concerns so that she wouldn't lose sleep over him or his duties.

"Just a little," Ann admitted with a broken smile.

The crestfallen look on her face confirmed his suspicion that she would worry—a lot. Taking her into his arms one last time, Houston pressed her against him. She came willingly into his embrace. Groaning, he rasped against her hair, "If you *ever* need me, Ann, all you have to do is call out my name. Okay?" He moved her away just enough to hold her startled gaze. "If you are in danger of any kind, just call out my name in your head."

"In my head?" Confused, she frowned.

"Mental telepathy," he explained gently. Trying to ease her confusion, he touched her head with his hand. "From your head to my head. Just call me. I'll get back here to Lima—to you—just as soon as humanly possible."

Stunned, she blinked. "Mental telepathy?"

Unwilling to get into a long discussion on it, Mike nodded patiently. "Yes."

"You—can do that? Read minds?"

"I'm a better receiver than sender," he said teasingly as he saw the wariness come back to her face.

"And how long have you had this ability?"

He ran his hands down her long, slender back, memorizing the feel of her. "About nine years. It happened after I almost died."

"Oh," Ann said, "a gift from a near-death experience? I've heard some people develop psychic gifts after encounters with death."

Mike raised his brows. "Well...something like that. The next time I see you, I'll share some other things about myself with you. Right now, time is gone. I have to leave...."

"You're serious about that, aren't you? This calling you mentally if I'm in trouble?"

"Very," Houston assured her in a growl. "Come here, *querida*. I need to feel you one last time...." He leaned down and captured her lips with his.

Lightning bolted through Ann as she was crushed against his hard, uncompromising body. Tears squeezed beneath her lids as she responded fiercely to his mouth moving against hers. This was their goodbye with one another. Maybe the last time she would ever kiss him. Perhaps the last time she would ever see him. Hot tears rolled down her cheeks, meeting and melding with their hungry mouths as they devoured one another. The saltiness combined with the utter male taste of him. Her world spun only around Mike, around his strong arms holding her, the beating of the powerful, loving heart in his chest against the firmness of her breasts. Oh, how badly she wanted to go to bed with him! To love him fully! She felt the same raw desire emanating from him.

As he tore his mouth from hers, he whispered, "Just stay safe, *querida*. Safe..." Then he turned, opened the door and left.

Ann stood there, swaying unsteadily. She wrapped her arms around herself as the door closed quietly behind him. She felt as if Mike was still embracing her in their final goodbye kiss. Tears flowed unchecked from her eyes. She *felt* his love. It was as real, palpable and surprising as her taking a sudden breath of air into her lungs.

In the next moment, he was gone like a silent jungle cat, leaving her heart pounding wildly in her breast. What had just happened? Unsure, Ann pressed her hand against her chest and went to the door to look out the peephole.

Houston was gone. There was no trace of him. Blinking, she moved away and slid the dead bolt back into place. That warm, loving feeling lingered around her, like a soft caress moving up and down her entire trembling form. Ann turned on her heel and walked slowly down the hall toward her bedroom. She was imagining things! She had to be!

Then why were there tears in her eyes? In that split second, she'd felt his fierce love for her, his raw, unbridled grief at having to leave her and his fear that he might never see her again alive. Picking up her black leather physician's bag from the closet, Ann shook her head.

"It's this damn country, Parsons. You're acting like you've had a temporary psychotic break from reality. It's Peru. Mike said it was a place where magic met reality. More to the point," she growled, grabbing her white smocks to wash them, "where delusions meet hard-core reality. Get a grip, will you?"

She picked up her smocks and headed out of the bedroom with purposeful strides. Houston was gone. Maybe forever. She had been crazy to think there was hope of a relationship with him. And yet, she'd been vulnerable with him. Something she'd never allowed with any other man except Morgan, who knew about her sorrowful past and understood how to deal with her. Yet Ann didn't regret her decision. As scared as she was, she felt exhilarated on another level. She knew then that she *did* have hope. Hope for a future with Mike. Could her feelings, which she'd never even spoken about to him, survive? And would Mike continue to evade Escovar? Her hands tightened around the smocks as she opened the door to the small laundry room.

Later, as she emerged from the laundry room, there was a knock on the apartment door. She looked through the peephole and saw a man in civilian clothes standing there. Who was he? Should she open the door? Ann removed the dead bolt, but left the chain in place and peeked through it.

"Yes?

"Dr. Parsons?"

"Yes?"

He was a young, dark-skinned man in civilian clothes, wearing a black leather jacket, standing relaxed in front of her. Giving her an apologetic look, he said, ''Orchid.''

She swallowed convulsively. This was one of Mike's men. Mike must have sent him up to her apartment for a reason. Quickly she opened the door and invited him to come in. He thanked her and moved just inside the foyer.

''Major Houston told me you needed a driver and escort while you are here in Lima. I'm Pablo Manuel. He asked me to be your bodyguard for the next six weeks while you are here with us. I am one of Major Houston's best soldiers. I got wounded two months ago and am not yet ready for duty with him, so he asked me, as a favor, to guard and take care of you.'' He held out the keys to her car. ''You are ready to work at the clinic, tomorrow morning?''

''*Sí,*'' Ann whispered, leaning against the wall, her heart pounding unrelentingly. ''He never said anything about you.''

Pablo smiled shyly. He opened his coat and produced the very same type of red-and-yellow orchid that Houston had given her. Only this one was in a small, plastic vial filled with water to keep it alive. ''Major Houston said this would convince you. Here, he said for you to wear this on your white coat, that it would bring out the color in your cheeks and make your freckles stand out.''

Ann was deeply touched by the parting gift. Taking the orchid, she held it gently.

Pablo nodded in satisfaction. ''That's a very special orchid, *se-ñorita,*'' he said.

''Oh?'' Ann replied. Even now she could smell the wonderful vanilla fragrance beginning to encircle her head. It was as if Mike was embracing her all over again.

Although Pablo seemed very young, maybe in his early twenties, he had a professional soldier's bearing. Ann felt safer, but not as safe as when Houston was with her. But then, she told herself, Mike was head and shoulders above any man she'd ever met in her whole life.

Only Morgan Trayhern was anywhere near to Mike's stature. The two men were different, though, and as Ann stood there, she tried to categorize *how* they were different.

"Did Major Houston tell you the story of that orchid?" Pablo inquired in a friendly fashion.

"No," Ann said.

"Ahh..."

She saw Pablo smile brightly, his strong white teeth a contrast against his dark, copper-colored skin. His black hair was cut military short, and everything about him spoke of his military background, from the way he carried himself proudly to the way he stood with his feet slightly apart for better balance. She decided she liked him. "I guess he didn't have time to share it with me, Pablo," she added.

"*Sí*, Major Houston can never remain in one place too long," he agreed somberly.

Every time Pablo mentioned Houston's name, Ann saw a shining awe come to Pablo's face, as if Mike were some kind of god come to earth to be worshipped. "What does 'ahh' mean in regard to this orchid?" she inquired.

Pablo laughed a little and gave her another apologetic look. "Dr. Parsons, it is not for me to discuss it with you. That orchid and her story should only be shared between you and the man who gave it to you."

"I see," she said. "Does everything in this country have a story attached to it?"

Pablo grinned. "*Sí, señorita.* What does an orchid mean otherwise? A tree? A bush? Without the story, you cannot appreciate it fully, no?"

"I guess not," Ann said lamely. Maybe the nuns would know. Or at least be more forthcoming about it. She could hardly wait to get to the clinic because she desperately wanted to work in order to soothe the loneliness that was cutting into her since Mike's departure. Work always kept her focus off whatever she was feeling. It would be impossible to put Mike and his parting kiss out of her mind—and heart—without it. Hard work always cured all her ills. And the clinic was certainly a place where she could spend twelve to sixteen hours a day doing just that.

"Eh, Ann, you must go home!" Sister Dominique came into the office where Ann sat going over the files of the patients she'd seen in the last twelve hours.

Ann smiled tiredly up at the old nun. Checking her watch, she realized it was midnight. "I lost track of time, Sister." She felt suddenly dizzy and reached out to steady herself on the nearby desk. Earlier in the day, she'd gotten a sudden nosebleed—out of nowhere. She attributed it to the altitude difference, though it was unlike her to get a nosebleed at all.

"Humph," Sister Gabby said, coming up alongside Dominique. "We are tired. We must say our prayers and then sleep. I've asked Pablo to take you home." She waved a finger at Ann. "You work too hard, Doctor."

"I'm used to it," she answered with a weary smile. She closed the file and stood up. Yes, work kept her heart from meandering and wondering about Houston...or the orchid she wore on her smock. When the two nuns first saw the orchid and heard that Houston had gifted her with it, they had cackled like a couple of broody old hens. Neither would tell her about the orchid, however, making Ann even more frustrated.

"The clinic opens at seven," Sister Gabby told her as they walked down the hall together. The gloom of the few lights along the corridor cast deep shadows on the hardwood floor as they walked.

"Okay, I'll be here at seven," Ann promised. She saw Pablo drive the car up to the front door and emerge. Again dizziness swept over her. She felt slightly feverish. Touching her brow, she placed her feet apart a little more so she wouldn't fall over from her sudden bout of weakness. She touched her brow and discovered her skin felt hotter than usual. It was just stress, she decided. Stress and a horrible, gutting fear that she'd never see Mike again. Tears burned in her eyes, and valiantly Ann pushed them back down—as she had all emotional wounds before this.

"Sleep in," Gabby advised gruffly. "Tomorrow we start renovations. *Mon petit chou* has employed bricklayers to build a new wing onto our clinic. Work begins tomorrow."

"And," Sister Dominique interjected with a wistful sigh, "we get a brand-new, much larger office with modern computers. Not that we know how to use them. But we'll learn!"

"Around here," Gabby said, "old dogs have to learn new tricks all the time."

Ann laughed softly. She found the two nuns inspiring and fun to work with. They flew around the clinic in their dark blue and white habits like angels without wings. Today, the first full day at the clinic for Ann, they'd processed over sixty people through the clinic's doors. "I know a lot about computers, so when they arrive, we'll set some time aside and I'll teach you how to use them. Fair enough?"

They nodded sagely and then both clasped their hands in front of them as she hesitated at the glass door.

"They are bringing water trucks tomorrow, too," Sister Gabby added excitedly. "Fresh water for the barrio! This is so exciting! The children will have fresh water to drink, not the stuff found in trenches or mud puddles. It will make our job much easier. There will be less infection. Twice a week, two huge water trucks will drive from section to section, giving away water to the people. Isn't that wonderful?"

Touched, Ann nodded. "This is all from the donations Major Houston got?" A chill swept through her. Looking down, Ann saw goose bumps forming on her lower arm. She was suddenly, inexplicably, icy cold. Was she catching something? It felt like flu symptoms to her. Great. All she needed was to get some acute illness on top of everything else.

"Yes," Dominique said. "He is a man of pure heart and action. We get a new wing on the clinic, which will give us a ten-bed ward in addition to the five-bed one. He has hired a part-time paramedic to help us, as well. His name is Renaldo Juarez, and he will be here tomorrow, too."

"It's shaping up to be an exciting day," Ann said, lifting her hand in farewell as Pablo opened the door for her. "Good night."

"Sleep well, child," Sister Dominique whispered, making the sign of the cross over her. "We will pray for you tonight."

Turning, Ann smiled gently. "I think Major Houston can use our prayers more than me."

Sister Gabby smiled. "He's *always* in every prayer session we undertake. Do not fear, he will not be bumped off our list. We're simply adding you to it."

Laughing, Ann said, "Believe me, I can use all the help I can get. Prayers are good. Any kind. Thank you...."

Her apartment was dark and quiet. Pablo insisted upon going in first and checking it out thoroughly. He was brisk and efficient as he looked for possible perpetrators, bombs or bugging devices. When he was satisfied her apartment was "clean," he said good-night and left.

Sighing, Ann wearily dropped her black bag on the sofa. In the kitchen, she gently removed the orchid, from her smock replaced the water it had used and then set it next to the sink. It looked bright and beautiful against the white tile background. And, as always, it reminded her of Mike. Turning, she saw the spray of orchids he'd given her himself sitting in the center of the table.

Why should I feel like this? So lost. Alone. As she moved unthinkingly to the breakfast nook and cupped the spray with her hand, she inhaled its fragrance deeply into her lungs. How was Mike? Was he in danger? Ann couldn't shake those questions even though she wanted to.

Frowning, she straightened and moved down the hall to her bedroom. She was almost dizzy from tiredness, not yet completely over the jet lag, she suspected. Removing the smock and pulling her pink T-shirt over her head, she sighed. Why was her heart feeling like this? There was an ache in it. She knew why but she wasn't willing to admit it to herself. Somehow, she had to climb back into that ivory tower of her mind and be free of her burning, painful emotions. Every time she closed her eyes and pictured Mike's craggy, scarred face, her heart opened like that orchid did. Stymied, she removed her gray woolen slacks and set them aside. It had to do with that invisible connection that somehow existed between them. Perhaps she was still able to feel his emotions toward her? That seemed impossible, yet Ann had no easy answers when it came to Mike. She wanted to find out about the rest of his mysterious past, which he'd hinted about, but feared she'd never see him again to ask such questions.

As Ann took a hot shower, scrubbed her hair and allowed the spray to gently massage her tense, tired body, her heart once again turned to Houston. Frustrated because she had no explanation as to why he was so much on her mind, stirring up her feelings like this, she wondered if she wasn't going a little crazy. As she toweled herself afterward, she swore she could almost feel a direct connection from him to her so that her every feeling was flowing to him and vice versa. It had to be a combination of sleep deprivation, stress and heartbreak.

"You're nuts," Ann growled, slipping into an apricot silk nightgown. And then she laughed at herself. A psychiatrist calling herself nuts. Now, that was the kind of humor Mike would appreciate immensely. He had a wry sense of amusement and would laugh with her about it. Then, as she walked from the steamy bathroom to her bed, Ann had the strangest feeling. Halting in the hall, she automatically touched her heart region with her fingers. If she closed her eyes, she could swear she heard Houston's deep chuckle.

"I take that back, Parsons, you *are* having a psychotic break. Now get your rear into bed and sleep. You're hallucinating." Or was it that mental telepathy Mike had said he could receive from her? Could he pick up on her errant thoughts? The whole idea was a little shocking to Ann. If he could read her mind, then he'd been able to read it since he'd met her. Oh! The embarrassment of that if it was true! That just couldn't be possible, her scientific mind told her.

As she jerked back the pale lavender quilt and sheet, Ann felt that laughter of his once again. The sensation was so warm and easy to surrender to. As she slid her feet beneath the covers and pulled them up, Ann released a weary sigh. Closing her eyes, she found herself wanting to be with Mike, wanting to know more—much more—about this enigmatic man. Today she heard the poor who came to the clinic call him the jaguar god over and over again. The people of the barrio worshipped Houston like a god, there was no doubt. He had produced so much for them, bettering the quality of their lives. Ann was sure that to the poor, his work seemed like a miracle only a god could pull off. He fed them, cared for them medically and often made the difference between life and death for them.

As the wings of sleep enfolded her, she felt as if she were drifting into the warmth of Mike's embrace instead. It was a comforting sensation and she surrendered to it, no longer afraid. Within that invisible warmth, she felt safe—and loved. Very much loved.

Chapter 7

In the days that followed Mike's disappearance, Ann discovered what hell was. The agony of losing him, not having him in her life, gutted her and bled her a little each minute of every hour of every day. Nothing had prepared her for this intense reaction, and she worked tirelessly at the clinic, sixteen hours a day, if possible—anything to stop the pain of her loss. She'd had several more nosebleeds, and though it was unusual for her to get them, she attributed it again to the altitude. The dizziness would come and go, too. And periodically, she'd run a fever for an hour, experience a bone-chilling sweat and then be fine. Her symptoms seemed to worsen, however, as the week wore on. Once, Sister Gabby tried to talk her into getting some blood tests, but Ann just waved off the idea, telling the nun it was nothing but stress, time changes and such. Ann didn't tell her that she was grieving for Mike—for what might never be between them.

For the next seven days, the nuns allowed her to open up the clinic in the morning and close it down at night. They were simply too old to keep pace with her youth. Little did they know her energy was a result of her restless attempts to hide from her aching need for a man she cared for deeply—though she had never told him how much.

I miss him. Oh, God, I miss him and I worry for him.... Ann wearily pushed some strands of hair off her brow as she finished stitching up a jagged laceration on the arm of a teenage Quechua boy, who sat very still on the examination table. Mike Houston had slipped inside the array of defenses she had worked so hard for so long to erect against males in general. In the last week, she'd heard more stories about the jaguar god from people who came through the clinic's doors. They were all eager to tell her of his power, his magic, his superheroic abilities. Of course, to herself Ann scoffed at them, but outwardly she just nodded her head, smiled a little and listened to their fervent stories about *him.*

She arrived back at her apartment at 1:00 a.m. that night. Pablo escorted her home and as always, checked out her premises and then left. She absently tossed the newspaper on the couch, remembering Pablo's words to her ten nights ago. He'd said the apartment was a fortress to keep her safe. Then he'd made a slip and called her "the jaguar's chosen mate" and when she'd stared at him, Pablo had quickly retracted his statement, apologizing profusely over and over again.

Though she'd been rankled by Pablo's faux pas, Ann continued to avoid the raw, twisting feelings of fear she felt for Mike's safety. Was he well? Hurt? How would she ever know? His whereabouts, she discovered, were one of the best-kept secrets in Peru.

Tonight, her head swam with exhaustion and she almost staggered down the hall to the bathroom to take her much needed hot shower. During it, she experienced another spontaneous nosebleed, to her mounting consternation. And then, almost as rapidly, she felt feverish, after which an icy chill worked its way through her bones.

While lying in bed, Ann opened the newspaper, as was becoming her routine, and quickly scanned the headlines. Her gaze was suddenly riveted on a large black-and-white picture with headlines that shouted *Escovar's Army Fights Back.* Sitting up, Ann felt her heart begin pounding as she rapidly read the text:

Escovar's hated enemy, Major Michael Sanchez Houston, has met him in a deadly confrontation in the highlands of north-

ern Peru, near the village of San Juan. According to reports,
Escovar was attempting to reclaim the territories of the co-
caine lord Ramirez, who was killed earlier in the year by
Houston's death squad. In a bloody battle, Houston, who is
a U.S. Army special advisor, took his squads of Peruvian
army soldiers into a trap laid by Escovar. Fighting is heavy
and there are reports of many wounded and killed on both
sides. Because the jungle is dense in that remote northern
region, no further information is available.

Ann stared at the photo of several dead bodies. Was Mike
among them? Suddenly, she felt nauseous. Her hands tightened
convulsively on the pages of the paper as she studied the photos
more closely. She saw two Quechua Indians, dressed in their cus-
tomary dark cotton pants and white shirts, lying dead. To the left
of them were three soldiers in camouflage uniforms. Her mouth
went dry. A machete had hacked the arms off the Indians, and
two of the soldiers had their throats slit open.

"Dear God..." She allowed the newspaper to fall off the bed
onto the floor. Ann pressed her hands against her face. She felt so
terribly cold as another chill swept through her. None of the men
in the photos looked like Mike, but how could she really be sure?

Anguished, she raised her chin and took a gulp of air. Tears
burned in her eyes and she angrily wiped them away. She jerked
off the covers and climbed out of bed. Reeling with shock, she
walked out to the darkened living room. There was a purple-and-
white afghan on the back of the couch and she took it, pulled it
around her shoulders and curled up on the sofa.

She tried to think rationally, logically, but it was impossible.
Her heart was pounding in her chest. She wanted to cry. She rarely
cried, not since— Ann savagely slammed the door shut on the
incident that had changed her life, changed how she reacted to
men. All men except Mike. He had captured her heart.

Ann sat there, rocking slowly back and forth, as she always did
when she was distressed and feeling out of control. The stories
she'd heard all week about Mike, about his mysterious "jaguar
medicine," as the Indians referred to it... They swore he'd stopped

people from bleeding to death with just his touch! *Baloney.* He was a paramedic. Direct pressure on a wound with his hand *would* stop most hemorrhaging. Ann gazed around the empty, silent apartment. She alone knew that he was just a man.

A sob rose in her throat. Her eyes burned. Bowing her head, Ann rested her brow against her drawn-up knees. The scratchy wool of the afghan felt somehow soothing. She ached for Mike's loving, intimate touch once again. From the beginning, he'd sensed her distrust of him, and he'd approached her slowly, allowing her to get used to him being in her life. He hadn't tried to get her into bed. Rather, his touch, his exploratory kisses, had laid a groundwork of trust between them. Now she was ready to seal her love with Mike completely and it was an impossibility.

Suddenly Ann felt Mike's brief touch on her skin—or at least she thought she did. Her flesh tingled in the wake of his grazing, invisible contact. As she allowed his craggy face to appear in her mind's eye, she felt comforted, the edge taken off her fear that he was dead. The sensation was not new to her; every time in the past week when she thought of him there would be almost an instantaneous returning warmth that soothed her, and she would feel undeniable love sweeping around her, as she did now.

Eventually, Ann fell asleep, curled up in the fetal position on the couch. In her dreams, she was back at the magical pool, wearing that vanilla-scented crown of red-and-yellow orchids in her loose hair. Here, she felt safe. Here, she felt protected from the harsh, brutal reality of the world that she had stepped unknowingly into.

"You are worried?" Sister Gabby inquired sweetly.

Ann had just finished examining a baby with a high fever from the flu that had hit Lima hard in the last week. The mother anxiously looked on. Slipping off the latex gloves which had been bloodied due to the severe nosebleed the baby had suffered during the high fever, Ann deposited them in the new waste container that had arrived only yesterday. "Just tired, Sister," she replied finally.

"Hmm, it is more than that, *mi pequeña*," the nun said, calling her by the nickname she and Dominique had given Ann on her first full day at the clinic. It meant "my little one" and they called her that because she was so thin. Even though Ann towered over them heightwise, the nuns saw her as small and vulnerable, like a child who needed to be protected. Ann had protested, of course, but when Sister Gabby explained that agewise, Ann *was* like a child to them, she relented. Now the words were said with such love that Ann surrendered without resistance.

Thinning her lips, she busied herself around the room, tearing off the soiled paper on the examination table and replacing it with clean paper after the mother and baby left. "Really, Sister. I'm just tired."

"Hmm," Sister Gabby said again, helping her to pick up the bloody gauze she dropped on the floor. "You must have seen the newspaper last night, eh?"

Ann froze. She slowly turned and regarded Sister Gabby.

The nun's brown eyes sparkled fiercely. "You must be going through a very special hell," she whispered.

Ann straightened. The pain in her heart almost exploded. She stood there, wanting to cry. Wanting to sob out her fear for Mike.

"Listen to me, child," Sister Gabby said, coming over and gripping her arms and giving her a small shake, "the newspaper often carries horrid photos. But those pictures may not have anything to do with *mon petit chou,* did you know that?"

Ann blinked. "What are you saying?"

"Oh, the account may be true, but this newspaper likes drama and tries to sell more copies by printing terrible pictures of death. Many are from years ago! I can tell you took that photo to heart last night. Your face is pasty today and your eyes show me grief and longing. But you shouldn't have let it bother you."

Trembling, Ann whispered, "It was horrid, Sister Gabby. I—I was afraid—for Mike...."

"Of course you were, *mi pequeña.*" She smiled tenderly up at her. "The heart has no brain, no eyes, eh? It only knows how to love. That is enough, *oui?*"

Love. Ann stared down at Gabby's kindly features. She instantly tried to reject the word, the feeling. It was impossible, because she felt so helpless and weak emotionally right now. "I worry for him, Sister Gabby."

The nun's mouth drew into a gentle smile of understanding. "Our Michael is a very special man, but I sense you already know that. At least your heart knows that." Patting her arm, she added, "You worry too much for him. He knows how to care for his men and himself. Do not put such great stock in the newspaper accounts of him, eh? You are working too hard. You need more rest."

Still, Ann continued to work endlessly to keep her mind and her aching heart off Mike Houston. What had he *done* to her? she wondered. It was as if an invisible umbilical cord was strung between them. Every hour, Ann could feel him. Actually *feel* his invisible, loving presence. It frustrated her. She couldn't get rid of the sensation or ignore it. Nor could her rational mind find any logical reason for the feeling. At night, in her dreams, when she was by that magical pool, was the only time she found a moment's peace and rest from her anxiety. Maybe she worried so much because she'd been in the military too long herself. She knew what kind of guerrilla tactics Mike was using out there. She knew in the jungle it was simple weapons like knives and machetes that took a man's life rather than bullets, because the foliage was so thick that bullets would easily ricochet off the trees. No, the kind of fighting Mike was waging was hand-to-hand combat in many cases. The worst kind.

On the fourteenth day, Ann closed the clinic early—before midnight—because she wasn't feeling well at all. Both nuns had left for the evening and were more than likely tucked in bed already. Every step up to her apartment was an effort and Ann tried to hide how she felt from the alert and discreet glances of Pablo, who was very concerned about her.

"Eh, Dr. Parsons, should you not take a day or two off? You have lost weight and you work your fingers to the bone. You must rest more, *sí?*"

It took too much effort to shrug. "Pick me up at 5:00 a.m. tomorrow, Pablo."

After he'd checked out her apartment, he nodded. "*Sí,* Doctor."

When she finally shut the door behind him, she sank against it, feeling terribly weak. A chill like she'd never encountered before worked its way up her spine. God, she was cold. Icy cold. Pushing away from the door, Ann picked up the newspaper and went to the kitchen. Despite Sister Gabby's warnings, she couldn't help herself from being driven by an almost obsessive need to check out the evening edition for information on Mike and his men.

There had been a blaring headline in every edition for the last seven days. Houston had launched a major counteroffensive operation against Escovar's attempts to invade and reclaim Ramirez's old territory in the highlands. Every night Ann read with eyes blurry from tears how the body count was rising on both sides. And horrific pictures always accompanied the text. Ann felt herself tense as she opened the paper.

Gasping, she felt her eyes widened enormously. The headlines blared Jaguar God Killed By Escovar!

"No!" Ann cried. Her startled shout sank into the silence of the apartment. She flattened the paper out on the table in desperation. She had to be reading it wrong! She just had to be! There was a photo of Mike in his U.S. Army uniform, the beret at an angle, his face hard, his eyes narrowed. It was an official military photo.

"Oh, God, no... No..." Ann rapidly skimmed the article.

During fierce fighting in and around the village of San Juan, Escovar personally led his men against Major Mike Houston's contingent, which was protecting the village from Escovar's attack. One helicopter was destroyed as troops disembarked from it and it was reported that the legendary Houston, known as the jaguar god to the people of the highlands, was on board. The helicopter had landed with Houston's squad, in an effort to reinforce embattled soldiers who fought bravely side-by-side with the villagers to stave off Escovar's well-planned attack.

A second black-and-white photo showed the twisted wreckage of what remained of a helicopter. White wisps of smoke floated upward from the gutted aircraft. Ann couldn't tear her gaze from the macabre photo. With a horrible, sinking feeling, she felt the pit of her stomach drop away. Uttering a small cry, she sat down before she fell down. Mike was dead! *Oh, God, no! No! It couldn't be! The paper had to be lying! Wasn't it lying?* Her mind reeled. Her emotions and heart exploded with wild, animal grief so raw that she cried out.

Hot, unchecked tears flowed down her taut features as she walked unsteadily to the living room. She had to get hold of Sister Gabby. "She would know...." Her hands shook badly as she dialed the phone. There was crackling and hissing on the line.

Groaning in frustration, Ann hung up and dialed again. There were very few telephone lines into the barrio. The one that led to the Catholic church was over thirty years old, and when it rained, as it had earlier today, the water seeped into the cable and calls would not connect until the line dried out. Every time Ann tried to call, the line hissed and went dead.

Ann sat there, wondering who else to call to verify the story. Pressing her hand against her head, she felt another violent chill pass through her. The icy coldness she felt was not to be ignored. It was then, only vaguely, that she realized she was burning up with a fever. She stood up, in a quandary. The earliest she could reach Sister Gabby, *if* the phone started working again, would be tomorrow morning. No one at the U.S. Embassy would tell her anything about Mike. He worked for the Peruvian government, and she knew they weren't about to talk to her, a stranger, to confirm his death.

"God..." She sobbed as she reeled down the hall toward the bedroom. As she stripped out of her clothes to take a shower and warm up, she knew she'd caught the viral flu going around the city. How many cases had they handled at the clinic in the last week? It must have been over a hundred. It was an upper-respiratory flu with a high, sudden fever, and though Ann knew there was no prescription drug to fight a virus, the sisters had homeopathic potions that seemed to arrest the deadly flu in its tracks.

Yes, she must have contracted the flu. She was run-down. Overworked. Getting too little sleep. Stress had lowered her immune resistance to the nasty virus. Moving in a daze to the shower, Ann turned on the faucets with shaking hands. Shivering, she avoided looking at herself in the mirror. Tears kept streaming down her face. She stood there naked, her arms wrapped tightly around herself as if to hold herself together so she wouldn't explode in a million, out-of-control pieces. She wanted to shriek and scream like a madwoman and give her grief voice.

She had never told Mike she loved him. She hadn't even been able to admit it to herself. Until now. When it was too late. That fact pounded throbbingly through her aching head. It hurt to move, the pain was suddenly so intense. Climbing into the shower, Ann thrust her head beneath the hot, massaging stream of water. She stood under the spray, trembling and shivering uncontrollably. The water was so hot that clouds of humidity filled the bathroom and her skin turned pink.

By the time she staggered from the bathroom dressed in her apricot silk nightgown and robe, Ann was feeling vertigo. She knew her temperature was high, maybe 104 degrees. She could feel her pulse pounding like a freight train through her body; her heart was pumping hard in her chest. Her hand against the wall, she managed to make it to the living room. The door was locked but the dead bolt was not in place. She should secure the door, but she suddenly didn't care any longer. Mike was dead. She felt as if she was dying.

As she crumpled to the couch and weakly drew the afghan over her shivering form, Ann could feel all hope draining out of her, as if someone had sliced open her wrists and was bleeding her dry. As she nestled her head on one of the pillows, she drew her legs up against her body, absorbing the warm comfort of the afghan. She was sick. Very sick. Mike was dead. Was he? Or was it a lie designed to sell more newspapers?

More tears leaked out of her tightly closed eyes. The fever was climbing. Her skin hot and dry. The chills racked her body every ten or fifteen minutes. Her mind turned to jelly beneath the violent assault of the burning fever. Tiredness, a spirit-weary kind of exhaustion, swept through her. Never in her life had Ann felt so weak, so alone...so horribly grief stricken. She lay on the couch, the sobs coming softly at first as her fever dissolved the massive control she usually kept over her emotions. Little by little by little, tears flooded her face and her sobs became louder and violently wrenching.

At some point, as the fever skyrocketed through her, Ann's sobs turned to weakened whimpers. The ache in her pounding heart was so painful that she no longer cared if she lived or died. Everything good in her life was now gone. Why hadn't she told Mike she loved him? Ann knew even in her delusional state that her feelings for him were real. *The past.* It was her past. Her fear had not allowed her to reach out, to admit even on some deep, intuitive level that she'd fallen helplessly, hopelessly in love with Mike during those eight weeks she'd spent with him at the ranch in Arizona. What a fool she'd been! A horribly frightened fool. As she lay weakly on the couch, in the grasp of the fever and hallucinations, Ann grieved.

At some point, she fell into a disturbed sleep filled with chaotic visions of the past, when she'd worked with Morgan's mercenaries in dangerous situations. Near dawn, with the apartment swathed in gray light, Ann jerked awake. She was burning up. She could not move, she was in such a weakened condition. Trying to think, she realized belatedly that what she had contracted wasn't the flu. It couldn't be; not like this... This was septic. Deadly. Trying to move her hand from beneath her chin, where it was tucked, Ann felt warm liquid flowing out of her nose. The warmth continued across her dry, parched lips. It tasted salty and metallic. What was it?

Barely able to move her hand, Ann laid her fingertips against her lips. The flow increased from her nose. Fighting to open her eyes, which felt like weights, she lifted her fingers just enough so that she could see them. In the gray light, she saw the darkness that stained her fingers.

Blood. It was blood. Her blood. What was going on?

This was no ordinary nosebleed, Ann thought blearily. No, the blood flowing from her nose was heavy, almost as if an artery had burst, but that was impossible. *I've got to get help. Now.* Ann used every ounce of her reserves and slowly sat up. She sank against the couch, a soft gasp coming from her. Blood flowed down across her lips, her chin, and began to drip down the front of her nightgown. Her panic escalated.

The fever had not broken. She was still burning up. The chills were racking her like birthing contractions every few minutes. *Septic. Somehow, I've gone septic.* Her mind fragmented; her vision blurred and became unreliable. Ann knew for sure now she hadn't contracted the flu. This was something far more deadly. A lethal jungle virus of some kind? Where—how had she picked it up? She'd had all her shots before coming down here. But there were many new viruses that had no vaccination protection available.

And then she recalled that yesterday, a little boy had come in with a broken arm that she had set and placed in a cast. He'd been a brave little six-year-old. His mother had been so grateful for her help and care. One of the last things that little boy did was pull a piece of half-eaten candy from his pocket and give it to Ann. She had ruffled his hair, taken the candy and thanked him. Without thinking, she'd popped it into her mouth and made big, smacking sounds of enjoyment for the child's benefit. The little boy had smiled bravely through his tears, and Ann knew that his priceless gift of candy, which few in the barrio ever got, had been a loving gesture toward her.

Reaching forward now, her breathing shallow and erratic, she knew she was going into septic shock. It was one of the most deadly kinds. She *had* to get help or she'd die! Something in her rallied. As grief stricken and delusional with fever as she was, there was a core in her that refused to give up and just lie down and die. Her fingers closed over the phone. The keypad blurred. Ann tried three times to recall the number at the clinic. *Oh, God, what was it?* Her fingers were shaking so badly that she kept missing the number pads on the phone as she tried to dial.

Everything in front of her began to go gray. She could feel a coldness stealing upward from her feet, flowing like a dark river into her ankles. No fool, she knew this was the shock...killing her. She was dumping.

The phone fell out of her nerveless hand.

Help. She had to get help.

Something drove her to try and stand. Caught in the grip of the fever, not thinking clearly, Ann leaned forward. Her knees buckled. The next thing she knew she was landing on the carpet. A groan rippled through her. She felt the carpet's springy texture against her cheek as she collapsed onto it. All her strength ebbed away. The blood was flowing heavily from her nostrils, unabated. *Dying. I'm going to die.*

It was one of the last thoughts she had. Her final thought was a weak cry for Mike Houston, for his help. That was all Ann remembered as she sank into a dark oblivion.

Ann heard Mike Houston's voice. It was deep and panicked sounding. She felt someone pick her up, the feeling wonderful. Floating...she was floating. Strong arms hoisted her upward. She heard Pablo in the background, the panic clearly audible in his voice as well. She was dying and dreaming. That was it. The hallucinations of fever. Oh, how she wished Mike was here! But he was dead. Dead.... How much she loved him...and he'd never know it...not ever.... Darkness overcame her again.

"What should I do?" Pablo asked, his eyes huge as he stood at the door to the apartment. "Call for an ambulance?"

Houston glared toward him as he held Ann in his arms, her limp form pressed tightly against him. "No, it's too late for that. She's dumping on us."

"I didn't know, Major! She looked very tired last night...but..."

Breathing hard, Houston shook his head. "Get the bedroom door open, Pablo. I'm taking her in there." He looked down. Ann's head lolled against his shoulder, her skin marbleized, cold with sweat. There was a faint bluish color around her parted, badly chapped and cracked lips. Blood was everywhere.

"Sí!" Pablo replied, and raced down the hall ahead of Mike.

"Hang on, Ann, hang on," Houston whispered urgently, holding her so tightly against him he thought he might crush her. She was like a limp child in his arms, there was so little life left in her. And whatever life there was was now only a dim flame. His mind raced with questions and possible answers. Somehow, she'd contracted a deadly hemorrhagic fever. Due to the filth, squalor and poor sanitary conditions she worked in, it was easy for her to contract one. He could barely feel her pulse.

Pablo jerked open the bedroom door, his breath coming in gulps. "What now, Major?"

"I'm going to work on her in here. Drive down to the clinic

and get whatever homeopathic remedy the sisters think Ann should have. Make it fast, Pablo. Bring IVs. She's not going to make it if we can't get them into her pronto...''

Pablo nodded brusquely and ran back down the hall.

Houston heard the apartment door slam shut as he looked around the small and feminine bedroom. He saw that the bedcovers had been twisted and thrown aside. The pain in his heart almost overwhelmed him. Ann was dying. It was that simple. That pulverizingly simple.

"You *aren't* going to die on me, dammit," he growled. He knew what had to be done. He'd done it before. Not often, but he knew the procedure, the effects—and the cost to himself. He sat down on the bed with Ann in his arms. Resting his back against the headboard, he spread his legs apart. Quickly, he positioned Ann's limp body between them with her back resting against his chest. He guided her head against the hollow of his right shoulder. He felt the cold dampness of her brow against his unshaved jaw and he pressed his trembling fingers against her carotid artery. There was a faint pulse, that was all. She was dying. Her blood pressure was falling through the floor. No amount of medical help would bring her back now. No, there was nothing known in the high-tech medical world, no drug powerful enough, to pull Ann out of this.

If he'd taken her to the emergency room of the nearest hospital, she'd have died on a gurney in front of him.

Houston breathed savagely, his eyes glittering like shards of icy blue glass. "No," he whispered fiercely, "I won't let you die, Ann. I won't...." He wrapped his arms around her slack form, which fit so heartbreakingly beautifully against his tall, lean form. *Get ahold of yourself, Houston. Get ahold...breathe...breathe in and out for her. Pick up the beat of her heart. Make it one with yours. Breathe with her.* And he did. He closed his eyes, his arms firm against her. He could feel the faint, weakening beat of her heart against his stronger, pounding one. They were one now, united. United in a death spiral. Houston knew what must be attempted. He knew the risks to himself. It didn't matter. He wanted her to live. He needed her, dammit, and that's all that mattered in his ugly, dark little world. Ann was his light. His hope, whether he deserved it or not.

His mouth thinned and he felt the power nearby. *Come on, come over me. I need you. I need to save her.... Help me! Help me....* He felt the power gather above him and then, like the sheath of a glove, he felt it move over him. As it did, he felt stronger than ten men. His heartbeat deepened and became five times the power of one human heart. The pulsing life that now embraced him was complete. Visualizing the golden energy now throbbing around and through him, Houston saw it move down his arms, through his hands and into Ann's limp, cold fingers.

He continued to breathe with her, slow, shallow breaths. He steadied her heartbeat and nurtured it. Now there was synchronicity; they were living, pulsing as one. Frightened by how far she was gone, he concentrated savagely on the life-giving energy flowing back into her. He wanted to rob death this time. And without apology. Little by little, he felt her heartbeat begin to pick up, and he felt her breath ease a little, deepen a little. Willing his life energy into her like a transfusion of a different kind, Houston let out a ragged, emotional sigh. He felt tears stinging the backs of his eyes. Ann couldn't die on him! She had to live! She had to! He needed her like he'd never needed anyone before. He'd found that out in the last two weeks while he'd been in that hell of a rotting jungle, fighting Escovar's men. He'd wanted to live—survive—to see her again.

His altered state deepened and he no longer thought, he simply felt. His heart entwined with her weak one. His breath filled her collapsing lungs with not only his oxygen, but his life force. Time ceased. He was no longer aware of the hard wood stabbing into his back or the firmness of the mattress beneath him. All he felt was his heart, filled with fierce emotions and love, as Ann lay in his arms, dying.

Minutes congealed and his world shortened to moments between the beats of her heart, to the time between each soft inhalation and exhalation of breath from her parted lips. He willed his life more surely into her. As he did, he felt the power surrounding him begin to vibrate in a familiar pattern. *Yes!* Yes, he could feel Ann's flesh beginning to warm beneath his hands. It was working!

The energy was flowing into her, giving her life, supporting her weakened heart and moving like a golden river through her, cleansing her, stealing her like a thief from death's grip. Behind his closed eyes, he could see it happening, that golden light flowing down through her thin body, reigniting her form with life instead of giving it over to death, which had hovered patiently, waiting.

Life and death. That was what this was all about and Houston knew it. A deep, throbbing pulse began to move from him directly into Ann's body. With each beat of energy, he began to feel a lessening of his own. He knew he could potentially die in the process, but he didn't care. If he couldn't save Ann, he didn't want to live, either. All his life, people he'd loved had died. He'd thought that by leaving her safe in Lima, it wouldn't happen to her. What a naive fool he'd been. He'd thought that by walking out on her life, he could protect her. But his plan hadn't worked. In that moment, he hated his life, hated what he was, what he had become, hated even the power within him—his taskmaster. It was both his burden and his gift that his presence could give life, or cause it to be destroyed. There was no in between. No trade-offs and never any compromise.

As the golden energy surged through Ann, he felt her body growing warmer by the second. Her breathing was deepening now as she absorbed the life-giving oxygen back into her lungs and fed the starving cells of her body. Her heart was beating strongly now, even as he felt his own solid heartbeat begin to diminish. The exchange was occuring. His mouth twitched. He tipped his head back and smiled faintly. Yes, she was going to live. *Oh, Great Goddess, she's going to live.* His spirit guardian was going to give her life, and not take her this time. Hot tears ran down his stubbled cheeks. He could smell the faint sweetness of Ann's silky hair against his jaw as the flowing, throbbing pulsations continued between them. He was giving her a transfusion of life. The only problem was that it was coming from him. Could he hold on? Could he give her enough to get her stabilized and still have enough left to cling to life himself?

Houston wasn't sure. He felt his guardian's presence even more now than ever before. A low growl of warning vibrated through him, but he felt no fear about death. He'd faced it so many times that it had lost any control over him. All that was important was the woman in his arms. The woman he needed as fiercely as his heart would allow him to need and want. Houston felt his consciousness slipping away. He knew he was at a precarious point in the exchange. He hadn't been this close to looking at death in a long time...

It didn't matter. He found himself sliding downward until he lay on his side on the bed, with Ann tucked tightly against him. Keeping his arm around her protectively, he sighed. Whatever had to happen would happen. He wasn't afraid of dying, but he wanted her to live. As the darkness closed around him, he knew that either he would wake up with Ann breathing easily by his side, or he wouldn't wake up at all.

Chapter 8

Ann felt a butterfly grazing her cheek. Or so she thought. The accompanying sensation was tender. Warm. Filled with love that made her heart pulse more strongly within her breast. She stood surrounded by shining gold-and-white light, absorbing a feeling of unconditional love that flowed not only around her, but through her. As bright as the light was, Ann was not blinded by it. Instead, the swirling, glittering, loving energy that embraced her made her feel carefree and joyous.

The light seemed to twist and become more opaque, taking on an identifiable shape. As it came closer, she felt no fear, only curiosity. Suddenly she recognized it—it was a jaguar with a dazzling gold-and-black coat. Ann could see the animal's huge, slightly slanted eyes, thin crescents of gold against the large black pupils holding her hypnotized. When the jaguar had moved halfway toward her, she watched the beast transform into the shape of a man. Her heart expanded like an orchid opening into full bloom when she realized it was Mike who stood before her. He was clothed in a dirty, bloody camouflage uniform. His face had two weeks' growth of beard on it. His eyes were shadowed and filled with a burning tenderness meant only for her.

A soft smile pulled at her mouth as she held his warming, life-giving gaze.

You came....

There was never a question that I wouldn't be here with you.

Ann stood there, torn between remaining in the embrace of the loving light and staying with Mike. There was no need for words in this realm, she discovered with a thrill. All she had to do was think and her thoughts were sent to Mike. And vice versa.

You have a choice, mi querida.

I know.... She felt his raw anguish, his need of her. Most of all, she felt his powerful love for her. It drew her like a beacon, called to her.

If you come back, there are terrible trials ahead.

Ann sensed that without knowing what those trials would be, exactly. But as she gazed into Mike's weary, battle-scarred face, she could feel the powerful beat of his heart in sync with her own. Every time his chest rose and fell, she inhaled and exhaled. The sense of oneness with him made her step forward. In a graceful movement, she extended her hand to him.

I'm not afraid, beloved. I have you. Ann knew she had expressed the truth, fully and without fear for the first time. It was a liberating moment for her. An empowering one. With Mike, she felt safe. He was someone she could trust. *I've searched for you for so long. It's been so hard, so lonely without you....*

You've held my heart for a long time. Longer than you know, he answered, lifting his hands. *Our search is over. Come back with me, Ann. Let's walk this last path together.*

Their fingers were inches apart. White-and-gold light surrounded them, pulsing with life. The urge to live, to remain with him, was suddenly overwhelming. The love emanating from him toward her was greater than the light that embraced her, such was his undying passion for her body, mind and spirit. It was an easy choice for Ann to make. As she reached across those last few inches toward him, and their fingers met, she felt a surge of energy tunnel through her. She felt his strong, caring fingers wrap more surely around hers, as if to steady her.

Come, Mike urged silently, *let's go home—together....*

Tears burned in her eyes. His face blurred momentarily as the tears formed and fell. Though he was a tired, weary warrior, his head was still held high, his shoulders thrown back with pride. Ann could only admire him. And love him.

I'm not afraid anymore....

As he cupped her hands, Houston smiled tenderly down at her. Squeezing her fingers gently, he leaned forward.

You don't have to be afraid. I'm here. I love you...and our love will keep you safe. He gently framed Ann's face with his hands and looked deep into her guileless eyes, which glimmered with tears. *I'm going to kiss you. As my mouth meets yours, drink my breath into you,* mi querida. *Take my breath into your body and you will live....*

As his strong mouth settled over her parting lips, the kiss felt so right to Ann, so warm and life-giving. Closing her eyes, she slid her arms around his broad shoulders and felt him move more surely against her. It was so wonderful to be drawn up against him, to feel her heart beat as one with his, to inhale his breath as her lips clung to his. Every sensation, from the rough, callused quality of his fingertips against her flesh, to the tender coaxing of his mouth sliding against her lips as he opened her to him even more, was exquisitely beautiful to her, causing fresh tears to stream down her cheeks and wash over their joined mouths.

How long she had waited for this welcoming kiss! Oh, the years, the decades she'd been searching without knowing that this man who held her now, was her one true love for life—her mate. Ann had never realized that until this moment out of time. The lonely, painful years, the darkness she'd carried by herself, began to dissolve beneath the tender ministrations of his mouth. She never wanted this kiss of shared love and incredible beauty to end.

Slowly, she began to feel herself growing heavy as she moved downward in a slow, spiraling motion. The light was dimming and they were moving into the darkness now. Somehow, she wasn't frightened by the dark, though as a child, she would have been paralyzed by fear if someone hadn't left a light on in her room when she went to bed. No, with this man, her mate, she could enter complete darkness and not be afraid.

As her body grew weighted, and different sounds and odors entered her peripheral awareness, Ann understood the true power of love. Love was the light that could cut through the blackness of hell itself. It could pierce the darkest of hearts. It could rescue someone from death and bring her back to life again. These thoughts remained with her as she relished the feel of Mike's arms around her, his strong, capable body against hers, steadying her descent. He was with her—inside her, around her, embracing her, their lips never parting, their hearts still beating as one.

Home, mi querida, *you're home now...open your eyes. Come on, my wild orchid, my woman, open your eyes. I'm here with you now. You're safe and everything is going to be all right....*

Mike's deep voice reverberated inside her like wonderful, ever-widening ripples of water moving down through her body. Her lids felt incredibly heavy and Ann struggled to hold on to Houston's voice as his hands framed her face. The moisture and warmth of his breath covered her as he spoke to her again, calling her back, calling her to his side.

Oh! How she always wanted to be with him! Ann struggled. She felt the terrible weakness of her body, but her heart pulsed strongly as his breath mingled with hers. He was giving her life, feeding her, nourishing her and rescuing her from the grip of death. Homing in on his low, trembling voice, on his hands as they gently held her face captive, she forced her lashes to move. But just barely. The lack of strength in her body scared her badly.

Don't struggle so hard, mi querida, he soothed. *Take your time. You're back with me. Just focus on my touch, my voice, and you'll be fine. Breathe more deeply now. That's it—nice deep, easy breaths. In and out...in and out...*

Ann felt his hands shift on her face, his thumbs removing the tears that continued to bathe her skin. Whatever she was lying on shifted. She felt his arm go around her shoulders and cradle her neck and head briefly. In a moment, she was propped up in a sitting position. Breathing became easier at that point. His roughened hand moved gently down her arm and he stroked her fingers.

Did you know that I dreamed of you when I thought Escovar was going to kill me and my men up in the highlands? I dreamed of you during that walk I took through the dark night of the soul. You were there, beloved. I struggled. I knew I could die if I wanted to, but you kept calling to me, teasing me and laughing with me.

You would dance like a butterfly around me as I stood in the light, unsure if I wanted to come back here or not.

Your laughter was like the beautiful music of the waterfall. Your eyes shone like the bluest of skies above the Andes. The shining love in your gaze was for me alone. You loved me. Fiercely. Protectively. You never gave up on me. You refused to let me die. You begged me, you broke down and wept for me, and I stopped, turned around and came back to you. Your tears were for me, not for yourself, and somehow, I knew that. You cried for me, for all I'd suffered, all that I had lost and would lose in the future if we could not meet again. You held me as I knelt down to take you into my arms to somehow try and comfort you.

I had never had someone cry for me before. As you sat there holding me, rocking me gently against your breast, you told me through your tears that you would willingly give your life for mine—that I had so much to do in the world yet. You told me that my path was hard and that if I had the heart, the courage of spirit to persevere, so many people's lives would be saved.

You cradled my face in your hands, and you looked at me through tear-filled eyes and said you would go in my stead. You would give your life for me, so that I might continue on. It was in that moment, my beloved, that you taught me something I hadn't learned yet about sacrificing for another, surrendering your life to a greater cause, a greater thing...far greater than either of us as individuals. You taught me humility, beloved, and the fierce love you held for me made me decide to live.

So you see, the scales are balanced now. You rescued me when I was ready, more than ready, to leave my life, my mission, behind. Only your undying love, your unselfish heart, taught me the difference, taught me what was really important. Now I've done the same for you. I was more than willing to give my life for yours. You are no less important than me. Your power, your commitment to doing good in this world, equals mine in every way. That is why we are together now. We have earned this gift from the universe, from the great Mother Goddess, to finally be with one another. Jaguar people have only one mate for life, beloved. You are my mate. I pray that when you awake and come back fully into your body, that you are able to walk beyond your fear and reach

out to me. Let my love dissolve those fears you will have to face.
Let me help you now, as you helped me....

Where did reality begin and hallucinations end? Ann wasn't
sure as she managed, finally, to force her eyes open to bare slits.
At first there was only darkness, but gradually, over heartbeats of
time, she began to make out light from shadow. She knew on
some deep level of herself that she had one foot in each world.
Only the stroking motion against her cheeks, the wet hotness of
tears trailing down her flesh, told her that she was still very much
alive.

Ever so gradually the light and dark began to take different
shapes and forms. Ann fought to keep her eyes open, but it was
such a tremendous battle. Struggling, she felt a shift against her
hip and thigh. What...? The movement was slight, but enough to
snag her wandering attention. Lifting her lids a bit more, she saw
huge black pupils ringed in deep blue staring back at her. Her
heart opened and joy cascaded through her. She knew these tender,
burning eyes; the love reflected in them matched her own.

With agonizing slowness her vision cleared and, the face that
held those eyes came into focus. It was Mike Houston. He was
here with her. Her sluggish mind whispered that it was impossible—that he was dead. That she must be hallucinating with fever.
But as Ann stared up at him in those warm, silent moments that
strung achingly between them, she saw tears trickling unchecked
from his eyes, rolling down his darkly shadowed, unshaved face,
and she knew that he was real.

Mike's tears grazed her soul as nothing else ever would. She'd
never seen a man cry before—not like this. In those pregnant
moments of clarity, her mind ebbing and flowing between consciousness and semiconsciousness, she knew in her heart his tears
were for her. Tears of love. Tears of relief. Of greeting. And
though her thoughts were coming so quickly that she couldn't
process them all, somehow she could feel Mike's every emotion
as he continued to gaze down at her.

She forced her badly chapped lips apart to form a word. One
word.

"*Mike...*"

She had to know if he was really here with her or if she was imagining all of this. Her heart beat harder, full of anguish at the thought that this was nothing more than a mirage, a last-ditch wish from her heart because she'd truly lost him forever.

Houston caressed her wrinkling brow. "Shh, *mi querida,* don't struggle so hard." He broke into a half smile filled with welcome. "I'm real. And no, you aren't dead. And neither am I." He picked up her right hand and brought it to his lips. Her flesh was no longer cool and clammy, but warm and full of life once again. Pressing his mouth to her soft skin, he could smell the faint fragrance of lilac soap she'd last washed with. He watched her eyes widen as he brushed his lips against her fingers.

"See? That was real." He laid her hand across her stomach, which was covered with warm blankets. Placing his hands on either side of her head, her sable hair a dark frame around her frighteningly pale features, he lowered his head until their noses almost touched. He watched her pupils dilate. She was watching him, holding her focus on him. Good, it would help keep her here. Keep her with him. Forever.

"No," he repeated, trying to smile, the corners of his mouth lifting, "you're not dead, Ann. You're here, with me, in your apartment in Lima, Peru."

He saw confusion cloud her eyes as she continued to watch him. She clung to each word he slowly spoke to her. When huge, new tears formed in her eyes, he understood that she was afraid he was nothing more than a fevered figment of her mind, of her broken heart. Lifting his hand, he brushed her tears away with his thumb.

"Reports of my death have been greatly exaggerated," he teased, his voice breaking.

A sob tore from Ann.

He felt his heart being ripped open. He had promised to take it easy and not rush her, but her eyes reflected such anguish that he couldn't stop himself. He couldn't help but reach for her as her sob knifed through him like the unsheathed claws of a jaguar striking out in defense.

"Come here," he rasped brokenly, leaning forward and gathering her limp form against him. She was alarmingly weak, and Mike gently guided her head against his shoulder so that her brow rested against his stubbled jaw. "There," he rasped, "does that feel real enough for you now, Ann? Feel me. Here." Lifting her hand because she was too weak to lift it on her own, he placed her soft palm against his roughened face. "Feel me. Feel my beard." He gave a short laugh, but it came out as a choking sound. "Can't you smell me? Cripes, I smell like the rotting jungle, like fear, sweat, blood and mud. That should tell you this is real. That I'm real."

He moved her hand in circular motions against his face. And then he placed her arm around his waist and he embraced her, so very much in touch with her chaotic jumble of feelings. There was a fine trembling in her as he gently rocked her back and forth in his arms. He felt so responsible for her safety that it nearly overwhelmed him. She shouldn't believe that he could always protect her. God knew, he wanted to, but he was only human. So terribly, vulnerably human. Turning his head, he pressed a kiss against her tangled hair.

"There. Did you feel that? I kissed your hair. How about another one?" Her hair was silky and he liked the feeling of the strands beneath his lips as he pressed a second kiss against her temple. Her arm lay limply against him, and for a moment, as he pressed a third, lingering kiss on her cheek, there was a slight response.

"Good," he praised huskily. "I see you're beginning to believe I'm real and not a figment of your fevered state." Sliding his fingers through her hair, he held her more tightly against him for a moment. "You came so close to dying...so close.... I heard you cry out for me. I heard you, *mi querida*. Everything's gonna be okay. Believe me," he rasped against her hair, "it is. You're very weak and you need to sleep. I'm going to lay you back down and I want you to stop struggling, okay? I can feel you. I want you to take my energy and let it heal you. Don't fight to stay awake or try to figure all this out. There will be plenty of time for that later, I promise you."

Mike eased Ann back onto the bed, keeping extra pillows beneath her because that helped her breathe easier. This time, as he straightened up after tucking her in, he saw that her eyes looked less cloudy. Her gaze clung to his until her lashes drooped shut.

"Sleep," he whispered, sliding his fingers through her hair in a caressing motion. "I'll be right here. I won't leave you ever again...."

The next time Ann awoke, sunlight was pouring through the curtains of her bedroom, making everything around her glow. As she lay there, she thought at first she was back in that gold-and-white light again. Then a broken snore snagged her drowsy attention. Barely turning her head to the right, she saw Mike Houston sitting, legs splayed, in a chair next to her bed. His head was tipped back, exposing his well-corded throat and Adam's apple, and his arms hung over the chair, which was too small for his large form.

She wasn't dreaming this time, she realized, though it took long, exquisite moments of simply absorbing his form into her wide-open heart before she could think straight. Thinking, Ann realized belatedly, took too much energy. Right now, on an intuitive level, she knew she had to be a miser with that energy in order to get well.

As he slept, Ann saw a depth of vulnerability in Houston as she'd never seen before. His dark hair was tousled and the exhaustion on his face wrung her heart. Dark, deep shadows lay beneath his eyes. His flesh, usually golden colored, was now pasty, as if drained of life. That frightened her. Was he wounded?

She had to examine him closer. As she struggled to try and sit up, the bed creaked in protest.

Instantly, Houston snapped awake, his eyes wide, his entire body tensing defensively. *What? Who?* He jerked a look toward Ann. She was awake. And she was looking directly at him, her eyes clear, her pupils huge and black and surrounded by the most incredible blue-gray he'd ever seen. The seconds strung palpably between them. When he realized there was no danger to guard against, he sat up straight. Then, raking her from head to toe with a searching gaze, he stumbled to his feet.

"Ann?" His voice was thick with sleep and undisguised concern.

She fell back, unable to remain up on her elbows for very long. As she closed her eyes, she felt his hands moving across her face, checking her temperature. And then he sat down next to her, his hip against hers as he picked up her wrist and felt for a pulse. It felt so *good* to be touched by Mike! How she wanted to tell him. She tried to form the words, but they stuck in the back of her dry throat.

"Good," Mike murmured, reaching for the blood pressure cuff on the nearby bed stand, "your pulse is finally strong and stable." Placing the stethoscope to his ears and wrapping the cuff around her arm, he pumped it up. As he released the air slowly from the device, he critically watched the needle. His heart soared.

"One hundred over eighty. Not bad," he said. "Not bad at all." He removed the stethoscope from his ears and the cuff from around her upper arm and watched as Ann slowly opened her eyes again. Smiling down at her, he rasped, "Welcome back to the real world, stranger." Getting up, he moved to the other side of the bed, where plastic IV bags filled with life-giving nutrients flowed into her left arm. Adjusting the drip, he felt relieved when she turned her head and continued to watch him. His heart pulsed with elation. Ann was out of the woods. For the first time in a twelve-hour period, her pulse and blood pressure were remaining stable. As he walked back around the bed, roughly wiping the sleep from his face, he felt exhaustion begin to avalanche upon him. Fighting it off, he carefully sat down on the bed and faced Ann. Should he take her hand as he had before? This time she was fully conscious, not floating in and out of this world.

To hell with it. Sliding his hand around hers, he squeezed her fingers. "Thirsty?"

Ann closed her eyes and drank in Houston's strong, firm touch. How did he know she desperately needed him to touch her? It felt like forever since she'd used her voice, and when she tried to force out a "yes" to answer his question, only a croak issued forth.

Nodding, Mike released her hand and quickly poured her a glass of water. "Hang on, I'll maneuver around here and help you sit up to take a sip."

His arm slid around her shoulders. How good it felt to lean against Mike as he positioned himself next to her. Raising her hand to hold the glass, she found, wasn't possible.

"Let me...." he whispered as he cradled her head against his shoulder, her soft hair against his jaw. "All you have to do is drink. Take all you want...."

Tears formed as she became privy to his incredible gentleness in the following moments. He pressed the glass against her lower lip and tipped it up just enough for her to drink without being drenched in the cool liquid. How good the water tasted! Ann slurped thirstily, some of the water spilling down both sides of her mouth. Houston couldn't tip it up fast enough for her to drink. Her throat was raw and so dry. And one glass was not enough. She saw the surprise in his eyes and then the grin forming on that wonderful mouth of his. She absorbed his warmth as she leaned against him. Just being held by him made her heart soar with joy. Just the strength of his arms around her, his body pressed to hers, fed her own strength.

"More?" Houston chuckled. "I don't have a beautiful woman in my arms, I've got a two-humped camel needing a refill at the oasis."

Ann laughed—or at least tried to. The sounds coming from her throat were raspy, but somehow Houston knew she was laughing. His grin widened enormously as he held her steady, his left arm wrapped around her while he reached for the pitcher on the bed stand. She watched him carefully balance the glass in his left hand while he poured more water into it. The errant thought that he could have laid her back down on the pillow and gotten the water more easily crossed her mind. Somehow, he understood that she didn't want to be physically separated from him just now.

After several glasses of water, Ann was sated. Houston replaced the glass on the bed stand. He should extricate himself and let her lie back down, but he was loath to release her. As he continued to hold her, he felt her tremble slightly and sigh.

"Okay?" he asked near her ear as he clasped his hands across her belly, above the thick blankets that covered her. She was warm and felt so good against him. Worried that he was taking advantage of the situation, he started to ease her up into a sitting position so he could move away from her.

He heard a mewing noise come from her, clearly a sound of protest. Looking down, he saw her raise her lashes. Her gaze clung to his. "No? You don't want me to leave?"

It took every bit of strength Ann had to lift her right hand and allow it to fall across his much larger, darker one. Words refused to come. Body language would have to do. As she tried to send out the impression she didn't want him to move, his mouth curved ruefully and his blue eyes danced with sunlight.

"Okay, I got the message. Just relax, you hear me? I'll sit here holding you for as long as you want, Ann. I'm in no hurry to go anywhere, believe me." And he wasn't. Mike watched as her lashes drifted shut and her lips parted. He heard a ragged sigh issue from her badly chapped lips. She sagged against him, and Houston realized just how much she'd struggled to keep him from leaving her bedside.

"Just lie here," he soothed, capturing her cooler hand between his own. "I'll be your blanket, okay? I'll keep you warm and safe so you can go back to sleep. That's what you need right now, you know. Lots of sleep. That and liquids." He pressed a kiss to Ann's hair and smiled with relief. She moved her fingers slightly within his hand.

Releasing a ragged sigh, Mike closed his eyes, too. He maneuvered himself fully onto the bed, his back against the headboard, his head tipped against the wall behind it. Exhaustion stalked him. He'd barely slept, snatching catnaps between taking her pulse, monitoring her blood pressure and watching over her during the endless hours, days and nights. But as he felt her shallow, slow breaths move moistly against the column of his neck, the hard line of his mouth relaxed. This was all he wanted for the rest of his life: Ann in his arms. Alive. Wanting him to hold her. Wanting him...

Chapter 9

"How long have I been out of it?" Ann heard how rusty her voice was, her words sounding more like croaks than the English language.

Houston stretched his long legs out in front of him. He'd managed to sleep with Ann in his arms, undisturbed, for nearly eight hours. She'd awakened first, and he'd quickly come awake seconds afterward. He'd eased her into a sitting position, given her several glasses of water and watched her orient herself completely to the real world once again. As he sat down, he knew the questions would come like a barrage. A part of him was afraid she'd reject him because of the answers he would have to give her.

Rubbing his face tiredly, Mike looked down at the watch on his left wrist. "Four days, ten hours and thirty-five minutes."

Her brows moved up. "Four days..." she managed in a whisper. She saw a lazy but exhausted smile tug at the corners of Mike's mouth as he regarded her in the dim light of the room, which was almost completely dark save for a small lamp on the Queen Anne dresser.

"Yeah..."

"What hit me? I..." Ann touched her hair with her trembling

hand. Weakness stalked her. "I remember having a fever. It was high. Sudden."

Houston lost his smile. Sitting up, he folded his hands between his opened thighs. "You got nailed with a hemorrhagic fever, Ann."

"What?" Her voice cracked in disbelief. She stared over at him. "But how..."

He shrugged wearily. "I don't know. You tell me. Do you remember anything out of the ordinary at the clinic? The granny nuns couldn't. God knows, we were looking for cause and effect. You had something that I've seen villagers get from living in lousy sanitation conditions. We had your blood analyzed at the hospital. It's actually a parasite. You pick it up from animal fecal matter."

"Yuck," Ann muttered. She pressed her hands to her face and tried to remember. Her mind wasn't functioning fully yet, not by a long shot. Emotionally, she felt completely raw and vulnerable. Having Mike here with her made her feel more stable, despite her weakness. "Wait..." She allowed her hands to drop away from her face. She told Houston about the little boy who had given her the piece of candy in return for setting his broken arm.

Mike's face darkened instantly. He straightened up and scowled. "You didn't eat it, did you?"

"Well, yes, I did eat it.... I mean, I didn't really, but you see, I wanted to make him happy. I know these kids don't get candy that often. I realized when he gave his only piece to me how much it meant to him. I popped it into my mouth and made lots of noises to show him how good it tasted."

Groaning, Mike raised his eyes toward the ceiling. "Ann...!"

"I spit it out into the waste basket as soon as he left," she muttered, defiance in her voice.

Houston got up. He couldn't sit still. "This is my fault, dammit," He began pacing the length of the room. "All my fault..." He ran his fingers savagely through his hair.

"How could it be?" Ann protested. "Mike, stop pacing. Sit here." She patted the side of the bed next to where she lay.

He halted and came and sat beside her once again. There was just a hint of a flush in her cheeks. How good it was to see her blush again!

"How did you know I was sick, Mike?"

He heard the fear in her husky voice. Holding her level gaze, which was filled with questions, he said, "You called me. Remember?"

Closing her eyes, Ann concentrated. Then she remembered something. Mike was here. Alive, not dead. "But," she said hoarsely, opening her eyes and fighting back tears, "they—the newspaper—said you were dead...."

Mouth pursed, he put his hand over hers. "Listen to me, Ann, these damn newspapers exaggerate a lot. Drama is their way of selling more copies."

"Then it was all a trumped-up lie?" Her voice was off-key.

"Not entirely," Mike muttered darkly. "I *was* slated to go on that chopper up to the village of San Juan with my squad. But something warned me against it. I settled for a convoy run up the mountain, instead. Another captain and his men were only too glad to get a lift to the top instead of marching through ten miles of jungle."

"And...they died instead?"

"Yeah...all of them, the poor bastards. Escovar's men have rockets they can launch from their shoulder. The chopper was just about to land when they began firing at it. I was halfway up the mountain with our convoy and saw it happen. We got pinned down, anyway...I lost most of my men...." His brows drew down and his voice faded. He didn't want to tell her how close to death he'd come himself. A bullet had ripped past his head, scoring his skull, and he'd fallen unconscious. Most of his men had thought he was dead because he was bleeding so badly. That was when he'd moved into the light—when Ann had come to him. The choice to live or die was his to make in that moment and he'd known it. Because of her, he'd come back, and thanks to his decision, his spirit guardian had healed the badly bleeding wound and he'd survived. Ann didn't need to know any of this. At least, not right now. She was too torn up already from the lousy newspaper report.

She gripped his hand as hard as she could, and he knew it was because she felt his pain and grief over the loss of his men. The moments strung between them, palpable and heart wrenching.

Never had Houston allowed her to see him like this. There were tears glittering in his eyes, but he refused to look up at her.

"I never realized just how dangerous your work really is...." she said thickly.

Twisting his shoulders to get rid of the tension and grief knotting them, Mike finally forced himself to face her. Her eyes were filled with such compassion. Suddenly Houston was tired of the life he lived. And though he'd found the woman he wanted to be with forever, his path would not—could not—change. The love he felt could never be expressed to her. "It's life and death every damn day, Ann. That's all I've ever known."

The flat finality, the grief behind his words, shook her. "This has been the worst two weeks of our lives. I'm so sorry, Mike—for your men...their families...."

Mike grimaced and admitted hoarsely, "I wanted to protect you from Escovar, from getting killed. Escovar has a sixth sense about people I—I care for. He's like a dog on a scent, and when he finds out who is important to me, he has them murdered."

"Escovar didn't get me," Ann stated wryly, "a damn parasite did."

"This time," he stated soberly. Mike knew he was scaring her, so he changed the subject. "Anyway, I heard you call me. Remember? The mental telepathy? And I felt you were in danger. I thought one of Escovar's killer squads had gotten to you." Releasing her hands, he stood up, frustrated. "It never crossed my mind that you'd contract a hemorrhagic fever and damn near die from it. I thought you were safe. I thought, for once, I'd outsmarted Escovar. He's a dark shadow in my life, always staining it, murdering those I care about. And when I heard—felt—you were in danger, there was no way I wasn't going to come back to Lima." He looked down at her, his voice heavy with weariness.

Ann swallowed hard at seeing the pain in his eyes. "I thought for sure I was going to die."

Rubbing his jaw, he muttered, "When we got here, about three in the morning, we busted down the door to gain entry. You were lying on the carpet, on your belly. You were bleeding from your nose, ears and mouth."

"Oh, God..." Ann connected back to the memory of that night.

"Then I wasn't imagining it? I was burning up with fever. It was at least 105 degrees."

"You had a temp of 106.5," he corrected grimly. "You were dumping. Your blood pressure was through the floor and your pulse was almost nonexistent. Pablo figured you lost two pints of blood on that carpet."

Her eyes widened. Ann heard herself gasp. "Then...I shouldn't be alive...."

With a shake of his head, Mike avoided her look. "No...you shouldn't be...but you are." His voice shook with raw emotion.

"But," Ann said weakly, "how? How did I come back? Medically, I should have died." She saw Houston's face grow closed, that hard mask returning. When he refused to answer her, fragments of memories began to trickle back—chaotic scenes and emotions. Groping, her voice cracking, Ann ventured, "Something happened...I remember being lifted up. I felt like I was in the clouds. I felt so light, so very light.... And I heard your voice. I told myself that was impossible. You were dead. It was then that I knew I was dying."

"Yeah," Mike said roughly, "you were dumping fast at that point. I was scared to death. I—" He stopped himself abruptly. He was afraid Ann would not believe the truth of what had happened. She was fragile right now, and he didn't want her upset. And if she knew the real truth, it would stress her out completely. That was the last thing he wanted.

Instead, he said, "I brought you here, to the bedroom. Pablo went and got Sister Gabby, who gave you a homeopathic remedy. I set up the IVs. When we realized how much blood you'd lost...well..." Damn, he didn't want to admit the rest of this, but he knew Ann was hanging on every word he spoke. He *had* to think of some kind of explanation. And he did—one that she, in her world, could accept.

"Sister Gabby said you were Type O blood. Of the three of us, her, Pablo and myself, I was the only Type O available. Sister set up a transfusion between us. It took one and a half pints from me to get your blood pressure stabilized...."

Pressing her hand against her heart, Ann whispered, "I see...."

The loss of that much blood was critical, she knew. "That's why you look so bad."

He grinned a little sheepishly. "Yeah, it kinda took me for a trip for the next forty-eight hours. I was a little weak after transfusing that much of my blood into you."

"Did Sister Gabby stay here?"

"No, she couldn't," Mike answered. He came back to the chair, and positioning it near the bed, he sat down. Ann was obviously accepting his version of the story of how her life was saved. Breathing a sigh of relief, Mike added, "I couldn't afford to have one of Escovar's spies zero in on this apartment. I know they follow the nuns around. I don't know if they followed Sister Gabby that night or not when Pablo drove her over. I wanted her out of here as soon as possible. I sent Pablo away, too."

"So, it was just you and me? You've been taking care of me through this whole ordeal?"

Houston nodded. Mouth thinning, he rasped, "I wanted to be here. I don't regret it, Ann."

"But," she murmured, "you said that it wasn't safe for you to stay very long in any one place—that Escovar's spies always tailed you...." And he'd been here, with her, going on five days now. Ann suddenly grew afraid—for Mike.

"That newspaper article probably covered my entrance into Lima," he said. "Escovar *probably* thinks I'm dead, too, but that won't last long. He'll send his spies in to see who was on that flight manifest."

"Five days is long enough for someone like him to find out the truth," Ann said. She suddenly felt very weak and very old. Worry for Mike's safety mushroomed within her. "And you look like hell warmed over. You haven't gotten enough sleep after losing nearly two pints of blood."

He lifted his head. "You must be feeling better. You're griping at me again."

Ann laughed spontaneously—a croak, really—but Mike's deep, answering laughter was music to her ears, a balm for her frightened heart. What had changed so much between them that she felt this close to him? Felt this desire to remain in his presence? She secretly hungered for his touch and wondered if she'd ever feel his arms around her again. It had felt so wonderful when he'd held her before.

"I guess," Ann uttered tiredly, "I had that coming."

He rose. "Yeah, you did, wild orchid." The name slipped out before he could stop it. Halting, Mike studied Ann for a reaction. There was a dull flush in her cheeks and she shyly looked down at her hands, clasped in her lap. In that moment, she was such a fragile, innocent young woman. It was torture not to kiss her, hold her close and feel her heart beating in unison with his. Torture not to think that someday.... Oh, Goddess...someday he could love her wildly, passionately, until they were joined on every level of themselves, from the physical to the most sublime. His heart ached for her. But it was a dream never to become a reality.

When Ann saw his wary look at his use of the endearment, her mouth softened. "Wild orchid. That's beautiful...."

"You like it?"

"Who wouldn't?" She laughed, a little embarrassed by the smoldering look in his narrowed blue eyes. Whenever he looked at her like that, she felt so incredibly feminine and wanton—two things she'd never felt before, really, except with Mike. And now, for whatever reason, his look stirred her even more deeply, ripening her yearnings as a woman who not only needed her man, but who wanted to make love with him as she'd loved no other man in her thirty-two years of life.

"I know I'm not beautiful, but I like the idea of being compared to such an exquisite flower."

Angry, but shielding her from it, Mike walked over to the dresser, toward the vase of red-and-yellow orchids that Pablo had brought before he left the apartment. Mike had wanted fresh orchids—Ann's orchids—by her side. They'd been sitting on the dresser through the long, dark nights of her illness, reminding him as he worked to save her that life was stronger than death. That love could delay death. And his love had.

"Here," he rasped as he placed the vase next to her bed, "you just look at these and know they're a reflection of you, okay? I'm going to take a shower, shave and probably keel over afterward."

Touched, Ann reached out and caressed one of the fragrant

vanilla-scented blossoms. "They're lovely," she admitted softly, meeting his exhausted gaze.

"So are you." His tiredness was making him say too much. "I'll check on you before I hit the sack, *querida*."

Ann nodded. "I'll be fine, Mike. You just get some rest. You look awful."

At the door, he hesitated. Placing his hand on the gold-painted frame, he looked over his shoulder at her. Already he could see that the old Ann was back. Her wry wit. Her sparkling blue-gray eyes filled with warmth—toward him. Heaven help him, but he absorbed it all like a greedy beggar stealing what wasn't rightfully his. "I'll take that as a compliment," he said, and giving her a sad grin, he left.

The phone was ringing. And ringing. And then it stopped abruptly after the second ring. Then it began again. Groaning, Houston rolled over on the couch and damn near fell off of it as he fumbled for the noisy device. Throwing out his hand, he forced his heavy lids open.

What the hell time was it? Sunlight was cascading through the western curtains of the apartment. The watch on his wrist read 3:00 p.m. Groping for the phone, he hesitated, even in his drowsy state. How many rings had it rung? If it was Pablo calling, they'd agreed upon two rings and then hanging up. Then the phone would ring again until the other party picked up. Mike had told his trusted sergeant to phone if, from his watch post in the apartment complex next door, he spotted one of Escovar's men hanging around the apartment. How many times had it rung the first time? Mike wasn't certain, as he knew the caller could be one of Escovar's spies trying to find out if he was here. Answering the phone could mean the difference between life and death. Or it could simply be Sister Gabby, worried about him and Ann. But the granny nun wouldn't be calling, he realized, because she knew it might put him in jeopardy.

Damn. To answer or not? How many times had it rung before he'd awakened? Something told him to do it.

"Yes?" he growled into the receiver.

"Major," Pablo said in a low voice, "Escovar has four armed

men in a car parked outside your apartment building. They've been here five minutes.''

All the sleepiness was instantly torn away. Standing up, Houston snarled, ''Pablo, get the car. Meet us around back, near the exit by the basement door, next to the trash cans. Make sure you aren't seen.''

''*Sí, sí!*''

Son of a bitch! Savagely cursing, Mike pulled on his shoulder holster. He always slept with the nine-millimeter pistol under his pillow no matter where he was. Grabbing his civilian black leather coat, and already dressed in a pair of jeans and a red Polo shirt, he hurried down the hall to Ann's room. They had to get out of here now! Escovar's men would be up at any minute. The yellow-bellied bastards were probably waiting for more backup, more men. More guns.

His heart was pounding as he opened the door to the bedroom. Ann was sleeping. As he hurried to her side, she looked like an innocent in a world gone mad. Shaking her shoulder, he growled, ''Ann, wake up!'' He didn't want to scare her, but time was of the essence. Moving swiftly, he unhooked the IVs and brought them carefully around the bed.

Groggily, Ann raised her head, disoriented. Mike leaned down beside her.

''Listen to me,'' he rasped, ''we've got to get out of here. Now.'' He quickly untaped the IV and pulled it out of the back of her left hand. Blood quickly pooled and he replaced the tape over it. ''We can't take anything. I've got to get you out of here.'' He took the blankets and pulled them around her.

Fear jagged through Ann. ''What—''

''No time to talk,'' he growled, and he slid his arms beneath her. Ann felt light. How much weight had she lost? He shrugged off the thought as his mind spun with tactics. With how to keep her safe.

''Hold on to me,'' Houston ordered as he brought her fully against him. ''Keep this blanket over your head. If I drop you to the floor, don't you dare move. You hear me?''

''Y-yes....'' Ann clung to his neck as he hurried out of the room, the blankets wrapped tightly around her. Terror seized her as she felt the sledgehammer pounding of his heart against hers. She smelled fear around him. She tasted it as she pressed her cheek weakly against Mike's neck. She knew she was a liability to him and the thought pained her.

Outside the door, Houston made a quick, cursory sweep of the hall. Nothing. Breathing harshly, he hurried toward the elevators. *No,* something inside him warned, *take the stairs.* Yes, a better, safer way. Turning on his heel, he jogged to the end of the carpeted hall. Leaning over, he jerked open the fire door. Gray concrete stairs with black pipe railing met his gaze. *Hurry! Hurry, there's no time left!*

The warning shrilled through him. Easing through the door, he rasped, "This is gonna be a rough ride. Hang on...." He gripped Ann hard as he began his rapid descent down the twelve flights of stairs.

Breathing hard by the time he'd gotten them to the basement, Houston ran for the rear exit. The dark, gloomy cellar was empty save for huge conduits, a lot of paper in receptacles and a massive furnace. At the rear door, he halted.

"Don't move," he rasped, and he stood Ann on the ground. He felt her legs begin to buckle. In one swift movement, he anchored her solidly against him, blankets and all. With his other hand, he pulled the pistol from his shoulder holster. He felt her arm weakly move around his torso as he eased the door open just a crack. There! He saw the black Mercedes-Benz. Pablo was only four feet from the door. *Good!* With a swift look in both directions, Houston jammed the pistol back into the holster and picked Ann up.

"Last step," he said huskily, kicking the door open with his booted foot.

Once they were inside the car, Pablo stepped on the accelerator. Houston forced Ann to lie down on the back seat.

"Stay down. Whatever you do, don't get up until I tell you it's safe."

"O-okay," Ann whispered as she felt the car begin to move. Houston's clipped, harsh tone scared her. If she'd been well, she might have handled this situation differently, but being ill made her vulnerable. Once again, she heard Mike's voice from the front seat, low and angry sounding.

"Let's get out of the city. Use all the back streets, Pablo."

"*Sí*, Major, *sí.*"

Houston slid down so he couldn't be seen. This was the lousy life he led. But he couldn't take the risk of anyone spotting him— especially Escovar's hundreds of spies, who salivated after that ten-million-sol reward on his head. Anyone on the street—vendor, beggar or businessman—could be a potential Escovar spy. And all the spy had to do was make a couple of quick phone calls and Mike would be history. Worse, Ann would be killed and so would Pablo.

"Major, where do we go? If Escovar knows you are here, he will have the airport cut off. He will have his spies at the army barracks...so where...?"

"*Aldea para los Nublado,*" Mike ordered. "The Village of the Clouds."

Pablo's eyes blinked, then widened. "*Qué?* Why?"

"Because," Mike snarled in frustration, "I don't have any other choice, so you'd better damn well make sure we don't get tailed."

"*Sí, sí,* Major..."

Ann lost track of time. She grew nauseous as the car twisted and turned down seemingly endless roads. All she could do was try to brace herself so she wouldn't fall off the seat. The blankets were heavy and she was hot in the stuffy vehicle. Perspiration soaked through the white silk gown she wore, making it cling to her. Trying to pull the blanket off her head so she could at least breathe, she felt Mike's hand upon her shoulder.

"We're out of the city now," he told her huskily as he removed all but one blanket from around her. He was leaning over the seat, his eyes narrowed and glittering as he rapidly checked her condition. She was very pale, her eyes huge and dark with fear. "Damn, I'm sorry for this, Ann. This wasn't in the plans...."

She rolled over and lay across the seat as best she could. Mike folded up one of the blankets and, lifting her head and shoulders, placed it beneath her as a pillow.

"Thanks.... What's going on?"

Houston never stopped looking around as he spoke to her. "Escovar got wind of my whereabouts. Pablo was keeping watch in the apartment complex across the way and he spotted a hit squad in a car out front of your place. They were probably waiting for backup before coming in after me.'' He saw Ann's face drain of color. How badly he wanted to protect her from all of this. Reaching down, he smoothed an errant curl off her wrinkled brow. ''It's okay. We're safe. We managed to get out of Lima without a tail, thanks to Pablo here.'' Mike gratefully patted his sergeant on the shoulder in thanks. Pablo glowed at the sincere compliment.

''Where are we going, then?''

Mike heaved a sigh and rested his arms across the seat as he regarded her. ''Home,'' he rasped. ''We're going home, Ann.''

Chapter 10

"Where are we?" Ann asked as she awoke and sat up on a pallet in a roomy hut, the morning light cascading through the window openings. Mike Houston was standing in the doorway, his massive frame silhouetted against the bright sunlight.

Mike turned toward her, smiling a little as he eased away from the door. They had driven for two days, with few stops in between. For Mike, outwitting Escovar was like trying to get his shadow to disappear on a sunny day. However, with more than a little help from the men and women elders here at the village, they'd successfully evaded him. And he was very relieved, he thought, studying Ann sitting before him, her legs crossed beneath the light pink cotton blanket. Her hair was beautifully mussed, her lips softly parted, her eyes still puffy with sleep.

Crouching down, he slid his fingers through her hair and eased errant strands away from her face.

"We're home," he told her huskily, catching her tender look as he caressed her cheek. "And we're safe here. No more running, ducking or dodging."

It was so easy to surrender to Mike. Ann was still healing from her illness and feeling excruciatingly vulnerable. Craving his continued closeness, his touch, she pressed her cheek against his open palm and closed her eyes.

"Home?" she whispered. Mike had been vague about where they were going. She only knew she was someplace safe from Escovar's murdering thugs and spies. She had slept most of the time during their escape because she was still recovering from the fever. Last night, in Tarapoto, they had left civilization behind, and Ann had heard Pablo say, as they slowly moved down a rutted dirt road in the darkness, that he saw a bank of clouds ahead. She vaguely remembered Mike carrying her from the car. She had seen stars overhead between the clouds. She had heard cries and greetings—some in English, others in Spanish and yet others in a language she was too tired to try and identify. Exhausted, all she could do was cling to him as he carried her to a hut and a soft, awaiting pallet. The last thing she remembered was Mike tucking her in with a warm blanket and pressing a kiss to her temple as she drifted back into the arms of sleep.

Now as he placed a feathery kiss on her wan cheek, a tremble raced through Ann and she lifted her chin, looking into his face, which was only inches from hers. "Hold me?" It took all her courage to ask. This was one of the few times in her life that she felt so nakedly vulnerable, so overwhelmingly in need of his protection. It must be the fear of Escovar finding them, coupled with the remnants of the fever, that made her feel this way. Ann searched his shadowed eyes. She had made it a point never to ask a man for anything because of her past. With Mike, it felt normal to ask for his help, his protection. "For just a minute?" she continued.

Houston saw the fear and worry in her drowsy blue-gray eyes. *Forever, if you want,* querida, he thought, though he dared not utter those words. Nodding, he sat down and positioned her between his massive thighs. It was so easy now, Mike mused, as Ann leaned against him trustingly. Her trust had been hard-won, he realized. And it could be shattered all too easily. One mistake on his part would destroy the tenuous connection between them. Especially now, when she was fragile and still mending. Her old walls hadn't been resurrected yet, but he was expecting them to be. Sliding his arm around her shoulders, he laughed softly against her hair. "I held you all night. Didn't you get enough of me then?" he teased.

Ann pressed her face against his neck. She felt the pounding pulse near his throat. He had recently shaved and she could smell the clean odor of soap still lingering on his flesh. She moved her head from side to side, content to be held within his strong, cherishing embrace. "I can't get enough of you...." she quavered. And she couldn't. Being in the back seat of a car for days that melted together like one nightmare had made coping with the ordinary things of life difficult. Mike had done his best to care for her under the harrowing circumstances, but they'd been on the run, barely ahead of Escovar's men, who had tracked them like bloodhounds. Ann had begun to truly understand just how hunted Mike was— and just how many of Escovar's spies were on his trail. Even when they'd stopped to get petrol, she'd had to hide beneath the blanket on the back seat, unmoving where Pablo, the least identifiable of the group, got the gas.

Mike heard the emotion in her voice and felt the stormy chaos within her. Sliding his fingers through her hair and taming it into place, he whispered, "Just tell me what you want, wild orchid, and I'll do my damnedest to give it to you." He bit back so much more he wanted to say to her. Every day they'd been on the run, he'd watched as reality struck Ann, reminding her about the price on his head and the raw danger he constantly dealt with. If anything, their experience on the road demonstrated why they could never have a life together. That made every moment he spent with Ann now even more precious, and like a greedy thief he absorbed her presence into his heart and soul.

The singing of many tropical birds added to the tender stillness ebbing around them as Mike held her. His heart sang, too. How often had he dreamed of Ann coming to him like this? Snuggling into his arms, seeking refuge? Seeking his reassurance? His love? Pain tightened his chest. Love? Yes, he loved her, but that was one thing he couldn't tell Ann. Pressing small kisses against her hair, Mike watched the sunlight strike the silken strands of sable, the red and gold highlights gleaming as the rays crept over the frame of the window and stole into the room.

Ann slowly lifted her hand and pressed her palm against the

center of Mike's chest. She saw that he was wearing civilian clothes still—a short-sleeved, white shirt and dark blue cotton trousers. He pressed his hand against hers.

"I remember...." Ann began in a husky voice as she closed her eyes. "While I was sick, I was dreaming, but I don't think it was a dream, Mike. When I was dying from the fever, I heard you break into my apartment. I remember you were holding me, willing me back to life. I saw the tears in your eyes. I heard your voice break. I saw this shadow near the bed. I—I don't know what it was, but then I saw it move above us. And then..." She opened her eyes and stared at the dried palm leaves that made up the wall of the hut. Ann pushed on, because she knew if she didn't, she'd never again find the courage to address it. "I'm a psychiatrist. This last week has been...bizarre for me. If I told any of my colleagues what I thought I saw, what I think really happened, they'd tell me I'd had a genuine, acute psychotic split from reality."

Mike eased away just enough to look down into her eyes in the warm silence between them. "What's reality, anyway?" he began. "Do any of us really know? I sure don't." His mouth curved ruefully as he studied Ann's shadowed, questioning gaze. He gestured to the door of the hut. "When I came here, to the Village of the Clouds, I was taught to lead with my heart first, *querida,* and my head second. I know I see things here—" Mike pressed her hand more firmly against his heart "—that my eyes don't see. So what's more important? A head's reality check? Or the heart's check of how you or I really feel on a visceral level?"

She managed a slight, strained smile. "I'm confused, Mike. And I'm scared. I feel lost in one way and so terribly vulnerable in another."

His smile dissolved. "I know you're scared. So am I," he confided in a low tone as he held her hands. "Not for the same reasons, though." He lifted his head and gestured toward the door. "We're safe here in the Village of the Clouds. Escovar will never find us here. It's one of the few places on Mother Earth where we're really safe. It's a haven where you can heal, Ann. That's why I brought you here."

She gazed through the doorway. The view outside looked like

any other village in the Andes. Chickens clucked contentedly; dogs yapped and ran among the huts, playfully chasing one another; women cooked over small fires with tripods and black kettles. Yet it felt different here and Ann couldn't figure out why.

"It's a beautiful name for a village," she whispered, returning her attention to Mike. In the light and shadow of the hut, his face looked harsh. She could still see remnants of exhaustion beneath his eyes, and in the way his mouth was set. She realized that Mike was trying to buoy her spirits, to help her feel more at ease here.

"I was brought here many years ago, Ann, when I was dying. My chopper had been shot out of the sky by Escovar and his men. I leaped out of it before it hit the ground and exploded. The blast knocked me into the jungle, but saved my life. Escovar's men were hot on my trail. I took a ricocheted bullet in this thigh," he continued, pointing to his leg. "The damn thing nicked my femoral artery and I lay bleeding to death in a shallow depression as they got closer and closer."

She felt anguish in her heart and she watched a somber darkness cover his face. "What happened?"

"Several things. This old shaman by the name of Grandfather Adaire appeared, almost as if by magic, out of the bush with two of his students, another man and a woman. He saved my life. He brought me here with the permission of Grandmother Alaria..." Mike's voice softened "...to mend. Only my week-long stay with them turned into a year-long stay."

"A year? Did the army think you were dead?"

He chuckled a little. "It was real convenient to disappear. I stayed here, fell in love with the village, with the people, found out a lot about myself that I'd been wondering about for years, and went into training with Adaire and Alaria, the elders here at the village. When I returned to Lima a year later, everyone believed I had died and been resurrected. They thought I was a ghost. I told them I'd survived the crash, but sustained a head injury and had amnesia until only recently. Once I realized who I was, I came back to the real world."

"And people believed you?" Ann demanded incredulously. She saw the mischievous smile creep across his face. There was such a little boy inside this man's body and she found herself starved for a little of his laughter and gentle teasing.

"Why wouldn't they believe me? I was a trained paramedic." Mike touched the left side of his head. "Look at this scar. I got it in that crash. That would have been enough to convince them."

"What were their options? Reality versus...what?"

"Not everything," Mike cautioned, "is a delusional episode, Ann."

"No? I can't tell if I'm dreaming or imagining things anymore."

"Well," he murmured, "there's another choice among the mystical people of Peru."

"This had better be good, Houston."

A fierce tide of emotion swept through him as he saw her rallying for the first time since almost dying. There was a fire in her eyes, her cheeks were slightly flushed and that luscious, orchid-shaped mouth was turned up in a hint of a smile, just pleading to be kissed again. He smiled at her returning spark of defiance.

"Adaire and Alaria would ask you to consider that shamans, such as they are, cross continually between the worlds. They stand with one foot firmly planted in the reality of the here and now that you are familiar with. And—" Mike raised his hand and made a circular motion around the hut—"they keep one foot in the other dimensions, or what they call worlds which intersect this very same space. Most people can't see them, shamans are trained to be aware of them."

"Worlds? I have trouble with just one reality. I'm sure I'd go over the edge if there was more than one continuously overlapping it. Anyone would."

"Patience," Mike chided. "Don't be so quick to judge just yet. Shamans have a special ability to move into what I call an altered state. They can tune in, sort of like a radio set, to one or more frequencies simultaneously. They can be here, with us, or out there, in the other worlds. And they switch back and forth by choice."

"Lately," Ann admitted, "that's how I feel—like I'm being flipped through a hundred television channels. I see so many different, shifting scenes. I hear things, smell and taste things.... I've never had this happen before, Mike.''

''If I told you that what you're experiencing is normal, would it make those worry lines on your brow go away?'' he asked, caressing her wrinkled brow with his index finger. Ann sighed and closed her eyes as he stroked her forehead. Mike understood the power of touch. Lately, Ann was wanting more and more of it.

''Sometimes,'' he began slowly, holding her gaze once she opened her eyes again, ''things happen in our life that throw us into chaos. We don't know which end is up. Or what is right or wrong. The only gyroscope I know that will hold the true course is here, in my chest.''

''The heart,'' Ann said, studying his softened expression. She was seeing another side to Mike now. Usually, he was always on guard, wary and alert. Here in this hut, this village, he was not shifting his attention from her to his surroundings continuously. Part of her truly began to relax and believe that they were safe.

''Yep. You're bang on, Doc.''

She grinned a little. ''I think I'm getting better.'' She patted her stomach. ''I'm starving to death, Mike.''

His brows rose. ''Really? You're hungry?''

''I feel like a starving jungle cat.''

''I see....'' Slowly extricating himself, he rose and said, ''I'll go get Moyra, then. She'll help you out of that nightgown and into some decent clothes. While she's taking care of you, I'll scare up some fresh hen's eggs and be just outside the hut here, cooking them over the fire.''

Who was Moyra? Ann was about to ask, but Mike disappeared out the door before she could say anything. To her total surprise, a young woman in her early thirties, her hair long, black and shiny, her eyes a lively forest green, skipped into the hut.

''Ah, there you are!'' she exclaimed. ''I'm Moyra. Of late, from Canada. I'm a student in training here at the village. You must be Ann.'' She knelt down, setting a colorful skirt and white blouse on the pallet. Holding out her slender hand to Ann, she said happily, ''It's so *nice* to meet you at last!''

At last? Ann slowly took her hand. ''Th-thank you.'' She regarded her. ''You're from Canada?''

Chuckling indulgently, Moyra nodded. "Originally I'm an Irish colleen. I emigrated to Peru. When I was older, I moved to Canada for two years to help a good friend of mine, Jessica Donovan, run her orchid greenhouse. I arrived here a year ago for further training with Grandmother Alaria. And you are from the States, we understand?"

"Yes...I am."

"Well," Moyra murmured, "while you're here with us, I've volunteered to be your maid-in-waiting. Michael isn't too well himself, yet. He did too much. I told the elders I'd step in and be of help when and where I could. Well, what do you think? Will this chemise fit you?"

Her upbeat, joyful mood and quick wit made Ann reticent. She saw the lively sparkle in Moyra's large, slightly tilted green eyes. Her face was oval, and when Ann looked at her, she felt as if she were looking at a cat's face.

"It—looks okay...."

"I'm so sorry," Moyra purred in her husky voice. "I'm rushing on like a wild creek in spring flood and here you are, feeling abandoned to a stranger. Michael isn't far away. He's just outside, as a matter of fact. He felt you might feel a little more comfortable with a woman helping you bathe and dress than him trying to do it."

Moyra was literally reading her mind. Ann stared at her as a red flush crept into Moyra's face.

"Dear me, there I go again. I owe you a second apology, Ann. Don't mind me, the blithering colleen from the Emerald Isle and all. I was just so charged up, getting to meet you. Michael has told us so *much* about you! About your bravery under fire. How you saved the lives of men and women who risked their lives helping others. How valiant and courageous you are." She moved her hands in a nervous, fluttering gesture. "First things first. You must bathe. We have hot springs located just a few steps behind this hut. Do you think you can stand? I'll help you walk to them." She grabbed at a woven bag. "Grandmother Alaria asked me to wash you with this very special soap she made. She said it would make you feel stronger. And heal quicker. It is from a very special orchid with healing powers. Well? Are you up to it?'' She tilted her head, her smile warm and engaging.

Ann managed a soft laugh. "A bath sounds like a dream come true." The feverish sweat had left her feeling very dirty, and she yearned for a warm bath to scrub away the memory of her deathly illness. "And is Alaria your grandmother?"

Moyra smiled gently. "We use the terms grandmother and grandfather to honor the elders who keep this village safe for all of us. They're also a term of endearment. In a greater sense, we are all connected by the invisible flow of life around and through us. Therefore, all elders are like grandparents to all of us."

Ann nodded. "What a beautiful concept." And it was. The warmth and sincerity in Moyra's eyes made Ann smile a little in response.

"Around here," Moyra said pertly, rising in one lithe, graceful motion, "where the clouds meet the other worlds, whatever you need will manifest. It's that simple and wonderful." She extended her hand. "Want to try to walk a bit, luv?"

Gripping Moyra's long, expressive fingers, Ann slowly stood up. Dizziness assailed her momentarily, but Moyra quickly wrapped her long, thin arm around her. "I've got towels and a robe waiting at the spring," she assured her. "Just look down and concentrate on putting one foot in front of the other."

"I'm stuffed, Mike," Ann protested as he tried to scrape some of his scrambled eggs onto her plate. They sat at a rough-hewn table on handmade chairs cut from mahogany and held together with thin, tough jungle vines.

"One last chance..." he teased.

With a quick laugh, Ann held up her hands. "*Finito,* Major Houston. I've eaten enough for three men."

Darkly, he spooned the last of the tasty eggs into his mouth. "You must have lost ten pounds. Maybe more." Ann was excessively thin and that wasn't good. Still, the bath at the hot springs, getting her hair washed and putting fresh clothes on, under Moyra's warm care, had perked Ann up considerably. But Houston wasn't fooled. He knew she was trying to rally, and that took a lot of energy she really didn't have.

"If I keep eating like this, I'll gain it back in a real hurry," Ann retorted good-naturedly. From the table she could look out the open window over the rest of the village. It was a beautiful place, with white, churning clouds hanging just to the north of them like billowing, constantly moving curtains. It was near noon, she supposed. The sun was directly overhead and shining brightly on the village, which sat in a flower-strewn meadow ringed on one side by jungle and on the other by grassy slopes that led up to the craggy, snow-clad Andes towering above.

Mike took the plates and set them aside. "I think you need to rest now, *querida*. You're looking pale." In fact, he could see the fine blue veins beneath her eyes, a telltale sign of impending exhaustion.

"I'm just a little tired," Ann protested.

Mike got up and pulled her chair back for her. The simple white peasant's blouse with short sleeves and a lace collar that revealed her collarbones made her look excruciatingly beautiful. The red-and-purple cotton skirt hung to her ankles, and Moyra had located a pair of open-toed sandals to protect her feet.

"Come on, I want to take you to one of the hammocks strung just outside our hut. You can let the soft breeze rock you to sleep."

The invitation sounded wonderful. Ann felt his hand settle around her elbow and steady her as she rose slowly to her feet.

"I wish I didn't feel like such a weakling," she complained as he placed his arm around her waist and drew her next to him.

"There's a time to be weak and a time to be strong, wild orchid." He studied her from beneath his dark brows as they left the hut. "I'll be strong for you now. It's your turn to lean on me, okay?"

She gave him a slight smile. "You know I'm not used to asking for help."

"I know." He sighed, squeezing her gently as they slowly moved around the hut. "Especially asking a man." He saw her frown. "I understand more than you realize."

Ann felt sadness and hurt move through her heart. Mike deserved her trust and love—she shouldn't be holding him up as a scapegoat for what another man had done to her many years before. "We need time to talk, Mike."

"And we'll get that—here," he assured her gently. "But not now."

"Okay..." The warm spring breeze wafted several strands of hair against her cheek. Ann noted more men in the village now, gathered around the tripods, eating and talking. Every once in a while she heard laughter. It was good, healthy laughter and she found herself smiling. There were two Pau d'arco trees no more than six feet apart near their hut. Strung between them was a woven hammock.

"Climb in," Mike urged, and he helped her sit down and then stretch out along the length of it. He took a white cotton blanket that Moyra had thoughtfully left behind, and shaking it open, he laid it across Ann. Her lashes were already closing.

"Thanks, Mike," she murmured. "I guess I'm more tired than I thought...."

He gently rocked the hammock, and within moments, Ann had spiraled into sleep. Moyra had made her a cup of herbal tea earlier. It had contained a natural sleeping aid. Right now, Ann needed rest in order to heal.

Mike wanted to remain there, standing over her and watching her sleep, but he felt Grandfather Adaire telepathically call to him. Reluctantly, Mike released his hold on the end of the hammock, giving it one more gentle tug. The breeze and birds would keep Ann company for a little while until he could return.

Moving around the hut, Mike wasn't surprised to see the elder waiting patiently for him. In the years Mike had known him, the old man hadn't aged one bit. Adaire's face was long, and lined like a road map, his shining gray eyes droopy looking, his white hair still peppered with strands of red to remind everyone of his Scottish heritage. His reddish white beard gave him the look of a sage, well deserved.

"She sleeps well," Adaire noted, shifting his wooden staff, topped with bright red, yellow and blue parrot feathers, into his left hand.

Mike sighed with relief. "Yes." He searched the elder's eyes. "Thank Grandmother Alaria for giving us permission to come here. I know you didn't have to allow us entrance. I didn't know what else to do. Everything blew up in our faces. Ann almost died.... I didn't ever expect to have to put all of you in danger like this.''

''It has been five years since your last visit, my son. Alaria said you were long overdue for a visit, and you are always welcome, no matter the reason for your appearance. And you did not put us in danger. We can only place ourselves in danger.'' He laid his bony hand on Houston's shoulder. ''Ann is not unlike us,'' he murmured as he led him back into the hut. ''Her heart is pure. What else can one ask for?'' They sat down at the table. Adaire moved very slowly but with ageless grace.

Mike folded his hands and waited as Adaire eased carefully into a creaking chair. To anyone else, he would appear to be a native of Peru, dressed as he was in a pair of threadbare pants made of dark brown cotton and a long-sleeved peasant's shirt too large for his tall, regal frame. Of course, Adaire's skin was white, as he was from Scotland. He had come from a long line of druid priests, Mike knew. Adaire's ancestors had taken care of the sacred oak grove on the Island of Mona, which had been overrun and destroyed by Caesar's army so long ago. Mike really didn't know how old the elder was. Not that it mattered, because Mike honored his wisdom and gentle form of leadership. Alaria, his wife, shared the leadership duties of the village with him. She was the primary emissary in physical form from the Great Goddess and was technically the leader of the village. All queries were taken to the main lodge, but in the end, it was Alaria who made the final decision. Both she and her husband were powerful shamans who led with their hearts.

Adaire's bushy white brows knitted as he placed his hands on his thighs. ''We must talk.''

Mike grimaced. ''I know what you're going to tell me.''

''You came very close to giving your life away for hers.''

Houston nodded and held the elder's gray, probing gaze. ''I did it willingly.''

''No doubt.''

Becoming grim, Mike flexed his hand and remained very still. ''I couldn't lose her, Grandfather.''

''Because?''

''I...'' He hesitated, his mouth growing dry. ''I care...for her.''

"You have loved twice before."

Mike held the elder's measuring stare. The word *love* grated on him. Adaire could be very intimidating when he wanted to be, and Mike could feel the man's mind probing his own. Houston offered no resistance to the gentle intrusion. He had nothing to hide from Adaire or Alaria. He knew Adaire was here to get the facts from him and share them with Alaria.

"You have loved two other women and they have been torn from you," Adaire said. "What makes you think Ann's fate will be any different?"

Mike's heart thudded with sudden fear. Pursing his lips, he rasped, "I don't think it would be different—that's why I'm trying to keep my distance from her...not letting her know my real feelings...." Hell, he'd barely admitted them to himself, much less Adaire. Mike knew he could never speak of them to Ann.

Adaire lifted his grizzled head and stroked his beard, the silence thickening. "Does she know?"

"About me? Us? No."

"She must know so she can make her own choice in all of this. You cannot lead her on."

A ragged sigh escaped from Mike's lips. "I know that, Grandfather." And he felt fear eating at him. What *would* Ann do once she knew the truth about him—his "kind"? Would she run in terror from him? Think that she'd gone insane in an insane world? Or would her care for him override the truth about him? And what if she *could* accept him? What did he think he was going to do—put her at risk of Escovar? *No.*

Scowling, Mike looked past Adaire and out the window toward the flower-strewn meadow. "I try not to care what she will think when she finally asks those questions, Grandfather. But I'd be lying if I said I didn't care."

"She's uncertain. And scared. You have little time among us before you must return to your duties in the other world."

Mike studied the old man. "I intend to take her out of here when she's recuperated and get her on the next plane for the States. And then I'm going after Escovar again. At least," he muttered, opening his hands, "that's my plan right now. How long can

Grandmother Alaria and the elders hold the power for us to remain here?''

''Two weeks.''

Two weeks. Mike knew that an outside energy such as Ann's could cause turmoil to the energy grid that made this village completely safe from any enemy encounters. It took the minds and hearts of many villagers meditating all day long to hold the protective shield in place and keep everyone who came here for physical training safe. Could he get Ann to accept him, his way of living, in that time? It was too short a period. Mike rubbed his jaw, and his voice hardened. ''She's been through hell already, Adaire.''

''I can see that. You know of her past?''

Scowling, Houston muttered, ''I've got an inkling. I haven't actively searched her mind. I wanted to let Ann trust me enough over time to tell me herself...to share it with me when she was comfortable.''

With a sigh, Adaire opened his long, bony fingers. The calluses on both his palms were thick and yellow. ''She is braver than you believe, my son. Don't treat her like a weakling, because she is not one. When you love, you protect. That is your nature. You cannot help it.''

Smarting beneath the accusation that he loved Ann, Mike pushed his chair away and stood. ''Yeah, well, it sure as hell didn't stop Escovar from killing the other two women I loved, did it?'' He lowered his voice and tried to control his runaway feelings. Adaire sat there, serene and seemingly unaffected by his stormy response.

''The path of jaguar medicine is not an easy one, my son.''

''No damn kidding.'' Mike raked his fingers through his hair and moved restlessly around the room. ''Don't you think I'm afraid it will happen all over again? Hell, it almost did. I heard Ann cry out for me and I felt her bleeding to death.... I got there almost too late to save her.'' He turned, studying Adaire. ''Yes, I'm protective. And I'd damn well go to the threshold of death again for her. I'm not sorry about my choices, Adaire. I can tell from the feelings I'm sensing around you that you aren't happy with me or what I did to save her life.''

"Please," the elder murmured gently, "be at peace with yourself, Michael. Come, sit down. Sit...."

The lulling baritone of Adaire's voice was like balm blanketing Mike's raging, unchecked emotions. He came and sat down, then he rubbed his face with his hand. "I'm sorry, Grandfather. I'm out of sorts."

Just then Alaria entered the hut. Mike smiled wearily up at her. She, too, was ageless in his eyes, the energy surrounding her like the pulsing of sunlight. Her unconditional love embraced him, and as he met her sparkling, dark green eyes, he felt her smile even though her full lips did not move. She stood nearly six feet tall, and her thin form reminded him of the most graceful of ballerinas. Her face was full and oval, her cheeks high and her nose thin, shouting of her aristocratic roots. Once, Adaire had told him, she had been high priestess of the sacred oak grove in England, though she was originally from Wales. How long ago she had come to Peru, Mike had no idea, but she, too, was descended from a long line of druids, and the stamp of leadership on her bearing was obvious.

"You are weakened by the considerable gift you gave to her, because of the bravery of your heart," Alaria said. "You will need these two weeks to recuperate yourself. Does Ann realize you need to heal, also?"

"No, Grandmother." Mike rose and pulled out the other chair for her. "And I don't want her to know. She's been through enough." He sat back down and stared at the rough, wooden tabletop. "Ann worries at the drop of a hat. If she even thinks I look ill, she gets upset."

"Must be love, eh?" Alaria teased gently as she laid her long thin hands upon the table.

He slowly raised his chin and looked into Alaria's large eyes, which were filled with warmth. As leader of the village, she wore around her neck a golden torque with a huge rectangular emerald of absolute clarity. Mike had been told by another student a long time ago that the torque was passed down to each successive leader of the Village of the Clouds. No one could remember how long Alaria had been leader. It was whispered that she was nearly a thousand years old and that because her heart was so pure, she aged very slowly. Right now, Mike thought she looked like she was near eighty, her gray-and-red hair plaited into two thick braids. "I...don't know when it happened. I swear, I don't," Mike rasped. Finally, beneath her gentle gaze, he admitted in a choked voice, "I wasn't expecting to fall in love ever again. Not with my track record." Grimacing, he muttered, "Ann walked into my life like a lightning bolt. I felt like someone jerked the rug out from under my feet."

"I can see that," Alaria said, smiling kindly. "Ann is your true mate, you know. You have shared your blood with her. She is a part of you—of us—because of that, whether she wants to be or not. I hope she will discover that being a part of the Jaguar Clan is not always harsh and challenging. We are glad to hold this energy for you—and her."

Mike reached over and gripped the elder's hand in silent thanks for her graciousness. He felt the parchmentlike skin, the bones of her work-worn fingers and the incredible strength they still possessed. More than anything, Mike felt life pulsing like a thousand suns through her fingers into him.

"Let us help you for a little while, eh?" Alaria suggested. "You need some care, too. You fight what lies in your heart. You are afraid to love again, with good reason. You are so torn now, my son."

Wasn't that the truth? In the past, Mike had had no one to turn to. His family in the Village of the Clouds was never far away, but to run to them and beg for help in every crisis wasn't his way. No, Mike respected what this village was and why it existed. He felt the warm energy begin to flow up into his arm. Within moments, he was very drowsy.

"Lay your arm on the table as a pillow," Alaria suggested, "and close your eyes and allow me to send you the healing energy you need."

Houston nodded and, without another word, did as the elder instructed. As he closed his eyes, head resting on his arm, his hand beneath Alaria's, a sense of utter peace flowed through him and erased all the anguish, pain and anger he'd felt earlier. Still, his last thought was: *How am I going to tell Ann about me? What will she do when she sees I'm not what she thinks I am? How will she react to being a member of the Jaguar Clan?*

Chapter 11

"This place," Ann began, "reminds me of the United Nations, Mike. It's not a simple agricultural village of Quechua Indians as I first thought." She sat with her back against a stout tree at the edge of a flower-strewn meadow, the shade of the tree shielding her from the sunlight. Above, churning white cumulus clouds drifted through the sky like a long roll of white cotton against the high slopes where the meadow met the magnificent snow-covered Andes. She picked at the ripe papaya that he'd peeled and carefully sliced to share with her.

"No one eats meat around here, I've discovered. Just fruits, vegetables and grains. And there are no babies here. Just adults." She met Houston's gaze as he sat less than a foot away from her, legs crossed, his arms resting on his thighs. "In the past five days, I've discovered a lot of what I'd call inconsistencies." She pointed to the fruit in his hand. "This is spring, not summer. This fruit shouldn't be available here yet. What did they do, ship it from somewhere? There are no automobiles, no trucks that I've seen to bring it here."

Ann looked around the meadow. "Yet it's a beautiful place. I love it here and feel so at peace." Her gaze traveled back to Mike.

"And I've never seen you as relaxed as you are here." Or as playful, she thought, realizing once more how precious his little-boy side, his frequent, teasing grins or the laughter reflected in his dark blue eyes, were to her. Frowning, she bit off a piece of the sweet, dark orange fruit.

"And now that I'm well and my brain's functioning again, I've got a lot of questions. Like, how did you hear me call you? I didn't pick up a phone and yell for help. And the nuns didn't know what was going on." She held his shadowed gaze. "So how did you know? I mean, I know what you told me about your telepathic skills, but still, it seems so unusual. And looking back and remembering more and more of what took place, Mike, I *know* without a doubt that I should be dead." Her voice lowered. "And I'm not. Something extraordinary—maybe an inexplicable mira-cle—happened, involving you...and...a large cat of some kind. This time, I don't want you to be evasive. We need to sit and talk about this. Every time I try to broach this topic with you, you start teasing me and we get to laughing, or you...well, you hold me, kiss me, and I lose track of where I wanted to go with the con-versation...."

Houston watched the puzzlement and confusion in Ann's ex-pression. It was time and he knew it. He'd been trying to delay this day, but he knew it would come. Ann was simply too intel-ligent, too curious, to let her near-death experience go without explanation. Before, he'd been able to distract her—with himself, with the attention he showered on her, the love he shared with her. At night, they slept in one another's arms. He would hold her and she would sleep like an innocent child in his embrace. It was sweet agony, because Mike would not take advantage of Ann or the situation. He wanted to, but he didn't dare. Things had to be that way between them or the solid trust that was being built would be seriously fractured. Mike knew this day of truth was coming and he hadn't wanted to let his raging hormones get out of control. Too many more important things were at stake.

Lifting his head, he gave her a strained smile. Today Ann wore a lilac-colored cotton blouse. It was very simple, the scoop neck accentuating her collarbones and slender neck. He watched as she nervously smoothed the folds of the dark blue cotton skirt again and again around her legs.

Setting the knife and the papaya aside on a small red cloth where they had placed the rest of their lunch, he moved to her side. Settling behind her, he drew Ann between his outstretched legs and allowed her to lean back against him. He savored these intimate moments with her. They were natural. And they both needed it—and each other. Her dark hair tickled his chin as she lifted her face to gaze up at him. Their mouths were a bare inch from one another. The urge to lean down, to take that wild-orchid mouth of hers was nearly his undoing.

"I have a story to tell you," he began in a low tone. "And it may sound like I'm making it up, but I'm not. You're going to have to trust me like never before. Don't ask questions until I'm done, and then I'll try my best to answer them as fully as I can. Fair enough?" His heart was beating hard and his fear sent a rush of adrenaline through him. In telling her the truth, he knew there was every chance she would leave him—today, forever. Yet Grandmother Alaria was right: Ann had a right to know. He would not live a lie with her. If she loved him enough, and he wasn't sure that she did, then her love would sustain her through this coming hour of bare-bones truth telling, and she would remain at his side. But even that thought tore him apart. Did he want Ann to love him? Mike was more scared now than at any time in his life.

"Fair enough," she whispered. Ann took his arms and guided them around her waist, placing his hands in her lap and covering them with hers. How she loved these special times with him, alone in this beautiful meadow. She was grateful Mike did not take advantage of her need to be held. On some level, he understood exactly what she needed.

"Okay," Houston murmured, easing her head back against her shoulder, "close your eyes and listen." He felt terror seizing him. Mike had known fear in his lifetime, but never this bad. The lump in his throat seemed to grow. To hell with it. He *had* to reveal who he really was.

"My mother was part Yaqui, part Quechua Indian, born in northern Peru. She was one of ten children, a middle child. When she was six, her parents moved the entire family to Mexico City. She got a job and worked hard. She literally pulled herself up from poverty, eventually making a middle-class living as a typist at the U.S. Embassy. It was there she met my father, a marine corps officer attached to the embassy.'' Mike nudged several reddish gold strands of hair away from Ann's cheek, where the breeze wafted them. How peaceful she looked. His heart ached with the loss he knew was coming.

''They fell in love with one another. It took a year for my father to get orders stateside, but once he did, they got married and she became an American citizen. I came along four years later, their only kid. When I was old enough, I realized I was different. For one thing, the color of my skin in a school of white kids set me apart, but it was more than that. It went a lot deeper. When I was nine, my mother sat me down and told me of her people's—her family's—unique history.''

Ann opened her eyes and looked up at him through her lashes. Mike was gazing away from her now. His profile was marked with tension. Why? Feeling his turmoil, she automatically smoothed her hand down his darkly haired arm. ''How were you different?'' she asked gently. Instantly, she saw his brows dip. His mouth tightened. Truly concerned, Ann eased from him enough to turn and place her arm around his broad shoulders. ''Mike?''

A ragged sigh tore from his lips. ''I—my mother said she was a priestess from the Jaguar Clan. I didn't know what that meant— at least, not at that time. She told me that one member of each generation could choose to become a member of that clan. It is the oldest continuing medicine line in the Americas. Jaguars used to roam the U.S., particularly the Southwest, until they were all killed off by white men who wanted their skins for their women to wear.'' He ran his hand through his hair in an aggravated motion and refused to look at Ann, although he could feel the probing heat of her gaze on him. Desperately, Mike searched for the right words, the right way to tell her.

''Among the Indian nations, there's always a family heritage of healers and doctors, just like there's a line of people with other finely honed skills, such as artisans, weavers, hunters or leaders. My mother was a healer and a member of the Jaguar Clan. From the time I was nine until I was eighteen, she gave me special training exercises to do every day. She told me that at the right time, I would meet a teacher who would help open these gifts within me, the ancient wisdom I carried, genetically, and I would begin to use this knowledge.

"I didn't know what that meant." Mike looked down at the grass beside him. "I do now..." His stomach tightened into a very painful knot. Unconsciously, he rubbed that area with his hand. Ann's fingers lightly stroking the back of his neck eased the tension there. But then, her touch was always healing to him. "My mother said that I would have to go to Peru to meet this teacher. Well, as fate would have it, I joined the army and was sent to Peru over ten years ago because I spoke fluent Spanish and I was good at what I did as a training advisor. I'd long ago forgotten about my destiny, the event that my mother had said would happen at the 'right' time."

Lifting his chin, Mike gestured toward the distant village shimmering in the sunlight. "When I came to Peru, I heard all kinds of myths and legends about jaguars down here. How they would track a man in the jungle for days, look directly into his eyes, freeze him so he couldn't run and then pounce on and eat him. I'd heard about the mysterious Jaguar Clan that lived up in the highlands, near the foot of the Andes. Things like that."

"When Escovar shot that chopper out from under me, and I was bleeding to death, it was Grandfather Adaire who rescued me. I was dying and I knew it. I was a paramedic—I knew the score. And I knew that a grizzled old man draped in a jaguar skin with two younger students in tow wasn't going to save my hide, either."

"Well," Mike rasped, "I was wrong. I've never told anyone about this, Ann. You're the first to know...." He met and held her somber gaze.

"Whatever you tell me, Mike, is safe with me. You know that." She reached out and laced her fingers with his.

He nodded, lifting her hand and kissing the back of it gently. "My life has always been in your hands," he whispered, meeting her widening gaze. "My trust of you is not the question."

Her flesh tingled and a slight ache began deep within her. Ann knew that feeling, for it often occurred when Mike touched her, or even kissed her fleetingly. "Unless Adaire had a surgical unit hidden somewhere in this village, there's no way he could have repaired your torn femoral artery," she agreed softly.

"Exactly," Mike said, turning and looking across the meadow. His voice lowered. "I passed out shortly after that, from blood loss. I had this wild, incredible dream that really wasn't a dream." He pointed toward the center of the large meadow.

"When I came to, I was in one of these huts like you found yourself in. Grandmother Alaria was with me, sitting serenely on a pallet next to me, just regarding me in a very kind, motherly way. She told me she was the leader of this village and that I was welcome to stay with them. As I got oriented, I realized there was someone else in the small hut with us, in the shadows. I was very weak, and it took everything I had to turn my head in that direction.

"I damn near had a cardiac arrest, for I saw this huge, stocky female jaguar suddenly appear and come toward me, where I lay. I thought I was a goner. She had a huge, flat head with the biggest, most incredible gold-and-black eyes I'd ever seen. I feared her. I started to look around for something—anything with which to protect myself from her charge. I knew I was fooling myself, because the jaguar is a massive animal. Before I could do anything, she was there at my side, licking at the wound on my thigh. I could feel her rough, pink tongue as she licked that area again and again. I felt this strange, hot wave of burning energy enter my leg. I remember moaning in pain, and then I lost consciousness again."

With a slight, strained chuckle, Houston shook his head. "Brother, was I naive back then. Grandmother Alaria laughed at my reaction. After I regained consciousness, that big cat lay down next to me, purring loudly and just watched me. I was so scared I didn't know what to do. The cat just lay there, switching her tail every now and then and watching me like a mother might her child. Gradually, my fear was replaced with...something else. It was then that Alaria told me it was about time I met my guardian, this beautiful female jaguar who had saved my worthless neck many times over. It was the first time I ever met her in this reality."

Puzzled, Ann stared at his profile. Houston's features were hard and uncompromising now, like those of the soldier she'd seen earlier in Arizona. "This guardian...does it have to do with your mother's medicine? Her predictions for you?"

Mike knew Ann would piece it together. "Yes...."

"But," Ann murmured, opening her hands, "how did this jaguar heal your torn femoral artery? That's impossible, Mike."

He slowly turned his head. "I was demanding the same answers from Grandmother Alaria. I told her I was dead, that this was heaven or something. I didn't understand. I couldn't have survived my wound. I should have bled out in four minutes or less, game over."

"Exactly." Ann saw a sheen of perspiration covering his dark gold skin. The suffering line of his mouth made her reach out. The act was intimate. As she brushed the tight line of his mouth, she saw the startled look in his eyes and the instant, burning desire for her. "I feel your fear," she whispered, again caressing his mouth. It was a strong, good mouth. One she wanted to kiss, to cling to and learn from forever. The day was coming soon, Ann felt, when she would walk beyond her last fear barrier and do just that: fully love him. If only he would stop pushing her away...if only he would admit what was so obvious in his touch, his eyes and his voice.

Ann's touch was unexpected. Searing. Hope suddenly threaded through Mike. He captured her hand and pressed a long kiss against her palm. And then he pressed it to his cheek. "Ann, I'm going to tell you something now, and I pray...I hope you'll believe me...."

The words came out filled with such anguish that she didn't know how to respond. "I know I'm pragmatic," she said softly, "and I can't explain how your guardian saved your life, but Mike, there's a lot in our world that can't always be explained in rational ways." She shrugged. "I believe in miracles. I always have, whether science can explain them or not. Things like this, what you've shared with me, make me curious. They don't scare me."

Taking the last of his fleeing courage, Houston met and held her warm blue-gray gaze. There was such compassion and love in her eyes for him. He felt it through every cell in his tense, frightened body. Still, he had yet to discover how much of his spiritual heritage she would truly be able to accept. "I want you to look out there, in the center of the meadow," he ordered her darkly. "And no matter what happens, know you're safe with me, Ann."

Puzzled, Ann watched him stand. He leaned down, grasped her hand and pulled her to her feet. She felt his arm go around her in an almost protective motion and a warm feeling spread through her. "Okay," she said "what am I suppose to see?"

As she stood beside Mike, their bodies lightly touching, Ann watched the meadow. Though she couldn't see it, she felt a strange shift of energy around Mike. And then she saw a dark, nebulous shadow begin to form no more than a hundred yards from where they stood. Frowning, she blinked. Was she seeing things? The darkness began to take a more identifiable form. In the next minute, there was a powerful female jaguar standing before them. Her gold-and-black coat gleamed in the sunlight.

Gasping, Ann took a step back. Instantly, she felt Mike's arm tighten around her.

"You're safe," he rasped. Would she run in terror? Risking a look down at her, he saw Ann's gaze riveted on the jaguar standing serenely in the meadow. His guardian looked at them, her tail twitching lazily from side to side. The terror, the shock on Ann's features, made his heart sink. His gut tightened painfully.

"Ann, listen to me," he pleaded, "that's my spirit guardian. That's the jaguar that saved my life years ago."

"But," Ann argued hoarsely, "she wasn't there a minute ago. She gave him a wild look and then stared back at the gold-and-black cat. "Or was she? Was she there, lying in the tall grass all along, and just stood up? The grass is four feet deep there..."

Turning, Houston gripped her shoulders. "No," he admitted, "she wasn't lying in the grass, Ann. I called her mentally. She came on my command from the other worlds. That's what really happened."

Ann gave him a strange, guarded look. Houston's eyes were narrowed and intense, and she felt the desperation in his voice. Peering around him, she stared at the jaguar in the distance. "What do you mean, you called her? I didn't hear your voice."

He smoothed some strands away from her cheek. Her face had gone pale. She was truly frightened. And so was he. He soothed her tight shoulders in a stroking motion. "You felt me call her, didn't you?"

Torn between the magical appearance of the jaguar and Mike's intensity, she muttered, "Well—yes, I felt *something*...but—"

"You felt me mentally call my guardian," he said slowly and firmly, "that was all. Mental telepathy, Ann. It's not something foreign to your understanding. I know it isn't."

She swallowed hard. "Oh, God, Mike, that's the *same* jaguar I saw when I was...dying, I'd swear to it." She gave him a confused look. "She came first. She was standing in the light with me. And then she changed—into you.... Now I remember. Yes, you were the jaguar—and vice versa. Oh, God..."

The way she looked at him made him want to cry out. He was losing Ann. He felt her slipping away from him as the fear, the realization sank into her. Grimly, he pulled her into his embrace. He felt her resistance and then it dissolved. "Just let me hold you, okay?" he rasped. When her arms went around his torso, he breathed a small sigh of relief. At least she hadn't run from his arms—yet. She still sought safety there, instead of running away from him.

"For a year in this village, Grandfather Adaire and Grandmother Alaria trained me to do what I can do now. They said I had the necessary skills and talents to become a member of the Jaguar Clan, if that's what I wanted. At first," Houston breathed harshly against her hair, "I was like you. I was scared. I thought I was going crazy or that I'd died and was trapped somewhere between heaven and hell in this insane place where the impossible happened every minute of every day. If you wanted a papaya to eat, all you had to do was think it, and it appeared physically in front of you. If you were hot, you could visualize a cooling shower from overhead, and it would happen within minutes." He caressed Ann's hair and felt her heart beating like a caged bird fluttering in her breast. Anguished, he wanted to somehow protect her from the truth, but it was impossible.

"This place," he began awkwardly, "is so very, very special. In North America, there is a similar place, a sister to this, on the East Coast, in North Carolina. It's called Spirit Lake. The Cherokee people are the guardians of it. Places like this—if you aren't supposed to see them, you won't. You can't gain access to them without...meeting certain requirements. That's why we're safe here. The Brotherhood of Darkness, our opposite energy, can't get to us here. This place is off-limits, in a sense, to them. That's why, when you awoke that first morning, you felt different. You mentioned it a number of times to me.''

Ann eased away just enough to look up at him. ''Y-yes.''

''It's the energy here, the people who live here or visit here,'' he said simply. ''That's the reason it's special. They are heart centered, very spiritually advanced, and they can hold or create an energy or reality. This village exists because of them.''

''That jaguar just appeared out of *nowhere,* Mike. How can you explain *that?*''

The trembling in Ann's voice tore at him. He gently turned her around so that they could watch the jaguar, which stood patiently out in the meadow. ''I can't...at least, not in a scientific way—a way you'd accept. Maybe later, when you understand more about us...''

''Is she always with you?'' Ann found herself wanting to know if the jaguar was a mirage or if she was physically real. Her fear was giving way to curiosity.

''Always.'' His mouth twisted in an effort to smile. ''Usually, she's invisible. I asked her to come and to appear so you could see her.''

''Would I see her if I wasn't here with you?''

''You saw her when you were dying of that fever, *querida,* didn't you?''

Ann nodded, so many more memories of that terrible night flooding her being. Throughout the last few days, more and more of that night had been coming back to her. Now she vividly recalled it in its entirety. ''She was there with me...'' Ann breathed raggedly.

''Yes,'' Mike admitted, ''I sent her ahead to help you, to stabilize you the best she could energetically, until I could reach you myself.''

''Then I wasn't dreaming it! I saw her next to the bed while you were holding me in your arms. I was lying between your legs and you were holding me against you. I felt your heart, your breath in me..."

"And at that point, my guardian came over me and supplied the extra energy, the gift of life to you through me," Mike said humbly. "That is the gift of the jaguar, Ann—life or death."

She gripped his arms and closed her eyes, caught up in the entire sequence. Mike held her steady. "My God...then it really did happen. I didn't dream it. I thought I was having hallucinations due to my high fever...."

"Nice medical explanation for the magic of possibility," he told her wryly. Ann opened her eyes and he watched as her lips parted.

"That's why they call you the jaguar god? It isn't just a myth?"

Gently, Mike turned her and, placing his arm around her shoulders again, drew her against him. "Some of the stories being told are true, Ann. Some of them are gossip. The myth builds, changes and becomes ridiculous."

"I heard Pablo say that you brought people back from the dead."

Mike laughed, but the sound was strained. With a shake of his head, he said, "No, that's something I can't do. Only the Great Goddess could do that, and I'm afraid I'm only a terribly flawed human being. No...I can ask for intervention for someone who's dying...and if it's allowed, my guardian will help me pour my own energy and hers into that person to help save them."

"And that's how you saved me? You not only gave me your physical blood, but you gave me part of...you?" Ann searched his harsh face, his shadowed eyes. "A transfer of—what? Your life energy along with a blood transfusion?"

His hand tightened briefly on her shoulder. "Yes, exactly. I couldn't do it if I didn't...care for you, Ann," he told her in a low tone. "There are two types of Jaguar Clan members—those belonging to the Sisterhood of Light and those belonging to the Brotherhood of Darkness. I chose the path of light, Ann. And in order to help someone who's hurt or dying, I have to be in good stead with my heart and my emotions toward them."

"And your friend Antonio? I saw the jaguar come over you that time in the airport."

"Yes," Mike admitted, "you did."

"And he lived."

"My jaguar spirit and I interceded on his behalf, Ann. And it wasn't his time to go. The Goddess allowed him to survive. My guardian and I were only tools, if you will, for that life-giving energy to flow back into Antonio and save him. It's not an unlimited source. If I give too much of my energy, I could die. It's a delicate balance."

She was very quiet, digesting his explanation. "And the same thing took place to save me?"

Mike held her steady, demanding gaze. "Yes." He saw her wrestling with his explanations. She was honestly trying to accept them—and him. He felt it. There was one more test to go, and he felt the fear eat away at him.

"There's one more thing I need to show you, Ann," he told her. "You don't know everything about me, and it wouldn't be fair to you if I didn't tell you the rest."

She stood back as he began to unbutton his white, short-sleeved cotton shirt. Her mind reeled with possibilities, with confusion. "What are you talking about, Mike?"

He stripped out of the shirt, let it drop to the grass between them, then faced her. "When I finished my training, when I took my guardian as part of myself, something happened... My body became marked for life, to identify me as a member of the Jaguar Clan. It happened during the initiation when the exchange of spirits—of hers—" he pointed to the jaguar in the meadow "—and mine occurred."

Ann tried not to stare at Mike as he stood barechested before her. This was the first time she'd seen him partially unclad. He always wore cotton pajamas when they slept together. His chest was magnificent, the dark hair spread across the broad, well-muscled expanse. There wasn't an ounce of fat on him, and when he moved, each set of muscles bunched with clear definition telling her how physically powerful he was.

She scowled at her wandering thoughts. "Are you saying you and the jaguar experienced a transfusion of some kind?"

"Exactly. I hope—pray—that what I show you won't scare you, Ann. It could—and..." He took a deep, ragged breath. "I'm going to turn around and I want you to look at my left shoulder blade...."

This was it. The final truth. Houston felt as if the guillotine was coming down on his exposed neck as he slowly turned around so that Ann could look at his back.

"Oh, my God!"

He froze. And he waited. His heart contracted in anguish over her terror-filled cry. Twisting to look over his shoulder, he saw Ann standing, her eyes huge, her hands pressed against her mouth to stop a scream as she stared wildly at him—at his shoulder.

"It's real," he soothed. "Just try and get ahold on yourself, Ann. There's nothing to be afraid of. Believe me, there isn't. How long have you known me? Have I ever done anything to make you think I'm not—Mike Houston? Not a man?"

As his words fragmented in her mind, Ann felt dizzy and she had to force herself to remain standing. She had to be hallucinating! She had to be! This was impossible! But Mike's words were filled with urgency, with fear. She fought her own fear. Fear of what was real and what was not.

"My God, is that—this—real?" she asked, finally looking up into his blue eyes, which glittered with pain.

"As real as you and me, Ann. Touch it—me...and find out. Whatever you do, don't run, okay? I'm not some kind of—of monster, I'm a man. The same man you knew before you saw this—this mark of initiation into the Jaguar Clan."

Heart pounding, Ann tried to allow his pleading tone to soothe her fear. The mark on his body seemed impossible, and yet it was there. And it didn't go away when she blinked her eyes. No, it wasn't a hallucination. There was a moon-shaped patch the size of her palm that was covered with sleek dark gold fur with black crescents—the same fur as that of the jaguar that stood out in the meadow watching them. Ann wanted to reach out, to touch it to see if it was real.

"Touch me," Houston demanded. "Touch *me*, not 'it,' Ann. Don't separate the jaguar fur from me as a man, because you can't. That fur is a part of my flesh. It's not pasted on, like you're thinking. The first time I saw fur on my body was during my near-death experience. On my arm. But that disappeared when my guardian's energy left me. Then, when I took the initiation into the clan, this—happened. That's why I never let you see my upper body naked before this. I was afraid that if you saw it, you'd run away from me. You'd—'' his brows dipped ''—you'd be scared of me....''

Ann allowed her hands to drop from her mouth. She took a step back. ''This is a lot to handle, Mike. You have to admit.''

He turned to her. Grimly, he whispered, ''Believe me, no one's more aware of that than me. I don't want to lose you...what we have, Ann. But I also know that I won't keep secrets from you, either. If you care for me...then you have to know. I can't live a lie. I never could.'' He avoided her searching gaze.

''And your wife? Did she know—about this?''

''I met Maria here at the village,'' he said wearily. ''She was from Spain.''

''And she was...part of this Jaguar Clan, too?''

He slowly bent over and retrieved his shirt. ''Yes. We met and fell in love with one another while I was here that year, in training. Grandmother Alaria married us. We took our vows and we left the village and went back to the 'real world,' Lima.''

''And she had that same...mark on her body?''

Grimly, he nodded. ''Same mark, same place. Those who go through the initiation receive this mark.''

Ann watched him knot the white shirt in his fist as he stood there before her. The suffering in his eyes tore at her and she felt his fear of losing her. ''And why didn't it save her and the baby when Escovar murdered her?''

Houston looked up at the brilliant blue of the sky above them. ''We have limits on our ability. We're not all equal in skills. Some of it is genetic ancestry, the rest has to do with where we are as a human being on our own spiritual path. We can be killed just like any other human being. When Maria was murdered, I went insane with rage. Escovar...'' Mike shook his head. ''He's pure evil. I don't know why I'm caught up in this death spiral dance with him, but I am. I didn't mean for his wife and children to die in that accident, but he believes I did it on purpose. I didn't. He even killed the man I sent to persuade him that it was an accident.''

''And then,'' Ann whispered, ''you met Tracy?''

''Yes. We fell in love. She worked as an intel officer at the American embassy in Lima.''

"And she was a member of your...clan?"

"No," Mike said, studying Ann's face. Did he dare approach her? Or would she back away from him, the fear he saw in her eyes multiplying. He ached to know if she cared for him enough to deal with this revelation, with him being more than a man in some ways, and in others, so terribly flawed and human.

"Did Tracy know about that?" She pointed toward his left shoulder.

He nodded. "About six months into our relationship, I showed it to her, and I told her the truth, like I'm telling you now."

Ann nodded and rested her hand against her beating heart. "H-how did she react to it?"

"She was scared at first," he admitted. "Like you are now. But she loved...trusted me enough to transcend her fear of the unknown, of something...different and unexplainable in her rational view of the world."

With a shake of her head, Ann muttered, "Houston, you sure as hell know how to throw a woman a real curve."

He didn't know whether to laugh or cry. "Translated, what does that mean?"

Ann dropped her hands. "I need time to think through this, Mike. All of it—my nearly dying, what I saw and felt. This is all just too incredible, and yet it happened. And it's real or I wouldn't be standing here today, alive, and I know it." Moistening her lips, she gave him a beseeching look. "I want to be alone for a while."

"You've got it." Mike tried to control his fear. He knew Ann's proclivity for cold, hard logic. She couldn't be a psychotherapist without that left-brain ability. But would she try and explain all of this away with that powerful and intelligent mind of hers? "I just have one thing to say." Opening his hand toward her, Mike rasped, "This one time, don't let your head do all the talking and deciding for you. Let your heart have a say in this, too. That's all I ask, Ann...just that..."

She wrapped her arms around herself and stood feeling very alone in that moment. Mike was suffering cruelly from her decision to separate from him in order to think all of this over, but it was the only thing she could do. "My heart is always involved in every decision I make," she said gently.

He nodded. "I know it is. It's just that..." Fear consumed him. He'd nearly said *I love you*.... The words froze in his mouth. His jaw ached because he so badly wanted to say them to her. "I know that it's your decision and in your hands—and heart." Mike tried to smile but didn't succeed as he pulled the shirt back over his upper body. "I'll move out of the hut for now. Whatever you decide, I'll abide by it, Ann. If this is too much for you to accept, I'll call Pablo and have him drive you back to Lima. You can catch the first flight going north, to the States, no questions asked. If you want to stay, on the other hand, I can't guarantee it's going to be a picnic. You know what's happened to the other two women I loved." Sadly, he whispered, "And I couldn't protect them...."

"But you did me," Ann said brokenly, tears welling into her eyes unexpectedly. Houston was terribly vulnerable right now. She'd never seen a man drop his guard with her as he had. He looked so lonely, so beaten down by life and its harshness, that in her heart, she knew he was a man of tremendous good. After all, she'd been privy to that side of him. He'd almost died giving her back her life.

Flattening his mouth, he rasped, "Yes, for once..."

"Maybe," Ann said, hope in her tone, "that means something has changed—for the better? I don't know, Mike. I have to think all this through."

Taking in a deep breath, he nodded. "I'd give you anything you want, Ann. Come on, let's go back. I'll move my stuff out of the hut."

Ann stepped aside as he walked over to her. Shamed by her reaction, she couldn't meet his eyes. She felt the hurt radiating from Mike by her actions. She couldn't help herself, but wanted to. Helplessly, she looked out at the meadow. The jaguar was gone! Quickly, Ann looked up at Houston. The agony she saw reflected in his eyes tore at her heart.

"I asked her to leave," he told her apologetically. "You've had enough shocks for one day."

Ann walked back with him, down the well-trodden path. They had walked out here arm in arm, laughing and talking animatedly about so many things. Now, as they walked back, each was well aware of the space between them. She saw Mike fighting himself not to reach out and hold her hand. God knew, she wanted to hold his. She wanted to be held by him right now, but that wouldn't make what she'd just seen or realized go away.

She stole a look up at his strong profile as they walked. Was he man or monster? A genetic freak? Something from Dr. Moreau's Island? A scientific project gone insane? And yet, as her mind clipped along, going over a hundred different events that had involved Mike during the last three months she'd known him, she realized he'd always treated her with respect, and that she had blossomed like an unwilling orchid beneath the sunlight of his personality...and his very large, giving heart. No, it wasn't fair to him to call him a monster. He'd be terribly wounded by that. He'd not acted like a monster toward her or anyone else she'd seen him interact with. If she didn't know he carried the mark of the Jaguar Clan, she would have said he was a normal human being just like anyone else.

Why couldn't she let herself see him for what he was? Maybe because he'd brought her in touch with a reality she'd never seen before—and understood very little about. Here at the village, everyone carried the mark, he said. And, the races and nations represented were as diverse and fascinating as any melting pot of human beings anywhere else she'd been on earth. She understood that hereditary Jaguar Clan blood had been shared around the world over the past millenium. It started in the Americas long ago and over time, due to inter-marriage, the genetic gift was passed on around the world, which explained the diversity of people who came to the village to receive their training. The people here were so uplifting, Ann had discovered. Everyone treated everyone else with such courtesy and genuine warmth and sincerity. There were never harsh words here. No, just the opposite, ever since she'd been here, harmony, beauty and an incredible peace had permeated her like a healing balm.

At the hut, she waited outside while Mike gathered up his few belongings. As he exited, she called, "Wait...."

Houston turned, his bag in his hands. Ann's face was shadowed and thoughtful. He could feel her thoughts, her heart as he could his own, though he'd try to shield himself from most of what was going on inside her. And it took everything to hide his reaction to

her wondering even whether he was some kind of monster. Some
genetic freak.

"You saved my life," Ann said.

"Yes," he answered, not understanding where she was going
with this.

"What do I owe you for that?"

His heart shattered. He tried to keep the disappointment out of
his voice. "Not a thing, Ann. Why?"

"I don't know," she began with an effort. "How do you pay
someone back for saving your life? I wouldn't be standing here
now if you hadn't done what you did."

He cocked his head, trying hard to understand her. There was
such a quandary within her presently. "Listen very carefully to
me, Ann," he growled. "What I did for you was a gift from my
heart to your heart. There are no strings attached to it. Do you
understand? Don't factor anything I did to save your life into whatever decision you might come to. That's separate. It has to be.
You owe *me* nothing."

She regarded his narrowed eyes. "I owe you the truth."

He raised his head and took in a deep, ragged breath. "Yes,
that's all. That's enough...." And it was. His life hung in a real
balance now. He could not share with her that she was his one
true mate for this lifetime. Even though he possessed paranormal
powers beyond most human beings, his life was led and dictated
by the Sisterhood of Light code. That meant that he would never
willingly force anyone into doing something he or she might not
want to do. As fiercely as he loved Ann, he would never allow
her to know she was his true mate until—and if—she decided to
accept him—all of him—for the way he was.

Mike could taste his love for her. They had so much to explore,
to share with one another—and yet he shielded Ann from all of
that. It wouldn't be fair to try and influence her like that. He knew
he could probably persuade her, but at what cost? No, it wasn't
his way. Ann had to decide on her own, based on the experiences
she'd already shared with him and the information he'd placed in
her hands about himself. His hand tightened around the paramedic
pack he held at his side.

''If you need anything, Moyra will be around. She'll help you, okay?''

Ann almost took a step toward Mike. She wanted to reach out, touch him and tell him everything would be all right, but she didn't know that. At least, not yet. The harsh mask was in place on his face. He was hiding a lot from her now.

''Okay....''

He turned and left.

Ann stood there for the longest time. Her need for him was so real that she felt tears form in her eyes. Turning, she sobbed and moved into the hut. Sitting down at the table, she buried her face in her hands and began to cry in earnest.

Chapter 12

"Grandmother Alaria..." Ann called out as she entered the elder's hut.

"Ah, my child, how are you this morning?" She turned slowly, a bowl of bread dough in her floured hands, her eyes crinkled with pleasure beneath her thin, arched gray brows.

Ann clasped her hands nervously. "I've made my decision." She glanced out the window at the clouds beginning to withdraw across the meadow, the sunlight revealing the brilliant colors of the flowers among the knee-high grass.

"I can see that you have." She set the bowl aside. "You are looking for Michael?"

In the last four days, Ann had grown accustomed to Grandmother Alaria's ability to read her mind. At first it had scared her, but during their frequent long talks, Ann had realized the elder would never take advantage of such knowledge. Now the old woman's ability simply reminded Ann that this world was foreign to her and that she needed to suspend her own beliefs. And, because everyone here was like Alaria, it was Ann who felt this great cosmic joke was on her.

"I—yes. Have you seen him?" Ann had seen Houston only

twice, and then only fleetingly. Since he'd left her alone at the hut, which stood on the eastern edge of the village, he seemed to have almost disappeared. Around here, that wouldn't surprise her.

Alaria gently patted her shoulder. "Why, I saw him just a few minutes ago." She pointed a bony finger toward a well-used trail that led down into the jungle near the village. "I think he was taking Sasha, his guardian, to the waterfalls to bathe her. She dearly loves her playtime with him. It's rare she gets it, so Michael is taking advantage of that time here with her."

"Sasha...that's a Russian name, isn't it?"

Alaria smiled kindly, her eyes twinkling. "Wasn't it you who said this was a village of the United Nations?"

Nodding, Ann slid her hand into Alaria's. The woman felt so old and fragile, yet so timeless. She was beloved by everyone here. And now Ann knew why. Something—a small voice within her heart—had urged her to see Alaria and Adaire after Mike left the hut, to ask them the questions that burned through her. She had needed answers. A lot of them. They'd willingly complied. Ann had lost count of the hours she'd spent in their warm, generous company over the last four days.

Releasing Alaria's hand, Ann stepped away. This morning she had awakened early after a deep, healing night's sleep, and had bathed in the hot springs behind the hut. Moyra had brought her a pale pink cotton blouse with short sleeves. Ann loved the tiny bits of lace around the throat and the pearl buttons down the front of the blouse. Nervously, she wiped her damp hands against the white cotton skirt that fell to her ankles.

"Grandmother, I have just one more question."

"Hmm? Yes?"

"I'm sure you already know what it is." She laughed a little out of nervousness. Here in the village, she'd observed, few people spoke because they were in constant telepathic communication with one another. Grandmother Alaria had hushed her worries that everyone could read her thoughts by explaining that in the Sisterhood of Light, it was part of the Jaguar Clan code never to enter another's space on any level without his or her conscious permission. Alaria had revealed to Ann the sensation of someone connecting with her thoughts. Once Ann recognized it, she was able to identify the brief, feathery touch. Because Ann always granted both Alaria and Adaire permission to enter her mind, neither elder spoke to her verbally very often. They usually answered her mentally. She, on the other hand, had no capacity for such a skill and had to use her voice to communicate with them.

"You carry Michael's blood in your veins now," Alaria confirmed. "And you wonder what that means. Are you one of us? One of the outsiders? Or neither? Or both?"

Ann moistened her lips and held Alaria's forest green gaze. "Yes...I wondered."

Picking up the dough, Alaria said, "Until recently, there was no way to share our blood with another. Michael is one of the first of our clan to have made the decision to do this. It is not against our code to do so, but heavy responsibility falls on the shoulders of the clan member who initiates such a process."

"Ever since that transfusion took place, I feel different, Grandmother. It's a little scary. Maybe it's this place...my imagination.... I don't know."

"What is different?" Alaria inquired kindly, plumping the dough on the table.

"I feel things more...more easily, I guess. And I can feel people's emotions and thoughts from time to time."

"And does that bother you?"

"Yes and no. Is that how it is with all of you?"

She chuckled. "Oh, yes, my daughter. It is not something we can turn off or on like a faucet. Like the jaguar, we sense and receive impressions that are so subtle that most humans would never be aware of them. But we are, at times, excruciatingly aware of them. *All* of them."

Ann shook her head. "It must be very painful to live among us."

"If your heart is in the right place—if you stand in balance with yourself—that is all the protection you need, my child. When you have compassion, it does affect how you respond to others, but it does not hurt you. Only if you are out of harmony will it tear you apart internally."

Ann hesitated for an instant. "I *am* different now? Changed?" she finally asked, waiting anxiously for Alaria's response.

"You are, let us say, in the midst of a great change." Chuckling, she pointed upward as a monarch butterfly with huge orange-and-black wings fluttered past the window of the hut. "Like the butterfly which waits within the cocoon until its time is ripe, your gifts will, over time, be revealed to you. But how you will utilize them remains unknown at the present. Michael's blood has mixed with your own. It is a gift of love, my child. Nothing bad will come of it. Later, you may want to return to the village for further training in the arts of the clan. That choice is up to you, though. There will never be pressure on you to develop your abilities or to come here to train. There is no coercion in the Sisterhood of Light. Not ever. Everything is always free choice."

Ann nodded. "Thank you, Grandmother." Now she understood that because of Mike's blood being transfused into her veins, she was considered a member of the clan as well. And she was the first person ever, according to Grandmother Alaria, to be permitted here without genetic ancestry. Ann had found out earlier from Alaria that clan members choosing to violate the laws of the Sisterhood of Light were no longer welcomed back into the village; and if they came without invitation, their rebel-like energy could destroy everything the clan had painstakingly built here over the centuries. Now Ann began to understand that her being here was a special privilege, granted because of Mike's actions. Otherwise, he would not have been able to bring her to the Village of the Clouds at all. That was the code. No one without Jaguar Clan ancestry could come and seek safety here.

"Go see him," Alaria coaxed softly as she kneaded the dough.

"Yes," Ann whispered. "Thank you, Grandmother." She saw the old woman nod, her eyes sparkling as she embraced Ann with feelings of love. Ann left the hut and headed down a well-worn dirt path through the village. Moyra had been showing her the many paths, the stream, and just yesterday she had shown her the rainbow waterfall, which had made Ann gasp with delight and awe. It, too, was otherworldly, more like an artist's rendering of some far-off place. And it, too, was real, for she had dipped her fingers into the warm, healing waters to see if it was. Her left brain, her mental faculties, were always questioning, testing and asking why. Of course, here that question was never asked. The

Jaguar Clan members had no such need; they simply accepted. She could not do that, however—at least not yet—and perhaps she never would.

Her heart pounded with fear and she forced herself to walk briskly even though she wanted to drag her feet. Mike had suffered long enough, and she knew these past four days had been hell on him as much as they had been on her.

The jungle enveloped her, and as she hurried down the sloped path, bushes and vines swatting gently at her legs, Ann prayed for the right words. She prayed for courage. She was so scared.

The path opened up. In front of her was the hundred-foot waterfall. In the morning sunlight the mist rising from around the tumbling water created a vibrant, colorful rainbow across the large, dark pool at the bottom. She searched for Mike and his jaguar guardian. There! Trying to compose herself, Ann forced herself to rehearse what she was going to say to him. Would he understand?

Mike was standing in ankle-deep water. In front of him, lying down in the water, was the huge female jaguar that Alaria had called Sasha. The cat was powerful, with thick, stocky legs and a broad, massive head. Her coat glowed gold, with black crescents over it. Ann swallowed hard as she realized Mike was stripped to the waist, and that the loose cotton pants he wore clung to his lower body emphasizing his powerful thighs. He and his guardian had obviously just been swimming in the deeper part moments before her arrival. His hair gleamed with rivulets of water. When her gaze fell upon his left shoulder, on the mark of the jaguar, Ann felt fear knotting her stomach once again. She was frightened as never before in her life.

Houston sensed Ann's approach. He forced himself to continue to sluice handfuls of water across Sasha's broad, strong back, though his heart was focused on Ann's presence. What had she decided? Mike had not allowed himself to invade her emotional field or her mind while they'd been apart. To have done so was against the highest code of personal ethics in the Sisterhood of Light. He respected Ann too much to breach that code even if the woman he ached for might tell him goodbye.

Slowly straightening, he turned around and met her shadowed, wary gaze. She stood near the bank, her hands clasped nervously in front of her. The soft breeze caressed her loose hair and the sunlight made strands of it come alive with red and gold highlights. He met her gaze and managed a tender smile of welcome. Sasha slowly rose and stood at his left side, her body touching his leg.

"She's so beautiful," Ann murmured, gesturing to the jaguar, which stood gazing up at her.

"What I'm looking at is beautiful to me," he said huskily. There was no more than six feet between them, but there might as well be a chasm. He saw a flush creep into her cheeks, but she avoided his eyes looking around the clearing instead.

"I need to talk to you, Mike. Can we sit down here?"

He nodded, feeling like a man before a jury as the judge was about to read the verdict. To him, it was either going to be a death sentence or a new life. And if it was a new life, what kind of life would it be? Did he really want to put Ann in danger by sharing his life with her? How selfish was he, really? Selfish enough to condemn her to death at Escovar's hands, sooner or later? A bitter taste coated his mouth. He reached down and slid his hand across Sasha's broad, sleek skull. Mentally, he asked her to leave them for a while. The jaguar moved sensuously out of the water and trotted up the trail that led back to the village.

Ann sat down, tucking her legs beneath her and smoothing the cotton skirt over them nervously. Mike sat down no more than two feet away from her, his legs crossed. The sunlight bathed him and he looked so strong and powerful compared to how weak and frightened she felt. Ann saw the ravages, the toll that waiting had taken on him. There were dark rings beneath his eyes and the slashes on either side of his mouth were deeper than usual, as if he were trying to protect himself from bad news. She realized he probably hadn't slept much at all.

Opening her hands, she forced herself to say, "I'm scared, Mike. More scared than I've ever been in my life." She closed her eyes because she couldn't stand the gentleness that came to his expression as she spoke. "You are so heroic, in my opinion. And I'm such a coward. You knew the risks you were taking when you brought me here. You could have left me in that apartment. You could have left me anywhere between Lima and this village." Ann opened her eyes and clung to what little courage she had.

"You didn't have to risk your life to come into Lima, either, when I got ill." Her hands fluttered in the air. "And most of all, you didn't have to risk your life to save mine. On top of it all, you gave me blood. Your blood."

Hot tears stung her lids. Ann looked up and willed them back. "I must have cried buckets in the last four days. More than I've ever cried in my life. And then I realized why. Something happened to me a long time ago. It was something I tried to forget. Something I wanted to forget. But now, more than ever, I realized that pushing it away, trying not to feel the pain it created in me, was staining my life in every possible way."

The tears wouldn't stop and Ann sniffed. She saw the anguish in Mike's features as she rattled on, speaking in hoarse undertones. It was so hard to look him in the eye. So hard. Ann knew she'd been a coward all her life and now was the time to meet Mike with the level of courage he'd shown her. "I know this sounds disjointed. I've done a lot of thinking about it. I cried so much my head ached, but the deeper I got into my emotions, the more I realized what was really going on inside me."

Mike forced himself to remain very still, his hands resting on his knees. How badly he wanted to reach out and touch Ann, to soothe away some of the fear he heard in her voice and felt around her. "What did you discover?" he asked her quietly.

Ann shut her eyes tightly and gripped her hands in her lap. "When I was in the Air Force, working as a flight surgeon, I was both a psychiatrist and medical doctor, helping pilots work through their fears after a crash so they could fly once again. But the military is a hard place for women. I loved flying and I liked the pilots, but I began to feel very vulnerable because of the way the men often harassed the women. It got so I feared men—the looks, the catcalls, the innuendos, the subtle and not-so-subtle ways they wanted to control me or any other woman who was in the military.

"I became so wary of men, of what they could do to me, that I put up strong walls to protect myself from them. I know behind my back they called me the Ice Queen but I didn't—couldn't—care. I lived inside my head. My world as a doctor was safe because I could weigh, measure, prove and see the different aspects of it with my own eyes. Science became my wall of protection.

By remaining there all the time, I could survive." She sighed raggedly. "And I did survive very well within that reality, Mike."

Opening her hands, she said, "Then I met Casey Cameron and I found myself beginning to love him little by little.... He worked hard to gain my trust." Some of the anguish began to leave the region of her heart and Ann knew it was due to Mike's warm, quieting presence. She ran her hand across his strong, firm arm. "Just as I was ready to trust, Casey died in a jet crash. He was torn from me. I stood there thinking that no matter what I touched or tried to love, it died. And then I had a disastrous affair a year after Casey died. Captain Robert Crane..."

Ann squeezed her eyes shut. "I was so horribly lonely after Casey died.... I had grown used to having him in my safe little life. Casey had accepted my world of logic and science. He didn't try to change it or me." Opening her eyes, her voice hoarse, she met and held Mike's compassionate gaze. "Crane was a manipulative bastard. He had seen me and Casey together. He knew the score, and like a predatory animal, he waited until I was at my most vulnerable and stepped into my life. He had all the right moves, the right words, the right everything. He took my reality and twisted it, used it against me. I'm ashamed to say I fell for it and him—completely."

Houston took a deep, raw breath. "He got you on the rebound, Ann."

Quirking her lips, she nodded, too ashamed to meet his gaze. His voice, though, was like a healing balm to her pain. "You could say that."

"The son of a bitch..."

With a helpless shrug, she whispered, "At the time, Morgan Trayhern contacted me and asked if I'd like a challenging position as part of his rescue operation. I leaped at the offer, because to stay in the Air Force would have reminded me too much of Casey—of what might have been with him—and I could no longer cope with the memories. Morgan's offer got me out of the mess with Crane, too. I just didn't have the guts to face him down and tell him what I really felt. That's one thing I've left undone. Morgan provided me an escape, an opportunity to move back into the safe little world of the mind. I could still do the job I loved and feel safe from my heart and feelings.'' She forced herself to look up at him. ''Until you crashed into my life, that is...''

He managed a sour smile in return. ''There's nothing safe about me, is there?'' And he realized more than ever how many changes and demands she'd encountered since being with him. And yet, miraculously, she was still here, with him. Houston felt the powerful connection between them. Would Ann be able to reach out and trust him based upon that? Was she willing to leave her safe little world forever for him? For a life that promised her only danger in the long run?

''Last night, Mike, I finally got it. I got the answer I needed about us.'' Ann eased away from him and, twisting around, she held his somber gaze. ''Your life has been just as rough as mine. People you loved were torn from you, too. The difference between us is that you didn't let your fear of losing me stop you from reaching out....''

Risking everything, he rasped, ''It hasn't been easy, Ann. My heart wanted to reach out to you. But my head, my experiences, told me I had no right to even try. All I could offer you besides my...love...was the threat of Escovar killing you.''

Her heart bounded with joy and dread. Mike had finally used the word *love.* She understood clearly why he had hesitated in using it with her and she knew now that he loved her enough to want to protect her from himself, from his dangerous way of living. She, too, had been afraid to use the word—but for different reasons.

Ann closed her eyes as he caressed her cheek. It hurt to breathe. It hurt to continue to feel on this so very raw, vulnerable level, but Ann pushed on. She met and held his tender, burning gaze as he continued to cradle her cheek. ''I wanted so desperately to reach out from behind my walls and love you in return, but I was afraid, Mike. So very, very scared. You made me happier than I ever thought possible. You've made me laugh more deeply than I ever have before. You've given me so much by having the guts to not let your past, those awful events, crush you, like they did me. I've been running scared all my life. I realized that, too, last night.'' She slid her hand over his and whispered brokenly, ''You were the one with the courage to confront me with the truth of who you are. And I was still hiding and running.''

She leaned forward and slipped her hand, palm down, across his shoulder. Instantly, she felt his flesh tense beneath her touch. ''You wear a badge of honor on your back. I wear scars of my past around my heart.'' Her palm reached the jaguar fur on his shoulder blade. She felt him tense again, as if to try and shield himself from her reaction. Throwing her fear to the wind, Ann moved against him, pressing her breasts to his chest as she slid her hand slowly, purposefully across the patch on his back again and again.

''The crosses you bear are many. The path you've chosen to walk is paved with risks and death. How can I, someone with so many emotional wounds, judge you?'' She moved her hand in a delicate, circular motion, allowing the sensation of his skin against her palm to course through her. His flesh was sun warm and firm. The jaguar fur was soft and thick in comparison, a seamless part of him. Ann eased back on her heels and allowed her hands to come to rest on her thighs as she looked at him. ''You never judged me, Mike. I have no right to judge you or this strange world you live within. Four days ago, you told me I had to make a decision about us. That's not true. We both had a decision to make—for ourselves, about ourselves. If you can love me, faults and all, then I can give myself permission to love you even if you are a part of a greater family known as the Jaguar Clan.''

Her words echoed through him like mission bells being rung on a cool, clear morning, like the music of the heavens and earth combined. Without a word, he slid his dark fingers around the whiteness of her wrists. Gently, he drew Ann's arms downward. ''The love and pain you held for Casey is not something to be ashamed of, *querida*. And what Crane did to you wounded you even more, made another scar on your heart. In a sense, those scars are medals of courage, purple hearts, if you will, that speak of the battles you were in, the wounds you sustained.''

Just his warming, firm touch eased her anguish. There was no mistaking his feelings for her as she drowned in his blue gaze. Tears glimmered in his eyes. Tears for her...

"They were battles I lost, Mike. I'm not proud of what I did, what happened...."

"You didn't lose any battles, Ann. Listen to me," he rasped fiercely, "you were frightened and alone. So very, very alone. I just thank the Great Goddess you didn't stop trying to reach out—especially to someone like me. But then, you're walking a unique path, too. And that path is the same as mine."

Hanging her head, Ann listened to the fierceness behind his words, which sounded like a growl. It wasn't a growl that frightened her, but rather moved through her, sustaining her, nurturing her.

His hands tightened briefly around hers. Ann's fingers were so cold and Mike knew it was because she had been so scared of coming face-to-face with her ugly past and sharing it openly, with trust and vulnerability, with him. "Your courage," Houston rasped, "is magnificent, Ann, in my heart, my eyes. There's not a damn thing you need to be ashamed of. You were young and you were impressionable with Casey. When he died, Crane took advantage of you and you believed in the bastard."

She pulled her hand from his and slid her fingers along his recently shaved cheek. "Walking wounded, aren't we?"

He took her hand and pressed a kiss into the palm. "But we aren't dead, Ann. And we sure as hell have hearts that belong to one another."

"I'm afraid," she quavered. "Afraid for you...afraid of a possible future between us. I'm afraid of the strangeness of your world compared to mine. In the last four days, I've come to accept it on some level, but it's very hard, Mike...so very hard...."

With a groan, Houston nodded. Her palm was so soft and yet so strong. He could smell the faint scent of the spicy orchid soap that she'd used. "I know...and it's your choice, Ann. I love you. For me, right or wrong, selfish as it is, there's no other answer except that I want you. All of you. For the rest of the time I have on our mother, the earth." He smiled tenderly at her. "I know it's not so simple for you, though.... By telling you I love you, I'm placing you in harm's way. Because of that, I can't and won't ask you to stay with me. This has to be up to you. Entirely."

Ann moved into his arms, curled up between his legs, wrapped her arms around his torso and laid her head against his chest. It was such a beautiful sensation—the strength of his sun-warmed flesh beneath her cheek, the powerful thud of his heart against her ear. Mike pulsed with such life, such hope, that it gave *her* hope.

"My whole life has been based upon my fears, Mike. I constructed my safe little world up in my head to avoid feeling. Well, I've found out the real world, reality, doesn't work like that. Every time I think I've got everything in place, life comes along in one form or another and destroys my order." She moistened her lips. "I think I finally got the message that there's no safety in living the life of the mind. I have to step outside of it once and for all. I'm willing to do that, to try that with you. Yes, Escovar is a threat to us. I've lived too much of my life with what-ifs, and with you, I have to surrender all of that. I can't have life on my terms, I've discovered. I have to learn to flow with it, not against it."

"My wild-orchid woman," he whispered huskily against her hair, sliding his fingers around the curve of her shoulder to the juncture of her slender neck. "We can live our lives in fear or we can walk free. That's the choice before you."

"I can be a coward like I've been all my life, or I can choose freedom, can't I?"

"Yes," he murmured, "and freedom always has a price. And in this case, the price could be very high. It could mean your life," he said soberly, his fingers stroking her head.

His touch was silken. Her breasts tightened in need of him, of the love he could shower upon her. Every time Mike stroked her hair, she felt joy replacing her fear.

"The other day, when I was out in the meadow trying to think my way through all of this," Ann told him in a low voice, "I watched a monarch butterfly land on some gold flowers at my feet. It stayed there, close enough for me to touch. I began to look at it in a different light. In a way, I feel like a butterfly. Almost a third of my life has been spent in a cocoon, Mike. And then—" she laughed a little breathlessly "—I met you. My chrysalis cracked open. My world changed. It was opening up and I grew afraid, because the only home I'd ever known was the prison of my orderly, rational cocoon. I'd equated that hard shell around me with protecting me, when really it was imprisoning me and stopping me from growing and being fully human...from being myself.''

Mike's hand stilled on Ann's slender neck. He could feel her pulse beneath his fingers. Smiling against her slightly curled hair, he said, ''So are you going to crawl back inside that prison or be a butterfly, *mi querida?*''

She twisted her head to look up at his wry, smiling features. His eyes burned with such tenderness and love that they melted the last of her fear and replaced it with a growing euphoria that made her feel as if she could do anything—anything in the world—and succeed at it. Even love Houston fiercely, fully when she'd never allowed herself to love at all.

''Butterflies are very delicate.''

''Yes,'' he murmured, leaning down and kissing her nose lightly, ''but they will fly two thousand miles on their migration journey to come back to their home. They might be delicate, but they're tough.''

Ann sat up and spontaneously threw her arms around his neck. ''Oh, Mike, I love you so much it hurts. Please, love me. That's all I need, that's all I ever want from you. Please...''

Chapter 13

The anticipation, the longing, was exquisite as Ann watched the tenderness burning in Mike's eyes turn to undisguised hunger and need of her. He eased up on his knees so that only inches separated them. As he towered over her, his shadow falling across her, her gaze was riveted on his eyes, on his mouth, which had become so terribly vulnerable looking in those seconds after she'd asked him to love her. Ann understood what their lovemaking meant, where it would lead. But today was the first day of forever for her. She was now a butterfly, free to fly, no longer imprisoned in a cocoon that hid her from life, from the man she loved. They had been in a sense like aliens from two very different cultures and times, but the language of the heart had been their mutual connection, the one language they both spoke and understood. It was enough.

His fingers, rough and callused, slid against the planes of her face, eliciting tiny tingles of pleasure. A ragged sound escaped her parting lips as he framed her face and gently angled her chin upward. He was going to kiss her. Ann allowed her hands to come to rest on his powerful chest, the dark mat of hair wiry beneath her fingertips. He had kissed her senseless before, and her body quivered with the memory of those stolen moments, heat flowing and pooling languidly in her lower body. But this was different. She was going to love Mike in return. She was going to breathe her breath of life back into him. This time, it would be an equal exchange as they shared with one another as never before.

Ann felt Houston lean over to claim her parted, waiting lips. Her fingertips dug into his chest as she anticipated—needed—him. She felt his large fingers curve against the base of her skull, strands of her hair tangled within his grasp. His body swayed slightly forward. His moist breath caressed her face. And then she strained upward to meet his descending mouth.

The first skimming brush of his lips against hers brought tears to her closed eyes. His touch was like that of a butterfly, so light and tentative. She could feel him restraining himself, and feel the leashed power vibrating within him as he took her mouth a second time. Hungrily, she opened her mouth as he rocked her lips open. He tasted of sunlight, of the sweet water of the rainbow waterfall, of the lush scent of orchids that grew in nearly every tree that surrounded the Village of the Clouds.

His breath mingled with hers. She took his breath deep within her, and she felt him tremble. As their mouths clung wetly, sliding greedily against one another, she allowed her own breath to flow into him. There was such a connection forged in those meltingly hot moments. She was no longer thinking, guided only by her heart, which asked her to give herself on all levels to Mike. Never in her life, had she done that—she'd always been too afraid. With Mike, with his tender mouth touching, cajoling and teaching hers, she gave as much of herself as she could, knowing that it would take time to surrender herself completely. Only time would help her to truly accept who and what he was.

Everything about him was primal—the pressure of his mouth against her own, the hunger building in his powerful embrace. She heard him groan, the reverberation moving through her like a drum being beaten as her hands slid upward across his bunched, tense shoulders following the curve of his thick neck. An explosion of heat begged to be released within her. As she brushed against him with her breasts, an incredible wave of pleasure shimmered through her. She felt her nipples tightening, clamoring to be touched, cherished and suckled.

Lost in the splendor and heat of his mouth, his breath warm and ragged against her, she buried her fingers in his dark, thick hair. She couldn't get enough of him, she discovered. Her body throbbed and cried out for him. With each movement of his mouth, his tongue sliding provocatively across her lower lip, she whimpered. He was trembling in earnest now, and it wasn't her fevered imagination. Slowly, very slowly, Houston eased away from her mouth.

Barely opening her eyes, her breath shallow and fast, Ann met and clung to his burning gaze. The raw power of him as a man, as someone who desired her, poured through her like cooling rain on a very hot day, it was so welcome. Ann tried to speak, but her heart was skittering wildly in her breast. She kept touching him, unable to stop from exploring his neck, shoulders and magnificent chest. It was as if she'd never realized how love could make her feel. But then, she understood that because of her past, she had never before trusted herself to open up to any man, never allowed herself to feel the divine pleasure that now exploded simultaneously through her body and heart.

"I want you to love me," she said unsteadily. "I want to love you..."

Houston nodded, unable to speak for a moment. Caressing her flushed cheek, he drowned in Ann's upturned gaze, which glowed with such life that he wanted to cry. Here was the woman he knew had lain dormant beneath that mask, that armor she'd worn so long to protect herself. Suddenly she seemed like an innocent in his eyes, not a mature woman with experience and life behind her. And he knew that emotionally she *was* terribly naive. Getting to his feet, Houston drew her upward. Not wanting to lose contact with her, he slid his arm around her and drew her against him.

"Come on, I know where we should go," he rasped.

Ann felt as if she were walking on air rather than the ground. The sunlight felt different, too. The breeze seemed to caress her like invisible hands, making her vibrantly aware of her body as never before. Each time she moved, she felt the action within her body. The sensation was so surprising that she lost herself in the fluidity, the gracefulness, of her own motion. Talk was unimportant.

At the same time, Ann felt Mike's every emotion. Alaria had made her understand that those of the Jaguar Clan had the very same senses as a jaguar; they were incredibly attuned to all living things and could absorb every impression, every emotion and thought without effort. This morning, Ann was glad to be in such intimate attunement with Mike. And even more surprising, she could feel his returning joy, his raw hunger for her, not only in her mind, but in her heart as well, and it left her reeling with euphoria.

They walked for perhaps half a mile down a winding, twisting mountain path in the jungle. At the bottom of the slope, a barrier of thick bushes and trees had grown like a dark green wall where the path ended. Mike halted and turned to her. He smiled knowingly.

"I think you'll remember this place," he said as he moved some branches aside to allow her entrance.

Puzzled, Ann slipped past him. Beyond the barrier of foliage, she saw an oval-shaped pool. Gasping, she halted, her eyes growing large.

Mike stopped beside her. Ann had pressed both hands against her lips, the surprise more than evident on her face. He chuckled softly and drew her against him as they viewed the pool together.

"This is the place in my dreams!" Ann whispered in awe, and she looked up at him. "I dreamed this, didn't I?"

Mike broke into laughter and pulled her fully against him, embracing her hard and swiftly. "Dreams are a part of our reality, *mi querida*. They are the stuff that helps us bring things into this physical manifestation, into the here and now." He kissed her hotly for a long, long time and felt her begin to melt bonelessly into his arms. Reluctantly, he broke away. How easy it was to love Ann. Even more joyful, more wonderful, was her ability to love him equally in return. Mike thought he might die of happiness. The threat of Escovar faded. At least, for a small space of time.

Ann sighed and looked at the pool, shaking her head. "So many times, Mike, I dreamed of this place! It was the only place I could come to—to...help myself. If I undressed and slid into the water,

I felt hope. I felt strength, as if I could keep on going, and I could survive...."

He heard the trembling in her lowered voice. Caressing her hair, he sighed heavily and simply held her. "This is known as the pool of life," he told her. "It's shaped like a womb to remind us that all creatures, two-legged and four-legged, come from the body of a woman, that we are all part of the tapestry of the Great Goddess, that we are all from her." He gestured to the clear water, which looked like glass, the sunlight reflecting off of it like dancing diamonds. "There are many legends about this pool among the Indians of Peru. It is said that anyone who can find it and bathe in it will become healed. Many people, dying of disease, try to find this place."

Ann studied his face and realized how happy he was; there was no longer any strain in his features. "And...do they ever find it?"

Houston smiled tenderly down at her. "The Village of the Clouds is accessible to anyone, two-legged or four-legged, whose heart is in the right place. The Great Goddess judges that, we don't. Many have found this beautiful place and some, with their last breath of life, have fallen into this water, only to be revived, healed and reborn."

She moved her hand against his lower back and felt the deep indentation of his strong spine, the tight muscles on either side of it. "This pool saved my life in my dreams. I knew that—every time I woke up and remembered being here, swimming in it."

"Your heart, *mi querida,*" he said huskily, framing her face and making her look up at him, "is so pure that I have no question as to why She allows you to come here any time you want."

Drowning in his tender smile, in the burning desire in his eyes, Ann took a deep, tremulous breath. It was so easy to lean against his strong, steadying body. "I love you so much," she quavered. "I'm so happy I think I'll burst, Mike."

Houston rocked her in his arms. "I love you, Ann. I always have. I always will." The deep timbre of his voice resounded around the intimate place, ringed by the wall of high, thick foliage. "I never knew I could feel this way, my wild-orchid woman. And it's because of you. You and that very brave, courageous heart in this tiny body of yours."

She eased away and studied him. ''I'm not tiny, Mike Houston—I'm five foot nine and one hundred and forty-five pounds. *That* is not tiny and you know it!''

His grin widened and he threaded his fingers through her hair. She leaned forward like a cat, desiring even more of his touch, and he felt her purr against him in sheer pleasure. ''Tiny compared to me,'' he whispered teasingly, capturing her mouth, feeling her respond like an opening orchid to his cajoling. His hand slid to the back of her head, which he angled so that their mouths fit deeply against one another. She tasted like the sweet honey that formed in translucent globules on the stems of blooming orchids. It was a heavenly sweetness that engulfed him, set him on fire with need of her.

In one smooth motion, he leaned down, and without breaking contact with her luscious, wet mouth, picked her up and carried her forward. The forest ground was soft and warm beneath his bare feet as he laid her on her back against the brown leaves and bark, naturally decaying to make more rich earth for seeds to take life within. He was again reminded of the circle of life—that even in dying, the body surrendered to the power of the Great Goddess, became part of her once again and nurtured and supported new life as a result.

Mike lay next to Ann, bathed by the warmth of the sunlight that fell over them like a loving blanket. In the distance, he could hear the roar of the waterfall. He saw colorful birds flitting among the branches of the tropical trees that surrounded this miraculous place, their songs swelling with joy, a musical tapestry proclaiming life and the sheer beauty of living.

The smile he saw lingering in Ann's eyes made him smile in return. She took his hand and pressed it against her pale pink blouse. The longing, the need for her, embraced him. Mike eased the first shell button from its buttonhole. And then a second, third and fourth. He knew he could not lose control over himself. No, he had to keep a close rein on those basic, almost violent needs. Over the years, with the blood of the jaguar coursing through his veins, he had learned to balance his primal urges and needs with the more refined ones of a human being. And now he understood that the test before him was a daunting one. In his heart, he was afraid that he'd wound his mate instead of drawing her out of that chrysalis and inviting her to be loved fully and without fear. Could he do it? Could he control the animal instincts surging and growing within him, straining to be released and expressed toward her? As the last button slipped free, he looked up and met her half-closed eyes. The softness of her parted lips, the longing in her gaze transformed and tempered his raging hunger for her.

It was all so simple, Mike realized in that moment as he slipped his fingers beneath the edge of the garment and moved it slowly away from her breasts. If he loved her from his heart, and did not allow his primal needs to drive him, he would know what to do. Within seconds, he felt that shift occur within him and his fear dissolved.

Ann wore no camisole beneath the blouse, and her skin shone white and almost translucent in the sunlight. As the fabric fell away, he absorbed the beauty of her breasts, and following his heart, he slid his fingers up around them, feeling her tighten deliciously in response to his caress. He heard her whimper, and she rolled to her side, against him, wanting more...much more.

Leaning over, he suckled her in slow, teasing sips. The honeyed taste of her body was an unexpected gift. Closing his eyes, he felt her arch against him each time he suckled her. The moan of pleasure coming from her only increased the throbbing of blood through his lower, hardening body. In a matter of moments, he had removed her blouse and devoted equal attention to her other breast. She trembled violently as he laid his hand against her bare midriff and eased his fingers beneath the waistband of her skirt, slipping it downward across her hips and legs.

He smiled to himself. Ann wore nothing beneath her clothes. Why would she? The veneer of modern civilization was gone and he was glad. He grazed the gentle swell of her abdomen to her flaring hips and down her firm thighs. He lifted his head and met her smoky eyes, which begged him to continue his exploration of her.

"You are so beautiful...." he rasped unsteadily, and he shed his cotton pants and pushed them aside. Now they were both naked, as it should be. This time, when he slid his arm beneath her neck and eased closer so that she could touch him at will, he saw the languor in her eyes, the heat in them. Leaning down, he felt her lift her head to meet his mouth, to kiss him. As her breasts grazed his chest, he groaned. Her lips were soft, hungry and searching against his mouth. He felt her shyly move her fingers against his chest, beginning to explore him. Understanding her shyness, the hunger driving her as a woman wanting to mate with her partner for life, he placed massive control over himself. Allowing his hand to fall upon her hip, he waited. It was exquisite torture for Houston; every fleeting touch of her fingers, every warm stroke across his hard, tightening flesh, made him feel as if he was caught between heaven and hell.

Nothing could prepare him for her butterfly touch as her exploring fingers ranged downward across his flat, hard belly to his hip. He clenched his teeth and groaned as she innocently caressed him. Perspiration beaded his brow and he trembled savagely as the warmth of her fingers surrounded him, lingered upon him. He drew in a deep, ragged breath. Blood pulsed and throbbed through him. How badly he wanted to open her thighs and thrust hard and deep into her!

Yet he knew that her exploration was motivated by more than just desire. In some part of her, she was still afraid. The errant thought that he was too large for her slipped through his dissolving mind as he sank rapidly into the bubbling cauldron of primal need of her. He knotted his fist in her hair and tried to concentrate on breathing, on controlling himself.

When her hand left him and she slid it around his waist and pressed herself wantonly against him, he had his answer. An explosive breath came out of him as he felt the warm satin of her skin against his taut, throbbing flesh. Capturing her mouth in one swift, hot motion, he eased her onto her back. This time, he would touch her in the most sacred of places that a woman could be caressed, a place of beautiful creation, of life, birth and love.

Lost in the exploding heat and strength of his mouth as he plundered her lips, Ann barely felt his fingers come to rest on her hip. But as he slid his roughened hand across her abdomen, she welcomed it. The ache between her legs intensified to such a degree that she began to moan, her body moving spontaneously at this point. She felt the strength of his hand as he caressed her left thigh, her skin feeling as if on fire beneath his stroking, exploratory touches. As he eased his hand between her damp thighs, she opened to him and gave him access to herself. It was so easy, so beautifully natural as she drowned in the searching splendor of his mouth.

She felt his fingers move in a caressing motion against her, and she moaned and tore her mouth from his. Lights and explosions went off behind her tightly shut eyes. She pressed her face against him and gasped for breath. With each wet, silken stroke, another jagged bolt of heat rippled up through her. It was sweet, unfulfilled agony and she writhed and twisted in his arms, wanting...wanting....

The moment his mouth settled over the peak of her left breast and he slid his fingers into her wet, moist depths, she cried out in startled reaction, but it was from the intense pleasure that gripped her in that moment. She opened completely to him, wanting more, much more of him, more of his stroking, fiery touch. The ache built so rapidly within her that she moaned. Each caress, each stroke made her cry out. Her fingers dug deeply into his shoulders and she arched against him like a bow too tightly drawn. As he suckled her strongly, she suddenly felt a white-hot explosion deep within her body. A little cry of surprise, of relief, tore from her lips.

Yes, yes, my beautiful orchid, open up for me...give yourself to me. Spill your honey over my fingers...spill your sweet, beautiful life over me....

Sobbing for breath, she clung to him in those moments afterward, not understanding what had occurred. She heard his low, growling laugh of raw pleasure as he moved over her, his body like a huge, heavy blanket across her. She felt him slide his hand beneath her hips and guide her fully under him. How natural it was to ease her thighs apart and welcome him to her throbbing, fiery entrance. As he placed his hands on either side of her head, she opened her eyes and looked up, up into his narrowed stormy eyes, burning with a savage fire that consumed her. His heart thundered against hers. Her nipples were tight and taut against the dark, springy mass of hair on his chest. He was smiling down at her, a smile so tender and yet so wild and untrammeled.

She felt his power for the first time. Every inch of his body was taut under his brutal control. Every time she touched him, he quivered. As she settled her hands on his hips and guided him against her entrance, he growled. It was a low growl of such utter pleasure that the sound traveled straight through her, to the heated cauldron boiling and throbbing with life in her lower body. She felt him press against her, and she moved her hips to invite him into her. He lifted his head, his teeth clenched, the perspiration standing out on the taut planes of his face. His fists knotted against her hair. She felt his massive control and began to dissolve it by following her heart, allowing the love she had always felt for him to flow out of her toward him in those golden moments.

Just as water gives nourishment to the dry, thirsty land, she understood that she was the water, the nourishment he sought, that he needed as a man. How easy it was to lift her hips and capture him, invite him into her most sacred place. Her lashes fluttered downward as she felt him surge forward, deep and swift, taking her, being consumed by her wet, warm depths. A cry tore from her—a cry of triumph, of elation as she rocked with him in a rhythm that matched the beat of their hearts.

His arms came around her, molding her against him. Crushing his mouth to hers, he clasped her to him, burying himself deeply in her welcoming, responsive body. The gliding, throbbing heat, the pressure and rhythm combined, and she felt the world slipping away as, locked in a tight embrace, their breaths ragged, their cries mingling, their slick bodies moving with the ancient, throbbing rhythm of the earth herself, they fused into oneness.

Sunlight danced and shimmered within her. She could not get enough of the taste of him, the smell of him, the texture of his roughened face against her own, softer one. He held her hard against him, thrusting into her, taking her, loving her and making her one with him. Why had she waited so long for this? For him? Those thoughts dissolved beneath the shattering, splintering explosion that occurred within her. His arms tightened. Breath rushed out of her. She arched against him, her head thrown back, her fingers digging deeply into his massively bunched shoulders. His responding growl of absolute pleasure, of absolute authority, resonated through her. A rainbow of colors continued to explode and expand through both of them as they gave each other the gift of themselves. Nothing else mattered in those raw, primal heartbeats out of time. Their love, so long denied, was finally satisfied, fulfilled. For Ann, it was like dying and being reborn all over again, the pleasure was so intense. So heartbreakingly beautiful.

The living warmth of the water being sluiced across her breasts and shoulders made Ann smile languidly. She lay in Mike's arms, floating bonelessly in the pool, the water like millions of hands touching her, healing her and making her feel every emotion within like a million blazing suns. He was lounging in the shallows, cradling her between his massive thighs. Each droplet of water that fell from him onto her made her sigh with pleasure as she nuzzled her face against the column of his massive neck.

"You have the most beautiful, giving body," Houston rasped against her ear. "You're just like an orchid—mysterious, closed until just the right amount of heat, sunlight and water are provided, allowing one lucky man to watch you grow, blossom and share the honey of yourself with him." He cupped his hand in the water and moved it down across her left breast. The nipple tightened automatically as he followed her luscious curves. She moaned and pressed a kiss to his neck as he held her tenderly.

"I like being an orchid," Ann whispered, resting her head on his shoulder and looking up at him. Mike gazed down at her. The undisguised happiness in his eyes embraced her as nothing else could. Did he know how young he looked now? So many of those stress lines had disappeared from his face that she marveled at what love, expressed and fulfilled, could do to a person. She wondered if she looked any younger, and then laughter bubbled up through her. She watched his mouth curve in response to her mouth.

"Do I look younger, too?" she asked playfully.

Chuckling, he smoothed her damp hair from her flushed cheek. "Love always makes you feel like living, *mi querida.*"

With a contented sigh, Ann took his hands and moved them across her belly. His dark fingers splayed out against the stark whiteness of her flesh. Light against dark. And hadn't they both suffered cruelly in their own personal darkness for so many years?

Alone? Hurting, yet trying to go on? Ann closed her eyes and rested completely against him. The solid beat of his heart was so steadying, so reassuring to her.

"I'm afraid to feel this happy, Mike," she admitted softly. "I've never felt like this before, ever...."

He caressed her face with his wet hand. Leaning down, he licked the droplets of water off her cheek. "Me either. But," he said with a laugh, "I'm not going to let my stupid head get in the way and ruin a perfectly beautiful day with my mate, either."

His laughter vibrated through her and she smiled winsomely. "You're right—I think too much."

Gently moving his hand across her belly, he whispered, "Think about this, then. Think about the child of love that will come from our being together today...."

Instantly, Ann's eyes flew open. With a gasp, she twisted around in his arms. "What?"

Mike regarded her through hooded eyes. "Didn't you know the other legend about this pool?" he asked as he drew her back into his arms.

She melted against him, her arms curving around his neck. "No, what?" Her abdomen tingled where he'd gently rubbed her with circular motions of his large, dark hand. She brushed several damp curls off his brow.

"That lovers come here, wanting a child to express their love for one another, and conceive?"

She lay very still in his arms for a moment. "I—I didn't know that..."

Mike eased her over him, positioning her so that he could look into her shadowed features. "Does it bother you?"

Ann shook her head and stroked his face. "No...it's just that...I felt something, too, when we...when we were loving one another. I thought that because I was finally able to love you so openly, so freely, that a baby would be created by us."

"Well," Houston murmured, satisfaction in his voice, "in about nine months, my wild orchid, I'm going to be here to help you deliver that gift into my hands."

She saw the tears glitter in his eyes as his hand splayed against her abdomen and he looked down at her belly. There was such raw hope and emotion in his voice.

"Oh, darling..." she whispered, and she pressed his face against her breast and just held him. Mike had lost his wife and his unborn baby. How could Ann have ever forgotten that? As happy as he was, Ann saw flecks of fear deep in his eyes and knew that Mike was afraid for her—for them.

Some of her euphoria dissolved as she held and rocked him in her arms. He trembled violently, once, and then she felt him release his fear. Sliding her fingers through his damp black hair, the sun warm and bright above them, she whispered, "I love you with my life, Mike Houston. And if I'm lucky enough to be carrying your baby in my body, then I'm the happiest woman on the face of this earth. Do you hear me?" She framed his face with her hands and forced him to look up at her. The fear was still there, maybe a little stronger than before. He was human, after all, she realized. Being of the Jaguar Clan didn't guarantee that life would be any easier. In fact, just the opposite was true. Smiling tenderly at him, she kissed his closed eyes, his nose and the corners of his suffering mouth.

"It won't happen again, Mike. I know it won't. Like you said before—we've paid all the tolls along the road. We got to meet...to love one another because we've *earned* this privilege. I don't believe for one moment that I'll be torn from you like Maria or Tracy were." Ann sniffed and blinked back tears as his lashes lifted and he studied her. Looking around at the beauty and peace of the pool, Ann quavered, "I may not know much about metaphysics like you do, but I know in my heart of hearts that we'll be here, nine months from now. I want to have our baby in this pool. I want her to be born into all the love she can possibly experience. Do you hear me?" She pinned him with a fierce gaze, her voice low and trembling.

Instinctively, in a protective gesture, Mike slid his hand across her belly once more. "I hear you, *mi querida.* I hear you..."

Another thought occurred to Ann in that moment. She decided to give voice to her fear. "Will this baby be like you?"

Tenderly, he smoothed the hair from her cheeks. "You mean, will the baby be 'different'?" He saw concern banked in her beautiful eyes and understood the nature of her question. It was one thing for Ann to try and adjust to his alien world. It was another to raise a child with special attributes.

"Does a baby who has the possibility of becoming a great artist or writer differ any more than the child we will have? No," he rasped, "our baby will be a blend of both of us. Whether or not he or she ever chooses to use the skills inherited from the Jaguar Clan is not up to us. Right now, I want to think of marriage, *mi querida*. I want our baby to have my name. I want it to have you as its mother and me as its father. Whatever talents or gifts it is born with remain to be seen. Let's take this one step at a time. It's all we can do."

Closing her eyes, Ann felt the safety of Mike's arms, heard the low growl of his voice, and they soothed her fears, her questions and uncertainties about their future. She was seeing his male side now, his need to fulfill his obligations to her. Mike would never be satisfied with just living with her; he wanted to marry her, to give her his name and what little protection he could offer her and the baby she now carried deep within her body. His possessive instincts were overpowering and she didn't try to combat them. There was something so primal about him, about those of the Jaguar Clan, that it would be useless to fight their sense about some things. *Marriage*. The word held such sweet promise and yet such fear for her.

"Marriage..." she whispered uncertainly.

Concerned, Mike gazed deeply into her blue-gray eyes. "You're worried that we can't make it as man and wife? That our worlds are so different that we won't be able to find any middle ground?"

Ann realized he was reading her heart and mind again. Gently, she slid her fingers across his roughened cheek. "Yes..."

"Life has to be lived one day at a time, wild orchid. One moment at a time. Outside the walls of this place, it's a crapshoot. There are no guarantees. Nothing. The moment we step back across that bridge, our lives are at risk." Leaning down, he caressed her mouth tenderly. As he eased away, his eyes burning with the passion of life that ran through him as surely as sunlight stroked the heated earth, he whispered, "The cosmic joke is that everyone's life is at risk every day. We don't know when our time will be up. We don't know how we are going to die. Billions of people on the face of Mother Earth live this way. Life is risky, Ann. I have an added danger in mine—Escovar. And yes, that does put you in greater jeopardy. All we can do is be careful, watchful, and stay ahead of him and his men. I promise you," he said in a deep, resonating tone, "that I will do *everything* in my power to keep you and our baby safe and shielded. With my life, I promise that to you...."

Tears stung her eyes as she closed them and pressed her brow against his thickly corded neck. His arms drew her tightly to him. All her senses were wide-open and she felt his fear, his suffering and anguish for her and the baby she carried. Mike was right—life was tenuous at best. She could step on a venomous snake and die. Or she could contract a hemorrhagic fever and bleed to death. Yes, he was right—life was a risk twenty-four hours a day. Again, she had to adjust her attitude toward living, toward marriage and becoming a mother and a wife.

A quivering smile touched her lips as she caressed his strong, naked shoulder. Mike felt so invincible to her, strong and pulsing with the power of life. She wished that same strength could live within her. Perhaps that was the gift of the jaguar. At least her baby would have that same powerful vital force, that sheer deter-mination and will to not only survive, but to live life on the edge and with passion—a passion she was only now beginning to un-derstand and appreciate by loving Mike.

"One day at a time," she promised him. "One hour at a time."

Caressing her hair, he pressed a kiss to the sunlit strands. "We can do this together. I know we can." His fingers curved about her skull and he closed his eyes as he rested his cheek against hers. "Love is the most powerful, the most healing emotion we have. It's ours, Ann. If we have the courage to embrace it fully, without reserve...if we can surrender to it entirely, then we've got more than most people will ever have...."

Raggedly, she whispered, "Yes, I understand that...and I'll try, Mike. I swear I'll try with every breath I take into this body of mine. I'm not there yet, but I'm going to try...."

Houston's fingers tightened on her silken hair. It was all he could ask of Ann. He knew she had not yet surrendered all the way to him—nor had she completely accepted the possibility of being his wife and the mother of his child. Only time...and the will of the Great Goddess...would allow her to cross that threshold between them. Only then would their love be strong enough to carry them forward into their new life together. The commitment needed to be at a soul-deep level, like a foundation being laid. For their lives to entwine fully, that foundation had to be there; otherwise, their relationship would deteriorate over time. He knew she didn't want that, and he didn't, either, so he would give her the time and space necessary to adjust, accept and then surrender to him, in all ways. He wanted this to happen naturally. Beautifully.

Chapter 14

Ann's heart was heavy. They were going to leave the Village of the Clouds within the hour. It was her understanding that because she was an outsider to the energy forces that kept all those within the village safe, she and Mike had to leave in order to ensure the protection of the villagers. Further, Mike had received disturbing news from his government sources that Escovar was mounting a campaign to take another village. No, real life was intruding upon them, whether they liked it or not.

Grandmother Alaria sat at the table in their hut as they packed their meager belongings. A number of new friends Ann had made over the last two weeks had dropped by individually and embraced her, blessed her and wished her a safe journey on her newly chosen path.

She was kneeling on the mat in the bedroom of the hut, folding clothes that she'd recently washed and sun dried. Mike was nearby, looking through the black paramedic pack he always carried with him no matter where he went, checking the contents and organizing items in case he had to use them.

Ann's body glowed from recent lovemaking they'd shared. She lifted her head to look at the man she loved. As if sensing her attention, Mike glanced in turn. Their gazes met. Her lips parted and she drowned in his tender look. His love for her was so strong and palpable that wave after wave of warmth embraced her. She sighed softly. Yesterday, they had been married by Grandmother Alaria, with the entire village in attendance. It had been a beautifully moving ceremony, the thought of which still made tears come to her eyes. Ann was beginning to understand on a much deeper level about the people of the Jaguar Clan. She knew now that the incredible loving power they held was centered in life and family.

Because she was now considered one of them due to her blood transfusion and becoming Mike's mate, she had to learn to accept the unsettling feeling of being in touch with the villagers' subtle emotions. And her own startling ability to share her thoughts and emotions with Mike was remarkable.

Mike didn't have to say "I love you" aloud. All he had to do was think about the love he held in his heart for her and a warm euphoria flowed through Ann just like a physical embrace. It was, as Grandmother Alaria put it wryly, a gift and a curse. There would be times, the old woman had explained the night before, as they shared their last meal with her and Adaire when they would fight and disagree, and Ann might want to ask Mike to shield himself from her. After all, that was the only fair thing to do, since she didn't possess his more advanced abilities.

Or did she? Ann wasn't sure. She eased back on her heels and continued to fold the clothes across her lap. Nestling her hand against her abdomen, Ann could sense the baby she and Mike had created down by the pool of life. She knew as a doctor that it was impossible to know this soon that she was pregnant, yet there was a warm flame of feeling, a thrilling joy that resonated throughout her belly and up to her heart ever since that day. Grandmother Alaria had confirmed that she was carrying a baby—a very special little girl soul, she had told them with a twinkle in her eyes.

Suddenly a voice startled her out of her reverie. "Have any names come to you yet, Ann?" Grandfather Adaire asked softly as he leaned on his staff at the door, watching her through kindly eyes. He then exchanged a tender smile with his wife.

Ann looked and laughed, a little embarrassed. She'd given

Adaire and Alaria permission to monitor her thoughts and feelings while at the village. They and Mike were the only ones, however, and everyone else remained shielded, as was the policy.

Mike smiled and placed his paramedic pack aside to welcome Adaire. He took the folded clothes off Ann's lap. "I know she's thinking about it, Grandfather."

"Aye...."

As Mike's hand settled over hers, Ann leaned against his strong, steady body. Today he was dressed once again in his combat uniform. That frightened her. It was a reminder that once they left the safety of the village, Mike would be a hunted man again—but so was she, now.

"How do you name a baby you haven't seen yet?" Ann teased them. "This is not fair. You know so much more than I do...." She leaned over and pressed a kiss to Mike's recently shaved cheek. Each minute here with him was precious, moments she wanted to brand into her heart and memory.

A rumbling chuckle rolled out of Adaire. "She is a child of the Jaguar Clan. She will come into your dreams very shortly, my dear. Believe me, she will become a pest to you each night you close your eyes. You think you will sleep?" He slapped his thigh and chuckled again. "This little girl is precocious. She will tell you exactly what she wants to be called when she arrives."

"That is true," Alaria said as she rose slowly to her feet. "I am being called," she told them. "I will meet you down at the bridge?"

Mike nodded. "Of course, Grandmother."

Ann saw the love between Adaire and Alaria as the old woman reached out and touched her husband's hand briefly and then was gone. With a sigh, Ann said, "I don't care what our baby wants to be called so long as she's born healthy." She cast a glance up at Mike, who had sobered slightly. "That's all I want. And a safe place to have her..."

Houston's arm tightened around her shoulders briefly. "I'm going to do everything I can to keep you—and her—safe." Frowning, he glanced at Adaire, then continued, "The best thing, we believe, is to have you go back to the States. Wait for me there.

Escovar won't follow you. I could fly up every few months and see you and—''

"Absolutely not!" Ann muttered defiantly. "I'm not leaving your side. I need you, too, you know."

"Ann," Houston soothed, keeping his voice purposely low and shielding her from his chaotic feelings, "we've discussed this before."

"Yes," Ann said firmly, "and we've agreed that I'll work in the villages as a doctor. My name will change because we know Escovar has linked me to you, as well as to Morgan, whom he hates almost as much as he does you. Yes, I know—" Ann held up her hand as Mike started to interrupt, "—that he'll try to find me and kill me because of that link. What is in my favor is that he doesn't realize we love one another, or that we're married. I can pose as a doctor from the Peruvian Red Cross, on assignment to this region. You said yourself that Escovar usually leaves the medical people in the villages alone. He won't kill priests or nuns, either."

"It's the only place of light in his dark heart," Houston growled. "I don't know what stops him. He kills everyone else— babies, children, women and men. His murdering soldiers don't give a damn about life, not at all...."

Ann felt his raw, cutting anguish even though she knew he was trying desperately to shield her from his worries about her safety. Moving her hand from beneath his, she pressed it against her abdomen. "Mike, don't do this to yourself. Please. I'm a doctor. I can help the people—your people. God knows, they need someone like me in every village, but that's not going to happen, either. I promised you that I'd stay in areas that you considered safe, far away from wherever you're going to engage Escovar as he tries to take over Ramirez's territory. I won't like not seeing you for weeks at a time, but I know you have a job to do. I'm not asking you to stop doing what you need to do, and you can't ask it of me, either."

Mike tried to protest.

Ann held up her hands. "I'm a doctor," she repeated. "I save lives in my own way, just as you do. Besides, I've grown to love the people of the villages—they are born and bred in the same mystical land that is our child's heritage. We're both committed. Neither of us is going to leave the field of battle we've chosen to take a stand on.''

''But,'' Houston said huskily, glancing over at Adaire for help, ''you're pregnant, Ann.'' He slid his hand across her belly in a tender motion. ''I lost one family—'' He stopped abruptly.

Ann reeled internally as his feelings deluged her. His terror over losing her and the baby were haunting him even more than she'd realized.

''Children,'' Adaire counseled soothingly, ''be at peace with yourselves. Each of you must trust and surrender to the other. Each of you must respect the needs of the other to pursue the goals you've chosen to work toward. It is that simple. You must make your individual decisions work for, not against one another.''

Bitterly, Ann admitted, ''I wish you could leave Peru, Mike. That would solve everything. If you could come back to the States, lead a normal life there—''

''My child,'' Adaire said in a low tone, ''Michael is in a death spiral dance with Escovar. No matter where in this world he tried to go, Escovar would seek him out, find him and try to kill him. It is better that this dance be played out here, in Peru, on the turf of the jaguar. It is to Michael's advantage that it be done here. I know that the constant threat to his life is very hard on you. But it would be a threat wherever you tried to live. You cannot outrun fate.''

Frustrated, Ann fought back tears. ''I keep hearing of this death spiral dance.'' She glared at Mike and then at Adaire. ''What is it?''

Houston sighed raggedly. ''It's something that was chosen by both of us—Escovar and I—before we ever came into physical bodies in this lifetime. There is some old karmic debt still unresolved between us. Only someone like Grandmother Alaria would know what that debt is. She is the only one allowed to see the Akashic Records, a place where all our deeds, actions and words in our hundreds, maybe thousands of lifetimes, are accurately recorded.'' Shrugging, Mike gave Ann a gentle squeeze. ''I don't know why Escovar is after me like this. I can't explain why his family died in that accident, or why he chose to murder my family in revenge...."

"It's like a stain on the soul," Adaire interjected gently, his gaze on Ann. "A stain can be caused by some terrible decision made by one soul against another in a particular lifetime. In order to remove the stain, the same event must be turned around, opposite of what it was before, and played out again. In that way, the scales of karma are once again in balance."

Struggling to understand, Ann whispered brokenly, "Lifetimes? Reincarnation? My God, I've never even considered them as possibilities. But then, to tell me that Mike murdered Escovar's family in one of these so-called lifetimes—"

Adaire held up his hand. "Wait, child," he murmured, "you cannot know all the possibilities that occurred between Michael and Escovar. I'm not at liberty to speak of it, either. To do so would be to interfere in the karma between them, and the clan can never interfere on that level. To do so is to break the code. Michael understands this, and I know it's very daunting for you to try and comprehend it all. A death spiral dance is a simple way of saying that Michael is locked in a life-and-death struggle with another person. In this case, Eduardo Escovar. And like actors, they must play out their parts. They must walk through the scenes, make decisions and work through their karma with one another."

Sniffing, Ann gave Mike a dark look. "And no one knows what the outcome will be, right?"

Unhappily, Mike gently rubbed her tension-filled shoulders. He wished that this topic hadn't come up. "That's right, *mi querida.* Look, don't worry about it. I've been evading that bastard for over ten years now. I'm slowly but surely getting the upper hand on him. We stopped him at the village of San Juan. I'll stop him at the next village he's preparing to attack in a couple of weeks. The people here are *worth* protecting, Ann, regardless of the death spiral he and I are locked in."

"Call it what it really is, my blood brother—a major death spiral confrontation between the Sisterhood of Light and the Brotherhood of Darkness," a woman's voice interjected. "It is the first of several clashes between the light and dark before the darkness descends upon all of us and we are hurled collectively into the pit of hell.''

Ann snapped her head toward the entrance to the hut. A woman, very tall, built like a lithe, well-muscled jaguar and dressed in camouflage combat fatigues just like Mike, stood there looking commandingly at them. The power emanating from her made Ann gasp. The woman had a rifle slung over her left shoulder. Her hair, backlit by the morning sun, was a shining blue-black waterfall, like a glistening raven's wing. It was her proud, almost arrogant carriage that made Ann tense. This was no ordinary woman. No, she was special...and dangerous.

Quickly, Ann perused her golden face, which glistened with a sheen of perspiration. Her willow green eyes were large, intelligent and slightly tilted. Her black hair framed her oval features, emphasizing her high cheekbones and full, grimly set lips. On the web belt around her slender waist were weapons of war. Ann saw: grenades, a deadly knife and a canteen. Across her shoulders were bandoleers of bullets for the rifle she carried.

Ann had seen female combat soldiers before, stateside, but never anything like this woman. She saw the glittering laughter in her eyes, the supreme, unshakable confidence in her proudly thrown back shoulders, and the way she lifted her chin at a cocky angle. There was no doubt in Ann's mind that this woman was, indeed, a member of the Jaguar Clan—she *looked* half human, half jaguar. One second Ann thought she saw a jaguar covering the woman soldier, the next, that stunning human visage reappeared. Power emanated from her in battering waves of such magnitude that Ann found herself recoiling.

''Shield yourself!'' Adaire growled. ''This woman is with child, Inca. You know better than that.''

Ann watched the woman give Grandfather Adaire a smile of annoyance, a one-cornered lift of the right side of her mouth. ''Old One, as usual, you are here to chide me.'' In the next instant, Ann felt the battering waves of energy cease, and she breathed an inward sigh of relief. Mike leaped to his feet, calling out Inca's name. Ann looked up at him in surprise as Adaire moved aside, scowling heavily in displeasure.

"You came!" Mike said, opening his arms to the newcomer a
he walked toward her.

With a husky laugh, she stepped into the hut, opened her arm
and gripped Houston hard, slapping him heartily on the back.

"Of course I did, my blood brother!" She buried her fac
against his shoulder and hugged him fiercely.

Ann blinked. Who was this woman? Even when shielding her
self, she was like a thousand suns radiating in the small space o
the hut. Her raw animal energy, her power was palpable. She wa
a leader, there was no doubt. And, Ann noticed, she was only a
few inches shorter than Mike. The woman's willow green eye
grew huge and black as she held Mike in her tight grip of obviou
warmth and welcome. There were tears in them, Ann realized
Slowly standing up, she felt very weak and terribly human i
comparison to this woman Adaire had called Inca. She was o
Indian origin, no question. Her dark golden skin, thick black hai
and classically beautiful face indicated that she was from some
where in South America.

"It is so good to see you," Inca whispered huskily as she finally
released Houston.

He laughed a little and gently cupped her shoulders. "I don'
believe it! I never thought I'd see you again, Inca.... Hell it's *goo*
to see you!"

Ann heard raw, undisguised emotion in Mike's voice. Confused
she looked from her husband to Grandfather Adaire. She'd neve
seen the elder angry before, but he was angry now. It was nothing
that overt, but clear in the way his brows were drawn down and
the line of his wide, usually gently smiling mouth spoke of dis
pleasure.

"You are not welcome here, Inca. You broke our code a long
time ago and you know our laws. You were never to step foo
back into the village."

Grandfather Adaire's voice felt like thunder to Ann. And she
reeled internally. Inca glared momentarily in the elder's direction
"I am not welcomed anywhere, Elder," she snarled back. "Do
not get tied in knots over this. I am leaving very shortly,
promise." Then she wiped the tears from her eyes. "I had to come
Michael. Your guardian told me you were here, that you'd taken

a new mate...." Inca turned, suddenly devoting her considerable attention to Ann, who stood uncertainly before her. Without hesitation, Inca strode over to Ann, her hand extended in friendship.

"I am Mike's blood sister, Inca. I am sure no one has told you of me. I am the black sheep of the Jaguar Clan—not quite pure enough of heart to be accepted and yet not dark enough of heart to be embraced by the Brotherhood of Darkness, either." She laughed heartily.

Stunned by her warm regard, Ann stared down at the woman's extended hand. How beautiful she was, in every way—full of such grace, such sinuous movement that it took Ann's breath away. There was an unearthly glow around her and Ann wasn't sure what that meant. Forcing a nervous smile, she lifted her hand and slipped it into Inca's.

"I'm Ann Houston. It's nice to meet you." Ann felt the strength in Inca's callused hand, realized the woman soldier had monitored the amount of pressure she used in her grip. Yet, as Ann met that willow green gaze, she felt an incredible joy embrace her. It was real. This woman was real. Her emotions were sharper, more ragged, less steady than Mike's or Grandfather Adaire's, but Ann felt only goodness radiating from her.

"It is good that my blood brother found the mate he has been searching a lifetime for," Inca told her in a low, purring tone. "I have prayed to the Great Goddess to ease his pain, his suffering and loneliness." She looked at Ann, her eyes narrowing as she studied her from head to toe. "Yes...you are the one." Inca turned and grinned at Mike. "This is truly a day to celebrate, my brother!"

Mike moved to Ann's side. He slid his arm around her shoulders and drew her gently against him as he met and held Inca's glistening gaze. "Yes, it is. I'm glad you could meet Ann."

"I am sorry I could not be here for the joining ceremony yesterday." Inca looked to the left and glared defiantly at Adaire, who stood tensely. "The Old One would probably have hemorrhaged on the spot if I had shown up, unannounced, on one of the five most sacred days a Jaguar Clan member can have." She laughed harshly. "Do not worry, I'm leaving, Old One. I can feel your anger stalking me."

Ann saw Grandfather Adaire's face grow shadowed. "You threaten all of us by coming here without permission, Inca, and you well know it. As usual, your own selfish needs and whims take precedence over the safety and consideration of others. You have not changed at all."

Scowling, Inca returned her attention to Mike. "There is trouble out there," she whispered tautly. "I ran into a couple of jeeps with Escovar's men not more than ten miles from here. They are like jackals hunting and sniffing around—for you." She placed her hand on his shoulder. "I must leave. I must journey back to Brazil, to my own death spiral dance, my brother. I wanted to be here, in person, to be a part of your happiness and to meet Ann—your life mate."

Ann felt the powerful love that Inca held for Mike. It was a stunning, fierce kind of love yet one that was very different from her own love for Mike. So many questions pummeled her, but she remained silent as the drama played out between the three members of the Jaguar Clan.

Gripping her hand, Mike rasped, "I had hoped to see you—but I knew the decision of the village elders about you, so I never thought you'd come back...."

Inca grinned wickedly. "Elder Adaire knows that I make and break rules as I need to, my brother. That is another reason why I'm not welcome here. Black sheep never are." She chuckled and released his hand. In one motion, she took a leather thong from around her neck.

"I have a gift for you, Ann," Inca said, her voice becoming a silken purr. "Here, this is for you—you are now my sister-in-law because you are my blood brother's mate."

Ann watched as Inca lifted the leather loop with a white claw hanging from one end of it and settle it over Ann's head, arranging it against her neck.

"I do not have much money." She grimaced. "I'm just a green warrior in the name of Mother Earth and the Amazon Basin which is being destroyed acre by acre. I do not have a job in São Paulo or Rio de Janeiro to make coins for anything fancy but—" she pressed her hand against Ann's upper chest, where the necklace now lay "—this is a gift from my heart to yours. This is a jaguar's claw. In time, you will understand what it is, what it means to you. Wear it—'' her eyes narrowed upon Ann's ''—*always*. Don't ever be without my gift, my sister.''

The heat of her hand was like a burning brand into Ann's flesh. Though Inca was not pressing hard, it felt like the thick, heavy claw was being pushed through Ann's flesh, into her bones and body. As she stood, riveted by Inca's closeness, she saw the woman's face change into that of the jaguar guardian who protected her. It was the face of a huge male with glittering green-and-gold eyes. Closing her eyes, Ann could barely contain the power and fierce sense of protection that Inca covered her with in wave after wave of heat and light.

As Inca slowly removed her hand, Ann swayed. She felt Mike's grip become more firm. Dizzy, she opened her eyes, stunned at the feelings in her chest. Without words, Ann lifted her hand. Yes, the claw was still resting there. No, it was not inside her, as it felt right now. She looked up at Inca. The hardness, the arrogance was gone in that fleeting moment. Instead, Ann saw a very beautiful woman, childlike in her terrible vulnerability and with eyes filled with such loneliness that it caught Ann completely off guard. She realized Inca was allowing her to see the *real* her, rather than the mask she wore. And suddenly Ann connected to her on a very familiar level. Inca was a lot like she herself had been all her life—a butterfly trapped in a cocoon. Yet as she met and held Inca's glittering gaze, Ann felt a depth of pain in her that was so overwhelming, she wondered how the woman was surviving it at all.

''I must go,'' Inca whispered hoarsely, self-consciously wiping her eyes and then stealing a look at Adaire, who stood near them threateningly. ''I have overstayed my welcome.'' Swiftly, she leaned forward and kissed Mike on the cheek. Then she carefully embraced Ann.

''Be strong, my new sister-in-law. Love him. He has gone too long without it. Having you strengthens all of us, believe me....'' She released Ann and shared a gentle smile with her. Then she extended her hand toward Ann's belly. ''May I? May I bless you and the baby you carry?''

Touched to the point of tears because she saw and felt Inca with such compassion, Ann nodded. "Of course…"

Kneeling down on one knee, Inca gently pressed her cheek against Ann's abdomen. "Little one," she crooned, "know that you are loved, so loved…. If I had parents like yours, I would be eager to come into this world, too. Even in the darkness to come, I am here. I am your aunt. I promise you, I will protect you with all my heart…my spirit…with the last breath I take. May the Great Goddess bless you, your mother and your father." Inca closed her eyes and pressed her hand more surely against Ann's belly. "I swear this…."

As Inca rose in one fluid motion, Ann felt an incredible sensation of love, of commitment, tingle up through her entire body. Even though Grandfather Adaire disdained Inca, Ann found herself admiring her. She was a woman of immense power, there was no question. Perhaps a woman who was not afraid to embrace her power fully, and thus threatened men. Yes, Inca would threaten most men—but not Mike. No, Mike loved her; that was obvious by the tears glimmering in his eyes as Inca raised her hand in farewell to them.

"I will see you in your dreams, my blood brother." She turned her gaze on Ann. "If you call me by name, I will come." She pointed to the jaguar claw around her neck. "Or call him." Giving Ann a mysterious smile, she turned around and with a deferential nod of respect in Adaire's direction, left as abruptly as she had come.

Suddenly dizzy, Ann whispered, "I need to sit down for just a moment, Mike…."

He eased her to the mat and knelt beside her. "You okay?"

With a slight, embarrassed laugh, Ann said, "I'm fine…fine. She's just a bit overwhelming, that's all. I'll be okay in a minute…"

Adaire hobbled slowly to the door. "There is less than an hour left, my children. Time is of the essence now…. I will meet you at the bridge over the stream."

"We'll be there," Mike promised.

Ann rubbed her brow as the dizziness slowly disappeared. When she looked up, Adaire was gone. Sometimes she wondered if these people just materialized from the surrounding air. She'd never seen it happen, but Adaire could not move that fast, for he had a bad limp.

"Wow," she murmured, giving Mike a wry look, "what a morning, huh?"

He grinned a little and knelt in front of her. "Inca doesn't exactly make quiet entrances," he agreed with a chuckle. Removing her hands from her brow, he said, "Hold still, I'll help steady you. Just close your eyes, take in a nice, slow breath while I hold you...."

It was so easy to surrender to Mike in this way, as he cradled one hand against the back of her head and pressed the other gently to her brow. Almost instantly, she felt the dizziness dissolve. In its place was a sense of stability again, of complete harmony with herself and with him. In less than a minute, it seemed, he withdrew his hands. When Ann opened her eyes, he was smiling tenderly down at her. Reaching up, she slid her hands up around his hard jaw and settled her palms against his cheeks.

"Thank you, Major. I think I like this form of medicine. Much quicker, less invasive than the kind I practice." She leaned upward to meet his descending mouth.

The moments slowed to a molten halt as his lips met hers. The joy of his mouth sliding, rocking her lips apart, was all that mattered. It was so easy to center her entire universe on Mike, on his touch, on the fierce love she felt in his heart for her alone. She drank from him, shared his breath within her and drowned in the splendor of his tender, searching kiss.

Gradually, he eased back from her lips. Ann's lashes lifted. "Now I'm dizzy all over again." She laughed softly as he caressed the crown of her head with his hand. She loved being stroked by him, touched and held. Feeling his unshielded love for her left her breathless and euphoric and filled her with so much hope.

Chuckling, Mike released her and sat back on the heels of his black leather boots. "I'm a little dizzy myself. But then, you're one hell of a kisser, *mi querida*...."

She flushed at his compliment and fleetingly touched her cheeks. She was not used to that burning look he shared so brazenly with her, that look of a man wanting his woman in every possible way.

Her entire body responded to his heated, smoldering gaze. An ache began to build deep within her, a yearning to be one with him again and again and again. Ann thought she'd never get enough of Mike, of what they'd shared every time they'd loved on these mats here in this hut.

Reaching out, he caressed her hot cheek. "There will be other mats, other huts," he promised her huskily.

"You're reading my mind," Ann said. And then she laughed, even more embarrassed than before. "Mike, I'm going to have to get used to this...."

He grinned broadly. "I can shield, if you want me to. It's not a problem, you know."

Slowly getting to her feet with his help, she said, "No...it's just different, that's all. I *like* our connections. In fact, when you shield yourself from me, I feel like we're only half-connected. It's an awful feeling...."

He moved the paramedic bag to the table and zipped all the compartments shut. "Now you know how a jaguar feels without his mate. The jaguar has that same kind of open mind and heart connection running between him and his mate twenty-four hours a day."

She picked up the folded clothes and brought them to the table where he was working. "It's a beautiful thing," she admitted, "like being fully alive, Mike, instead of half-alive. Do you know what I mean?"

He saw the quizzical look in her expression. A love so fierce and pure welled up in him that he couldn't speak for a moment. Ann might not be a genetic member of the Jaguar Clan, but her heart was so pure that it rocked him as nothing else ever had. Raising his hand, he eased several strands of reddish brown hair from her wrinkled brow. "Yes, I know exactly what you're talking about because we share it."

With a sigh, Ann looked around. "Will it still be there when we leave here, Mike?"

Hands stilling over his black canvas bag, he held her gaze. "What we have will be with us until the day we die and even beyond mere physical death, *mi querida.* It will only grow stronger, more sure and more beautiful with each passing day, week and month. Love, once it takes seed and you surrender completely to it, does nothing but grow.''

She nodded and sat down on the chair, her hands resting on the pile of colorful clothes Moyra had loaned her. "In some ways, that's scary. In others, it makes me feel so hopeful about the future for us." Ann knew she had not yet given over, surrendered completely, to Mike yet. Time...they had to have time....

"Yeah, I feel scared and hopeful, too," Mike agreed wryly. "The future is iffy. But then, it's always been that way with me." His expression sobered. "It's you who's going to go through some tremendous adjustments because of it." His brow wrinkled. "And that's what worries me."

Ann saw and felt his agony over having to subject her to his life on the run from Escovar. She knew he worried that the drug lord might put two and two together and realize their connection— and then murder her to get even with Mike for the death of his family. It was all part of the death spiral dance.

Anxious to distract him, Ann said, "Tell me about Inca. What an incredibly powerful woman she is! What did she mean when she called you her blood brother? Is that another custom here in the Village of the Clouds?"

She saw him release his worry and focus on her questions. Folding his hands on the table, he said, "Over time, you'll get to understand a lot about the Jaguar Clan and its customs. When I came here to this village after being wounded and nearly bleeding to death, it was Inca who cared for me. She was in training with Adaire and Alaria at the time. She'd been Adaire's prize pupil for two years, and she was one hell of a powerful woman even then.

"At the time, I didn't know I was one of the Jaguar Clan. I lay on a pallet in a hut like this, and I fought against the energy, the healing, that Adaire was trying to send to me, to pump into me, to save my worthless neck. I fought it—and him—every step of the way because I was scared and I didn't understand." He gave Ann a humored look. "Like you, my left brain, the paramedic in me, said I should be dead, and I wasn't. When you believe something like that to that degree, you can stop healing energy from coming in to help save you.

"I was semiconscious from losing so much blood. I kept fading in and out, and yet Inca devoted herself to caring for me. She *refused* to let me go. Adaire released me. She did not. He ordered her to let me die. Inca defied his direct order and said no, which helped create more problems for her. At that moment, she broke a basic clan law—you cannot save someone who is supposed to die. That is what brought her banishment from the Village of the Clouds. Adaire wanted her not only banished, but her jaguar guardian stripped from her for disobeying. Alaria said no—that banishment was enough.

"Adaire has yet to forgive Inca for this, I think. They were so close before that. Inca had never had a father figure until she came here, at age sixteen, and Adaire loved her like the daughter he'd lost many years earlier. Inca more or less replaced that lost daughter in Adaire's heart. When she defied him, it cut him to his soul. He'd never entertained the possibility that she could do that to him. He thought her love and respect for him was more powerful—but he was wrong.... She took things into her own hands and fought for me on every level to get me to accept the healing energy. I don't know how many nights she bathed me with a cool cloth, or talked to me or...sang to me. She has a beautiful, angelic voice...." Houston smiled at Ann. "Back then, Inca was...different, and she usually obeyed the laws of the clan. But one night, as I was slipping away, dying, Inca broke clan law."

Mike frowned heavily. "She shouldn't have done it, but she did anyway. Inca was only eighteen at the time, young, impetuous and rebellious. I don't know whether it was out of spite for Grandfather Adaire, who had released me to make my choice to die, or if it was just that damned stubborn streak of hers to save a life.... Anyway, Inca joined with me...as I joined with you to save your life in Lima. My spirit was too weak to fight her, and so she was able to stop me from going over the threshold, into the light, and dying.

"The next morning, I awoke and I was coherent. I remember weakly sitting up, and I saw her lying curled up in a fetal position, next to me. I saw blood all over the damn place around her. She'd bled out. I was terrified. About that time, Grandmother Alaria appeared and quickly went to her side. I saw her do something that just blew me away. She knelt over Inca, gently cradled her in her arms like a child and held her face very close to hers. Inca was a gray-blue color. I knew she was dead. I saw Alaria breathe into her slack, parted lips. I watched—and saw—this golden, living energy flow back into Inca. I was transfixed. I knew that what I was seeing was a miracle. There was no question of it.'' His voice shook with emotion. ''Alaria brought Inca back to life.''

''My God, Inca died giving you life? Is that what you're saying?''

Mike nodded. ''I'm going to skip the technical stuff with you and just say that Inca struggled to stop me from choosing death *and* tried to heal me, and she didn't have the necessary power to do both. She'd had two years of training with Adaire and Alaria, and she knew a lot of different healing methods. With her energy, she managed to stop me from crossing over the threshold. She had very little left with which to heal me, though. Instead, what Inca did was transfer my wound, my condition into herself. She gave me her own life-force energy so that I could live. That's what killed her.''

Ann's eyes widened. ''Then...she acquired your wound?''

''Yes.'' Houston sighed. ''Inca knew if she could bring me back, that I'd still die. I'd bleed to death on the floor of that hut. Grandfather Adaire had released me, so that meant I'd be the way I'd been before he found me in the jungle.''

''And Inca willingly sacrificed her life for yours?'' Ann quavered.

''Exactly.'' Houston raised his eyes to the roof of the hut. ''She was a wild, impetuous young woman then. I think she thought that she could pull it off and heal herself of the wound she took on from me. She bit off more than she could chew. Usually she is very good at taking care of her own needs first, above anyone else's. She still is.''

''Even if that's true,'' Ann said, feeling the truth of Inca's goodness in some deep intuitive level of herself, ''Inca gave her life for you.''

''No question,'' Mike murmured.

''And Grandmother Alaria really did bring her back to life?''

He nodded, then frowned. ''Grandmother Alaria is very, very ancient....'' Awkwardly, he continued, ''Alaria and Adaire are role models here at the village of what we can become, if we follow our heart's path. But we're all terribly human, too, and each of us has our own flaws, problems and weaknesses to overcome, first.''

''Yet,'' Ann said, ''it's obvious Adaire didn't want Inca here.''

''That is his karma, something he must work through with her,'' Mike explained. ''He has yet to do it, or she with him. It's still an open, bleeding wound between them. Alaria has forgiven Inca, which is why I suspect she allowed her back here to see us just now.'' He smiled a little. ''Grandfather Adaire isn't happy about it, but there's not much he can do. I pray that he and Inca make peace between themselves. The sooner, the better.'' He opened his left hand and showed Ann an inch-long white scar in the palm of his hand. ''Once I understood what Inca did for me, when I'd mended and finally accepted that I was one of the Jaguar Clan, I sought her out. I asked her what I could do to balance the scales of karma between us. To thank her for fighting for my life and saving me even when I'd given up and was ready to leave this body. She said she wanted me to be her blood brother. She had no family of her own and she wanted to be part of my family.''

''So, you shared one another's blood?'' Ann asked.

''It's more than that, but yes, it's one of five powerful ceremonies we have: life, death, birth, joining and adoption. The adoption ceremony is like a linking between our spirits, but not like the marriage that took place between you and me. It's different, but in some ways similar. She loves me and I love her—sister to brother and vice versa.''

''And Inca came here when she wasn't supposed to? To see you?''

Houston smiled thinly. ''Inca comes and goes where she damn well pleases. She treads where angels and spirit guardians fear to go, believe me. She's a hellion, a rabble-rouser, a zealot, an extremist, but I love her and admire the hell out of her for what she's been able to do...for what she is doing to save the rain forests of Brazil.'' He opened his hands. ''Because she's so driven, so focused, she's out of balance. But she doesn't care. She has the power of the Jaguar Clan in her veins, she has her guardian and she knows how to use—and abuse—the power she has. As she said earlier, she walks a fine line between darkness and light. To her enemies, she's the devil incarnate. To the people of Brazil, who love her, worship the ground she walks on, she's known as the jaguar goddess.''

"Like you're known as the jaguar god here in Peru," Ann ventured.

"Similar, though I play by the rules set out by the Sisterhood of Light. Inca plays by her own rules. But then, if I'd gone through the living hell she did when she was a child, and later as a young adult, I don't think I'd be half as good as she is about it. I'm afraid I'd have been very tempted to side with the Brotherhood of Darkness and go after my enemies, one by one, to even the score...."

Sliding her hands over his, Ann said, "I like her, Mike. I don't care what Inca's done. When she leaned down and pressed her face to my body, I felt and saw the real her."

Mike entwined his fingers with hers. "Yes," he rasped, "you did. That's only the second time I've seen Inca unshield herself completely. I was stunned that she'd do it here, with Adaire present. But..." he gazed at her "...she can see how pure your heart is, how pure you are, and she knew she could entrust herself entirely to you without fear of reprisal. And Inca runs on fear.

"She gave you two gifts. The first was her friendship, her heart, and the second is something that I know you don't understand—that jaguar claw. It's half of her protection, something she always carries with her. She gave it to you...to our baby...." He blinked a couple of times, his voice suddenly emotional. "I don't know about her. She's so damn unreliable, and yet she turns around and does something like this. I saw and felt her just like you did. We were seeing her good side, the side of her that's whole and not shattered by what life's done to her."

"It was a real privilege, then?"

Mike slowly rose, wanting to continue the conversation but knowing it was time to go. "It was a gift, *mi querida.* A gift of such unselfish proportions that I would never in a million years have expected it from Inca. I know she put herself on the line for me once, but she has been very protective of herself ever since." Mystified, Mike held his hand out to Ann and helped her stand. "Inca knows something we don't. But then, she's farseeing, like Grandfather Adaire, whether he admits it or not. She's got tremendous skills and abilities in place—far more than most of the Jaguar Clan members. More than I do, that's for sure. I know she saw something...and that's why she gave you that gift, that protection...."

Ann slid her arm around Mike's waist and leaned on him. She hated to leave, yet it was time. "Then, darling, she's given the gift not only to me, but to our baby and you."

Mike caressed her hair. "I know," he murmured worriedly. "I know...."

Chapter 15

"Ann, you must rest," Pilar Lachlan pleaded, guiding her over to a rough-hewn chair in the hut where Ann had been seeing patients all day. "Eight months along and you work like you're not pregnant at all!"

"I can pretend, can't I?" Smiling wearily, Ann allowed Pilar, who was married to one of Morgan Trayhern's ex-employees, Culver Lachlan, to sit her down. It was late afternoon and Ann was tired and thirsty.

As if reading her mind, Pilar, a petite woman, of Quechua and Spanish heritage, poured her a glass of water from a clay pitcher on the table. "You can try, my friend, but I see dark circles under your eyes. I can tell your tiredness goes to your bones." She frowned and handed Ann the glass. "I know it has been a month without a visit from Mike. I'm sure it's been hard on both of you. But he'll be here tomorrow morning." Reaching out, Pilar patted Ann's hand.

Ann moved her other hand gently across her very swollen belly beneath the pale pink cotton smock she wore. "I think we're both excited about seeing Mike. She's kicking up a storm in here."

Grinning knowingly, Pilar murmured, "I remember the feeling well. My daughter Rane, who is ten now, was our first child."

She cast a glance toward the straw cradle in the other room of the hut. "Maria is only four months old. She is our second heart child."

Smiling softly, Ann studied the tiny little baby with reddish hair sleeping soundly in the cradle. "She's so pretty, Pilar."

Squeezing her hand, Pilar laughed and said, "Yes. All children born of love are beautiful. Yours will be, too, though you won't think that when she gets you up every two hours to be breast-fed!"

Ann smiled. She didn't know what she would have done without Pilar's help during her pregnancy. Ann had traveled on a monthly circuit to five different villages in the highlands, all within a hundred miles of the nearest fighting that Mike waged against Escovar's men. During that time, Morgan had put Ann in touch with Culver, who lived in the village of San Cristobal. It was Culver's wife, Pilar, the daughter of a jaguar priestess, who had not only helped Ann establish a circuit and routine, but had been her right hand all these months, even while she'd been carrying her own baby! Ann had helped Pilar deliver the strapping eight-pound Maria four months earlier, with Culver there to catch his second daughter as she crowned and slid into his large hands. It was in Culver's hands that Maria drew her first breath. It had been a beautiful birth.

Ann sighed and blotted the perspiration from her brow with a pink linen handkerchief. It was September, and it was hot and humid. She felt the heat more than usual because of her pregnancy. "You need to get home," she murmured, looking out the door at the angle of the sun on the horizon. Pilar drove ten miles over heavily rutted roads to be with her each day, her daughter in tow on some days. The rest of the time, Rane and Culver took care of Maria, providing Pilar had stored up enough breast milk to make that possible.

To look at Pilar, who wore a blue cotton skirt and white blouse, her black hair long and flowing, one would think she was like any other Indian villager. Yet she was a college graduate and once had worked for the Peruvian government as an undercover spy, as well as for Morgan Trayhern. She and her *norteamericano* husband had met and fallen in love ten years ago. But it wasn't until they had rescued Morgan Trayhern from Ramirez's fortress in the highlands that they finally admitted their love and married. Everyone had said Morgan's rescue couldn't be done, but this brave woman had teamed up with a giant of a man—a hardened mercenary—and accomplished the impossible.

Mike had played a role in Morgan's rescue, too. And he knew Culver and Pilar very well. Ann was glad to have such friends, because Mike was gone more than he was at her side. It had been a terrible period of adjustment for her in many ways. Yet every few nights Mike entered her dreams, and she made love with him at the pool of life, or they walked hand in hand in the Village of the Clouds. Sometimes they sat by the rainbow waterfall and talked over what their day had been like. She loved this added form of communication, another hidden plus to his being a member of the Jaguar Clan. His visits in her dreams didn't take place every night, because often, he was attacking Escovar's holdings in dangerous night raids.

"Tonight," Pilar said, standing and smoothing her skirt, "is the first night of the jaguar moon."

Ann tilted her head. "That's a term I've never heard before."

Pilar went over and gently eased her baby daughter from the straw cradle and nestled her against her breast. "The jaguar moon is the seven days before a new moon, when the moon sheds no light on Mother Earth." She walked back and stood near the table. "It is said that this is the time when the Brotherhood of Darkness is at its greatest strength because the Great Goddess and her symbol, the moon, cannot shed her light of protection across our mother, the earth, and all her relations. It is the time when evil spirits have power over the force of light. The Goddess cannot protect us as this evil stalks our land."

Ann raised her brows. "I don't feel anything different," she said.

Pilar caressed her sleeping daughter's chubby little face. "Soon I will know more of these things. I am going into training, my grandmother Aurelia told me. I'll become a member of the Jaguar Clan."

"What do you do for seven days in the dark of the moon?" Ann teased. "Hide?"

With a chuckle, Pilar shook her head. "My grandmother, who is in her nineties, is a very wise woman. She told me to tell you that when the sun goes down, you must remain inside this hut and meditate or pray. Do things that allow you to go inward. These seven days are a time of introspection, of moving deep within ourselves, to see our truth and to feel our way through this time of darkness. It's not a time for many external events, or to start new projects. This is, she has told me, a time when a seed is planted in the ground. It's very dark for that seed in the soil, no?''

''Yes,'' Ann said, pouring herself more water, ''it certainly is as dark as a night with no moon for that little seed buried in fertile earth.''

''So,'' Pilar said, ''use this time to plant new seeds of awareness within yourself.'' She smiled and raised her hand in farewell. ''I will see you tomorrow morning? Mike said he will be here no later than noon?''

Ann nodded. She held up her crossed fingers. ''If everything goes according to plan, he'll helicopter in.''

''And I will do what I can here tomorrow, at your clinic, to help out until he arrives.''

Ann waved goodbye, thankful for Pilar's care and love. Without her friendship, she knew that she wouldn't have fared half as well. Sitting at the table, she gazed down at the white-and-purple orchids that Pilar had brought that morning. Though they were beautiful, they had no scent, not like those gorgeous red-and-yellow ones Mike had given to her in Lima. With a sigh, Ann rested her head on her arms on the rough-hewn table. Exhaustion ate at her. How she missed her husband! She never knew when he would visit until a day or two beforehand, because he feared Escovar finding out.

This time, however, was going to be different. Mike was coming to take her to the Village of the Clouds for the last month of her pregnancy. He wanted her to have a month of serenity, with him at her side. Grandmother Alaria, bless her, had given Mike permission to bring her ''home.'' Ann understood enough to know that the village was indeed a very special place. It was available only to those of the Jaguar Clan, or to a person whose heart was in the right place and who sought healing at the pool of life. Otherwise, one could look at the slopes of the Andes and never even see the village. Ann couldn't explain how that could be and had given up trying. All she knew was that the village was real, and she was eager to be a part of incredible peacefulness and joy that always resided among the heart-centered people who lived there.

In the distance, Ann heard a car entering the village. Frowning, she wondered if Pilar had forgotten something. Or perhaps it was Mike? Her heart lifted a little at that thought. Sometimes he came by car, with Pablo as his driver.

Ann heard the chickens clucking and squawking in protest as the car slowly came to a halt just outside her hut. She didn't sense it was Mike and swallowed her disappointment. She would know if it was him; he always sent his jaguar guardian ahead to tell her of his approach. At those times, Ann had felt the guardian's warmth and strength like an embrace. Hearing two car doors open and then shut, she straightened up in the chair and waited.

Sometimes people in the surrounding villages brought their sick to her. Some of the farmers who made a better living could afford some old clunker of a car to get around in, instead of traveling by foot or donkey, which was the usual means of transportation up here in the highlands.

A man, very lean and around six feet tall, dressed in a short-sleeved white shirt and tan slacks, stepped into the doorway.

Instantly, Ann went on guard. She met his dark, narrowed eyes as they settled on her.

"Yes?" she asked firmly. "May I help you?"

He suddenly smiled. His thin face lost its hardness.

"Ah, are you...Dr. Barbara Forest?"

Ann nodded. Her "other" name was what she went by. No one knew her real name, except for Pilar and Culver. "Yes, I am. Are you ill?"

"Well." He laughed apologetically. "I was driving to my land holdings, up east of here, and I suddenly got very dizzy. Very dizzy." He touched his brow. "They said there was a Red Cross doctor here in the village. So I said, 'Why not stop?'" He walked into the hut and stood in front of her table. "What could cause my dizziness, Doctor?" His gaze moved to her left hand, where there was a plain gold wedding ring on her fourth finger.

Ann slowly rose. "If you'll have a seat, *señor,* I'll take your blood pressure and pulse. We'll see if maybe it's due to high blood pressure. Are you on any medications right now?" She reached for her black physician's bag, put the stethoscope around her neck and drew out the blood pressure cuff.

"No...no medications, Doctor. Ahh, I see you are with child. Soon, eh?"

Ann smiled her perfunctory doctor smile as he pulled out the chair and sat down. Something bothered her about this man. He was, for this area, very richly attired. His shirt was not made of cotton, but of silk, and it clung to his rounded chest. As she approached him, she judged him to be in his middle forties. His skin was a pale gold color, and she guessed that he might be of Spain's Castilian aristocracy. From a very rich family, no doubt. His features were sharp, almost gaunt looking, and his dark brown gaze ferreted around the silent hut.

"Well," she murmured, affixing the blood pressure cuff to his right arm, "let's see what we've got...." She pumped it up, let off the pressure and watched the dial as she listened for the first beat of his heart. He was watching her with great interest, and that bothered her. She had pinned her hair up to keep it off the back of her neck because it had been exceedingly hot of late, and suddenly she felt very self-conscious.

"*Señor,* your blood pressure is normal," Ann informed him, removing the cuff. She saw him nod and appear relieved.

"That is good." He looked around some more as she put the cuff and stethoscope back into her bag. "I had heard of a doctor up here. They said she was very beautiful. A *norteamericana.* I said, 'No, how could that be?' And the gossip was that you'd appeared one day, like an angel from heaven, in February of this year." He snapped his fingers and grinned, showing a row of clean, white teeth. "It's quite unusual for a doctor to be up here. A blessing, yes, but very, very rare."

Ann didn't like him—at all—but she hid her irritation. Moving around to the other side of the table, she said, "I work with the poor, *señor*...."

"Eduardo," he said genially, "you may call me Eduardo. After all, your husband, Major Mike Houston, knows me very well."

The icy grating of his words shattered her. Ann froze. She stared at him. He was relaxed, sprawled out in the chair, his arms across his chest. He smiled up at her, but it wasn't a pleasant smile. It reminded her of a predator's smile right before it killed its frozen prey. That was how Ann felt right then—absolutely unable to move. Her heart thudded harshly in her chest. She felt as if she couldn't breathe.

"Eduardo Escovar at your service, Dr. Ann Houston." He rose and made a sweeping gesture as he bowed in her direction. As he straightened up, he snarled an order in Spanish. Instantly, two armed guards entered the hut, their gazes locked on her.

With a gasp, Ann tried to move. Escape was impossible. Eight months along, she was about as fast as a lumbering elephant. Besides, Ann knew that any violent exercise could induce premature labor. She rested her fingertips on the edge of the table, feeling the blood flowing out of her face.

"*Señor,* I don't know what you are talking about. My name is—"

"Silence, bitch!" he snarled, his lips lifting away from his teeth. "I have tracked you for eight months. Ever since that bastard, Houston, stole you from your apartment in Lima, I have had my loyal spies out, searching." He made a stabbing motion toward her. "My spies have discovered you are Ann Parsons. You work for Perseus. For that slimy Morgan Trayhern." He smiled a little, picking at some imaginary lint on the front of his shirt. His voice softened and became cajoling. "You are Houston's wife. That, I have no doubt." His dark, angry gaze settled on her swollen belly.

Instinctively, Ann shielded her baby with her hand. Terror ate at her. She tried to think, tried to find a way to escape, but it was impossible. Her only help would have been Pilar, but she was gone until tomorrow morning. A coldness flowed up through Ann, more chilling and haunting than she'd ever experienced. Escovar was going to kill her—and her baby.

"Listen," she pleaded hoarsely, "don't hurt my baby! I'm eight months along...can't you—"

In one lightning motion, Escovar lunged forward and with his open hand, slapped her as hard as he could across the face.

Her head exploded with light and pain. Ann cried out and staggered backward. She felt herself falling from the unexpected blow. Somehow, she threw out her arm as she was knocked sideways, and her hand struck the wall of the hut, breaking her fall. She crumpled heavily to the mat beside the table. Liquid flowed hotly out of her nostrils and across her parted lips. She tasted the salty, metallic taste of her blood. Automatically, she pressed her fingers against her throbbing nose and cheek.

"Get her up!" Escovar rasped.

Instantly, his two guards, heavily armed with modern rifles, moved forward.

Their hands bit savagely into Ann's arms as they jerked her to her feet. She cried out as pain serrated her belly. *No! God, no!*

"In the car!"

Semiconscious, Ann was literally dragged between the two guards. She saw several villagers hiding behind their huts, their eyes huge with terror. The door was opened and the men shoved her into the back seat. Sobbing, Ann was sandwiched in the rear seat of the white luxury sedan by the two large, muscular guards. The air in the car was hot and humid. She watched through narrowed eyes as Escovar's driver quickly opened the front passenger door for him. Escovar looked down before getting in.

"Comfortable, Señora Houston? I hope so. We are going for a little ride to a place not far from here that's very, very famous." He grinned savagely and slid into the leather seat.

Ann tried to compose herself. The guards were tense beside her, and when she tried to wipe the blood from her nose, they glared at her. Emotionally, she was in such terror that her mind was frozen, and she could taste death in her mouth. She had to try and think! *Think!* Mike wouldn't be here until tomorrow, at noon. Did Escovar know he was coming? Oh, God, she had to keep his arrival time a secret at all costs! A sob caught in her throat as she protectively covered her unborn daughter with her hands. The glittering hate that Escovar had for her—for Mike—was palpable.

"W-where are you taking me?" she demanded in a wobbling voice.

Escovar turned his head and smiled generously. "Ah, Señora Houston, this is a place you must visit." He turned in his seat and devoted all his attention to her. "Tell me, when does your very famous husband come home, eh?"

Ann avoided his piercing gaze. "I—I don't know. I never know...."

Chuckling, Escovar nodded. "Yes, well, that's very wise of him. He always operates on a need-to-know basis. I thought," he said with a sigh, "that since you are the one he loves most, he'd certainly let you know when he was coming for a visit. My guards persuaded several of the villagers where you have your clinic to talk. Pity. None of them seemed to know when the jaguar god was going to appear."

Coldness crept over Ann. She knew Escovar was prone to use torture to get the information he wanted. Yet she'd not heard of his arrival in the village. That was a clue to her of how lethal he was at what he did. He was almost like a jaguar in some ways, a shadow until he wanted to be seen.

As they bumped along the rutted road, the bouncing and jerking was hard on her. Ann could feel telltale pains around her belly. As much as she could, she held her abdomen, held her daughter from the jolting motions on the rutted road. Soon they were on another dirt road, one lined by a thousand-foot dropoff into the jungle below on one side and in a thousand-foot cliff of yellow-and-red soil on the other.

Escovar hummed a tune and seemed to be enjoying the scenery. Ann shook in fear. She couldn't help it. Without a doubt, Escovar would kill her—and her baby. It was only a matter of time. Her mouth was cottony and dry. She tried to call Mike, but the terror broke her concentration. Again and again, Ann tried to call him. She knew he would hear her, but it had to be an intense, concentrated thought before he could pick it up. Oh, dear God, what was she going to do? Closing her eyes, she felt hot and nauseous. Ann knew there was no talking Escovar out of anything. She felt the full extent of his rage and hatred and it battered her senses.

As the sun was setting on the western horizon, the sky becoming gray with gathering clouds, Escovar snapped at the driver to stop. Ann looked around. They were parked in the middle of the dirt road, its green, grassy edge littered with bushes and big gray rocks before it fell away into space.

"Get her out!" Escovar ordered as he left the car.

Her legs wouldn't work and Ann was dragged between the guards to the edge of the cliff. Her eyes bulged as she struggled to push away from the precipice. Dirt and stones tumbled down with her movements. The first hundred feet was nothing but rock, littered with branches from trees and bushes that had tumbled, over time, from the cliff above them.

Escovar sauntered over. He lit a cigarette and took a long, deep drag of smoke into his lungs. His eyes glittered as he studied her.

"You know this place, Señora Houston?"

Her skin crawled. Wildly, Ann looked around. "N-no, I don't."

He smiled a little and took another drag on his cigarette. "I'm surprised, frankly, because your husband has made this a very famous place." He stabbed with his cigarette down the slope. "Look," he snarled. "You see those four white crosses down there, about five hundred feet below? Just before the edge of the jungle?''

Ann tried to gather her composure. Sweat was dripping into her eyes and they burned with pain. Tears of terror ran down her cheeks. Blinking rapidly, she tried to concentrate on where he was pointing. Halfway down the slope, she saw four white crosses with huge bunches of fresh flowers around each one.

''Y-yes, I see them,'' she whispered hoarsely. The guards' hands bit deeply into her arms, the pain constant.

Escovar took another drag on his cigarette. He looked at her, his face raw with grief. ''Those four crosses are my wife, my two sons and my daughter, *señora*,'' he rasped. ''Your husband murdered them in cold blood! Look at them, damn you! Look at them because it is the last thing you are going to see!''

With a cry, Ann jerked her head toward him. ''Señor Escovar, please, don't do this! Mike didn't murder your family! I swear it! It was an accident! He was following them in a helicopter and trying to land in front of them. The driver of your family's car panicked. He was going too fast for this road. The car flipped!'' Ann sobbed as she felt the guards move her within inches of the cliff edge. ''Oh, God, you've *got* to believe me! Mike never meant to harm your family. I swear it....'' She sobbed as she clung to his angry features with tear-flooded eyes. His gaze was black and glittering as he stepped toward her.

''Do you know how *much* I loved my wife?'' he screamed into her face. Reaching out, he wrapped his hand through her hair and jerked her head forward.

Ann felt his breath against her face, hot and nauseating. She was held captive, her neck and head twisted at a painful angle as Escovar glared down at her. Her scalp radiated in pain. She tried not to cry out as tears slipped from her eyes.

''My children. The babies my beautiful Juanita carried in her belly, which I tenderly caressed every day she carried them....'' His voice cracked. ''I *loved* her. I loved them! Your murdering husband took them from me. The coward didn't come to me. No,'' he rasped, his spittle splaying across her face, ''he picked on innocents who could not protect themselves.''

Suddenly, he released Ann's hair.

With a cry, she was jerked upright by the guards once again.

Escovar was smiling, but there was no life in his eyes. Only death. "Let me see..." he murmured, composing himself. "I have killed his first wife and I understand she was pregnant. Too bad. I counted that as one death. To make up for the death of my sweet little daughter, Elizabeth." He shrugged. "And then the second woman he loved, that *norteamericana* who worked in the embassy. Poof!" He threw up his hands and laughed.

Ann winced. She thought he was going to strike her.

"Her death paid for Ernesto's death, my youngest son...."

Escovar reached out, gripping her belly hard.

Ann screamed and kicked out, trying to protect her baby from his clawlike hands.

Escovar dodged her attempt, his hand loosening on her belly. He grinned savagely.

"I should have both your legs broken for that," he snarled, staying just out of range of her flailing feet. "Ordinarily, I would," he told her archly. "But I am not a man without honor, not like your bastard husband...." Again, he inhaled deeply on the cigarette, regarding her from hooded eyes.

Ann sobbed for breath. She hated his touch on her belly; she felt his hatred and revenge and tasted it in her mouth.

"So, you will pay for my Juanita, my heart, who I grieve for daily." He turned and pointed to the largest of the four crosses at the bottom of the cliff, the one with the most flowers around it. "Every day, did you know? I have one of my men come here and place fresh flowers near these crosses. Oh, they are not buried here. No, they are at the compound, in proper graves where I can go and talk to them daily. It is a custom, you know, *señora?* To place a cross to remind everyone that they died a needless death at the hands of a murderer."

She saw Escovar's eyes glitter with tears. His voice became laced with grief and grew harsh with emotion as he turned back to face her.

"Well, now, Houston can place a white cross of his own down there." Escovar smiled, showing his white teeth. "You and your unborn baby will be an even trade for my wife and my other son's death. Yes, that feels right to me. When he finds you—if he can find you—he will understand it all...my plan. I knew someday he would fall in love again. And I waited.... I have the patience of a jaguar, also." He dropped the cigarette to the yellow dirt and crushed it out with the sole of his expensive loafer.

"I will not torture you, *señora*. Ordinarily, I would. But you are a woman, I can see, of great courage. Most people who are dragged in front of me lose their bowels and scream for mercy. You did not. You begged only for your baby's life. I find that— commendable. Houston, when he finds you, will find your body eaten by buzzards. There won't be much of you left to grieve over." He smiled. "Say your prayers, *señora*. For you are going to die...."

"Nooo!" Ann shrieked, her voice cracking. She tried to yank free of the guards, but they were simply too strong, and she too far along to do anything more than struggle in their grip. She saw Escovar's face grow cold and expressionless. His eyes went dead. She dug her heels in as the guards propelled her forward, toward the edge of the cliff.

And then everything slowed down. Ann closed her eyes. She drew a deep, quavering breath into her body. Opening her heart fully for the first time, she pictured Mike's hard, scarred face in front of her. She sent out a cry for help that reverberated through her, through everything surrounding her in that moment. For the first time, Ann surrendered fully to her love for Mike. She felt all her emotions build, felt the thunderous power of feeling grow within her, and as she pictured him, she sent everything she felt to him. Within those long, drawn-out seconds, she surrendered fully to the magic of possibility, to his world, his belief in the mystical, the unseen. This was one time when she must reach out, embrace him fully and believe—for her baby's sake...for any chance of survival....

Seconds later, she was hurled out into space. Her last view was that of the sharp, gray rocks racing up to meet her. Her scream was for Mike...and then darkness was upon her and she remembered no more.

Chapter 16

The dawn was a thin, bloody ribbon along the horizon. Houston tried to keep his focus, his concentration, but the pain in his lower body, on the left side of his rib cage and head kept shredding what little composure he could muster. The shaking of the helicopter around him, the humid wind whipping into the open craft where his squad of hardened soldiers sat as they flew toward their destination, didn't help.

Hours earlier, he'd heard Ann scream for help. Far south of her in the Andes, in the middle of a firefight with some of the heaviest opposition Escovar had thrown against his men to date, Mike knew she was dying. He could feel it throughout his body. He'd known it the instant he'd felt her scream rip through him. And he knew...oh, hell, he knew.... Sweat trickled down the hard planes of his features, across his stubbled beard as he anxiously sought out the grayish black ground a thousand feet below him.

His jaguar guardian was with Ann and he could feel everything that Ann was experiencing. She was unconscious and bleeding to death. The massive pain he was feeling in his abdomen were savage birthing contractions. Trying to keep his anguish at bay, his need to sob, Houston sat in the copilot's seat, gripping his fists in his lap. He'd tried to withdraw from the firefight when Ann's cry shattered him, but it was impossible. Escovar's men had launched such a massive counterattack that Mike had finally had to call in army reserves from Lima itself to come and help extricate him and his squads.

Now, as the bloodred color on the horizon thickened to announce the coming morning light, Houston had managed to get two chopper loads of men—his handpicked, well-trained soldiers—out of that hellhole and into the air to fly to Ann's side. He knew where she was and it sickened him until he wanted to vomit. Escovar had planned this so well, so very well.... Mike couldn't believe Escovar had found out his connection to Ann, they'd tried so carefully to hide her status. The spies in the Peruvian government on Escovar's payroll had won again.

Over and over, Mike sent Ann energy. But he had to be there in person, he had to be there at her side for it to make a real and lasting difference. Judging from all the pain in his body he was picking up from her own, he knew she had broken ribs and a wound on the side of her head. The cutting pains in his abdomen told him his daughter was in the process of being born—alone to die if he could not reach them in time. Closing his eyes, Houston tried to steady his reeling emotions, his love for Ann, his terror in knowing that he was feeling her life slowly leaking away from her.

His mind spun wildly with plans and tactics. It wouldn't be unlike Escovar to set up a trap, as Mike came to rescue the woman he loved more than life. Escovar could be waiting for him on the cliffside his own family had accidentally driven over, rolling end over end and dying five hundred feet below as the car smashed into the jungle.

Rubbing his face savagely, Houston took deep, gulping breaths. Never had he expected Escovar to make a stand against him over the graves of his lost family. That was sacred ground to him—and to Mike. But he'd broken that taboo. Escovar's hatred of him was so complete that he'd captured Ann, taken her to the spot where his family's car had run off the road, and he'd either shot her, tortured her or pushed her off that cliff. Mike didn't want to consider that he might have done all of those unthinkable things to her and then hurled her down the slope, thinking she was dead or dying. Then he had left her for the black buzzards to find as the sun rose this morning.

Choking on bile, hatred consuming him, Houston struggled to clear away his emotions and remain focused on Ann and her rapidly deteriorating condition. The plan he'd formulated swam in his head. He would leap out of the helicopter just above the ground when they located Ann. And then he'd deploy the two chopper loads of men above him—just in case Escovar was laying a trap for him. Once his men had secured the area, both choppers would land.

Mike had his paramedic pack; he had his other skills.... If he could stabilize Ann and the baby, they could possibly fly them to Tarapoto, the nearest city with a hospital, a hundred miles west.

So much could go wrong. Mike knew Ann had been injured at dusk yesterday. For six hours, she'd not received any stabilizing medical help. He wondered how, with the severity of her injuries, she'd held on this long. Alone, abandoned by him in her greatest hour of need... He felt her life ebbing away rapidly now. Mike felt her fighting, but she didn't have the necessary strength to do it much longer. His eyes narrowed as the helicopter rose over the last jungle-clad hill to that road where Escovar had lost his family.

The bloodred ribbon was turning a deep pink color as the sun's rays neared the horizon. Houston ordered Captain Sanchez, the pilot, to bank away from the road they paralleled and head toward the jungle below. There was an abandoned car on the dirt road, the doors open and no sign of life around the vehicle. As the helicopter turned steeply the spinning of the thick blades sending out heavy, drumming sounds in the humid morning, Mike anxiously searched the slope below for Ann.

In the meantime, the other helicopter, armed with a door machine gun, began to prowl the territorial limits of the area Houston had laid out for them earlier. They would be the guard dogs—in case Escovar was waiting...waiting to spring his trap. Mike's mind raced with questions. Why was there a car abandoned up on the road?

Houston would not endanger his men for his own personal needs any more than necessary. He would try to locate Ann, leap off the chopper and send them high enough, far enough away, to stay out of the range of rifles and rocket fire as he worked to save her life.

"There!" Pablo cried from the rear of the aircraft. He made

stabbing motions out the door of the helicopter. "Major Houston! *¡Commandante! ¡Commandante!* See?"

Mike got out of the copilot's seat and made his way through the tightly packed squadron of heavily armed men. Kneeling down at the door, where the wind whipped into the cabin, he gripped Pablo's shoulder. The young soldier was jabbing his finger repeatedly toward the edge of the jungle. Squinting, Mike could make out nothing at first as the helicopter bobbled and shook in the early morning air currents rising off the humid land.

Yes! His heart slammed in his chest. Mike saw it—he saw— Wiping his mouth, he leaned farther out the door. In the grayish light, he could barely make out Ann's still form. She was on her back, seemingly unconscious. And alone. So alone...

No...wait! As the helicopter skidded closer, descending rapidly in altitude, Houston blinked away the sweat stinging his eyes. Heart pounding, he saw a soldier in green-and-black fatigues jogging down the road toward the abandoned car.

Inca! It was Inca! But—how?

Stunned, Houston froze momentarily, his eyes widening. Inca halted and lifted her face toward them, her expression one of rage mixed with terror.

"Get closer!" Houston roared to Sanchez. "She's one of us." He leaned down and grabbed his paramedic pack. The helicopter dropped rapidly, within fifty feet of the grassy slope. His mind spun with questions. If Inca was here...how the hell had she gotten here? She didn't have the ability to physically transport herself from one place to another. Or did she? *No, impossible.*

The battering air slammed against Mike as he made a five-foot leap off the lip of the helicopter to the earth below him. Houston had thrown out his paramedic bag first. It landed and rolled twenty feet away from where Ann was located. The instant Mike leaped, he bent his knees to absorb the shock of contact. The slope was too steep and he'd have to roll. As he hit the wet, slippery grass, he heard the helicopter's engine rev to full power and pull up high and fast.

"Michael! Michael!"

He threw his arms and legs out to halt his roll. The wet grass soaked his clothing. He sprang to his feet. Inca's call was hoarse. Desperate. Turning, Houston grabbed his black paramedic bag and dug the toes of his boots into the soft, wet earth, heading for Ann.

He whipped a look to his left as he ran. Inca had leaped off the road, rifle in hand, and was scrambling down the rocky slope toward him.

With each running stride, he wondered if Escovar was nearby and waiting. But his gaze was riveted on Ann, who lay unconscious on her back, looking like a splayed-out, broken doll in the dreary gray light of dawn. He heard Inca approaching. Her green eyes shone with tears and utter desperation.

"I got here just as fast as I could," Inca sobbed. She dropped her rifle as she hurried toward Ann. "Get the baby! The baby's coming..." she cried over the noise of the helicopter's departure.

Pushing for breath, Houston dropped to his knees beside Ann. He tore open the paramedic pack. Inca fell to her own knees, breathing heavily. She immediately placed her hands on the sides of Ann's bloodied head.

"How long have you been here?" he rasped, jerking out the labor supplies. His gaze shot to Ann's pale, unmoving face. How pasty she looked! Her lips were parted. He saw dried blood from her nose, the bruise around her left eye. Inca was holding her with all her strength, all her energy, he realized.

"A few minutes after Escovar threw her off that damn cliff. She must have hit the trees, which broke her fall. I've been trying to help her hang on. At one point, I think she regained consciousness." Inca rasped. "I'm tired, Michael...I'm almost out of energy. The baby is being born...Ann's bleeding to death from the inside...."

"The placenta has been torn away from her uterus," he whispered raggedly, quickly examining Ann. He saw the bloody mass on the right side of her head. He feared the worst: a deadly head injury.

"Can you keep stabilizing her?" he asked anxiously. If she'd become conscious earlier, that meant that even though the head wound looked bad, it wasn't a subdural hematoma, which could cause brain damage.

Inca laughed hoarsely. "Even I run out of energy eventually. It took nearly everything I had to get her to this point."

Mike spread the silver-lined blanket beneath Ann's hips. He moved her as gently as possible. He saw the baby's head crowning. It was a matter of moments before his daughter would be born. He had to hurry. Snapping on latex gloves, he grabbed the scissors and clamps that would be necessary. Positioning himself between Ann's legs, he placed his hand on his daughter's head. Life and death. It was so horribly entwined. He knelt there, sobbing for breath.

As his daughter entered the world, her tiny head resting in his large hands, joy filtered through Mike's terror. Her tiny face was flushed pink with health. In the next contraction, he allowed his daughter to turn on her shoulder, and then the rest of her perfectly formed body appeared and slipped into his awaiting hands.

"I've got her!"

Inca nodded. She rested her brow against Ann's hair and closed her eyes. "Thank the Great Goddess..." she whispered unsteadily. Tears choked her voice.

Rapidly, Mike placed a small blanket around his daughter, keeping her cradled in his arm, against his body. The last of the blood pulsated through the cord. He placed the clamps on the umbilical cord. His gaze went to Ann. Tears blurred his vision.

"She's slipping," Inca cried. "Oh, damn, I can't hold her anymore.... Michael!" She collapsed beside Ann, her features pale.

There! Houston quickly cut the umbilical cord. Just as he did, the rest of the placenta delivered. That was good. Quickly tying off the cord, he wrapped his daughter tightly in the blanket. Rising up on unsteady legs, he moved forward. In one motion, he gripped Inca's shoulder as she lay there, sending Ann the last of whatever energy she had left in her.

"Here," he rasped, pulling Inca away. "Lie down on your side. Hold the baby next to you. Just hold her against your chest and keep her warm. That's all you have to do...." He looked into Inca's watering eyes. He saw the devastation, the hopelessness in them. She did as he instructed and rolled over. As he tucked the baby into her arms, against her bandoleer-laden chest, he gave her an unsteady smile of thanks.

"Save her...." Inca sobbed. "Save Ann—you have more energy than I do...."

Houston wasn't sure Ann could be saved this time. As the light grew from the coming dawn, he saw the dark stain of blood around her lower body. How much blood had she lost? With the birth of the baby, the bleeding should stop. Gently, he gathered his wife, the woman he loved so fiercely, into his arms. He was careful, because he knew she had broken ribs, and any movement might puncture her left lung.

He heard the helicopters droning above him. He sensed that Escovar was nowhere around. For whatever reason, the man was not going to engage him in a firefight on his family's graves. As he moved his hand across Ann's limp hair and closed his eyes to make contact with her spirit, Mike knew that Escovar wanted him to feel the same anguish that he had when he'd discovered his family dead at the bottom of this slope. No more than fifty feet away from where Ann clung to life in Mike's arms were the four crosses ringed in fresh flowers, a poignant reminder of that terrible event of so many years ago....

Tears stung his eyes as he worked to forge the fragile connection with Ann. There was so little life left in her. He heard a baby crying piteously and realized belatedly that it was their baby— their daughter—crying out for Ann, for her nourishing milk, her loving arms. A sob ripped through Houston, shuddering through his entire body. Ann couldn't die! She just couldn't! Yet compared to the time she'd nearly died from that hemorrhagic fever in Lima, she was much weaker.

The baby's cries became stronger. More insistent. Houston concentrated. He focused on holding on to Ann, on to her spirit, which stood at the threshold of death. Did he have the power to pull her back? He felt his composure shredding. He felt his anguish over the possibility of losing her. Ann couldn't die! He needed her! He loved her! Their daughter had to have a mother, dammit! Ann had to come back! The sobs ripped out of his contorted mouth as he leaned over her, cradling her helplessly in his arms. She was so cold, her body limp, without life. No! He'd just found her! He didn't care what laws of the code he had to break. He wanted her back! He loved her too much to let her go!

The cry of a baby made Ann fight for consciousness. She struggled against the weighted feeling of her eyelids as the baby's cries became more plaintive. It was her daughter—she knew it. As she barely lifted her lashes, Ann saw someone leaning over her, staring down at her. The effort to try and see who it was was almost too much for her. She felt a hand, strong and firm, on her arm.

Mike...it had to be Mike! Her lips parted and she tried to smile. He'd come...he'd come for her....

"Ann?"

Yes, that was Mike's voice. Off-key, ragged sounding, but his voice. Ann rallied and tried to open her eyes once again. This time, she was more aware of her surroundings. The white walls behind Mike as he stood leaning over her, anxiety written in every plane of his dirty, perspiration-streaked features, told her she was in a building of some kind.

Again, she heard the cry of a baby. Her baby...their daughter.

Her mind wasn't functioning well. She saw Mike's grim mouth part. He reached over, and with a trembling hand, kept stroking her head.

"*Mi querida?* You're safe. You're in a hospital...."

Safe. The word rang through her like a breath of life-giving air. Mike was here, with her. He was dirty. He was in uniform. His face was deeply lined with exhaustion. His eyes were red rimmed and she knew he'd been crying. Why? And then the entire series of events with Escovar came flowing back through her. It was too much. Ann tried to take a deep breath, but it hurt too much, the left side of her rib cage reminding her that she'd broken some of those bones in the fall after Escovar had pushed her over the cliff.

Closing her eyes, Ann focused on Mike's hand, which gripped hers so tightly. She remembered Inca. Opening her eyes, she looked up at him. Inca was not there with him. Had it been her imagination? Ann did not know where reality began or ended anymore. It didn't matter. Not at all.

The cry of her daughter made Ann rally. Her gaze moved left, toward the sound of her baby.

"You hear her?" Mike asked hoarsely, praying that Ann could. She'd sustained a nasty concussion from the blow to her head, near her ear. The doctor had given her twenty stitches to close up the wound.

Ann opened her chapped, dry lips.

Mike smiled a little. "Hold on. I'll get her," he whispered unsteadily.

Closing her eyes, Ann wished for more strength, and had none. Incredibly weak, she could feel the IVs in both her arms, sending life-giving fluids to sustain and stabilize her. She became aware of throbbing pain every now and again in her lower abdomen. Her baby, at some point, had been born. She watched through half-closed eyes as Mike moved away. He returned moments later with a tender look on his face. In his arms, in a soft, pink blanket held gently against him, was their daughter.

Anxiously, Ann looked. She tried to lift her head.

"Don't struggle," Mike whispered unsteadily. He sat on the edge of the bed, facing his wife. Very carefully, he laid their daughter across her abdomen.

"You've got broken ribs on the left side," he warned as he held their daughter so Ann could look at her for the first time. The joy in Ann's eyes, the tears that sprang to them, made him smile tiredly. "She's healthy and doing just fine, *mi querida*." His voice broke. "And you're going to be fine, too..." Houston allowed his tears to flow freely down his stubbled, dirty face. They had arrived here at the Tarapoto Hospital three hours earlier. With the help of the emergency room doctor, Ann had been stabilized and whole blood given to her by himself and Inca. He had been right; as soon as their daughter was born, Ann's internal bleeding ceased. The birth had been the biggest threat to her life. She had been bleeding to death with each wave of contractions.

Ann sobbed. It hurt to move, but she weakly lifted her hand and placed it on her tiny daughter's dark-haired head. She saw Mike's mouth curve tenderly upward. He gazed down at her.

"I love you," he rasped, and he leaned forward and placed a very gentle kiss upon her mouth, welcoming her back, welcoming her into his heart once again.

Ann drowned in the splendor of his mouth. Mike was so strong and cherishing as he moved his lips against hers. His breath gave her life, and more energy. In her hands, on her belly, she held their baby daughter, who had stopped crying the moment she was with her mother. Ann was alive. Mike was here, with her. And most important, their baby was with them—alive and well. As he eased his mouth from hers, hot tears spilled from her eyes.

"I...love you..." Ann whispered brokenly, clinging to his stormy gaze. In that moment before she'd been hurled off the cliff by Escovar, she had surrendered fully to his love, to him. Ann understood now, as never before, what Grandfather Adaire had talked about, and what Alaria had hinted at. The complete surrender of herself on all levels to the love she felt for Mike had occurred. She was stunned and warmed by the strength and nurturance of his love for her as she lay there. She felt Mike grip her shoulder momentarily as he looked down at their baby.

"She's beautiful," he said hoarsely, his voice cracking, "just like her mother...."

Outside the private room, Houston sank against the white-washed wall of the small hospital. His knees were weak. He could barely think. The hospital personnel moved around him in a ceaseless flow of traffic up and down the hall. A bone-deep weariness struck him so hard that for a full minute he didn't think he could move, much less walk. Down the hall, in another private room, Inca was sleeping. Right now, Ann was breast-feeding their daughter for the first time. The baby would sleep, and then so would she. They would be together. And now he had to get some sleep or he was going to keel over right here.

Shoving himself away from the wall, Houston blinked back the last of the tears burning in his eyes. As he headed toward the room where Inca slept, his heart felt bruised with all the emotional upheavals he'd experienced in the last twenty-four hours. Opening the door, he entered the room and saw Inca sitting up on the edge of the bed. She was still in uniform, like him. The bandoleers of ammunition she always carried across her shoulders were hung over a chair nearby, with her rifle. Her black hair was mussed, an ebony waterfall spilling over her slumped shoulders as she sat there, head bowed.

Forcing himself over to her bedside, Mike drew up the chair with the bandoleers hanging across it. Searching Inca's pale features as she lifted her head, he realized for the first time what it had cost her to try and save Ann and his baby. Being able to transport herself physically, from one country to another was known as bilocation. The power it took to do it was beyond his comprehension, but she had that ability and had used it to try to help Ann. He drew the chair under him and sat down, his arms resting across the top. "How are you doing?" he asked huskily. He was slurring his words.

Inca shrugged weakly. "Like hell itself ran over me," she joked tiredly.

"Makes two of us," Houston teased huskily, and shared a one-cornered smile with her. "I don't know how you did it, but I owe you more than I can ever repay you, Inca.'' And he meant that. Mike watched her shadowed, willow green eyes narrow briefly as she sat there, her hands gripping the edge of the bed.

"You owe me nothing."

"How did you know?" He searched her pale, exhausted features.

Lifting her head, Inca took a deep, shuddering breath. "When I touched Ann's belly, when I laid my head against her to bless your baby, I saw it...." Her voice deepened with despair. "I saw all of it...."

Houston scowled. It was on the tip of his tongue to ask why she hadn't told him, but he knew why. As many laws as Inca might break regarding the Sisterhood of Light, some she would never break because it would mean permanent excommunication from the village, and from the Jaguar Clan. She would be stripped forever of her guardian and become a rogue clan member, only to be hunted down by the Brotherhood of Darkness. Even she did not want to lose her status, though at times she fought against the elders of the village like a rebellious, headstrong child.

"I—I wanted to, my brother." Her voice broke with fervency. "Believe me, I wanted to."

Mike nodded and rested his chin against his hands as he held her glistening gaze. "So you did the next best thing—you teleported from Brazil and then came in and picked up the pieces?"

Her mouth stretched a little. "I did what I could within our laws, my brother." She slowly sat up and pushed her thick, black hair away from her face.

Houston cocked his head, regarding her quizzically.

Inca laughed. The sound, faint in comparison to her normal husky laughter. But she seemed close to her old self. "Less than thirty seconds after Escovar threw Ann off that cliff, I took him down." Her eyes glittered. Her voice lowered to a growl as she met Houston's widening eyes. "He is dead, my brother. And so are the two thugs who were with him. I appeared there, ten feet away from them, right after they threw Ann off the cliff. They picked up their guns and shot at me."

Stunned, Houston stared at her. The silence was like a sharp knife ready to fall between them. His mind whirled.

"Then that's why the car was up there...but no bodies."

Her mouth twitched. "I called in the jaguars. They disposed of the bodies. Fitting end, don't you think, to this death spiral dance you've been in with him?''

Mike shut his eyes tightly. ''Inca....''

Reaching out, she gripped his arm. ''By the time Ann had stopped rolling, I was being fired upon. Escovar ran. His two henchmen hid and there was a firefight on the road. It took more than ten minutes before I could kill the two of them. I called the local jaguars, a male and female who own the territory, and told them to carry off their bodies. I didn't care what happened to them.'' Her eyes flashed dangerously. ''Then I went after Escovar. I knew you were on your way to Ann. I saw your guardian with her and knew that what could be done was being done for her. So I set off after Escovar, to track him down and make sure he would not be there when you arrived. To take care of him once and for all.

''I tracked him down with my guardian.'' Her green eyes glittered with satisfaction. ''Escovar shot at me, missed, but I did not. He died with a bullet in his head.'' She lifted her chin imperiously. ''A fitting end to a brother of the darkness, do you not think?''

Mike was stunned. He could only nod.

She chuckled. ''The local jaguar had her fill of Escovar, I'm sure. The rest of his carcass is buzzard bait out there right now. His men will never find him. That I am sure of. A good end for a murdering bastard like that, is it not?'' She slowly flexed her hand, pleased with herself, and stared at Mike.

Houston lifted his head. He saw the glittering hate in Inca's green eyes, and the satisfaction in them, too. ''He's dead?'' Stunned, he saw Inca nod and then give him a lethal smile. It was the smile of a jaguar that had won a heated battle.

''If you think for one moment that I was going to let that murdering son of the darkness take Ann and your baby's life, you are mistaken, Mike. The Great Goddess did not give me that vision of Ann's future for nothing and you know it.''

''I didn't know you had that kind of power,'' he murmured, still shaken by the fact that Escovar was dead.

''Ahh, brother, you are so dense sometimes!'' Inca slowly unwound, like a sinuous jaguar, from the side of the bed. Ruffling his dirty hair, she stepped over to him and slid her arm around his heavy, slumped shoulders. ''If it had not been for the fact I gave Ann that jaguar claw, my guardian's symbol, I would never have been able to do what I did.'' She patted Mike's shoulder gently. ''You see, the last thing Ann did before she hit the ground was grab for that necklace she wore. She called you...and then she called my guardian.'' Grinning tiredly, Inca held his gaze. ''I did not break code for once, my brother. By giving Ann my second guardian, I made sure she had every right to ask for divine intervention and help from me—and them. I could come once she called me. Before that, I was helpless to intervene—even though I wanted to.''

''So she had two guardians working to save her?''

''Yes,'' Inca said, satisfaction purring in her husky voice. ''That is what saved her, my brother. Elder Adaire will not be appearing before me to chew me out over this mission.'' Inca chuckled indulgently and raked her fingers through her thick, dirty hair. ''I am filthy. I am going to take a shower and then I am going to eat. I'm starving! You, on the other hand, look like hell warmed over.'' She slapped his shoulder and pointed to the other narrow hospital bed. ''Go lie down. I'll keep guard over your wife and daughter. After all, I am the little one's aunt. And this is the first time I get to practice being one. You sleep. I will guard and take care of your family for you....''

Ten hours later, Houston awoke. He felt groggy, but he had much of his strength back. The smell of the jungle, the mud and dried blood, was too much even for him, so he stripped out of his fatigues, took a quick, hot shower, shaved, put on a fresh set of clothes and quickly headed back to Ann's room. The watch on his wrist read 0300. The hospital hall was deserted except for one nurse at the desk. At both ends of the hall, Houston had stationed guards—his own men—in case Escovar's thugs tried to make an attempt on their lives.

He had business to attend to and that had to come first, even though he wanted to peek in on Ann and their daughter. Using the telephone at the nurses' station, he reported in to a top official in Lima that Escovar was dead. The satisfaction Mike felt was small in comparison to the relief. With Escovar out of the picture, that meant an end to the death spiral dance for him—and more important, for Ann and his baby daughter.

Finishing his call to the official, Houston ordered his two squads to fly back to Lima for a well-deserved rest. He himself had been given a month's leave, on the spot, by the official. As he walked back down the hall, toward his wife's room, his heart felt lighter and lighter. For the first time since everything that had happened, Mike felt joy replacing dread. Hope replacing fear. As soon as Ann was well enough to travel, he would take her and his daughter to the Village of the Clouds. Grandmother Alaria had promised them a month there, and he was going to take her up on it, without question and with gratitude.

Houston quietly opened the door to Ann's room and slipped in. The harsh light from the hall flooded in around him. He saw that Ann was sleeping soundly, their baby daughter nestled in her arms. A soft smile tipped the corners of his mouth. Inca lay on the floor, next to Ann's bed, only a blanket for a mattress beneath her. She, too, was sleeping deeply. Her rifle, which was never more than a few inches from her, lay at her side, her fingers draped across it. That was the way of Inca's life: she was a green warrior in Brazil, a hit-and-run specialist against those who would destroy her rain forest home, which was really the womb of Mother Earth.

His gaze moved back to Ann's shadowed face. Already she appeared to be stronger and have more color. He felt her growing strength as he unshielded to allow himself to feel her and their baby fully. Yes, life was pulsing through them once again. The ache to be with them overwhelmed Mike. Quietly crossing the room, he was careful to move slowly. If Inca sensed any danger, she'd snap awake and grab that rifle so fast that he knew it would make even the head of a seasoned military man like him swim.

But he had jaguar blood and could pad so softly as to never be heard—not even by Inca. Easing himself onto the bed, Houston settled his bulk gently against his wife's form. Sliding one arm beneath Ann's neck, he lay on his side and placed his other arm across her until his hand closed over his baby daughter, wrapped in the fleecy pink blanket. Tiredness flowed over Mike once more as he pressed his brow gently against Ann's hair. How good it was to feel her soft, shallow breath against him. An exhausted smile tipped the corners of his mouth as he closed his eyes and allowed the peace, the joy, to thread through him. In moments, Houston was asleep, with the woman he loved so fiercely in his arms and their baby daughter beside them.

Chapter 17

Ann shared a secret smile with Mike, who sat on the edge of her bed, his arm draped casually around her shoulders. Next to him was Grandfather Adaire, who had materialized before them little less than fifteen minutes earlier. Mike had warned her he was coming and *how* he would come. Teleportation was something that only a few of the Jaguar Clan could accomplish.

Grandmother Alaria had other duties to fulfill, so she'd asked her husband to come in her stead. Ann was disappointed, but knew that when they reached the village, Grandmother Alaria's love and support would be there for their daughter. One of the many things Ann was getting used to was the ebb and flow of situations and not to assume or expect. As Mike always told her, "Expect nothing, receive everything." And judging from Grandfather Adaire's expression and tender regard for their new baby daughter, he was the perfect person to perform the ancient ceremony they had gathered together for.

Grandfather Adaire stood beside Ann's bed, leaning heavily on his staff, which had colorful parrot feathers attached to it. Everyone's attention went to the door as it slowly opened.

Ann held out her hand. "Inca...come join us." She saw the

woman warrior's hesitation as her gaze settled darkly on Adaire. "Please," Ann murmured.

"You are invited to the naming ceremony," Adaire rumbled. "Enter!"

"I thought Grandmother Alaria would be here," she said stiffly. But the flash of rebellion in Inca's eyes softened immediately as she closed the door and centered her focus on Ann.

"It should not matter who is here," Adaire said to her sharply. "We are gathered because of this child. *That* is what you should be focused upon."

For whatever reason, Ann knew that Inca trusted her with the very core of her wounded being. And she could literally feel Inca's distrust and dislike of Adaire. As Ann held out her hand, the woman warrior walked around the bed and grasped her fingers.

"I'm so glad they found you," Ann told her.

"I was in the hospital cafeteria, eating."

Houston grinned. "Is there any food left?"

Chuckling, Inca released Ann's fingers, leaned over and very delicately touched the baby's soft black hair. "I left you a little, my brother. Ahh, look at her. She is so beautiful!" Inca smiled up into Ann's eyes. "She has your beauty and this ugly guy's stubborn personality. What a combination!" She laughed fully in that husky, purring tone as she straightened up.

Ann cradled her daughter in her right arm. She gazed from Inca to Adaire. "Now we can begin, Grandfather."

He nodded his aging head. Placing his staff against the wall, he drew out a small glass vial with a cork in the top of it. "Let us bow our heads in prayer, in grateful thanks for this child's entrance into our lives, that she is alive and healthy."

Ann closed her eyes. She felt Mike's arm move comfortingly around her shoulders. This was all she wanted, all she would ever need: him and her daughter. Three days after the horrendous event, Mike had suggested the naming ceremony. She was still too injured to be moved, to make the trip to the Village of the Clouds. Another week here, in Tarapoto, was what the doctors recommended. Ann didn't like the idea of staring at four white walls for another seven days when she could be "home" in the village, but she didn't fight Mike on the decision.

Adaire's low, rumbling tone filled the room. "Allow the light of the Great Goddess and her heavens to come through you, Cath-

erine Inca Houston.'' He reached over and gently touched the
baby's hair with the fragrant orchid oil. Moving it in a clockwise
circle, he pronounced, ''Your connection to this life, in this body,
is now complete.''

Ann watched through glistening eyes as Grandfather Adaire
rubbed a tiny bit of oil on Catherine's brow, her throat, over her
heart, stomach and abdomen. Adaire's hands were so gnarled and
aged looking against Catherine's new, pink skin. The little girl
slept as he touched her, as if she knew he would never hurt her.
And throughout the moving ceremony, Ann saw tears in the elder's gray eyes.

More surprising to Ann, as Grandfather Adaire called out the
baby's name, was that Inca's head jerked up, her eyes widening
in total surprise that her own name was part of it. Just as quickly,
she hid her reaction by placing her hand across her eyes, bowing
her head so no one could see how she really felt about it.

Adaire then raised his hand and placed a drop of the oil on
Ann's heart region. ''From daughter to mother, the Great Goddess
bless this union between you.''

He then moved around the bed in slow, limping strides. Mike
eased off the bed and unbuttoned his white cotton shirt to expose
his chest. Adaire placed a drop of oil above his heart and rumbled,
''From daughter to father, the Great Goddess bless this union between you.''

Ann felt Inca stiffen. She hoped her friend would not rebel,
would not refuse the gift that they had given her. Mike had told
Ann earlier that those who accepted the drop of oil at a naming
ceremony accepted an unbreakable bond with those who shared
the oil; becoming, in essence, an extended family even if they had
no blood or family lineage in common. For Inca, who was an
orphan, and almost an outcast of the Jaguar Clan, this would mean
that someone wanted her enough to invite her into their family
unit. Honored and loved no matter how bad her reputation was,
or what she had done in the past. Mike had warned Ann that Inca
might balk and refuse to be part of the ceremony because Grandfather Adaire would be overseeing it, instead of Alaria. Inca had
always gotten along with Alaria. Her quarrel was with Adaire.

Although it hurt to move her left arm because of her broken
ribs, Ann reached out, entangling her fingers in Inca's strong ones.

Inca snapped her head to the right, looking down at her.

Ann tried to smile through her tears, silently asking her to be a part of their family. She saw Inca valiantly try to shield emotions, but for whatever reason, she could not. Maybe it was the baby that had exposed Inca's deeply hidden vulnerability. Ann wasn't sure.

As Adaire approached her, Inca stiffened, but turned her attention upon him.

Ann squeezed her fingers in a pleading gesture. She saw Mike nod gently at Inca, as if encouraging her to allow the ceremony to take place. She also saw Adaire wrestling with his own judgment of his former apprentice. There was such bad blood between them.

Inca wore a sleeveless, dark green T-shirt. With her left hand, she yanked it down enough to expose her heart region between her small breasts. Her lips were set as Adaire moved forward to place the oil on her skin.

"From daughter to aunt, the Great Goddess bless this union," he rumbled.

Ann closed her eyes as Adaire placed the oil upon Inca's chest. She thanked her friend mentally. Little Catherine stirred and opened her eyes. They were so large and blue-green in color. Ann knew without a doubt that her daughter would have her husband's deep blue eyes as she grew older. Smiling, she placed a soft kiss on her tiny brow. Catherine's bowlike mouth curved in a smile.

Adaire moved around to the other side of the bed. He leaned down and carefully bundled Catherine into his arms. Ann watched as he cradled her daughter against his thin chest, his gray eyes glittering with tears as he placed his trembling hand upon her small chest beneath the blankets.

"This is a child of our hearts. She has her family here with her now. She also has her extended family of the Jaguar Clan. May she be blessed by the Great Goddess to walk a path of light in harmony with her heart. May she always see through the eyes of her heart. Blessings upon her, her family and the Jaguar Clan, into which she is welcomed."

Ann sniffed. She glanced over at Mike as he went and stood beside Inca. There wasn't a dry eye in the room, though Inca tried to hide her tears. It was impossible. Adaire was beaming as he held Catherine, rocking her gently in his arms.

"Thank you, Grandfather," Mike whispered, extending his

hand across the bed. "Ann and I are grateful you could do this for us...all of us...."

Adaire carefully cosseted Catherine as he reached out and shook Mike's hand. "My son, I would go wherever Alaria asked me to. This is a blessed moment." He released Mike's hand and turned his attention to Ann.

"It is a custom of our people for the elder who blesses the newborn to tell you something of her future. I know Alaria wanted to be here, but circumstances prevented her from doing so. She sends her love to all of you."

Ann nodded and leaned back against Mike as he sat down on the bed and placed his arm around her shoulders again. "I hope Catherine has a good future, Grandfather," she quavered, sniffing and blotting her eyes with a tissue.

Inca came and carefully sat down on the same side of the bed, near Ann's blanketed feet, facing her. She placed her hand across Ann's ankle and looked at her through tears that she refused to allow to fall.

Adaire sighed. "For once, I can tell you with great assuredness that Catherine Houston will be a catalyst in our world as she blossoms into an adult."

"Don't you mean Catherine *Inca* Houston, Old One?"

Adaire scowled and refused to look down at Inca, who had prodded him unmercifully, with blatant sarcasm in her voice.

"Of course—Catherine Inca Houston."

Mike reached out and gripped Inca's hand as if to tell her to let the slight go, that he and Ann loved her and that was all that mattered. Adaire, as spiritually advanced as he was, was not perfect. Inca was still his open wound, one that he had not been able to heal within himself. Mike fervently prayed that someday these two would make their peace with one another.

"Catherine Inca Houston," Adaire intoned gravely as he held her, "you will become a light among lights. A woman of great and balanced power who will help our mother, the earth, and bring two-leggeds in harmony with all our relations."

Leaning down, Adaire kissed her brow. "The Great Goddess blesses you, little one. Go in peace, in step with her heart, for you are made in divine image of her."

Gently, Adaire handed Catherine toward Ann.

"Please, allow Inca to hold her," Ann murmured.

Instantly, Inca gasped and recoiled. She released Mike's hand. "But—"

"Hold her," Mike ordered quietly. "You're her godmother now. More than an aunt, you know." He saw Adaire's scowl, but the elder controlled his reaction and managed to tame whatever feelings he had toward Inca as he limped around the bed to stand before the woman warrior.

Ann smiled through her tears. Mike gripped her hand gently and they watched Adaire set Catherine into Inca's arms. Maybe, just maybe, this little innocent baby could help begin to heal the rift, the chasm between them. Ann knew Inca never wanted to be touched by Adaire. But now, as they carefully passed the baby between them, they had direct contact. She hoped the baby would become a bridge and connection between them.

Inca's face changed instantly as she cradled Catherine very carefully in her arms. All the anger, the distrust, melted away. As she held Catherine, she bowed her head, her black hair falling across her shoulders and acting as a shining curtain, hiding her face.

Adaire moved away, but there was a kinder expression on his face as he watched Inca's unexpected reaction. It was as if he was surprised but pleased by her acceptance of the baby.

Ann felt a tremendous unleashing of emotions from Inca. There was no need to see her features; Ann felt her tears. Catherine started to move very actively in Inca's arms, her tiny hands flexing, as if to reach up and touch her face.

"Kiss her," Ann urged brokenly. "She wants you to kiss her...."

Inca slowly raised her chin. Tears were streaming down her taut face. "N-no...I cannot.... I do not deserve such a gift—"

"Nonsense," Ann whispered. She gestured firmly toward her child. "She wants you to kiss her. You're her aunt. Her godmother. If anyone should be holding her and kissing her and loving her, it's you."

Inca's shoulders sank. She struggled hard not to sob as Ann reached out to her, heart-to-heart. "You do not realize all I have done—how bad I really am—"

Mike sighed raggedly. "Listen to us, Inca," he said in a low, emotional tone. "Ann and I don't care what you've done. We don't stand in judgment of you or what's happened in your past. Our daughter wouldn't be alive today—" he looked tenderly down at Ann "—nor would my wife, if you hadn't been there...if you hadn't helped to save their lives by protecting them against Escovar and his men. This isn't about karmic payback or balancing things out among the four of us. Two people are alive here today because of your courage and bravery. Catherine belongs to you as much as she does to us. You're her family now, you know. You're not an orphan anymore, Inca."

Inca winced, shutting her eyes tightly for a moment, then carefully lifted Catherine so that she could look at the baby's face and waving, active arms. "She is so precious. So clean and innocent...without sin...."

"We were all like her once," Mike reminded Inca gently. "Life changes us, but somewhere in your heart there's light, Inca, or our baby daughter wouldn't be happy to be in your arms, and you know that. Babies sense who's good or bad. If Catherine didn't want to be with you, she'd be screaming her head off." He grinned a little down at Ann.

Ann agreed. "We love you, Inca, sins and all. We aren't perfect, either."

Inca cast her a tear-filled look. "You are not anything like me. You know nothing of the blood that stains my hands or what I have done.... I am not a good person like you. I have acted in revenge, which is against clan code, and I have not yet learned my lesson—"

"Tell that to the baby in your hands," Adaire rumbled warningly, scowling at Inca. "Can you not allow the purity of a baby, newly born, to wash away some of that eternal darkness that stalks your soul?"

Shaken, Inca refused to look up at Adaire. Lowering her head, she pressed a hesitant kiss against her soft, ruddy cheek.

Ann watched as something magical occurred when Inca allowed herself to kiss Catherine. She felt a shift, a dramatic one, in the room. Whatever demons, guilt or darkness Inca was fighting dissolved within that moment. Ann was mesmerized as Inca's drawn, pain-filled expression disappeared. And for a second time that day, Ann felt the shield completely fall away from her friend. Ann wasn't sure what had happened, but she understood that something very powerful and healing had taken place between Inca and Catherine. Her daughter cooed and waved her arms, as if excited by the touch of Inca's lips upon her cheek.

Inca smiled brokenly as she brought the baby to rest against her breast. In a tender motion, she wrapped her arms around little Catherine, closed her eyes and rocked her gently.

Mike shared another tender look with Ann. Then he turned to Inca and saw huge tears squeezing from beneath her thick, black lashes, her lower lip trembling with a sob that desperately wanted to be released. He watched Inca fight against being human and vulnerable. He knew it was because Grandfather Adaire was in the room that she wouldn't cry, wouldn't allow her feelings to be displayed. Mike looked up to see the expression on the elder's face. No longer was Adaire scowling. No, the old one was staring at Inca with such compassion and love that it shook Mike. Wave after wave of emotion emanated from Inca. It was as if she could no longer control them, and on some level, Mike understood that this was good because Inca rarely released her feelings freely. But this innocent little baby did. Babies were pure love, as far as Mike was concerned. Pure, radiating love, so clean and innocent in this insane world they lived in. And only something as pure as Catherine would be able in some unfathomable way to reach effortlessly into Inca's dark, wounded heart, and help release her past.

Mike felt Ann press her cheek against his chest. Leaning down, he threaded his fingers through her clean hair and gently held her against him. Yes, whatever they were sharing in this miraculous moment, it was a powerful healing for Inca, made possible by the daughter whom she had saved. Kissing his wife's hair, Mike lifted her chin a little and met her widening blue-gray eyes. There was such love burning in them for him...for her new, extended family. Mike smiled brokenly as he caressed Ann's pale cheek. He couldn't wait until he was within the sanctuary, the serenity of the village with his family.

"Look at her," Mike said with a chuckle, "she's a hungry little jaguar today." He sat with his back against the huge silk cotton tree, the long, thin gray roots surrounding them like protective arms. Ann was curled up between his legs, resting contentedly against him. Catherine lay suckling noisily from her left breast. Mike's arm was positioned below Ann's to help hold their daughter in place as she fed.

Dappled sunlight filtered down through the leaves, dancing

around them like gold, glittering coins. Mike listened to his daughter's noisy, happy sounds. He grinned down at Ann. Her face mirrored her happiness, her absolute contentment. Watching Catherine suckle, Ann softly caressed her daughter's curling black hair. "She is hungry," she said with a laugh. "Every day since we've been here Catherine gets stronger, hungrier and more active."

Mike agreed. He moved his hand in a caressing motion across Ann's sable hair, the reddish gold highlights gleaming in the sun. "One more week," he said with a sigh, "and then we have to leave."

"I know..." Ann tried to keep the disappointment out of her voice. She looked out across the wildflower-strewn meadow. There were red, purple and white flowers mixed with the verdant green of the grass. This was their favorite place to come, besides the pool of life. Mike had surprised her earlier by making a picnic lunch over at Grandfather Adaire's hut before picking her and Catherine up and bringing them here to the ancient tree they enjoyed so much.

"I think Grandmother Alaria is sad that we're going to have to leave," Ann whispered. "She is so taken with Catherine." Without fail, the elder would walk over to their hut midmorning shortly after Catherine's feeding, to sit with Catherine in the hand-hewn rocker outside the hut and rock her in her arms for an hour. Inevitably, all six elders would come over, touch, hold and love Catherine. It seemed the child had several doting grandparents.

"Alaria might be the leader," Mike said, "but she's lonely, too. I think, with us, she can be more herself—just another human being."

"Yes," Ann said softly, gazing out across the meadow. It was near eighty degrees, the sky a deep, cloudless blue. To the north, she saw that white roll of clouds hanging against the grayish blue snow-covered Andes. The day was perfect. Everything was perfect. "Members of the Jaguar Clan come and go from here constantly. She is their leader," Ann noted, "and she has that role to fulfill for them."

"Not with us, though," Mike whispered, and leaned over and kissed Ann's brow.

Closing her eyes, she nestled her face against the curve of his neck and hard jaw. "I don't care where we go when we leave here, Mike. I just want to be with you."

The trembling in her voice touched him deeply. Easing his arm around her, Mike held Ann tightly against him. Catherine continued to suckle noisily, her small arms waving every now and again, as if cheering for that rich, nutritious milk she was gobbling down.

"Yesterday, I left the village and met Pablo down below the bridge," he confessed in a low voice.

Ann opened her eyes. "So that's where you went. I wondered...."

Chuckling, Mike slid his fingers along the smooth curve of her cheek. He ached to make love with Ann, but the time wasn't right yet. She was recovering from the birth and her ribs were mending nicely, but she needed to recuperate fully, first.

"So what were you conspiring with Pablo about?" she demanded wryly. Gently she moved Catherine to her other breast to continue feeding. Mike drew the edge of Ann's blouse away to expose her other breast and helped position the baby against her. Just having his strength, his support and assistance meant the world to Ann. He'd helped deliver so many babies over the years in the villages of the highlands that he knew a lot more about them than she did. However, the women of the village, many of them mothers many times over, had also helped her pick up the necessary mothering skills, and Ann was more than grateful for their knowledge and guidance.

"I know you're worried that when we leave here, we'll be in the same danger as before," Mike began quietly. He watched Catherine's little mouth suckle strongly. Smiling, he felt his daughter's strength, her determination to latch on to that nipple and feed. A drop of milk formed at the corner of her mouth, and with his finger, he rescued the bubble. In one motion, he placed the milk onto his tongue. He heard Ann chuckle.

"Two hungry jaguars here," she teased, smiling up at him.

He grinned. "I'm hungry, all right, but it's not the same hunger little Cat here has," he growled darkly.

Blushing fiercely, Ann held his burning blue gaze and knew exactly what Mike meant. She felt her lower body respond to his look. How badly she wanted to love him! Waiting was necessary, but it was a special, unfulfilled agony. With a frustrated sigh, Ann muttered, "Let's talk about the future, shall we?"

Laughing deeply, Mike cradled his wife and child more securely against him. "Okay, okay...." Then he sobered. "I've been talking to Morgan off and on. He's made us an offer we can't refuse."

Ann felt her heart squeeze a bit in terror. "What do you mean, Mike?"

"I told Morgan I'd talk to you about his proposal first. And then, when we decided, I'd get back with him with a firm answer one way or another."

"This had better be good, Mike," she warned.

He grinned a little sheepishly and caressed her flaming cheek. "Oh," he whispered conspiratorially, "I think you'll like his offer...."

Ann relaxed in Mike's arms. Happiness continued to flow through her. What else was there besides lying against the man who loved her with a fierceness that defied description, while holding the child created out of that love in her arms? "Okay, what did he offer you?"

"Us," Mike corrected. "Morgan knows the score down here. He's had mercenaries working with all the governments in South America for some time now. He has a plan—a big one—to go after all the drug kingpins at once in one massive concerted effort. To do so he needs people like myself, who have been in the field for a long time and know the score, to help develop tactics and strategies that will break the grip of the drug lords once and for all."

"That means he want you to help him come up with a battle plan."

"Yes," Houston murmured, "but not like you think." He smiled a little. "Morgan has got the guarantee of the U.S. government to form a top-secret department under the code name Jaguar."

Ann gave him a significant look. "Now, I wonder who came up with that name?"

"Hey, I'm innocent—for once," he said. "Morgan came up with this all on his own."

"Does he know about you...the Jaguar Clan?"

"No. He might have an inkling about us, but as an outsider, no, he doesn't have much information."

"I see...."

"He wants to move us to Montana, where he lives, near Philipsburg, a small town deep in the Rocky Mountains. He has key

government officials from ten countries coming there, with their
families. This is so damn secret that only the president and two
members of his cabinet know about this plan, Ann. And it's going
to be kept that way. We'll work at an office in Philipsburg during
the day, forming plans, and we'll be staying in contact with each
of these governments at the highest of levels. This minimizes possible leaks to spies who are moles for the drug lords.''

Ann considered his plan. ''Montana?'' She looked around. ''A
far cry from the humid jungle, isn't it?''

He nodded. ''Yes, it is.''

''Will you miss it? This?''

Shaking his head, Mike placed a kiss on her wrinkled brow.
''No. I have exactly what I want in my arms right now,'' he
whispered huskily. ''As long as I'm with you, I don't care where
I live, *mi querida.* Do you?''

Ann closed her eyes and rested against him. ''No,'' she whispered softly, ''I don't care either, Mike. I just want our baby—
and you and I—safe, that's all.''

Sighing, Mike nodded and held her gently. ''I know,'' he said
heavily. ''Going north will be safer for us. If word ever gets out
about the organization we're planning, it won't matter where we
live, we'll be in maximum danger. Escovar is dead, but someone
will take his place. It's only a matter of time. The difference is
my death spiral dance is over. If we continued to live in Lima,
you and Cat would be exposed to the same dangers. Drug lords
go after family members of people like myself. I want you *out* of
that danger as much as possible. By moving to Montana, we'll
have a modicum of safety and a chance at a peaceful life.''

''I know....'' Ann raised her head. ''But we have an advantage,
Mike, and you know it.''

His mouth drew into a slight smile. ''It might be hell sometimes,
being a member of the Jaguar Clan, but in some ways it's a blessing, too.''

''Your guardian will tell us if trouble is coming. That can be
an early warning system for all of us—even for Morgan and his
family.''

''Yes, but they'll never know that we're operating on a different, invisible plane.''

Ann shrugged. ''It doesn't matter. We'll be able to tell them if our cover is blown. Then we can still get out in time and keep our families safe.''

Mike nuzzled her cheek. "Well? Want to move to Montana, Mrs. Houston?"

"Yes," Ann whispered, her voice emotional. She gazed down at Catherine, who had stopped suckling and was now asleep in her arms. "I want as normal a life as we can have for her, Mike. And for ourselves..."

"Well..." He sighed, smiling against her cheek. "Being a member of the Jaguar Clan isn't going to guarantee total normality, but for the most part, we can have it."

Lifting her head, she met and drowned in his deep blue gaze. A fierce sense of love overwhelmed her. "Kiss me?"

"Any chance I get...."

As she met his descending mouth, felt the power of his lips upon hers, she gave herself completely to Mike in every way. When they gently drew apart, he began rummaging in the loosely woven sack that he'd brought the lunch along in.

"I have something for you," he murmured, and he withdrew a red-and-yellow orchid from the sack.

Gasping, Ann eyed the blossom. "Mike, that's the same kind of orchid you gave me in Lima!"

He grinned and pinned it in her hair. "Yep, the same one you saw in your dreams a long time ago. Remember that?" He carefully affixed the flower so that it rested against her left ear. The vanilla scent enveloped them.

"Yes, the same one you gave me when you first came to my apartment in Lima."

Chuckling indulgently, he said, "You were mine then and you didn't even realize you'd been caught."

"What's that supposed to mean?"

Very pleased with himself, Mike said, "You don't know the story of this particular orchid yet, do you?"

"No, but you're going to tell me, aren't you?" Ann flashed him a smile. His eyes danced with a mischievous glint in their depths.

"It's called the marriage orchid," he told her, his smile widening. "A man who wants a woman to marry him will bring her this orchid. It's a proposal. If she accepts the orchid, well, it's a done deal—she has, in effect, agreed to marry the poor slob."

Ann gave him a dirty look. "No fair, Mike. I didn't know what

I was taking from you when you handed me that spike of orchids in Lima!''

"Oh, yes, you did, *mi querida*. On some level of yourself, your spirit knew. That's why you grabbed them.''

"I did not grab them, Michael Houston, and you know it! You always embellish things so much!''

Laughing deeply, Mike rocked her in his arms and gave her a swift, hot kiss on her parted, smiling lips. "You can never outwit a jaguar. He will *always* trap you.''

"Pooh!'' Ann muttered. "You were being just plain sneaky, Major Houston, and you know it!'' She fingered the orchid in her hair. "But it's a beautiful gift and a beautiful way to say that you love someone.''

"Sneaky?'' Mike muttered, pretending to be wounded. "I'm not sneaky.''

"Okay, how about another adjective, like underhanded?''

His laughter rolled across the meadow, absorbed by the inconstant breeze and warming sunlight. As he held his wife and baby, he realized he had never been happier. The life that stretched out before them wouldn't be easy, but Mike knew they had the strength and courage to weather whatever was thrown at them. And more important, they had love. Forever.

* * * * *

More MORGAN'S MERCENARIES
are coming!
Don't miss Ty Hunter's story,
coming in July 1999
to Silhouette Special Edition,
only from Lindsay McKenna!

Here's a sneak preview....

Just the way he walked reminded Catt of a lithe animal, like a jaguar, perhaps. He had dark brown hair, shortly cut and close to his skull. He wore sunglasses, so she couldn't see his eyes, which would have told Catt everything she needed to know about him. What was this man hiding?

It was his face that drew her. An oval face with a hard, uncompromising jaw. There wasn't a handsome bone to this man's face, Catt decided. He hadn't shaved and the darkness of his beard gave him a decidedly dangerous look. Who *was* he?

He slung a large canvas bag over his broad shoulder as he strode confidently toward her. He walked like he was in the military. Catt's mind spun with questions. Was he sent by some government agency? Warning bells went off within her. She was no stranger to CIA or military types because in her business, she frequently rubbed elbows with them out in the field. They were instrumental and necessary—even if they were sometimes arrogant about the role they played in helping Catt get medical attention to those who suffered.

Once again, Catt sensed an air of danger around him. Why did he look so familiar to her? Her heartbeat sped up. The shape of his face...that arrogant, confident walk...she couldn't shake the feeling she knew him. But from where? *Where?* She was almost ready to hurl the first words at him and demand his name when he slowed down and took his sunglasses off. When his icy-cold cinnamon-colored gaze locked on to hers, Catt gasped.

Her eyes widened. Her hands dropped from her hips. Her lips

parted. And then her anger surged through her like a volcanic explosion as her voice cut through the humid afternoon air.

"You bastard! I told you I *never* wanted to *ever* see you again!"

Ty's heart slammed against his rib cage like a punch being delivered by a boxer. He halted, his mouth dropping open. The woman glaring at him like an Amazon warrioress was Cathy Simpson. *His* Cathy.

The red-haired beauty he'd fallen hopelessly in love with ten years ago.

The woman he'd left behind.

But never forgot....

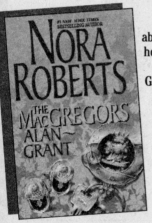

If you enjoyed what you just read,
then we've got an offer you can't resist!

Take 2 bestselling love stories FREE!

Plus get a FREE surprise gift!

This March Silhouette is proud to present

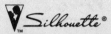

SENSATIONAL

MAGGIE SHAYNE
BARBARA BOSWELL
SUSAN MALLERY
MARIE FERRARELLA

This is a special collection of four complete novels for one low price, featuring a novel from each line: Silhouette Intimate Moments, Silhouette Desire, Silhouette Special Edition and Silhouette Romance.

Available at your favorite retail outlet.

Based on the bestselling miniseries

A FORTUNE'S CHILDREN *Wedding:*
THE HOODWINKED BRIDE

by BARBARA BOSWELL

This March, the Fortune family discovers a twenty-six-year-old secret—beautiful Angelica Carroll *Fortune!* Kate Fortune hires Flynt Corrigan to protect the newest Fortune, and this jaded investigator soon finds this his most tantalizing—and tormenting—assignment to date....

Barbara Boswell's single title is just one of the captivating romances in Silhouette's exciting new miniseries, **Fortune's Children: The Brides,** featuring six special women who perpetuate a family legacy that is greater than mere riches!

Look for **The Honor Bound Groom,** by Jennifer Greene, when **Fortune's Children: The Brides** launches in Silhouette Desire in January 1999!

Available at your favorite retail outlet.

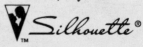